DEVIL'S DUE

OVERWORLD CHRONICLES BOOK 19

JOHN CORWIN

RAVEN HOUSE

ENTER THE VOID

Baal has assembled nearly all the major relics of Juranthemon.

Once the final pieces are in place, the realms will collapse, killing billions and erasing countless others from existence. Even the afterlife may be wiped into oblivion. Only two or three relics remain, and the sword of Jura, Unmaker, is in the worst place imaginable—the Void.

Thanks to the insane goddess, Eve, it's possible Baal already knows where Unmaker is, pitting Justin and gang in a race against time and the grand overlord of Haedaemos.

The Void swarm presents a challenge even for gods. It consumes everything organic right down to the soul. Opening a portal to the Void is dangerous enough. Entering the barren realm is suicide. But Justin may have a secret weapon—an unlikely ally with a way to enter the Void unharmed.

But as Justin and the others delve deeper into the mysteries of this barren wasteland, they soon discover there's far more to the Void than hideous bugs and the swarm. And the secret it hides could be the key to victory or annihilation.

BOOKS BY JOHN CORWIN

CHRONICLES OF CAIN

To Kill a Unicorn

Enter Oblivion

Throne of Lies

THE OVERWORLD CHRONICLES

Sweet Blood of Mine

Dark Light of Mine

Fallen Angel of Mine

Dread Nemesis of Mine

Twisted Sister of Mine

Dearest Mother of Mine

Infernal Father of Mine

Sinister Seraphim of Mine

Wicked War of Mine

Dire Destiny of Ours

Aetherial Annihilation

Baleful Betrayal

Ominous Odyssey

Insidious Insurrection

Utopia Undone

Overworld Apocalypse

Apocryphan Rising

Soul Storm

Devil's Due

Assignment Zero (An Elyssa Short Story)

OVERWORLD UNDERGROUND

Soul Seer

Demonicus

Infernal Blade

OVERWORLD ARCANUM

Conrad Edison and the Living Curse

Conrad Edison and the Anchored World

Conrad Edison and the Broken Relic

Conrad Edison and the Infernal Design

Conrad Edison and the First Power

STAND ALONE NOVELS

Mars Rising

No Darker Fate

The Next Thing I Knew

Outsourced

For the latest on new releases, free ebooks, and more, join John Corwin's Newsletter at www.johncorwin.net!

CHAPTER 1

The blink stone on the ground behind the burned-out husk of the mansion was solid evidence Conrad and Ambria had been there. Shelton knelt and examined footprints captured in dried mud.

"Conrad always answers his phone. Something must have happened to him." Max knelt next to Shelton, eyes wandering the ground leading toward a copse of trees that hid the crack in the world between Queens Gate and the Glimmer. "They must have blinked."

Shelton picked up the abandoned blink stone. It was flat with rough edges and pockmarked sides, unchanged since the instant of its conception when the fabled city of Juranthemon was destroyed by the Sundering. "How do you blink and leave the damned stone behind?" He shook his head. "Something ain't right."

Then again, no one really understood how blink stones or any of the relics of Jura worked. Maybe something had gone terribly wrong. Maybe the poor kids had been whisked off to oblivion.

"You think someone kidnapped them?" Max stood and brushed dirt off his jeans.

Shelton grunted and examined a ragged black line that ran across a patch of grass. He stood and followed it behind shrubs along the back wall of the former mansion. He did his best not to think about what had happened here all those years ago, but unwanted images pushed past his defenses. Mr. Bigglesworth, a shapeshifting Flark, had killed Shelton's adoptive father only feet from where he stood.

In his rage, Shelton had destroyed the mansion with battle magic. In all the years that had passed since then, no one had tried to rebuild it. He cleared his throat and pulled himself back to the real world. The backside of the shrub was charred, and ash covered the ground.

Max gasped. "Oh no!"

"It ain't enough ash for bodies." Hoping he was right Shelton stooped down and cleared a spot of earth. Even the dirt beneath was blackened. "The weeds and vegetation were flash fried."

"By what?" Max reflexively ran a hand through his white-blond hair. "Maybe Conrad fired a spell at someone hiding in the bushes?"

"Nah this is something else." Shelton sniffed the ashes. The odor was faint but unmistakable. It didn't reek of brimstone as he'd suspected it would, but of burned electronics. He walked around the shrub, examining the area from all angles. After a few minutes, it was obvious he didn't have a clue what could have caused it.

Max mimicked Shelton's method, even sniffing the ash for himself. He wrinkled his nose. "It stinks like lightning."

Shelton nodded. "Something like that." It had been a long time since his bounty hunting days, but he had all his old spells saved. He took out his arcphone and flicked through several screens before finding his archives. It took another few minutes to remember what he'd named the spell he was looking for.

Max walked toward the copse of trees. "Maybe they're just lost in the Glimmer."

Shelton grunted. "Cora or Evadora would've found them by now."

"Yeah." Max's voice quavered. "I'm really worried. I just don't see how they could vanish without a trace."

"I used to make a living finding people who vanished without a trace, kid." Shelton offered him a smile. "We'll find them." He located the spell he was looking for and activated it. Focusing his willpower through the phone just as he would a wand, sparkling particles rained down from the end. As he'd hoped, they glommed onto the magical signature of whatever caused such an intense blast.

Shelton sprinkled the particles all around like a chef over-seasoning a pork roast, and they began to reveal the invisible residue. Within minutes, it was clear a rune or demon pattern hadn't been the cause of the discharge. He'd expected an object or even a diagram to become visible on the ground, but instead, the particles outlined the shape of a short humanoid holding onto an equally short staff.

After a few minutes of dusting, Shelton figured the outline was about as detailed as it would get. The person and the staff were about five feet tall. The top of the staff was rounded with two prongs curving up from the sides. It was a strange configuration for a magic staff. The outline was too vague to determine if the figure was male or female, much less determine an identity.

"What's wrong?" Max watched him intently.

Shelton frowned. "The magic dust sticks to magic signatures, not the people who cast the spells." He pursed his lips. "Whatever happened here saturated the caster with magic discharge."

"Maybe he's a channeler not a caster. That would charge the entire body with magic."

"Exactly!" Shelton clapped Max on the shoulder. "That's using your noggin."

Max grinned at the compliment. "The caster was hiding in the bushes."

He walked along the blackened line and pointed where the blink stone had been lying. His grin vanished, replaced by a look of horror. "Blink stones can't be damaged or destroyed because they're relics of Jura."

Shelton saw where he was going. "There's no residue to indicate Conrad and Ambria were vaporized, Max." That didn't mean anything, of course. Then again, if the burst of magic was sufficient, it might have left a signature on both ends. He continued sprinkling particles along the blackened line. Before long, the entire scene was outlined.

A jagged line ran from the bushes to the outlines of two human forms holding hands. There wasn't enough residual energy around them to give more than a general outline, but there was plenty in the hand that had been holding the blink stone. The discharge from the spell had interacted with the stone somehow.

But how and why?

Max wiped tears from his eyes as he walked around the outlines of his friends. "They can't be dead, Shelton. They just can't be!"

"Son of a bitch," Shelton growled. Something terrible had happened, and he had no explanation for it. Bouncing ideas off Adam would've been nice but he was busy with other matters.

Baal only needed a few more relics of Jura to cause a grand reset that would slam all the realms back together and kill billions, so Conrad and Justin decided it was best to gather the ones they knew about and find better places to hide them. Conrad had gone to the Glimmer to collect the dagger of Jura. Someone had apparently been lying in wait.

Max broke the long silence. "Conrad would only use a blink stone in an emergency. He didn't like how dizzy it made him."

Shelton nodded and grunted. "Did you see where Conrad hid the dagger?"

"Yes, in the roots of the Soul Tree." Max bit his lower lip. "Should we go get it or do you think Baal already got it?"

That was a damned good question. Baal had read Justin's mind during his transition to the afterlife, but Justin didn't know exactly where the dagger was hidden. The Soul Tree was massive, and the roots jutted from the ground, forming countless hollows and crevices where the dagger could be concealed.

Cora, the Glimmer Queen, usually knew when someone entered her domain because she controlled most plant and animal life within. But Conrad knew ways around that. What better way to sneak into the Glimmer undetected than by kidnapping Conrad and forcing him to help? It seemed likely something had gone terribly wrong with that plan.

It had been a while since anyone had heard from Conrad. At best, he and Ambria were being held and interrogated somewhere. At worst—well, he didn't want to think about that, and he sure as hell didn't want Max thinking about it because those kids were the closest thing to family Max had.

Max looked up at him with big eyes. "What are you thinking, Shelton?"

"Hang on, kid." Shelton paced back and forth, conjuring a plan that would put them on the right path. The ambusher wouldn't have waited here for days on end, hopes based on the random chance that Conrad would waltz by. Baal had eyes and ears around Arcane University and down in the town of Queens Gate, meaning someone had spied on Conrad and had known he was coming here.

Shelton scrolled through the spells on his arcphone and ran one designed to detect magical and science-based surveillance. After several minutes of scanning the environs, it came back negative. That lent more credence to the theory someone had been following Conrad.

He looked at Max. "You last saw Conrad five days ago?"

"Yes." Max nodded. "Ambria was complaining that she was hungry and wanted to eat before they went to the Glimmer for the dagger." He smiled. "She complains a lot."

Shelton snorted. "I'm aware."

"Ambria had been begging him to go on vacation too." Max shrugged. "That's why I wasn't worried when they didn't come back right away."

"You were also busy training with me," Shelton said. "Don't blame yourself for not checking on them."

Max sagged. "What if they were kidnapped and they've been captive all this time?"

"Nothing we can do about that," Shelton said. "Focus on what you have control of."

"Like what?"

"Let's backtrack their last steps before this point." Shelton pursed his lips. "Where's the most likely place they would have eaten before coming here?"

Max didn't even think about it. "The Copper Goose is Ambria's favorite place."

"Then we'll start there." Shelton walked into the copse of trees. A wide crack in the rock wall led through a short tunnel to a bridge that spanned a sea of stars. He strolled through the tunnel and to the lip of the invisible bridge, looking for clues. There were no recent footprints in the dust or any sign that Conrad and Ambria had been through here anytime recently.

If he continued onto the bridge, a pair of glowing orbs would make a quick appearance. Conrad had supposedly told the rift guardians to let his friends pass, but Shelton didn't feel like testing his luck.

There was no need to enter the Glimmer anyway since there were no indications of recent traffic. The answers he needed would be in Queens Gate. He peered into the bottomless chasm and wondered what would happen to anyone unfortunate enough to fall in. A shudder ran up his spine.

"Makes you feel small, doesn't it?" Max said.

"Fighting the Apocryphan makes me feel small." Shelton chuckled. "This just gives me the willies." He turned around and went back through the tunnel.

Shelton grabbed his broom where he'd leaned it against a crumbling wall and hopped on. "Let's grab lunch."

Max frowned as he climbed on his broom. "It's only ten thirty."

"Brunch then." Shelton wheeled his broom east and zoomed off, flying high enough to clear the trees. He glanced back at the charred remains of the mansion one more time before urging his broom to top speed.

It didn't take long to clear the stone wall guarding the Fairy Gardens. He curved south to fly around Colossus Stadium and continued past the rising white spires of Arcane University. A moment later, the ground dropped out from beneath him, opening into a wide green valley. Nestled in the middle of farms and homesteads was the city of Queens Gate. To the far south and north, rock walls rose into the skies, marking the end of the pocket dimension.

The organically curved buildings of Science Academy glittered in chrome splendor on the cliff to the east of the valley. The academy once again bustled with life after having been shut down for years. Shelton had a feeling he'd be making a visit over there soon enough. Team Justin needed all the help they could get in the fight against Baal.

He dove toward Queens Gate. Much of the outer city was still in ruins from the battle against Xanos. The city center didn't look much better thanks to Overworld refugees from all over the world storming into it after Max's father, Xander Tiberius had been killed and his surviving family, with the exception of Max, banished for being assholes. The Overworld was still in chaos thanks to the war against Xanos, and rebuilding would be a long row to hoe.

The merchant quarter was thankfully intact. The giant copper goose in the southern quadrant of town was an easy target to find. The broom parking was relatively empty since the breakfast crowd was gone and the lunch crowd wouldn't arrive for another hour. He slid his broom on the rack and went inside, Max close behind.

"Sit where you like," a bored looking host said.

Shelton did a circuit of the restaurant. A young couple, Arcanes by the look of them, sipped mimosas and stared into each other's eyes. An older gentleman sat on the balcony reading a nom newspaper. The Goose was otherwise empty of patrons—no surprise at this hour.

Max waited in the hallway while Shelton checked the bathrooms. Then they sat at a table near the back of the main room so Shelton could sit facing the door.

A young woman approached their table. "You can get bottomless mimosas for ten tinsel and the brunch special is a goat-cheese omelet for seven tinsel."

"Does it have bacon?" Shelton asked.

"You can add it for only a few tinsel extra," she said.

Shelton grunted. "I'll have the omelet, add bacon, and a four-shot blackeye with Irish crème."

"I'll have the same," Max said.

Shelton raised an eyebrow. "I don't need you running up the walls, kiddo." He turned to the waitress. "Make that an orange juice for him, okay?"

The server wrote it down and left.

Max leaned his elbows on the table. "I can't wait until the new Mansion is finished. The Ranch is okay, but it's weird living in the middle of a nom city. You can't use brooms or magic or anything."

"I love the city." Shelton leaned back in his chair. "But I miss the original Mansion."

Max nodded in the general direction of the university. "You looked upset when we reached the old Primus residence. Did seeing that old place make you think of your dad?"

Shelton grunted. "Yup. Been a long time ago, but it feels like the blink of an eye." It felt even shorter since they'd passed nearly half a decade in only a few months' time thanks to time dilation in Utopia.

"What now?" Max said.

"You have pictures of Conrad and Ambria on your phone?"

Max nodded and showed Shelton the gallery. There were photos of Max, Conrad, and Ambria standing together grinning. Images of Evadora and Ivy clowning around. Justin and Elyssa sparring as the sun rose behind them. Nightliss hugging the ghost of her dead sister, Daelissa, in Nowhere, and group photos taken during the small after party of David's return to his body.

Shelton chuckled and took the phone to look through everything. "Hot damn, we've been through some shit, haven't we?"

Max nodded. "Yeah. It was so cool seeing Jeremiah Conroy and finding out about the afterlife, but I think it made Conrad really sad."

Shelton understood. "He wanted to see Delectra."

"Yeah." Max looked down at the table. "She's probably in there somewhere, but Daelissa and the others are too busy trying to rescue consumed souls from the infernal fount to go hunting around the afterlife for lost people."

"Probably so." Shelton found a picture of himself grinning madly at Bella while she tweaked his nose playfully. "I like this one." He showed it to Max.

"Oh, that was when you put hot sauce on her pizza as a joke."

Shelton snorted. "Didn't even faze her. That woman has a cast iron stomach."

"So do you," Max said with a grin.

The server returned with their drinks, nuclear coffee for Shelton, and OJ for Max. Shelton showed her the picture of Conrad and Ambria. "You recognize either of them?"

She frowned, looked at Max, then looked at Shelton. "Oh, I know you guys!" She gasped and called out across the room. "Cheryl, come here!"

Shelton and Max exchanged confused looks.

"You know us?" Shelton said.

A redhead hurried across the room and joined her. Her eyes flared. "Holy farting fairies! It's Harry Shelton!"

"Can you believe it?" the other server giggled. "And this is Miracle Max!"

Max blinked long and slow. "Miracle Max?"

"How in the blazes do you know us?" Shelton said.

"You guys led the fight against Xanos," the first server said. "You're famous here in Queens Gate."

"Heroes," Cheryl said.

"Just doing our job, ladies." Shelton took a sip of his coffee and found it exactly to his liking. He showed the servers the picture again. "Have you seen either of these kids in here?"

Cheryl nodded vigorously. "It was so cool having Conrad Edison and Ambria Rax here. They've been coming here even before they were heroes." She looked at Max. "No offense, but I served your brothers and hated their guts."

"What a coincidence," Max said. "I hated them too."

A pair of cooks and other wait staff slowly gathered as word spread. Shelton took advantage of the situation and asked them questions about Conrad and Ambria. The story was pretty much the same from all of them. The couple had come in, been embarrassed by all the attention, eaten, and left.

"Did you notice anyone about five feet tall with a staff following them or taking notice?" Shelton asked.

Most of the staff shook their heads, but the hostess filled in the missing link.

"There was this woman who came in asking about them a few minutes after they left," she said. "I'm five foot one and she was about my height."

"What did she ask you?" Shelton said.

"She'd heard through the grapevine that some famous people were here and wanted an autograph."

"Anyone else ask for autographs?" Shelton said.

Cheryl nodded. "Us and several patrons, but then Clark told everyone to lay off and leave them alone so they could eat in peace."

A tall, burly cook nodded. "Yep. I could tell the poor kids were uneasy about all the attention."

Shelton pursed his lips. "What did the woman look like?"

The hostess's forehead scrunched. "She was blond, wore glasses, and had this real know-it-all tone. Kind of made me want to slap her."

Shelton didn't need to hear another word because he knew exactly who the hostess was talking about.

Serena Thain.

CHAPTER 2

"**H**oly farting fairies," I muttered. "That's a lot of people."

Dozens of men and women in matching t-shirts wandered aimlessly around the hellish landscape. What was especially puzzling was *where* they were wandering, namely the Abyss, formerly the eternal prison of the Apocryphan.

"What in the hell?" Elyssa shook her head like a wet dog. "Are they bussing in tour groups now?"

Elyssa and I were perched on a cliff ledge overlooking the otherworldly landscape. We'd only arrived a couple of hours ago with the intent of searching for a mysterious relic of Jura that the Apocryphan had supposedly kept here for Eve. During our initial flyover, we'd spotted the group and taken cover since there was no telling who or what they might be. There were demons, monsters, and other nasty entities who called this place home.

Elyssa peered through a set of spectacles and grunted. "Oh, now it makes sense."

Even with my super vision, the tour group was too far away for me to make out who they were. "What makes sense?"

She handed me the spectacles. I focused on a busty brunette with a brainless expression as she examined a rock. The words, tastefully scribed on the t-shirt in Comic Sans font, came into focus: *Baal's Little Bitch.*

"Well, shit." I lowered the spectacles. "Baal must really be desperate if he's using noms to search for relics."

Elyssa pursed her lips, took the spectacles back and turned a dial between the binocular lenses. "Baal doesn't do desperation. He's using noms as bait." She passed them back to me.

The view was no longer in color, but in gray-toned spectral mode. Ghostly, inhuman shapes crawled around the fringes of the group, unseen monsters looking for warm flesh to inhabit. Some were demon spirits banished to the Abyss as punishment, recognizable by their shapes and colors. I had no idea what the others were and didn't want to find out.

"This is monstrous." Elyssa bared her teeth. "We need to get these people out of here."

"Easier said than done." I continued spying on the noms. "How long do you think they've been down here?"

"My guess is Baal sent them in not long after he found out the Apocryphan were dead," Elyssa said. "He's had a little more than two weeks."

"Not a lot of time to search this place from top to bottom." A maze of ravines rose in the middle of the Abyss not far from the group. Though the flat-topped cliffs obstructed the view, I caught a hint of what looked like tents. "We need to get closer without being seen."

Elyssa nodded. "There are others without matching t-shirts. I have a feeling they're not noms."

"Infernus?"

She nodded. "No doubt."

"I don't see any Hell demons at least."

Elyssa grimaced. "Those are the worst."

During my little jaunt into the afterlife, I'd learned a lot about souls, spirits, and the true nature of Haedaemos. The entire realm was a spiritual afterimage of the world as it had once been before the Sundering. The demons who called it home required physical hosts to remain on our plane. But there were also physical demons from Hell. Hellfire demons towering twenty feet tall, red-skinned manikins with stubby wings and hooves, and rolling balls of tentacles called octopods were among the starring cast from that place.

Hell demons were powerful and nearly impossible to kill by ordinary means. If not for Emily Glass and her godlike powers, we would have died during our last confrontation. Then again, I'd killed myself by overusing the powers she'd stolen from an Apocryphan and given to me.

The Abyss was shaped like a giant bowl, encircled by mountains that rivaled Everest. The first couple hundred feet of cliffs were polished smooth, preventing anyone without serious climbing equipment from scaling the surface.

Past that, the rugged mountainsides were guarded by tentacle monsters and giant stone crabs. If someone made it to the peaks, the dark gravity fringe would crush them. Though the Apocryphan could easily climb the mountains, even they couldn't withstand the extreme gravity of the fringe.

The living area of the Abyss consisted of rocky plains in the outer ring. A maze of cliff walls bisected the bowl, running east to west. In the center of that maze was a bubbling lake of fire, the underside of the infernal fount. It served as the physical doorway between the Abyss and Haedaemos.

Elyssa and I were in the outer ring on what I referred to as the northern side. Baal's little bitches strolled around the central cliffs almost directly ahead. There wasn't much cover between us and them, so we elected to fly low and stick close to the cliff walls.

It took us half an hour to creep close to the canyon maze. From there, we used our brooms to reach the top, so we'd have a good vantage point from which to spy. And, boy did our little eyes spy something awful. Bird cages large enough to hold ostriches lined the canyon floor. The cages held humans.

Demon symbols were scribed in the rock beneath the cages. I shifted to demon vision and took another look at the prisoners. Superimposed over the dull human auras were monstrous shapes, demons and spirits that clung to the human souls like parasites. Infernus, easily discernable by their black uniforms, stood before some of the cages.

"They're questioning the spirits about the relic." Elyssa bit her lower lip. "This isn't good."

Baal had tricked me into giving him the general whereabouts of three relics just before I'd died. Conversely, he'd also let me know exactly which relics he was missing, though I wasn't sure if there were more he hadn't mentioned.

"Underborn has the heart, Eve has the sword, and the dagger is in the Glimmer." I shook my head. "What relic is Baal looking for here?"

"Before we attack the infernus, we need to find out." Elyssa quirked her lips, looked around the camp, and pointed to the closest interrogation. "Let's start there."

We backed away from the ledge until we were out of sight and then plotted a route. The buttes forming the canyon maze were flat across the tops, like a large plateau carved into puzzle pieces.

We flew our brooms in a roundabout pattern, flying over the narrowest gaps in order to avoid being seen. Every time we crossed a chasm, I waited to hear a shout of surprise when someone saw us, but apparently no one bothered to look up. It also helped that we didn't make any rookie mistakes, like knocking loose gravel or dust over the ledges.

Moments later, we settled onto our stomachs and low-crawled to the ledge directly above the infernus we'd spotted earlier. He was gone.

"You've got to be kidding me," Elyssa groaned. She looked around and shook her head. "I don't see any other interrogations."

"Me either." I sighed and laid my head on my hands. "What now?"

She worked her lips back and forth. "These look like the infernus Baal personally uses, which means they won't be taking notes or sending texts to their master."

"He knows everything they know."

"Yep." Elyssa scanned the area with her spectacles. "Which also brings up something I hadn't considered earlier. If we try to free the humans, Baal will know the moment we attack. Unless we take out the infernus quickly, we'll have to fight reinforcements."

"Baal might personally join the fight." I backed away from the ledge so I could sit cross-legged on the ground. "We'll have to be stealthy." I grinned. "What if I open portals beneath their feet and drop them into the carnivorous realm?"

Elyssa joined me and put a hand on my arm. "No Apocryphan powers, Justin. Opening a portal to the Abyss was hard enough."

I scoffed. "Not really. Opening small portals isn't a big deal."

She scowled. "In the Abyss, it's a huge deal. Your knees wobbled when you made it."

"Yeah, because the Abyss was designed to resist portals."

"Which means dropping infernus through portals out of here will be a struggle you don't need to make." Her hand squeezed my arm harder than necessary to get the point across. "I will kill you if you kill yourself again."

I held up my hands in surrender. "Fine. But it means rescuing these people will be a lot harder than it has to be."

Elyssa smiled. "Remember the good old days when all you had were demon powers?"

I nodded. "Yeah, and I remember how hard it was to fight giant scorps and all the other monsters the bad guys threw at me. It'd be a fun change to drop bad guys through a portal every now and then."

"I agree." She chuckled. "It was pretty funny seeing Baal and his demon horde fall through the hidden portal on the beach."

"Ooh, that was nice." I took a moment to savor that memory. "I'll bet he's still pissed at me."

"No doubt." Elyssa leaned over and pressed her lips to my cheek. "You like how that feels?"

I sighed gently. "Boy and how."

She patted my cheek not quite hard enough to be considered a slap. "Then don't die again, *capisce?*"

I slumped. "*Capisce.*"

A man's screams echoed through the canyon.

"Got another one!" a deep voice shouted.

We peered over the edge as infernus rushed down the canyon toward the voice. Elyssa watched three others race after their companion and then looked down at the caged person.

I read her mind. "What if the demon tells them you were asking questions?"

Elyssa blinked. "You knew what I wanted to do?"

I snorted. "We've been together long enough for me to figure out a few of your cues."

She grinned. "Aw, that's sweet. I taught you well."

"Only you would think learning battle tactics and strategy is sweet."

"It's the sweetest." She winked. "I think questioning the demon is a risk worth taking."

I bit my lower lip. "Fine. I'll stay up here and keep watch."

Elyssa produced a carbon fiber spike from her fanny pack and drove it into the ground with a swift downward stroke of her heel. She tied a climbing rope around it and rappelled down the side, landing behind the cage. The possessed woman inside hissed and made buzzing sounds that I quickly realized was a language.

"What are you saying?" Elyssa asked in English.

The woman's eyes flared, and she began speaking in Cyrinthian. "Voxx knows only this primitive language." She spoke slowly, as if the sounds felt alien to her.

"You know Cyrinthian," Elyssa said.

"You will release Voxx or suffer." The woman hissed again. "A mere demon pattern will not hold Voxx forever."

Elyssa pursed her lips. "I am not the one who imprisoned you, but perhaps I can help set you free."

I couldn't see the woman's face, but she hissed as if considering the offer. "Voxx is listening."

"What questions are those people asking?"

"They ask if Voxx knows what relic of Juranthemon is hidden in the Abyss, but Voxx knows nothing of it."

Voxx was obviously one of those kinds of people who referred to himself constantly in third person.

Elyssa frowned. "Anything else?"

"They offered Voxx a reward for information leading to the relic, but Voxx knows nothing." The woman turned in a circle, hissing angrily.

"How did you get here, Voxx?" Elyssa asked.

"Voxx comes from the outworlds." The woman held a hand toward the sky. "Voxx is a scout, seeking inworlds that still glow with life. Voxx seeks for the devourers."

Elyssa's mouth dropped open. "Outworlds?"

"Yes, the ones outside of the inside." The woman began to dance. "Voxx was captured and sent here by an inworld god until Voxx died. This place traps Voxx's spirit. Voxx cannot report to the outworlds."

The woman gripped the bars of the cage. "Now, you set Voxx free?"

Elyssa was obviously having second thoughts about it. "Only if you promise to never report to the outworlds."

"That was not the bargain," Voxx hissed. "You asked. Voxx answered."

I thought about calling down to Elyssa, but a shout would likely carry far from up here and I didn't want the infernus forewarned.

Elyssa used her foot to scratch out the pattern where it protruded beyond the border of the bird cage. The woman cackled gleefully, and then slumped like a rag doll. I switched to demon vision and regarded the spirit of Voxx. It looked like a giant locust, hungrily buzzing above its next meal.

My breath caught in my throat. *What if it tries to possess Elyssa?* But Voxx wasn't taking any chances. The bug creature flew away and vanished from sight. Elyssa clambered back up the rope and quickly coiled it as the shouts of infernus grew closer.

The echoing voices grew closer, but not by much, indicating the infernus had chosen another canyon for the new possessed prisoner. Elyssa and I crept across the plateau toward the voices and spotted the infernus heading into a branch of the maze a few chasms over. The gap from here to the next plateau was too far to risk flying over, so we'd have to plot a new course.

"We should just use the brooms," I muttered.

Elyssa shook her head. "We'd be spotted in an instant flying across a forty-foot span."

"Maybe." I peered across the broken tableau and found where we could cross. "But this is like solving a puzzle."

"Aw, does it hurt your brain?" Elyssa elbowed me. "You used to like being a nerd."

I puffed out my chest proudly. "Hey, I'm still a proud nerd."

"Then nerd onward and get us where we need to go."

Finding a path wasn't easy without a bird's eye view, but I picked out a route that seemed promising and started flying. We had to fly all the way down to where the wider canyon narrowed before we could cross it and made our way where the infernus were still shouting at each other as they wrestled with whatever entity they'd just captured.

I wondered how they prevented the spirits from fleeing the bodies before they trapped them with a demon pattern. Even the strongest of spirits couldn't enter and exit a body in an instant. It took time to nestle into flesh and then to untangle from it. My question was answered when we finally spied the infernus. A metallic band glowed around the neck of a pudgy man.

The band crackled and the man shouted in pain. He began shouting in Cyrinthian. I imagined most of the entities trapped here spoke the original language because that was just how long they'd been around.

One of the infernus, a tall, muscular male, shuddered violently. "My lord approaches." He stiffened and the timbre of his voice changed. "Well, another one, finally."

"Baal is in the house," I whispered.

Elyssa's forehead scrunched with concern and she put a finger to her lips.

Baal gripped the arm of the possessed man for a moment, then knelt on the ground and began carving a pattern into the stone with a claw-like fingernail. Despite the complexity of the pattern, he knocked out the pattern in less than five minutes. Then again, scribing demon patterns was old hat for the grand overlord of Haedaemos.

Other infernus picked up a nearby cage and set it down in the middle of the pattern, then Baal shoved the man inside.

One of the infernus knelt. "My lord, the spirits grow increasingly hard to bait, for they see how we question the prisoners."

"Perhaps I we should use a carrot instead of the stick." Baal put a finger on his chin. "A reward of freedom for information leading to the relic might be in order."

The other infernus nodded obediently.

Baal held up a finger. "But not yet. So far, we know that the Apocryphan were indeed guarding a secret relic, one that is of vital importance to completing my collection." He pursed his lips. "But that is all hearsay, overheard from conversations between the Apocryphan."

"Perhaps not all." Another infernus spoke in the same tone as the other, as if Baal were controlling him as well. "One spirit reported seeing Eve visit Zon so she could confirm the relic was still safe."

A third infernus joined in. "Xanos likely knows, but she'll never talk to us even if we could find her."

The other infernus began speaking in Baal's voice, throwing ideas back and forth with each other. He was talking to himself on a grand scale and it was a little scary seeing how effortlessly he could do it.

It also made me realize how futile this search was. If Baal, the grand overlord of Haedaemos, couldn't find this relic, how in the hell were we supposed to?

CHAPTER 3

The chattering infernus abruptly went silent. One of them began questioning the new prisoner. His voice no longer sounded as if Baal was controlling him.

"What is your name?" the infernus asked.

"Why couldn't I resist?" the man paced in a circle in the cage. "Oh, the temptation of warm flesh." He moaned and began stripping off his clothing. "I would gladly trade this greater prison for a new prison of flesh yet again, though my flesh be trapped by a cage." He started fondling himself and the infernus stepped back, watching, and waiting.

I suspected they'd seen this happen a few times as the spirits enjoyed their new bodies. But once the novelty wore off, then the real questioning would begin. Until then, I didn't feel like watching the shit show happening below and neither did Elyssa.

We backed up and spoke in low whispers.

"Maybe we should visit Eve," I suggested.

Elyssa scoffed. "After you dumped Xanos on her front lawn I doubt she'll be in the mood to talk."

"Worth a try. If she knows Baal is close to finding the secret relic, maybe she'll tell us what it is."

"Or she'll just give you her old non-interference speech." Elyssa scowled. "Right before she interferes."

Eve was unstable, to put it lightly. She'd murdered three Apocryphan just to keep us from freeing them from the Abyss in the fight against Xanos. It was even worse knowing they were her creations, her own children, and she'd been content to leave them trapped in the Abyss for eons, then killed them rather than let us set them free.

I wondered if Xanos still lived or if Eve had murdered her too. Considering the death toll from the war, Xanos's death wouldn't be the worst thing in the world.

I considered our options. "Do you still have an ASE on you?"

Elyssa nodded. "There are barely a handful left in the entire Templar organization, so I felt guilty about taking it."

"Feel guilty no more. Let's leave it here while we go visit the mother of creation."

Elyssa rolled her eyes. "Eve is not the answer."

"No, but maybe, just maybe, Xanos is."

Her lips peeled back into a scowl. "You think Xanos knows about the secret relic?"

I nodded. "I'm counting on it."

Elyssa worked her jaw back and forth. "After everything that bitch did, I'll be more likely to punch her in the face than ask her questions."

I grimaced. Elyssa thought Xanos had gotten off lightly after everything she'd done. I thought being stripped of her powers and banished to spend time with her crazy goddess mother was a sentence worse than death. I shrugged. "I know you hate her, but she might know something."

Elyssa rolled her neck as if trying to loosen tension in her shoulders. "Fine. It's worth a try, I guess." She looked at the sky of eternal dusk and shuddered. "I'm ready to be back in sunshine again anyway."

"Yeah, me too."

Elyssa plucked a marble-sized object from her pouch, spun it, and let it hover in mid-air. She pulled up a holographic screen and programmed it to keep an eye on the area. Unfortunately, it didn't have a wide range of options, so it would hover over the prisoner below and record what it could until we returned.

I watched it shimmer into camouflage as it drifted into place, then turned my gaze toward the glow on the horizon. That glow was the underside of the infernal fount. It could be opened like a gateway, allowing passage into Hell, the likely place where Baal was keeping all his stolen relics. I didn't know how to open it, but Baal's infernus probably did.

Elyssa pursed her lips. "You've got that look, Justin."

I nodded. "It's my brilliant idea look."

"Is it though?" She patted my shoulder. "Most of your off-the-cuff ideas are pretty bad."

I shrugged. "Just because I think it's a brilliant idea doesn't mean it'll end up being one."

"Oh, I know, believe me." Elyssa sighed. "What is it?"

"Why don't we make a side trip to Hell before going to see Eve?"

Her eyebrows tried to fly away with incredulity. "You're cray."

"To the max." I grinned. "It's on our bucket list, right?"

She snorted. "Literally going to Hell is probably the fastest way to kick the bucket."

"Maybe so." I pointed toward the infernal fount. "My guess is that the infernus can open the doorway between here and Hell. If we wait there for a few hours, maybe one will open the doorway and let us through. Then we can sneak through and find Baal's relics."

Elyssa tapped a finger on her chin. "There's a hitch in that plan. Hell is probably crawling with octopods, manikins, phegors, and hellfire demons. There's no way we can waltz in there unnoticed."

"Stop using logic on me." I sighed. "Stealing those relics would reset the countdown and set Baal back to square zero. Maybe we should at least try."

She frowned. "I suggest we recon the area and see how frequently the infernus go back and forth. I can send the ASE through the gateway and use it to gather information. Once we're fully informed, then we plan our infiltration."

"Once we find the relics, I can portal us out with the Apocryphan powers." I mimicked snapping my fingers because I didn't want to alert the infernus below. "It'll be a snap."

"You say that, but what if he has portal blockers? What if the relics are physically inaccessible?"

I didn't have a response to that. Elyssa was great at planning. I was too impulsive, and my success rate reflected that. The old me probably would have bulldozed over her objections and gone ahead with it. Elyssa would have come with me if only to save my ass when my plan failed.

But I'd seen too much and been through too much to be so foolhardy on a whim. Baal was the ultimate plotter and planner, always a step ahead of us at every turn. But with my resurrection and removing Cain from his arsenal of resources, it seemed for the first time that we'd drawn even with the infernal bastard.

Every moment we delayed was a moment Baal had to pull the countless threads he'd woven. His complex tapestry of deception was not only a work of art, but the key to his ultimate victory if we didn't find a way to unravel it first.

Stealing the relics right out from under his nose would be the master thread that might undo all others. At the very least, it would royally piss him off. And that was enough for me.

I took a deep breath to curb my enthusiasm and nodded. "Let's do the recon, babe."

Elyssa's luscious lips spread into a beautiful smile. "Aw, I'm proud of my boo-bear for listening to reason."

I rolled my eyes. "Just because I act like a kid doesn't mean you have to treat me like one."

She pinched my cheek. "You're so cute when you're indignant."

I let her have her fun, then got back to business. "Probably be best if we circle wide to stay out of sight."

Elyssa recovered the ASE she'd just released. "Let's do it."

We retraced our steps then headed west where the plateau met the mountains. Giant spider webs blocked portions of the canyons below, reminders of Araxos, the spider-like Apocryphan who'd once lived there. She along with Posthanied and Couriondral were the ones killed by Eve, their eternal imprisonment cut short by an act of betrayal.

Since the infernal fount was in the middle of the Abyss, we followed the curve of the mountains until we were on the opposite side of the fount from Baal's concubines and infernus, then made our way toward the objective. When the craggy plateaus ended, we swooped low since the only cover between us and the crater around the fount were random boulders and a few craggy trees.

I felt hungry eyes on us the entire way and could only wish it were the ghost of Patrick Swayze wanting to dance dirty with us. Those watching us were voracious spirits who wanted desperately to pounce on us but sensed my demonic powers and doubted their ability to overwhelm me.

The flat, rocky terrain slowly morphed into rolling hills that shielded our approach. The ridge of the crater around the infernal fount rose into view moments later, so we slowed for a look around. There were no sentries, no patrols marching the perimeter. With the Apocryphan dead, Baal probably had supreme confidence neither us nor Emily Glass would have a reason to revisit this dreadful place.

We dismounted our brooms and set them on the ground, then climbed the rise on foot. When I peeked over the edge, I couldn't believe what I saw. Elyssa emitted a soft gasp, echoing my own surprise.

Gone was the bubbling lake of fire, replaced by a hole leading into a rocky cavern, its walls glittering with diamonds. The orientation was strange since, from this side, a person would drop into the hole where reversed gravity would flip them upright and set them on solid ground. We were looking at the literal doorway to Hell.

And it was wide open.

A small group of red-skinned manikins hopped around the bottom of the pit, fighting over the corpse of one of Baal's male concubines. I grimaced and repressed the instinct to swoop down and kill them all.

Elyssa ducked behind the ridge and programmed the ASE. "I hope the demons aren't perceptive enough to see through the camouflage."

"It's worth a try, regardless." I wished I could see further through the doorway, but there was no good angle from up here.

The ASE shimmered into camouflage, leaving the barest hint of a ripple where it spun, then zipped down into the crater. I lost sight of it quickly, but figured it'd be through the doorway in a few seconds. The manikins continued screeching at each other as they tore the body apart.

I wanted to throw up. War had shown me a lot of ugly things, but sights like this still hit me where it hurt. Baal's minions probably kidnapped these poor people. Some of them might even be former government officials he'd replaced with infernus. They didn't deserve the fate forced upon them, but to preserve the element of surprise, we'd have to wait before trying to free them. I didn't want to think about how many more of them would die or be possessed by malevolent Abyssal demons before we returned.

"I think we're done here for now." Elyssa gave me an expectant look.

"Yeah, for now." I glared at the demons below. "But we'll be back."

"All right, Arnold." She managed a small smile. "We'll be back to save the day, provided we survive what comes next."

We made our way to the cover of a large boulder a good distance from the crater so we could portal to Eve's world. Dropping in unannounced on a somewhat insane goddess was probably not the smartest idea in the world, but time was ticking down to doomsday. It wasn't just the end of the realms and billions of lives on the line, but even the afterlife itself. Reversing the Sundering would also likely wipe out the vast majority of souls in the afterlife.

We had to take every reasonable chance we could to stop Baal. I said a silent prayer to the Flying Spaghetti Monster and his son the Swimming Ravioli Beast and summoned the Apocryphan powers. The world took on a greenish hue and my veins thrummed with energy. It took every ounce of control to limit my scope and focus. As someone once told me, I was a fifteen-amp fuse trying to channel a hundred amps.

I'd burned myself out once and knew better than to let that happen again. Even so, the power required to open a portal was enormous. I could barely open a pinhole to another realm with my Seraphim powers and the last time I'd tried, I'd been useless for a day afterward.

I traced the symbols for Eve's realm in the air, filled them with power, and envisioned the cottage. It was ornate but simple. Gray stone, arching wooden gables with intricately carved designs, and a green slate roof. It was something out of a fairy tale, a home that could have been crafted by the seven dwarves. It sat in a meadow of yellow daisies basking in warm sunlight.

Drawing upon the power boiling in my veins, I slashed vertically through the air, slicing open the very fabric of space and time. The slash widened into an oval of bubbling black liquid. Passing into and out of the Abyss was a bone-chilling experience thanks to the dark gravitational fringe touching the quantum tunnels.

I steeled myself and pushed into the darkness. It was like diving into freezing molasses. I sank into the portal for a seeming eternity. For a heartbeat, existence winked away, leaving me in deafening oblivion. And then I stumbled from the other side into warm daylight.

Elyssa stepped out a moment later, rubbing her arms for warmth. "I'd be happy if we never have to do that again."

"You and me both," I said.

The cottage lay right in front of us. A woman rocking in a chair on the front porch stared at us. Recognition flared in her eyes and the stare mutated into a glare. She rose, and the glare morphed into resignation. She was much shorter than I remembered, no longer towering nearly ten feet tall. Now she stood Elyssa's height. Otherwise, she was much as I remembered her, flaming red hair, lavender skin, and a perky nose over rosebud lips.

"You've come to finish me." Xanos sighed and walked down the porch to us. "Make it quick."

CHAPTER 4

"Gladly." Elyssa looked all too happy to end the Apocryphan. She even went for the sai swords sheathed on her back.

I held up a hand. "We're not actually here to see or kill you." It was awkward seeing Xanos again, especially with Elyssa staring daggers at her.

Xanos flinched. "You're not?" A heavy Cyrinthian accent colored her English.

"No." I raised an eyebrow. "Are you Eve's houseguest now?"

"No." Xanos worked her lips back and forth. "She was furious to find me in her realm. Told me I was a failure."

"A failure?" Elyssa scoffed. "Why would mommy dearest say that?"

"Because I did not succeed at conquering the realms." Her lip curled up and her nose twitched, an almost comical expression that had me mystified until she abruptly sneezed twice in quick succession. Tears pooled in her eyes, but she quickly wiped them away. "Now I am left in this cursed meadow with my allergies, all alone."

I repressed a grin. "I can bring you some Benadryl."

Her eyes narrowed. "That would be most kind."

Elyssa folded her arms and looked her up and down. "Did you shrink?"

Xanos nodded. "Eve saw fit to make me frail and weak as punishment."

I pinched the bridge of my nose. "Going back to this whole conquering thing—you're saying Eve is upset that you failed?"

"Yes." Xanos's shoulders slumped. "She believed my quest for world domination was the best way to keep Baal at bay. But now she believes Baal will win and recreate the world in his image once he is reincarnated as Elohim."

"She's a goddess for, uh, God's sake." I wondered if I should even capitalize that anymore. "Why doesn't she fight back?"

"I don't know, and I no longer care." Xanos went back to the porch and dropped into a chair. "For centuries, I used my vast intellect and cunning to bend others to my will. I freed my spirit and then my body from an inescapable prison. I rose from the ashes and nearly conquered Eden. But for all my successes, I underestimated the resolve of the Overworlders."

"You're not the first would-be conqueror we've defeated." Elyssa practically spat the words. "You're obviously not the last."

"Whatever you want from Eve, she will not give it to you." Xanos crossed her arms and watched us intently. "You are here for the weapon that killed my kin, are you not?" Losing her powers and shrinking to human size hadn't dulled her wits a bit.

"Do you know where it is?" I said.

"It is not here. Eve cast it into a place she thought not even Baal could reach."

Elyssa's eyes widened. "The Void?"

Xanos blinked in surprise. "You are perceptive for a human."

"I don't know why I didn't think of storing relics there before," Elyssa said. "The Beast devours anything living, so theoretically, Baal couldn't retrieve anything from there, right?"

"I told Eve she was wrong, but her mind constantly wars with madness." Xanos tapped her temple. "The Sundering broke her creation and cracked her mind. She lived among humans multiple times, not by choice, but because she forgot herself and her powers. And she also forgot what happened to Elohim when the world splintered."

"He became a spirit in Haedaemos." I leaned against a post.

Xanos frowned. "Of course, he did. But that is only a part of it. Most of his being went to Haedaemos, but other bits and pieces ended up in various realms. The best part of him went into the realm of Utopia. The darkest, most corrupt part of him fell into a realm and lay dormant for eons before it awakened."

I tried to wrap my mind around what she was saying. "You mean Utopian humans are so cool because of Elohim's good bits?"

"Naturally." She shuddered. "It has infused their beings."

Elyssa had already pieced together the rest of the puzzle. "The worst part of him eventually became the Beast."

"Darling child, you are wise beyond your years." Xanos's forehead creased. "The beings of that place were tainted, twisted, cursed. Due to my long imprisonment, I was unable to witness what happened there, but after my escape from the Abyss I captured a part of the Beast and examined it."

"Captured it?" I shivered. "We fought the Void swarm before. If part of it is separated from the Beast, it dies."

"Yes," she said. "It's a hive mind controlled by the malevolent core of the part that was once Baal. Once it cannot communicate with the brain, it quickly dies. That is why I examined it in its home environment."

Elyssa gasped. "In the Void?"

Xanos scoffed. "It is not truly a void at all. The realm still exists, stripped bare of all organics. Only barren cities remain."

I wasn't quite as adept at deduction as Elyssa, but that was when I saw Eve's mistake. "In other words, Unmaker can be retrieved if you enter the Void with protection."

Xanos nodded. "Eve confronted Baal and told him he would never have Unmaker. Baal told her there was no realm he couldn't conquer, even her own. He told her she could not hide it since the relics talk to each other."

"Then why did she throw it in the Void?" I said.

Xanos shrugged. "She said it was the only realm Baal couldn't conquer, not even with an army of dragons. There are worse things than the swarm in the Void."

I didn't want to imagine what those could be. "How likely is it that Baal knows where Unmaker is right now?"

Xanos didn't hesitate. "One hundred percent."

I flinched. "Are you kidding me?"

"I am not." She sighed. "Eve told him where she would put it and challenged him to retrieve it."

"Son of a biscuit eater." I groaned. "Eve needs to see a shrink."

"I think she is correct in thinking Baal cannot retrieve it any time soon." Xanos shrugged. "Even with my considerable resources, it took a long time to overcome the hurdles."

"But what if Baal can communicate with that lost part of himself?" I said. "What if the Beast hands over the sword willingly?"

"That is a possibility, but the odds are very low." Xanos tapped a finger on her chin. "The Beast acts on sheer reflex from what our experiments revealed. He cannot simply grant safe passage."

I wanted to punch Eve in the throat for her stupidity. "True or not, we've got to get it before Baal does."

Elyssa pursed her lips and stared at Xanos. "We have no reason to trust you. You're trying to lure us to our deaths."

"I have no reason to see you dead," the Apocryphan replied.

I snorted. "Bullshit. You hate us because we stopped you from world domination."

"I am ashamed and angry at myself for my failure." Xanos looked me in the eye. "I am only telling you this because I truly desire to stop Baal."

My jaw went slack. "Oh, now you want to join the team?" I threw up my hands. "Damn it, Xanos, you could have joined us a long time ago and saved thousands of lives. Now that you're a powerless midget Apocryphan you suddenly want to help us?"

"I am a prisoner, trapped and isolated in a tiny realm." Tears welled in her eyes. "I am going mad with boredom and loneliness."

"You survived eons in the Abyss," I said.

"Because I could openly plot against my father and siblings." She laughed. "I had my powers and knew I could escape from the prison. But without powers, there is no escape from this lonely place. That, and I also hate my mother."

"And there it is," Elyssa said. "She wants to prove her mother wrong."

"You and every teenage girl." I mulled it over. "How do you plan to help us without powers?"

"I have been to the Void. I know the most likely place where the Beast would keep the sword."

"What controls the swarm?" I asked. "Is it a giant brain?"

She shook her head. "I will say no more until you agree to take me."

I looked from Xanos to Elyssa. Elyssa bared her teeth. "You've got no leverage, you sanctimonious purple bitch."

Xanos shrugged. "On the contrary, I have a great deal of leverage."

I shook my head. "I say we run some tests of our own on the Void just to confirm she's telling the truth, and then we go forward. I can guarantee she's lying about something."

"Tests?" Elyssa scoffed. "That could take days or weeks we don't have. Let's just toss her into the Void and see if she talks."

She wasn't wrong. Cinder and Adam would be the first people to tell me that extensive testing needed to be done before attempting a mission into the Void. On the other hand, trusting Xanos as a partner was problematic. She might not have her powers, but she was still cunning and dangerous. For all I knew, she had a way to rip away the Apocryphan powers Emily had given me. The last thing I needed was another double threat to the realms. Her war had given Baal tons of space and time to build on his already considerable advantage.

But Xanos wasn't perfect. Despite her superior intellect, she'd had fallen into the same trap as others before her. Hubris and greed could bring down even the mightiest. Baal had also demonstrated that weakness, but the difference was he'd stacked the deck so heavily in his favor that he could afford a few failures without losing the entire war.

I looked at Elyssa. "I think we might have to consider her offer."

She scowled. "I don't like it, but we might not have a choice. She might already know things that would take us months to discover. And experimenting means repeatedly and recklessly exposing our realm to the Void."

I felt as if we were reasoning ourselves into a very dangerous corner.

Xanos watched me confidently. She already knew what my answer had to be. I almost wanted to say no just out of spite.

Instead, I sat on the porch and looked out at the meadow, letting the tension simmer a bit longer while I considered the other threads we were chasing. Conrad and Ambria were supposed to retrieve the dagger. Emily and Tyler were tracing leads on Underborn since he had the heart of Jura, but were also going to Aquilis. Vitania, former queen of the Sirens, hadn't been heard of since she went to petition Queen Dactia for help against Baal.

Unmaker, the sword of Jura, was supposedly the third and last remaining piece of the puzzle needed by Baal, but the unknown relic hidden in the Abyss made me wonder if that was true.

"You have made a decision," Xanos said.

"Yes." I looked at her. "You will help us retrieve Unmaker, but only if you answer this question."

She watched me expectantly. "That depends on the question."

"What is the secret relic hidden in the Abyss?"

Xanos stared blankly for a moment. "I heard Posthanied mention it once, but I don't know where or what it is."

Elyssa's eyes glittered with anger. She obviously didn't believe Xanos. "Baal's agents are hunting the Abyss for it. We could beat them to it if you help us."

"I truthfully don't know what might be hidden there," Xanos said. "Baal would occasionally send agents into the Abyss searching for hidden relics, but my siblings and other inhabitants would quickly dispatch them."

"How could you possibly not know?" Elyssa said.

"I was an outcast, banished to the fringe." Xanos shook her head. "I only learned what I did from spying on the others."

It was impossible to determine if she was lying or not, and I didn't feel like going through a long interrogation. "Well, let's just hope Baal doesn't figure out what it is before we do." I crossed my leg, leaned back in the chair, and rocked it back and forth a couple of times. "What do we need to enter the Void?"

"I am on the team?" she asked.

I nodded. "You're on the team."

A pleased smile crossed her face. "There is a hidden Razor Echelon base in Italy." Xanos steepled her fingers. "We can find the proper equipment there."

"How about you tell us where to find it?" I shook my head. "I'm not giving you access to a stockpile of weapons." Razor Echelon's anti-magic weapons had driven the Overworld to its knees and nearly exterminated supers. "For all I know, you've got a reserve army hiding out there."

"I have no more forces," she said. "Once you banished me here, my influence over the humans began to wane and fade until it was nothing more than a dream to them."

Elyssa blurred across the space between them in an instant, her face full of rage. "A dream that murdered thousands!" She gripped Xanos by the arm and yanked her out of the chair before flinging her off the porch and to the ground. "You led them like sheep to a slaughter and now you talk about them as if they were nothing. Do you know how many good people died to stop you?"

I watched in astonishment. Elyssa almost never lost her cool no matter how much she despised someone. "Babe, are you okay?"

Xanos lay on the ground nursing her arm. A deep bruise was already forming beneath the lavender skin.

Elyssa glared at her, shoulders heaving with anger. "Tell us where to find the base."

Xanos struggled to her feet. "Please, take me with you. I will make a soul oath if necessary."

I recovered from my shock. "Did Eve strip your Apocryphan strength?"

"I am not even a shadow of my former self." She straightened herself proudly despite the grimace of pain on her face. "Certainly, I am no match for either of you."

Elyssa took a deep, calming breath. "Make a soul oath."

I shook my head. "She has no powers. How will a soul oath help?"

"A soul oath will bind me regardless of powers," Xanos said. "But you will have to mingle your soul essence with mine since I no longer have the ability to do so."

She seemed almost eager to do it and I couldn't tell if that was because she was desperate to leave Eve's realm or if there was another ulterior motive. What if forming a soul oath helped her in ways I didn't understand? I really hated dealing with someone so conniving because it made me second-guess myself at every turn.

Maybe there was more to it I didn't understand, but as far as I knew, this was the best way to ensure Xanos didn't try to double-cross us later. She'd made Zon swear a soul oath before freeing him from the Abyss, so maybe it would work as advertised.

I shifted to demon vision. Xanos's aura no longer thrummed green and bright. Now it was a muted white, not much brighter than an ordinary human's. I extended a tendril of my essence and wrapped it around hers. She gasped softly at the contact. I was tempted to feed my demon side from her essence but got straight to business. I gave myself a moment so I could phrase everything in airtight turns.

Elyssa had already taken care of it. She turned the screen of her arcphone toward me, displaying the oath we'd designed for Posthanied, Araxos, and Couriondral. She'd marked through a couple of sentences and modified it for the current situation.

"Xanos, swear on your soul that you will not betray us in any way shape or form while you help us retrieve Unmaker. Once we have completed the mission and you've returned to this realm, your oath will be completed."

Xanos nodded. "I swear it."

An electric tingle passed between us and it was done. Elyssa raised an eyebrow, silently asking if it had worked. I nodded.

There wasn't much else to do here, so I set my hands on my hips. "Where in Italy is the Razor Echelon base?"

Xanos rubbed her bruised arm. "The north side of Mount Vesuvius."

I didn't have any pictures stored on my arcphone or an aethernet connection in this realm, so we'd have to return to Eden first. I traced the patterns for Eden and pictured Big Creek Ranch since it'd be best to report back to headquarters before attempting a jaunt into the Void.

Before I could slash open the portal, a golden beam speared into the ground before me, melting the dirt instantly. I yelped and leapt backward.

Eve landed next to me hard enough to shake the ground. Dirt and debris scattered into the air. Before I could utter a word, she gripped me by the shirt and flung me across the meadow. "Trespasser!" she roared. "Elohim holds no sway in these lands!"

CHAPTER 5

I skidded through the flowers and rolled to a stop against a distant tree. Eve was already blurring across the field. I knew my Seraphim powers weren't nearly enough to stop her, so I drew upon the Apocryphan magic and cast a shield. Eve slammed into it and rebounded with a thunderous boom.

"Eve, it's Justin!"

Her eyes glowed bright as the sun. Yellow flames billowed around her as she lifted from the ground. "Elohim." She spat the name. "You have tainted my works to satisfy your hubris, now you dare sully my new world?"

Her new world? What was she talking about?

"Eve, I'm not Elohim." My hands trembled under the strain of holding the shield and because I was scared shitless. Eve was even more unhinged than Xanos had claimed.

"Enough of your trickery." Eve curled her hands and miniature suns began to form around them. "You destroyed Earth. I will not let you do that to Alden."

Despite my fright, I nearly lost my concentration at that statement. "What's Alden?"

"Do not mock me," Eve growled. "Leave now or we will battle to the death."

"I yield!" I said. "I will leave."

The fiery nimbus around Eve began to fade. "Go now before I change my mind."

"I must return to my minions," I said.

"Take them and go!"

I lowered my shield and ran like my life depended on it—because it one hundred percent did. Eve continued hovering in the air, rotating to follow me as I raced back to Elyssa and Xanos.

Elyssa looked like she had a million questions, but she held them in. Xanos looked as if she might have soiled her pants. I traced the patterns for Eden as quickly as possible and slashed my hand vertically toward the ground. The portal blossomed before us. Elyssa and Xanos leapt through and I followed. The instant my feet touched the floor in the underground bunker at the Ranch, I closed the portal.

"What in the actual hell?" I grabbed Xanos's arm. "I thought Eve was gone!"

"She was." Xanos trembled in my grasp. "Her world is likely warded against intruders. She must have sensed your arrival."

"Eve is certified insane." Elyssa leaned against a stone wall. "We can't count on her help at all."

"That's putting it mildly." We were in the travel room, an empty chamber that was part of the warren of tunnels making up the underground Templar compound. This room was specifically cleared out as a convenient portal destination for me and Elyssa. It was certainly easier than using the designated portal locations in the garage beneath the barn especially since those were in such heavy use these days.

I turned to Xanos. "What's Alden?"

She shook her head. "It was rumored Eve began designing a new world after the Sundering within a new realm space. It was to be a recreation of Earth but the strain of doing it alone caused her such mental strain that it was never completed."

"A whole new world?" Elyssa said.

I nodded. "A new fantastic point of view. No one to tell us no, or where to go."

Elyssa groaned. "Justin, this is no time to joke around."

It wasn't, but it was the only way for me to manage my sanity in these insane times. "Xanos, do you know how to find Alden?"

She shook her head. "It was said Vitania helped her in the early stages. Perhaps she knows."

"Maybe Baal doesn't know where it is either." I tapped a finger on my chin. "It might be a good place to hide relics."

"Let's shelve that for later," Elyssa said. "We've got more immediate problems, like retrieving Unmaker before Baal does."

"Agreed." I blew out a breath and stepped into the corridor outside. We were already on command level, so we made our way toward Thomas's favorite strategy room. Templars in black uniforms narrowed their eyes when they saw Xanos, but none gasped or drew swords. They were too well trained for that.

The strategy room was empty, so I dropped into a seat at the conference table and motioned Xanos toward one. "Make yourself comfortable."

She sat in the leather chair and looked around, probably memorizing every detail.

Elyssa phoned her father and spoke with him. "He'll be here in a few minutes." She held up a trembling hand. "I'm going to get a blood pack before I get full-blown jitters."

"I'll be here." I took out my arcphone and dialed Shelton. He, Cinder, and Adam were working on a solution to the infernus problem, rooting them out of nom governments without causing total chaos along the way.

"Well slap my ass and call me Sally," Shelton said when he answered. "Just the man I needed to talk to."

I leaned back in my chair. "We've only been gone a few days. What's wrong?"

"Oh, I'll tell you what's wrong." Shelton grunted. "Conrad and Ambria vanished. Max and I found a blink stone near the entrance to the Glimmer. There were some burn marks in the vicinity that makes me think they were attacked and maybe kidnapped."

My heart skipped a beat. "By whom?"

"That's what I'm looking into." He paused. "Serena Thain is in Queens Gate. I don't think it's a coincidence."

I jolted to my feet. "Serena? You need to capture her and bring her in."

"Yeah, I could do that, but that'd be useless." He scoffed. "You know she'll clam up and not give us anything. But if I follow her, I can see exactly what she's up to."

"You're right. Unless you lose her."

"I ain't gonna lose her." Shelton grunted. "What's new with you?"

"Oh, nothing. Just sitting in a conference room with Xanos."

He gasped. "Xanos? Are you nucking futs?"

"Eve shrank her to human size and took away her physical abilities," I explained. "Aside from her ruthless cunning, she's practically harmless."

Xanos slumped as I talked about her in front of her back. I didn't even feel bad about it.

"I hope you're right." Shelton blew out a breath. "Why is she with you?"

I snorted. "You're going to love this next part."

He groaned. "Yeah, I'll bet. You plan on raiding Hell with her as your sidekick?"

"No, that comes later." I let the tension build for a moment. "We're going to the Void."

"What?" Shelton shouted loud enough to just about rupture my eardrum. "You can't be fucking serious!"

"Dude, calm down." I walked to the end of the oval-shaped table away from Xanos. "Eve put Unmaker in the Void, but according to Xanos, Baal knows where it is and might mount an expedition to recover it anytime now."

"I find that hard to believe," Shelton said. "The Beast devours everything. Nothing will last two seconds in there."

"Xanos claims there's a way to safely enter the Void." I told him everything she'd told us.

Shelton took a moment to digest everything. "You mean bits and pieces of Baal are scattered throughout the realms?"

"According to Xanos, yes." It would have been nice having confirmation from Eve, but that wasn't about to happen. Thomas entered the room alongside Elyssa. "Look, we're about to debrief Thomas. I'll let you know how it's going down."

"I want to go with you," Shelton said.

"If Conrad and Ambria have really vanished, you need to find them." I shook my head. "According to you, you used to be the best bounty hunter ever."

"Fine," Shelton said in a resigned voice. "I might have embellished my reputation a little, but I'll find them."

"I know you will." I sighed. "See you on the flip side."

"Yeah," he said in a rough voice. "Don't die." Then he ended the call.

Thomas looked from Xanos to me. "Elyssa debriefed me on the way here. If that was Shelton, I assume you know about the disappearance of Conrad and Ambria?"

I nodded. "He just told me."

"Emily Glass has not reported in for over a week," Thomas said. "Our efforts to protect the final relics are not going well."

"Understatement of the year." I shrugged. "If Emily can't find Underborn, then Baal probably won't have any better luck. Maybe he'll never find the heart."

"For all we know she's been held up in Aquilis while trying to help Vitania." Thomas settled into a chair at the end of the table near Xanos and regarded her with his icy blue eyes. "Not so long ago you delivered an ultimatum to us. Had you instead accepted an alliance we could have ended the threat of Baal already."

"Perhaps." Xanos straightened in her chair. "I did not see it as advantageous at the time. I erroneously thought there was little you could do to halt my progress."

Thomas simply nodded, apparently seeing no reason to debate the matter further. "Now, about the mission into the Void. What equipment will ensure your safety?"

"The swarm devours organic matter, absorbing it entirely into the greater whole. It drains energy sources quickly, even magical ones." Xanos leaned back and steepled her fingers. "Razor scientists sent drones into the Void to study it and winnow out any weaknesses in the swarm."

"Please elaborate." Thomas held his chin between thumb and forefinger. "I want to be absolutely sure of this."

"The Void is a realm with a mass only slightly smaller than Mars." She approximated a circle with her hands.

Thomas slid an arctablet across the table to her. She tapped the screen and a holographic whiteboard appeared. Xanos drew a circle then pinched the edges to expand it into a sphere upon which she traced several small landmasses. She shaded water blue and most of the land-masses in various shades of red. Only the small continents at the poles were left white.

Some realms more closely resembled Eden than others. This one looked nearly identical to Utopia with two separate super-continents on opposite sides of the globe and a few smaller land masses in between.

Xanos leaned back from her work. "It's only a rough drawing, but it illustrates the layout well enough."

I blurted out my only observation. "It looks a lot like Utopia. Is that because one realm got the good and the other got the bad?"

"There may be a correlation." Xanos shrugged. "But I don't know for certain."

"How did you obtain a global map?" Thomas asked.

"High-speed drones flew over the swarm and captured footage." Xanos rotated the globe. "The swarm is fast, but not fast enough to capture drones and drain their power supplies."

"Why were you studying the Void to begin with?" Elyssa asked.

"Curiosity and to see if it might be a useful weapon." Xanos shook her head. "I determined it was too dangerous."

"Duh." I rolled my eyes. "Why are some areas redder than others?"

"Concentrations of the swarm were greater there for reasons unknown."

Xanos clasped her hands. "What you must understand is that the tiny locust-like creatures are only a portion of the swarm. There are worse things lying beneath the outer layer."

I gulped. "What could possibly be worse than those?"

"Hang on." Elyssa held up a hand. "Every time we've opened a portal to the Void, it's been by accident, and when we have, there's nothing but darkness. How did your drones see anything?"

"There is dim sunlight in the Void except for one place—the heart of darkness, the lair of the Beast." Xanos shook her head. "We never discovered a reason why incorrectly visualized portals open there."

"It would make more sense if portals didn't open if you couldn't visualize the destination." My forehead pinched. "I assumed the Void was a literal name—that there was nothing there."

"The Void is certainly not a void," Xanos said. "There are ruins of a former civilization and even life."

I frowned. "I can't quite wrap my head around that concept."

Elyssa wrinkled her nose. "I thought the realm was entirely consumed by the Beast."

"It would seem so, though it doesn't explain many things." Xanos shook her head. "Our studies were incomplete. There are still many unresolved mysteries about the Void."

Elyssa waved a hand dismissively. "Let's get back to the meat of the discussion. What do we have to worry about when we get inside the Void?"

"The atmosphere is barely breathable, toxic to all but the hardiest life-forms. There are places covered in smothering darkness with no sense of direction." Xanos's hands trembled. "The swarm covers the world in a dense blanket like ash. Now that I consider facing it without my powers, I am admittedly nervous."

My heart was already palpitating. "Why are some areas pitch black?"

"Unknown." She looked down at the table. "There is dim sunlight that penetrates the thick cloud cover, but some places are inexplicably black, as if the very light has been corrupted and turned to darkness. Not even artificial or magical light can penetrate it."

"Freaky." I shuddered. "Maybe the laws of physics are being subverted somehow."

"That is one theory." Xanos shrugged. "After losing people in the areas of darkness, we simply avoided them."

I nodded. "Are they like the heart of darkness you mentioned?"

"The lair of the Beast is dark because the concentration of the Void swarm is incredibly dense there." Xanos met my eyes. "It is not the same as the pockets of anti-light."

"Anti-light." Elyssa blew out a breath. "Maybe Unmaker is safe after all. Do you really think Baal can overcome these odds?"

"If the Beast is truly a fragment of Baal, who's to say he can't control it somehow?" Thomas pursed his lips. "He might simply be able to send in an infernus and retrieve Unmaker. We need to beat him to it."

Elyssa nodded. "Agreed. At the very least, we'll confirm he took the sword."

I leaned toward Xanos. "We need to do this ASAP. How are you going to help?"

"The equipment I'll provide will mitigate the effect when the outer swarm comes for us." Xanos bit her lower lip. "We will have to fight for every inch of progress. Believe me when I say the outer swarm will be the easy part."

Elyssa tapped a finger on the table. "If we do get the sword, how will we protect it any better than the Void?"

Thomas nodded. "A valid point. I believe the Glimmer is the best place to create a repository for the relics. Cora commands every plant and creature in the place. Provided she can eventually awaken her people, we can form it into an impenetrable fortress."

"The Glimmer would be adequate," Xanos said.

"Eve might have created a new world within its own realm space that could be a safe haven for relics." I told Thomas about Alden.

"Another good possibility." Thomas turned to Xanos. "I want all the details about your equipment. I need to know Elyssa and Justin will be safe."

"We will be wearing armored body suits composed of murkonium crystalloy." Xanos wiped the whiteboard clean and sketched a suit that looked like something out of Iron Man but with a clear glass globe around the head. She colored the armor dark purple and dotted it with small nodes.

That was enough for me to form a connection. "That looks a lot like Daskar armor. Is murkonium crystalloy a fancy name for crystalline Murk?"

She shook her head. "The design is heavily influenced by Daskar armor, but because Murk is the force of creation, it contains too many organics to withstand the swarm." Xanos began writing out a complex chemical equation. "We extruded the organics and replaced them with titanium, forming a new crystalline metal that the swarm cannot penetrate."

I shook my head in disbelief. "Think of the good you could've done in the world with your arcnology."

Thomas inspected the illustration. "What about life support?"

"Our agents utilized Mzodi arcnology to adapt black aetherium as a power source." She drew a small backpack on the suit. "It is buried beneath a thick layer of armor to prevent the swarm from siphoning energy."

"How in the hell did you have access to Mzodi arcnology?" I said.

Xanos pressed her lips into a flat line. "We captured Mzodi and learned the secrets from them."

"By torture." Elyssa pounded a fist on the table and bared her teeth.

For a moment, I thought she was about to go ham on Xanos again.

"It was war." Xanos's voice cracked like a nervous teenage boy trying to convince a father he had only the best intentions for his daughter. "I thought of nothing but gaining the ultimate advantage."

Elyssa took deep breaths, but her violet eyes glittered with rage.

I'd seen Elyssa pissed off plenty of times, but she was always in control. Seeing her lose it with Xanos made me wonder if something else might be happening. If maybe Xanos still had her powers of persuasion and was using them to unbalance Elyssa.

Elyssa's glare softened and she sat back down. "Tell us more about the armor."

"As you wish." Xanos pointed to the nodes. "You can channel magic through these, though it won't do much good against the swarm since they consume the energy." She tapped the arms. "Arcphones and arctablets integrate into the armor so you can continue using them. They are also protected from power drain." She listed off a few more aspects of the armor and went silent.

Thomas nodded. "The mission to the Void may proceed."

Xanos didn't look happy to have swayed him. If anything, she seemed to regret coming along now that she'd highlighted just how dangerous the mission would be even with the equipment.

I stood. "Well, let's get going."

Elyssa nodded. "I'm ready."

Our small group had barely made it into the hallway when a wide-eyed Adam Nosti rushed around the corner and nearly collided with us. "Justin? Oh, thank god you're here."

I staggered back in surprise. "What's wrong?"

He threw up his hands. "This entire facility is about to blow up!"

CHAPTER 6

Thomas didn't even look surprised. "What is it this time?"

"No time to explain!" Adam grabbed my arm. "Come on!"

We ran down the corridor after him, took a few turns, and ended up in a vast open space Thomas had converted into a lab for Cinder and Adam to use. I saw and felt exactly what the problem was the moment I entered the room.

A small, but rapidly growing crystalline sphere had already burst from the confines of a null box it had been stored in. Jagged spikes grew from the sphere, their tips crackling with power as it soaked up all the ambient aether. I switched to demon view and watched in horror as the glowing veins of aether in the ground pulsed and dimmed.

It was a crystoid, a weapon designed to drain the aether from the world and redirect it to the former mastermind's headquarters on Seraphina. Cephus, the bastard behind their creation, was long dead, ironically consumed by the Void swarm.

"Hello, Justin." Cinder stood a few yards from the crystoid. "I'm afraid Adam and I made a terrible mistake."

"That's a freaking understatement." There already wasn't enough aether in the air for me to use for levitation, so I cast around for something to stand on. I located a stack of crates that would do the trick. There was only one way to neutralize the crystoid before it gathered enough energy to blow a hole in the roof and cause a cave-in. The crates were heavy, so I summoned my inner demon and partially manifested. Muscles coiled around my arms and my body swelled. My clothes stretched and began to rip, so I figured I was big enough and started pushing the crates.

Elyssa and Cinder ran to my side and helped, though I didn't really need it at that point. We shoved the stack in front of the crystoid. Just as I clambered up the side, the bottom crate groaned and cracked. Water trickled between the seams and suddenly it burst out. The stack toppled. I leapt out of the way as the pile crashed to the ground and all hell broke loose.

"That crate was full of soggers!" Elyssa dove away as dozens of small grenades bounced from the other crates and began bursting into flames. "And the other one is full of scorchers!"

Everyone took cover as the grenades demolished the crates until only soggy ashes remained. As a final insult, the icer grenades went off last, covering the floor in frozen gray puddles.

"Shit!" I watched the energy building up in the crystoid with my demon vision. The spikes on the top were already beaming energy toward the ceiling. Before long, it'd reach critical mass, bouncing the energy back in a loop that would either blow a hole in the ceiling or cause the crystoid to overload and detonate like a nuke.

Unless I positioned myself directly in the beam of aether emanating from the spikes, I'd have no magical energy to neutralize the crystoid. "Please tell me there's at least a stepladder around here."

"Not here," Cinder said, "but perhaps in another room."

"You have Apocryphan powers, do you not?" Xanos turned to me. "Simply touch it and channel the energy away."

"My body can't handle that kind of power." I'd touched a crystoid before and blown a hole through a hill. The energy surge had nearly killed me, and I'd only touched it for an instant. The only safe way to get power from a crystoid was by standing directly in the tight beam of aether it projected from the top. Without anything to climb, I didn't know how to pull that off in time.

The crystoid had already swelled to over ten feet tall. Not even a stepladder would do the trick anymore.

Elyssa grabbed my hand. "I've got an idea." We skirted around the icy puddles and made our way in front of the crystoid. Elyssa knelt. "Get a running start. I'll launch you into the air when you get here."

"And then what?" I said.

"Levitate."

I hadn't even thought of that. "Let's do it." I ran back about fifty feet, lined up, and sprinted toward Elyssa. My right foot landed in her cupped hands. She thrust upward and I jumped at the apex of her momentum. I arced through the air, soaring higher than the crystal meteor. Just as my momentum began to fade, I felt the rush of aether as I met the beam coming from the spikes.

Wings of pure energy sliced painfully from my back, one ultraviolet, the other white as snow. I spread them and held myself aloft before I fell back to earth. Flying and levitation weren't exactly my strong suits, so I took a moment to stabilize my position. It had been a long time since I'd neutralized a crystoid and my memory was a bit foggy.

"Be careful," Adam shouted up at me. "It'll try to suck you in when you neutralize it."

That was when I remembered how much of a pain in the ass these things had been. I levitated diagonally higher, keeping myself in the beam of aether to give myself some wiggle room for what was going to happen next. The ceiling was smooth-carved rock—not the ideal surface for what I needed, but I channeled four threads of Murk and adhered them to the ceiling and myself, then tied off the weaves.

I didn't know if my anchors would hold, but there was no way to test them except by doing what needed to be done. I cupped my hands. An orb of ultraviolet Murk formed in my left hand and a star of white Brilliance glowed to life in my right. When they each grew roughly the size of my head, I began to weave them into a ball of gray Stasis.

"Why do you not channel Stasis directly?" Xanos said.

I blinked. "How?"

She shrugged. "You just do it."

"Wow, great advice, Xanos." I rolled my eyes. "That's exactly how I learn to do anything I've never done before."

Xanos frowned. "I cannot put the process into words."

"I'll just do it my way, okay?" I continued weaving Stasis until it was large enough to give me some buffer, because the next part was going to be tough. I channeled a beam of Stasis into the crystoid. The meteor sucked greedily at the incoming energy, like a fish snapping a lure. But instead of catching a trout, I'd hooked a whale. The sudden intake jerked my arms down and yanked me toward the crystoid. My tethers snapped tight and my arms felt as if they were about to pop from the sockets.

The outer spikes shaded gray as the Stasis began to neutralize the crystal, but the drain continued unabated, a black hole sucking me inexorably into its gravity. My body ached at the intense strain, both mentally and physically. I cried out as the crystoid hungrily soaked in every ounce of aether I could channel.

The tether around my waist broke free from the ceiling. The one securing my chest snapped. The crystoid was only halfway gray.

"Hold on," I groaned. "Don't break on me now."

The third tether failed and the fourth one couldn't take the strain. I began falling toward the crystoid. All I had to do to stop my fall was to cease channeling Stasis. But I couldn't stop now or the crystoid would recover and everything I'd done would be for nothing. My wings flared in a desperate attempt to slow my descent, but it wasn't enough.

Slowly but surely, I drifted lower and lower. I couldn't stop myself. I gritted my teeth and summoned every ounce of power I had. The beam of Stasis widened. Sweat trickled down my forehead and into my eyes. I considered using the Apocryphan powers, but they'd interrupt channeling Stasis, causing more harm than good. I clenched my teeth and gave it everything I had.

I heard my friends calling out. Felt my heart pounding in my chest. The strain finally overwhelmed me, and my wings puffed away. I fell. Crystal shards bit into my skin and the roar of shattering glass filled my ears. My shoulder slammed against the rocky floor. Weakly, I pushed myself up and found myself in a mound of gray shards.

Elyssa reached me first. "You did it!"

I tried to stand but couldn't muster the strength. "I want ice cream."

She laughed. "I'll get you all the ice cream you want, big boy." She pulled me to my feet and steadied me, wiping broken crystal from my arms.

Adam looked at his feet. "Man, I'm so sorry. I must have mislabeled one of the null cubes when we put that thing into storage."

I took a few deep breaths. "Why in the hell do we have crystoids in storage?"

"We found tons of them stored in Cephus's lab on Seraphina." Adam shrugged. "We didn't know what to do with them, so we dumped them in null cubes. With everything that's happened since then, I forgot all about them."

"They were coated with a protective material that kept them from activating," Cinder said. "When Cephus launched them through sky portals toward Eden, the friction in the atmosphere was enough to burn that away. I believe the coating must have worn away while in storage."

"So, we've got only god knows how many of these things sitting in storage?" I threw up my hands. "That's insane!"

"We can get rid of them." Adam held his chin between thumb and forefinger. "We'd just need someone to channel Stasis the instant we open each null cube and destroy the crystoid."

I blew out a breath. "That's exactly how I want to spend an afternoon."

"It can wait." Thomas surveyed the disastrous mess in the lab. "Finding Unmaker is the priority."

"The sword of Jura?" Adam scratched his head. "I thought Eve had it."

"Not anymore." I scuffed a pile of gray dust with my shoe. "Now it's in the Void."

"Oh, snap." Adam grinned. "No way Baal can get it there." His eyes settled on something behind me and grew wide as dinner plates. "Holy shit, it's Xanos!"

I put a hand on his shoulder. "She's with us."

Adam put a hand on his chest. "She doesn't have any powers, right?"

"No, the big bad Apocryphan can't hurt you now." I looked him in the eye. "She's even been shrunk to bite sized now."

He scratched his head. "Wow, she is a lot smaller."

Xanos's shoulders slumped. "I do not appreciate the constant reminder that I have been reduced to nothing."

"Good." Elyssa smiled humorlessly. "You deserve it for all the heartache you caused, you purple bitch."

"Damn." Adam drew out the word. "You're not usually so savage, Elyssa."

"Her anger is appropriate," Cinder said. "Xanos nearly destroyed the Overworld."

Adam recovered his wits. "Why is Xanos here?"

I hesitated a second. "We're going to the Void with her."

"Wait, what?" Adam looked back and forth between me and Xanos. "That's a suicide mission!"

"Maybe not." I explained the mission and Xanos's part in it.

He stared at us in astonishment. "Can I come? Pretty please?"

"You want to come to the Void?"

Adam nodded fervently. "Dude, that would be the most interesting field trip ever. And maybe I can help."

Xanos looked him up and down. "Doubtful, mortal."

He looked her up and down. "Yeah, well you're not such hot shit anymore, so why are you going?"

She stared sullenly at him, apparently lacking an answer.

"Can I come, Justin?" Adam clasped his hands beggar style.

"Xanos, are there enough suits?" I asked.

"Enough suits for all the fools in the world," she replied. "How many more shall we cast into the Void with us?"

"I would like to be cast into the Void," Cinder said.

I shook my head. "I'm not risking all our brains in one go. Cinder, we need you here."

He looked from Adam to me. "It pains me to admit that you are correct."

"You speak strangely," Xanos said. "As if you lack emotion."

"I am a golem," Cinder explained. "Fjoeruss crafted me in his image as a gray man, but something happened when I was a captive of the vampire, Maximus, that gave me sentience."

Xanos blinked. "Accidental sentience? That's nearly incredible."

Adam shrugged. "He may not emote very well, and he may be a golem, but he's a better person than you are."

She stiffened but didn't reply.

I mulled over Adam's request for a moment and concluded that having our brainy friend on hand during an expedition into the unknown would be a good thing. He'd saved our asses on numerous occasions. He might not be the most powerful Arcane in the world, but he could hack his way out of just about anything.

I clapped his shoulder. "Adam, you're on the team."

"Yes!" He fist-pumped. "I'm looking forward to seeing the Razor facility."

"It's a science facility." Xanos regarded the mess left from the crystoid. "A clean and orderly environment."

"Wow, did you just diss our lab?" Adam shook his head. "A real lab gets dirty. Anyone who tells you differently is selling you something."

"She probably killed anyone who made a mess," Elyssa growled.

"My scientists were the best and the brightest." Xanos lifted her chin proudly. "I provided them with proper environments for experiments." Her lips peeled into a sneer. "Not a reallocated warehouse."

"I agree with Xanos," Cinder said. "These facilities are not favorably predisposed to science."

"Wow, Cinder." I shook my head. "You sided with the former bad guy?"

He blinked. "That is no endorsement of her attempt at world domination."

I snorted. "Well, as long as we're clear about that."

Elyssa checked her arcphone. "It's getting late. I suggest we get some sleep. We can go to the facility tomorrow."

I nodded. "Sounds good to me."

Thomas regarded Xanos. "I believe it would be best if you spent the night in our secure facility."

Her eyes flared. "In a prison cell?"

"I'm certainly not giving you free roam of the compound." He motioned her toward the door. "Unlike the Overworlders your people experimented on, I promise you'll be well-treated." He escorted her out of the room.

Fair cheeks flushed with anger, Elyssa glared at her until she vanished around a corner.

I took her aside. "What in the hell is going on with you? I've never seen you act so irrationally angry toward someone no matter how rotten they were."

She blew out a breath and looked down. "Daelissa was a saint compared to Xanos. Even that bastard, Baal, has more honor than that purple bitch."

I nodded. "You're not wrong. The experiments her people did on living prisoners was unconscionable. But Daelissa drained innocent people until they were husked, and Baal has kidnapped thousands of noms, using some of them for concubines and simply killing the others. They're equally bad."

Tears welled in Elyssa's eyes. She turned and abruptly left the room. I hurried to catch up. "Elyssa, what's really wrong?" She continued marching down the hall.

I grabbed her arm and turned her to face me. "You never keep things from me, but I feel like there's something you don't want to tell me."

Elyssa wiped at her reddened eyes. "Xanos is a monster! After everything I saw in her prison laboratories, I don't think she deserves anything except a painful death. I can't believe we're collaborating with her."

"And that's everything that's bothering you?"

She looked up at me and nodded. "I don't like hating someone this much, but I absolutely despise her. She used her powers of manipulation to brainwash humans and made them commit atrocities."

"I understand, I do." I wiped a tear from her cheek. "We'll be done with her after this, I promise. How about you think of a good way to punish her when we're finished?"

A smile shone through the tears. "I'd like that a lot, Justin."

"Hey, I know what makes my bae happy."

Elyssa snorted. "That's messed up."

I kissed her forehead. "Yeah, well, life keeps bending us over and ramming it up our butts without lube. Maybe we can return the favor."

She sighed. "If we beat Baal, do you think we'll finally have peace?"

"At this point, I'd be happy with a two-week vacation before the next major crisis."

Elyssa leaned on my chest. "Me too."

It was hard seeing her like this. Elyssa was my strength, always there when I faltered. She'd rescued me countless times, not just from physical danger, but from the depths of despair. I needed her at a hundred percent when our mission started.

Otherwise, the Void would eat us alive.

CHAPTER 7

Using a picture Xanos found on Google Maps, I opened a portal to the city of Pompeii, Italy. We stepped into a small alley, hidden from the prying eyes of noms. The facility was hidden beneath a grocery store just around the corner. Xanos wore jeans, a long-sleeve shirt, and a ballcap to hide as much of her lavender-colored skin as possible.

Considering the wild tattoos and modifications I'd seen on noms, I doubted she'd stand out much. At her current size, she looked like a cute girl, not a formerly murderous giantess hellbent on world domination. I had to keep reminding myself what Xanos had done so I wouldn't lose sight of that.

It was the middle of the day, but the streets were practically empty. People watched us from their balconies, some of them calling out angrily as we walked to our destination.

I smiled uneasily at my friends as an old grandma shouted in Italian at us. "What the hell is going on?"

Adam looked at his phone and frowned. "Fascinating. The entire nom world is on lockdown due to a pandemic."

"Say what?" I looked at his phone screen and glanced at the headlines.

"Italy was hit hard." Adam shook his head. "It's no wonder those people are upset. They think we're breaking the stay-at-home orders."

"So much for blending in." Elyssa looked up and down the road. "How much further?"

"Not far." Xanos took a right and pointed to a small stone building on the other side of a roundabout.

We hurried that way even as people watched us through open windows or called down to us from their balconies. We'd nearly reached the roundabout when a police car screeched around the corner and stopped right in front of us.

A pair of officers stepped out. One held up a hand and began speaking in Italian.

"No speako Italiano," I said.

He frowned and motioned his partner over.

I spoke slower as if that might help. "We aren't from here."

"Americans?" the other officer said.

"Yes." Maybe in a past life, I thought. "Americans." I pointed to the store ahead. "We need milk and bread."

He shook his head. "No. Stay home, no go anywhere."

The other guy was already breaking out handcuffs, motioning at Adam to turn around. He did a double-take when Xanos stepped into view from behind Adam.

"We don't have time for this." Elyssa looked ready to throw down.

I shook my head. "Everyone and their abuela is watching us. We can't throw down with the cops and walk away. They'll see us enter the grocery store and send reinforcements."

"The correct term is nonna," Xanos said. "Abuela is Spanish for grandmother."

I blinked. "Now isn't the time for language lessons."

Xanos smiled reassuringly at the police officers and shook her head at the one preparing to handcuff Adam. She spoke slowly in Italian, pointing at the grocery store and then back down the street.

The officer shook his head, but his partner put a hand on his shoulder and apparently talked him down. The other one looked Xanos up and down then spoke while making a variety of gestures that looked rude. Xanos's smile made me think maybe they weren't so much rude as suggestive of something else.

Then the second officer motioned us onward. "Fast," he said. "Fast and go home."

Xanos smiled and nodded, replying in Italian.

The officers climbed in their car and drove away.

Elyssa looked suspicious. "You used your powers of influence over them."

Xanos shook her head. "I told them it was my parents' store and that I had to bring home as much as possible so we could use it before it goes bad."

"What did they think about you being purple?" I said.

"I told them it was a rare skin condition." She shrugged. "The first officer wanted to know who my parents are, and the address. His partner told him he just wanted to know so he could ask me on a date. I told them they would have to fight over me."

"That explains all the gestures." I looked uneasily at the people glaring at us from the comfort of their homes along the narrow street. "Let's go before they come back."

The sign above the door looked as if it had been hand-painted by a child. I couldn't even decipher the messy cursive. The windows were blacked out and there were no posters or signs anywhere indicating the place was a grocery store. Then again, maybe that was the point. It was doubtful any noms would ever enter the building if they didn't know what it was.

Xanos bypassed the front door and walked around to the back. Elyssa took me by the arm to slow us down. "Don't let down your guard," she whispered. "This could be a trap."

I nearly stopped in my tracks because I'd completely let down my guard. Razor Echelon had created weapons that countered just about every kind of magic and supernatural being in the Overworld. They had drones that could knock us out, cubes that tracked supernatural signatures, and rifles that shocked us into submission. For all I knew, this place was rigged with traps that would render us unconscious and then Xanos would be free upon Eden again. Though, unless she had a way to steal my Apocryphan powers for herself, I didn't know what good it would do her.

"Why did you learn Italian?" Adam asked Xanos as he walked alongside her. "Doesn't seem like you'd even need to bother."

"I had an Italian host for a time when I was a spirit." She stopped at a heavy-duty steel door in the back. "I absorbed the language naturally."

"Naturally." Elyssa scoffed. "That's about as unnatural as it gets."

"Must be handy." Adam sighed. "The only other language I know is Cyrinthian."

Xanos raised an eyebrow. "Low Cyrinthian, the language of Arcanes."

Adam shook his head. "I know conversational and High Cyrinthian. We spent years in Seraphina, after all."

Her other eyebrow joined the first. "Impressive, for a human."

Elyssa huffed. "Just open the door."

"As you wish." Xanos slid open a hidden panel in the back wall to reveal a number pad.

"I don't think she realizes she just said she loves you," I whispered in Elyssa's ear.

Elyssa rolled her eyes but couldn't repress a snort. "You never miss an opportunity, do you?" Her shoulders stiffened as the steel door swung open. "Get ready. Xanos will go first so she can spring the trap on us behind her. Be ready for anything."

I had a better idea. "Hold up." I went to the door and peered inside with my demon vision. I didn't see any magical traps, which made sense considering Razor's anti-magic stance.

Xanos sighed. "You don't trust me."

"Hell to the no." Elyssa's warning had filled me with paranoia. I needed to take even further precautions. I stared at a spot in the rough asphalt and reached through the window of my soul into Haedaemos where I quickly found a good candidate.

I sensed my inner demon but didn't stop to say hello. Ever since our adventures in the afterlife, we hadn't had as many conversations as we used to. It was as if our personalities were merging to the point where there wasn't a clear delineation like there used to be.

A bubbling pool of tar formed in the asphalt. A form began to rise from it, jerking and twitching spasmodically. It took on the shape of a large canine and tore its way free from the primordial ooze.

I am here, the new hellhound announced.

Xanos scoffed. "A hellhound. How quaint. I recall you using me in such a form once."

"You were a good girl when you were a dog." I sighed. "Then you turned into a bad girl."

"She was always a bad girl," Elyssa said.

Xanos scowled but held her tongue. "What now?"

"The hound goes with you. We'll follow close behind in case there are any traps." I motioned her onward. "Let's go."

Adam gave me an uneasy look. "Do you really think it's a trap?"

"This is Xanos we're dealing with." I watched as she and the hound entered the door. "Let's not take any chances."

Adam gulped and followed Xanos inside. Elyssa and I brought up the rear. I readied my Seraphim powers in case I needed to blast anything or shield us. We passed through an empty stockroom and into a room with a large stainless-steel refrigerator. Xanos reached around the side of the unit and tapped in a sequence on a number pad. The fridge slid aside, revealing another door. Xanos opened it and stepped into darkness.

Adam held his arcphone at the ready and poked his head into the door. A light flicked on and he jumped back a foot. "Shit!"

Xanos stood next to an elevator door, an amused expression on her face. "I don't suppose it would do any good to tell you there are no traps?"

The hellhound sat on his haunches, red eyes watching the Apocryphan intently.

"Nope." Elyssa stepped into the room and punched the button next to the door. "I'll slash your throat the instant you try anything."

"How do I make it clear to you that my own self-interests are at stake?" Xanos folded her arms and cast an angry look at Elyssa. "If Baal undoes the Sundering, I may be among the billions who die. Just because Eve reduced me to nothing does not mean I am ready to give up."

In that instant I realized exactly what drove Xanos. She had been the outcast, the one the others looked down upon, and had been bullied by her siblings. She was the only one not to have ruled nations when the other Apocryphan dominated the Earth. They had brawn, but she had brains.

In short, Xanos was the outcast nerd of the Apocryphan bunch.

As the black sheep of the family, Xanos felt the relentless need to prove herself. She'd tricked her brethren into attacking Elohim and sundering the world, thus throwing their rules into disarray. When the Sirens lured the Apocryphan into the Abyss, Xanos spent eons searching for a way out until I unwittingly freed her spirit.

Now she was powerless and no taller than a human, but she hadn't given up. Xanos would never give up, no matter the odds. She was a survivor. Unfortunately, that didn't mean she was trustworthy. If anything, it meant she'd use us until she didn't need to anymore.

Somehow, I had to channel Xanos's survival instinct into a force for good. I didn't know if that was possible or not, but even someone as rotten as her had to have some sliver of good left inside. For our sake, I hoped so.

The elevator door slid open and we crowded inside.

Xanos wrinkled her nose. "It reeks of brimstone thanks to this dog of yours."

"Nah, I just farted." I winked.

She frowned. "I've never understood why bodily functions are so humorous to humans."

I pursed my lips. "Do Apocryphan poop?"

Adam snickered.

"We eat, we drink, so of course we urinate and defecate." Xanos shook her head. "Most physical beings operate by similar standards. Even beings of pure energy still shed waste, but in a different manner."

"Really?" Adam looked intrigued. "Is it like heat waste, or maybe vapors?"

"Both and more." Xanos launched into a dissertation on various entities and how they pooped.

Just as the elevator ride threatened to go on forever, the doors opened, and I groaned with relief.

"Fascinating." Adam wasn't done learning. "What do you know of Flarks?"

"A great deal." Xanos looked ready to dish everything about the disgusting creatures when Elyssa snapped her fingers.

"Save the lectures for later, please. I'm about to fall asleep."

Adam looked like he was bursting at the seams with questions, but he clamped his mouth shut and nodded. "Sorry."

We stepped out of the elevator and into a large white warehouse space lined with large white cubes. It looked nearly identical to the underground prisons Razor used to house and experiment on supers during the war. With a loud *snikt*, Elyssa drew her sai swords and pressed their points against Xanos's throat.

The Apocryphan gasped and backed into a wall. Blood trickled from the hollow of her throat. "What are you doing?"

"You bitch," Elyssa growled. "How many did your people murder here?"

"Not a prison." Xanos trembled violently causing the sword points to scratch her skin. "We manufactured devices here."

I gripped Elyssa's wrist. "You're going to kill her."

Elyssa's white-knuckled death grip on the swords relaxed slightly. After a long moment of hesitation, she stepped back and sheathed the swords. "I am going to kill her if she's lying."

Tears of pain trickled down Xanos's cheeks. She gingerly touched the cuts on her throat and looked at the blood. But she didn't glare at Elyssa or cast any threats. She did what she'd probably done when bullied by her siblings—put her head down and complied.

She opened the first door and stepped back to let us see inside. The cubes in this facility were notably larger than the ones in the prisons I'd seen. This one housed a long machine with tiny robot arms along a conveyer belt. I stepped inside and examined the components. A funnel at one end held hundreds, maybe thousands of metal casings. A crate at the other end held magazines filled with bullets.

"This manufactures electro-bullets and inserts them into magazines." Xanos pointed to another cube. "That one stamps the rifle components and assembles them." She pointed out other cubes and explained what they did.

Adam nodded. "Isn't everything designed to self-destruct if a super tries to use them?"

"Yes." Xanos looked up demurely. "May I show you to the suits?"

I'd seen that look in the eyes of bullied nerds in high school. I knew how powerless she felt right now, because I'd felt that way when Nathan Spelman and his football cronies bullied me in high school.

Dude, you're sympathizing with a psychopathic former demigoddess. I wondered if Xanos would have become such a terror if her Apocryphan siblings had been nicer to her, or if Eve had protected her.

I felt like slapping myself just to stop this line of thinking. I was trying to humanize someone who hadn't been even remotely human for thousands of years. She'd seen us as mere worker ants who could be used to further her agenda. If Xanos had been treated kindly by her siblings, she probably would have followed in their footsteps. The Sundering might never have happened in the first place, true, but that was the only silver lining.

I cleared my throat. "Please take us to the suits."

Elyssa gave me a *really dude?* look for being polite.

Escorted by the hellhound, Xanos began walking down the aisle.

I considered asking why her facilities were so oddly designed. It seemed inefficient to make a warehouse-sized room and fill it with smaller cube rooms that didn't even come close to using all the overhead space. Maybe she did it for the aesthetics.

Elyssa abruptly stopped an instant before a squad of Razor soldiers rotated out of cover behind cubes on either side of the aisle and sprayed us with gunfire.

CHAPTER 8

Xanos threw up her hands as if they might save her.

I reflexively channeled a shield in front of her and the bullets pinged off the invisible barrier. Radios chirped and soldiers began shouting commands. Echoes of boots on concrete told me enemies were circling around behind us. I spun to tell Elyssa just in time to see her leap fifteen feet, catch the roof of a cube, and pull herself up.

She must have drawn her light bow, because bolts of energy began flashing down the aisles, exploding on impact. Soldier shouted in alarm.

Xanos was still frozen behind my shield, but it wasn't going to last long. A pair of soldiers with energy-draining rifles were already lining up for a shot. A couple of blasts would put a massive drain on my shield and take it down in seconds.

I tied off the weave to the shield so I could turn my attention toward an escape route. Adam grabbed Xanos by the arm and dragged her back toward me.

Hellhound, search and disable any attackers.

The hound bounded back past me and dashed down a corridor. Razor possessed weapons that could disperse the demon flesh of hellhounds, but he could at least do some damage before they took him down. Shouts and cries of alarm told me he was doing just that.

"Cease fire!" Xanos shouted even as Adam dragged her behind a cube for safety. "I am your leader!"

It was obvious that this hadn't been a trap prepared by Xanos, but a completely unexpected attack. I doubted they would listen to or even recognize her in her current form. Sure, they'd seen her as a full-fledged giant Apocryphan, but now she didn't look much different from any other super, aside from the purple skin.

A squad of soldiers burst around the corner on the opposite side of the cube and opened fire. Adam tapped his phone and a shield shimmered into place.

One of the Razor agents tapped the side of his full-faced helmet and his voice emerged from speakers on the helmet. "Your magic won't do you any good, freak. Surrender if you want to live."

"Cease this attack!" Xanos shouted. "I am Xanos!"

The man flipped up the blacked-out visor for a clear look at her. "I wish you were that bitch. I'd kill you with my bare hands for what she did to us."

Xanos's face paled. "What do you mean?"

"She controlled our minds. Turned us into her slaves, and then threw us into battle without caring how many of us died." His eyes narrowed. "You look like a toy compared to that giant purple monstrosity."

"Maybe it is her," another soldier said. He cast his hidden gaze over us. "Is that Xanos?"

"No," Adam said. "Now, lay down your weapons and surrender. I don't want to hurt anyone."

The first soldier burst into laughter despite the distant shouts and screams from his comrades as Elyssa and my hellhound ripped into them. "Hey Baskins, light up this shield with your rifle."

"Gladly." A mountain of a man bearing one of the energy-soaking rifles stepped into view and aimed the wide muzzled weapon from the hip.

Adam shook his head. "You really don't want to do that."

Baskins fired. Gray rings of energy rippled out of the muzzle and struck the shield with a loud crackle. The shield should have crumbled like broken glass, but it didn't. Instead, the charge bounced right back in soldiers' faces. The magazines on their rifles glowed. The electro-bullets inside detonated. Electricity raced up and down their bodies. The soldiers convulsed violently and began dropping like rag dolls.

The only one to escape electrocution was Baskins. His mouth dropped wide open. Before he could turn and run, Adam dropped the shield and ran another spell on his arcphone. Ropes of energy lashed out and wrapped around the man's feet, tripping him up.

In the distance, a few more people cried out and then the facility grew quiet except for the panicked breathing of Xanos.

"I was wrong," she said softly. "It was better for me to stay in Eve's realm. I am weak. I am nothing. Even a stray bullet could end my life."

Razor bullets didn't usually kill, but in this case, the overload of the magazines in the soldiers' rifles had electrocuted them all to death.

Elyssa leapt down from a nearby cube, lips pressed into a grim line. "Your hellhound is gone, but we took out seventeen soldiers." She looked at the downed men in front of us. "I think that's the last of them."

Baskins rolled over and raised his rifle. Adam kicked it out of his hands, then secured the man's wrists with another spell from his arcphone.

"What the fuck?" Baskins shouted. "My dispersion rifle destroys magic and my armor is magic resistant." He looked at the crackling bands of energy around his wrists. "How did you do that?"

Adam shook his head. "Your dispersion rifle and magic-resistant armor operate on similar theories—that aether bonds can be broken down at a molecular level. I turned the theory on its head."

Xanos snapped out of wallowing in self-pity. "But how?"

"I created a spell with malaether, a corrupted form of magical energy." Adam shrugged. "Technically, it shouldn't be done because malaether is extremely unstable. But when properly stabilized, it creates a reversion field that rebounds dispersion fields back at the source." He looked at the bodies of the other dead soldiers. "I certainly didn't expect that to happen."

I clapped him on the back. "Hot damn, Adam. That brain of yours saved us again."

Elyssa nodded. "Good work."

"You didn't do so bad yourself." I winked. "It helps having a kickass ninja guarding our backs."

I thought about summoning another hellhound, but Xanos looked pretty shaken up. It seemed she hadn't planned any treachery after all. She was too busy questioning life right now to be much of a danger. Or...was it yet another plot of hers to draw us into complacency?

Now I'm second-guessing my second-guessing.

I had to remain vigilant without giving myself a stomach ulcer from the stress.

Elyssa knelt next to Baskins. "Why are your people still here? The war is over."

"It'll never be over until freaks like you are dead." He tried to spit in her face, but Elyssa dodged it with ease.

"Try that again and I'll cut off your nose." Elyssa whipped out a sai sword and flicked the tip of his nose with the point.

"Ouch!" He winced and tears of pain filled his eyes.

"So, you and your buddies decided to keep the gang alive?" Elyssa said. She prodded him with the point.

"Yes, yes!" He winced with each poke. "The Overworlders destroyed most of our facilities, so we only have a few remaining. We came here because it's the one with all the weapons and ammo. We haven't been able to do much with the pandemic keeping everything locked down."

Elyssa nodded. "How many other companies of soldiers are there?"

"I don't know." He watched the tip of her sword fearfully. "I swear it. Only Colonel Jameson knew." He glanced at the man who'd lifted his visor earlier. "I think there might be two more companies, but I don't know where they're located."

"I have a good idea where they are." Xanos knelt on the other side of the man. "For I am Xanos."

Baskins glared at her, then looked at Adam. "Is she really Xanos?"

Adam nodded. "When we defeated her, we took away her powers and sent her back to her mom's house. Her mom is a goddess, so she shrank Xanos down to human size and took away her strength."

A smile spread across Baskins' lips. "Really?" He burst into laughter. "This purple shit stain is our glorious leader?" Baskins laughed until it sounded like he wanted to cry.

Xanos's face turned about as purplish red as it could get. "Why do you mock me when we could have ruled the realms?"

"Because you're no better than the other freaks, you purple-faced bitch!" He spat in her face. "I hope you die painfully for using us."

Xanos fell back on her ass, wiping away the thick spittle.

Elyssa laughed. "I'm just about willing to let you go free for that."

Baskins glared at Elyssa. "Xanos betrayed us and her own kind. Why are you with her?"

"Because another entity wants to destroy the world and remake it." Elyssa shook her head. "I don't know how much you know, but the Grand Overlord of Haedaemos plans to recombine the realms, killing billions in the process."

Baskins paled. "What the fuck is it with you freaks and your hunger for world power?" He shook his head. "Screw it. Just kill me now and get it over with."

I shook my head. "Nah." I turned to Adam. "Cut him loose."

"Sure, okay." Adam shrugged and tapped on his phone.

I pictured a lovely little town in Iceland I'd never forget and slashed open a portal. It was still cold there, but the flowers in Vitania's front yard were bright and blooming.

Baskins stood and stared in awe at the portal. "Where is that?"

"It's a surprise." I shoved him through and closed the gateway. Then I looked down at Xanos where she still sat on the floor wiping spittle from her face. "Baskins has a point. You screwed over everyone."

Tears welled in her eyes, but she remained quiet.

"No need to pile on." Adam reached down a hand. Xanos reluctantly took it and he pulled her upright.

"She doesn't deserve a helping hand," Elyssa said.

Adam shrugged. "Sorry, but I've been hanging around with Justin too long. He sees the best in even the worst of us and never gives up. I'd like to think that anyone can be redeemed no matter how shitty they used to be."

For the first time since seeing Xanos again, Elyssa looked ashamed. She looked away from Adam. "Fine, but don't be surprised when she turns the tables on us." Elyssa spun and jabbed a finger at Xanos. "Because I know you will!"

I cleared my throat and rubbed my hands together. "This has been the best family trip ever. The perfect capper would be suiting up and entering the Void. Whaddya say, kids?"

Elyssa scowled.

Adam chuckled.

Xanos nodded somberly. "I am ready."

I felt bad about leaving the dead lying where they were, but we couldn't exactly take them aboveground for a proper burial. We put the bodies into one of the manufacturing cubes and Adam used a preservation spell to keep them fresh for a few days.

"Why don't we just feed them to the Void?" Elyssa said.

Xanos shook her head emphatically. "The point of this is to avoid attracting the Beast. If it senses flesh, it will focus all its attention on that location."

"Won't opening a portal grab its attention too?" I said.

"Normally, yes." Xanos traced the symbols for opening a portal to the Void in the air. "Opening a portal the right way will take us to an oasis—a place untouched by the swarm."

Adam's eyebrows arched. "There's a place the Beast hasn't destroyed?"

Xanos nodded. "We took photos so opening a portal with the symbols and the image will allow us safer entry than portaling to a random location."

Elyssa scowled. "Why didn't you mention this earlier?"

"Because then you wouldn't need me." Xanos led us to a cube at the far end and opened the door. "Without technology, I am now useless."

"Doesn't matter." Elyssa gripped her arm and led her into the room. "You're coming along."

Adam winced. "Damn."

I took him aside before he entered the room. "Look, I understand. I want to see the best in Xanos and so do you. Hell, I just came back from a little adventure with Daelissa, and it was damned hard to see anything good in her."

"But she eventually redeemed herself," Adam said.

"No, she took her first step toward redemption." I sighed. "She consumed countless souls during her long life and sentenced them to an eternity of torture. If she can restore them and bring them to the after-life, I'll consider that penance."

"Well, she's dead at least." Adam shrugged. "If and when Xanos dies, she'll end up the same place. Wouldn't it be better for her to earn penance while she's still alive?"

I opened my mouth to debate the point, but he was right. Redemption was so much harder while alive. Maybe Xanos would redeem herself, or maybe she'd fall flat on her face. Only time would tell.

Adam and I entered the room. Transparent cases lined the walls, each displaying one of the suits Xanos had illustrated for us. They all looked about the same size, which seemed problematic. Elyssa guided Xanos to the first one. "Put it on."

Xanos pressed the side of the case and the front section slid into the floor. She looked uneasily at us, then stripped, revealing a curvy, compact body with a little bit of pudge in the belly. It seemed Eve had stripped her of her supernatural metabolism as well.

Damn, that's harsh.

Adam cleared his throat and averted his eyes, but it was obvious he wanted to look. I'd seen Xanos naked when she was still a giant. As Shelton had noted, her boobs were each bigger than my head at the time. Eve had reduced them to little more than A-cups.

Xanos turned her back to the armor, seemingly unconcerned that it was about a foot too tall for her. "Bonding sequence initiate."

79

The suit hummed to life and a robotic voice spoke. "Sensing parameters. Parameters set. Adapting." The crystalline armor shrank. "Bonding ready."

Xanos backed into the armor and seemed to melt into it. When her head was centered in the neck hole, the suit shrink-wrapped around her body, forming a perfect fit.

"That was cool." Adam stepped closer, inspecting the fit and finish. "How does the murkonium transition from a solid to a gas?"

"It's a process similar to what the Darklings on Seraphina have used for eons." Xanos lifted her chin a little, as if recovering a fragment of her dignity by being smart. "These suits use gems to change the physical state of the armor, but it's tied into an arcnology framework."

"Brilliant." Adam whistled. "How much of this is your work and how much came from your scientists?"

"I came to them with the magic theories. They helped me bind it to scientific principles." She looked at the arcphone in his hand. "Arcnology was the missing link that bound them together."

Elyssa rolled her eyes. "Adam, go clean up your pants and get into a suit."

"Don't make fun of my nerdgasms." He opened the display case next to Xanos's. "Should I keep my arcphone outside the suit?"

"No, keep it in your hand." Xanos stepped out of the display case, her movements fluid despite the armor. "The suit will bond with arctablets and arcphones, allowing you to use them with the external display. The Void swarm will drain arcphones of power if you keep them outside."

"Ah, I see." Adam stepped up to the armor in the case and looked at us. "Could you guys turn around?"

Elyssa laughed. "And deprive us the fun of seeing you awkwardly strip?"

"I can put on a show," Adam said. "But you need to make it rain."

"Well, at least I know who has the jokes when Shelton isn't around."

Elyssa walked around the display cases in the middle of the floor and out of sight.

I turned away because the last thing I wanted to see was Adam's hairy ass. Xanos watched without expression.

A moment later, Adam said, "Bonding sequence initiate."

I listened to it go through the checklist and waited until Adam exclaimed, "Wow, it's really comfortable in the crotch. And I can use my phone like normal!"

I turned around and inspected the suit. The screen of his arcphone was on the right arm of the suit.

Xanos smiled. "I'm glad you like it."

"Like it?" He flexed his biceps. "Dude, this is almost as good as being a superhero."

I stripped and suited up while Adam enjoyed another nerdgasm. As the suit formed around me, the phone slid out of my hand and moved to the top of my arm where the suit molded around it. It was admittedly cool. I decided to give it a test. "Nookli, what's the weather like in Italy?"

My phone replied in its choppy synthesized voice. "Justin, there is an Indian restaurant four miles away."

Adam chuckled. "If I didn't know better, I'd say your phone likes to mess with you. You've had it long enough that it's probably achieved sentience."

Elyssa walked around the corner looking curvy and delicious in her bonded armor. "His phone is nearly a decade old and hopelessly outdated, but he refuses to upgrade."

"I'll never give up Nookli!" I shot back. "Just because she has a slightly defective chip or two doesn't mean I should replace her."

Elyssa snorted. "At least we'll always find an Indian restaurant when we need one."

"True." I rubbed my belly. "But I don't want to risk explosive diarrhea while we're in the Void."

Xanos's forehead scrunched with confusion. "Is this how you allay fear? By discussing irrelevant subjects?"

Elyssa shook her head. "You wouldn't understand."

Adam scratched his nose. "Man, I hope I don't get any itches while we're all sealed up."

"What if we have to pee?" I asked.

"You may urinate and defecate to your heart's desire," Xanos said. "The suit will contain and eliminate waste using the same process Darklings use in their bathrooms."

"Even farts?" Adam said.

Xanos stared at him and slowly shook her head. "Your attempts at levity are not helping me."

I snorted. "Helping you what?"

She clasped her hands. "My stomach hurts with fear."

"We're all nervous," Adam said.

Xanos looked down. "I have never known such intense fear. It is because I know I have no power to defend myself or escape should the mission go awry."

"Welcome to the club." I shrugged. "One screwup in the Void and we'll earn a one-way ticket to the afterlife."

"No." Xanos shook her head. "The swarm consumes all, even the soul. There is nothing but oblivion should we fail."

CHAPTER 9

"**W**ell, shit." I hadn't realized that the Beast ate souls right along with the body. "I guess we'd better not screw up."

Elyssa tapped the side of her head. "Where are the helmets?"

"Initiate full seal," Xanos said. Ultraviolet mist covered her head and congealed into a clear dome. "Deactivate full seal." The dome misted away.

I looked around. "Do we need anything else?"

Xanos produced a black cube—the devices her troops used to hunt for supers. "I will configure this to ignore your magical signatures. The relics emit a very strong magic field. If the sword is close enough, the cube should detect it."

"How close?" I said.

"For a magical signature that strong, perhaps within a few hundred miles."

I grimaced. "Travelling a hundred miles on foot isn't going to work out."

Xanos nodded. "Agreed."

"What about weapons?" Adam asked.

Xanos shook her head. "None of our weapons had any effect on the swarm, so there is no point to bringing them."

I examined the gems on the palms of the armor. "Why did you include magic channeling nodes when Razor's entire purpose was to quash magic users?"

"We planned to weaponize the nodes using arcnology, so we left them in the design." Xanos shrugged. "Your Seraphim magic will have little effect on the swarm."

"What about Stasis?" I asked.

She shook her head. "I cannot say as we didn't have the ability to test such things."

I had a lot of other questions, but at this point, it seemed like I was stalling for time. "Man, I'd hoped to eat authentic Italian before we went into the Void."

Xanos held out her hands helplessly. "There are nutrition packs available in storage."

I rubbed my belly. "Good, because I'm starving."

We helped ourselves to some grub—it wasn't very tasty—and then prepped for launch. There was no way to bring food or other supplies with us since opening our suits to eat would invite a quick death.

Xanos showed us to a room set aside for travelling and gave me the Cyrinthian symbols that would open a portal to the Void even though I could have looked them up on Nookli. She activated a screen on the wall and scrolled through several images before settling on one with a copse of trees.

"I didn't think vegetation could survive in the Void." Adam pushed a finger up the bridge of his nose even though he no longer wore glasses. "Is that the right picture?"

"It is an oasis." Xanos stepped beside him. "Others like it are scattered throughout the realm."

"How did it survive?" Elyssa asked.

"We don't know." Xanos pursed her lips. "We ran experiments on the trees and the land but couldn't discern what made the swarm ignore it."

"Do you have images of other oases?" I asked.

Xanos nodded. "We will start here and see if the cube detects anything. If not, we will portal to the next and so forth."

Adam turned to her. "Do we need our helmets on while in an oasis?"

Xanos shook her head. "The air inside the oasis is breathable, but outside of them the air is toxic."

"That is so freaking weird." Adam bit his lower lip. "I really want to understand how these little islands survive."

"It's magic." Elyssa made jazz hands. "The Glimmer is nothing but chunks of a broken planet floating in out space and you didn't question that."

"Oh, I questioned it," Adam said. "Magic is the answer, but I want to understand the underlying reason for it."

Xanos nodded. "The mind of a scientist knows no rest."

"No one asked you," Elyssa said.

"Actually, I did." Adam sighed. "Well, let's get on with it."

I traced the symbols in the air, imbuing each one with power as I did, then closed the circuit and fixed the image of the oasis in my mind. I slashed my hand vertically through the symbols and the portal ripped open. The world on the other side looked normal, serene even. A gentle breeze whispered through the leaves of a purple-leafed tree. Grass and flowers swayed.

"I'll go first." I tentatively poked my head through and looked around. A violet sun smiled down from a green sky filled with blue clouds. I'd seen plenty of bizarre color combinations, so that didn't faze me. The air smelled fresh and the vegetation didn't try to eat me. That was a win in my book.

Perhaps fifteen feet away, the air rippled like water. I materialized the helmet, took a few deep breaths, and walked toward the anomaly. I reached out and my hand passed through it without resistance. I pulled back my hand and was relieved to find it still there. Then I poked my head through the ripple.

The pristine glade vanished, replaced by a wasteland. There had once been a city here, but not like one I'd ever seen. The buildings resembled spikes jutting into the sky at odd angles. Some might have been temples, judging from the idols and statues adorning them. There were normal buildings, their rectangular shapes something of a relief among the chaos, but even they were built in ways that made me go cross-eyed.

It was as if someone hired M.C. Escher to design a city that would drive mortals mad. Crooked streets wended through the buildings, a serpentine maze that would confound even the strongest minds.

Ashes stirred beneath my feet, drifting lazily as if the gravity wasn't quite normal. A faint buzzing tickled my eardrums. I noticed a bit of ash floating near my head and glanced at it. I realized that it wasn't ash at all, but a small locust-like creature hovering nearby as if observing me.

Others rose from the ashes, some settling on my armored hands and arms. A chill ran down my spine and I hastily backed into the oasis. The rippling curtain of air swept the locusts off me. It seemed the Beast hadn't devoured this place because it simply couldn't penetrate the barrier.

Elyssa regarded me with wide eyes. "Justin, you look like you saw a ghost."

I turned to Xanos. "The city—it's enough to make me feel slightly crazy."

She nodded somberly. "The civilization that once occupied this realm slowly devolved into chaos and madness. Their earlier buildings are normal by comparison."

I shuddered. "I don't even want to look at the buildings if I can help it."

Elyssa frowned. "I don't understand how buildings could make you feel that way."

"Oh, you'll understand, believe me." I motioned toward Xanos. "Can you get a reading with the cube?"

She stepped through and activated her helmet. "I'll check."

"Hey, I want to look too." Adam stepped through the gateway and Elyssa followed on his heels.

They activated their helmets and passed through the barrier. I took a deep breath and followed suit. Xanos stood on the other side holding the cube in her palm and slowly rotating south—or maybe north, it was impossible to tell in this bizarre place.

Elyssa and Adam stared with slack jaws at the city.

"My eyes!" Adam abruptly turned away.

Locusts buzzed to life around us. Xanos ignored them, but Adam and Elyssa swatted at them as if they were mere bugs to be squashed. The locusts circled us as if probing what we were.

"Remain still and they will go away," Xanos said, her attention fully on the cube. She turned to me. "There is a faint pull coming from the southwest. We should travel to another oasis and triangulate until we lock onto the location."

"Sounds good." I took another look at the city and felt dizzy. "Let's go."

We stepped back into the oasis and went through the gateway.

"The barrier cleans off the bugs." Adam inspected his arms. "Fascinating."

I closed the portal.

Xanos summoned a map on the laptop. It closely resembled the one she'd drawn for us and Thomas back at the Ranch, but this one had dozens of small blue dots.

"Those are oases?" I asked.

She nodded. "The ones we mapped." Xanos touched one in the middle of the continent that resembled Utopia. "This is where we were. Now we will try this one further north, and another one due west."

"I'm ready when you are." I watched as she pulled up another image. I noticed the file name matched the numbered label on the map. This oasis had no trees; rather it resembled a section of the crazy city we'd seen in the distance. But the buildings were small enough to resemble a model of the city.

"God, it hurts to look at." Adam looked away. "You were right, Justin. That architecture is whack."

"This is a children's playground." Xanos regarded it without apprehension. "Or so we deduced from available data."

I forced myself to look at it, figuring a miniature version of chaos might allow my mind to assimilate it more easily than the full version. I opened a portal and we stepped into the oasis on the other side, activating our helmets as we did. Ignoring the playground from hell, I passed through the rippling barrier and into the wasteland.

I instantly regretted my decision. Twisted buildings jutted all around us. Cubes, spheres, and stairs formed mazelike patterns, some seemingly floating in the air. I tried to understand what supported the structures and what purpose they served, but the harder I tried, the dizzier I became.

Xanos didn't seem bothered at all and began scanning. Adam took a couple of deep breaths and joined her.

I averted my eyes from the structures to maintain my sanity.

"It literally hurts my eyes to look around." Elyssa stared at the ground. "I feel so disoriented and dizzy. It's maddening!"

"I know." I risked another look and regretted it. "At some point, we have to walk through this landscape, and I'm concerned that my mind can't handle it."

She squeezed her eyes shut. "You and me both."

The ground was carpeted with dust and, of course, the locusts. They buzzed to life and began inspecting us. Some were tiny as gnats or mosquitos, others the size of flies, but many were larger, with barbed legs and grinding mouths filled with sharp rending teeth. One hovered right in front of me, the O-shaped orifice opening and closing as if chewing.

I stared in horror at the little monster, resisting the urge to smash it between my armored hands.

Elyssa flinched. "We're not alone."

"Yeah, these locusts are everywhere."

She shook her head. "No, over there."

I followed the tip of her finger and saw a long shadowy figure crawling toward us. A cloud of locusts rose where it stepped, but they settled back down almost immediately.

"Uh, Xanos?" I turned toward her. "Do we need to worry about that thing?"

Her eyes settled on the creature. "We're done here. Go back inside the oasis immediately."

The shadow darted toward us at incredible speed, giant black wings buzzing. I screamed. Adam screamed. Xanos stumbled into us, nearly bowling everyone over in her haste to retreat. Elyssa yanked her back across the threshold as Adam and I dove back to safety.

I rolled over onto my elbows and tried to see through the rippling air, but the other side wasn't visible. That was probably a good thing, considering even the architecture in the Void screwed with my mind.

Adam removed his helmet. "What was that thing?"

Xanos sighed. "As I said, the locusts are not the only thing in the Void. There are other creatures, all presumably linked to the Beast."

I took a breath to calm my racing heart. "Why do I get the feeling that you're not telling us everything you know?"

"There's plenty she's holding back." Elyssa scowled. "She's waiting for the right moment to seize the advantage."

Xanos laughed mirthlessly. "What advantage could I ever hold over any one of you, much less all three?" She shuddered and walked back through the portal to the lab.

I watched Xanos and wondered if all of this was simply a chess game to her or if she was being truthful. Elyssa's gut feelings were rarely wrong. The rest of us went through the portal and back to the lab.

Xanos tapped another blip on the map, this one about a hundred miles west of the last one. When she double tapped it, a picture of the oasis appeared.

I examined the image for a few minutes, giving myself some recovery time. Opening these portals was more of a strain than I wanted to admit to the others.

Elyssa patted my shoulder. "You okay?"

I nodded. "Yeah. Just can't go too crazy or I'll be worthless."

"Take all the time you need."

I was tired, but also eager and curious to push forward. Despite the last scare, I wanted to learn more about the Void, and maybe even get a clear look at whatever scared the crap out of us. I focused on the picture and opened a portal.

This oasis was little more than a patch of dry mud. The bare earth looked crimson, but it was hard to tell if that was due to the ultraviolet sun or not. I stepped through and grabbed a handful of dirt, then brought it back to our side. The red looked paler beneath the white light in the lab. I set the sample down on a nearby table just in case I wanted to analyze it later, then went back through.

Xanos and the others had already stepped through the veil, so I continued after them. There were no buildings on the other side. The landscape consisted of little more than barren hills covered in the locust ash. The bugs rose around us, buzzing, but eventually settled down when we didn't move for a minute or two.

"It's further west." Xanos held the cube in the same direction. "We'll need to travel to another oasis."

We returned to the lab where Xanos inspected the map. The first two points of the triangle were spaced hundreds of miles apart out of necessity since there weren't enough oases to keep them any closer. The one we'd just tried was only about eighty miles from the last two. The next one Xanos picked out was over four hundred miles away from the previous oases, meaning we'd have a very long walk when it came time to venture into the wasteland.

The image of a small patch of grass no wider than five feet in diameter appeared when Xanos tapped the marker for the next destination.

"Why is this one so much smaller?" I asked.

Xanos shrugged. "The oases vary in size, but we couldn't discern why."

"They're probably natural formations, some kind of interdimensional tears," Adam said. "That would account for the variances."

Xanos nodded. "We also hypothesized that to be the case."

"I'd love to look over the notes." Adam pushed a finger up the bridge of his nose. "Maybe I could extrapolate answers from the data."

"I would be interested to hear your thoughts," Xanos said.

I snapped my fingers—or tried to. The suits weren't exactly designed to allow for it. "Stay on task, kids. We've got a lot more to worry about than variations in the sizes of oases."

"Of course." Xanos cleared her throat. "I am ready."

But she wasn't, and neither was I. No one could really be ready to experience the Void. I slashed open the portal. There was no purple sunshine, no patch of orange grass. The only thing that welcome us was pitch black and the deep, reverberating growl of the Beast.

CHAPTER 10

"Close it!" Adam shouted.

Beneath the growl was the skittering sound of insectoid limbs. The darkness squirmed and began to bulge out of the portal toward us. I closed my fist and willed the portal to close. But something fought my will, powering the portal from the other side. A long, spiked limb pierced the darkness and swiped just inches away from my face.

I clenched my teeth and fought the opposing force. The clash felt like a vice in my head. Whoever was testing my Apocryphan powers was holding their own. The clash of wills wasn't a stalemate. I was winning, but the fight would take too long. More limbs slashed through the barrier. Something was trying to come through.

Elyssa drew her light bow. "What's wrong, Justin?"

"Someone's fighting me." My head began to ache. "Jesus, it's like a battle of wits with a Sicilian."

"Not the time for jokes, Justin!" Elyssa drew back and a bowstring of energy formed beneath her fingers. A sizzling orange arrow blossomed to life on the string. She held it a moment to let it charge and fired as four spiked limbs grasped for a foothold on our side.

The arrow exploded on the other side, but the black veil across the portal didn't reveal what was hid behind it. Horrific shrieks echoed from the darkness. The mind fighting me faltered for an instant and that was all I needed. I slammed the portal shut.

The closing portal slashed off the limbs and they fell to the floor, twitching. Xanos and Adam were back against the far wall, eyes wide. Elyssa aimed another arrow at the limbs, then released the tension on the string once it became evident they posed no further threat.

I spun toward Xanos. "What the actual fuck, woman?"

She held up her hands. "I don't know! Are you certain you focused on the picture?"

"A hundred percent." I clenched a fist and pounded a table to keep me from punching her in the face. "I've done this a million times with omniarches."

"Maybe the grass in the oasis died," Adam said. "Maybe something altered its appearance enough that the picture is out of date."

"No." Xanos shook her head. "The oases don't change. Even when we've tried altering them, they revert back to their original state by the next visit."

Adam bit his lower lip and stared into space. "Did you keep measurements of every oasis you visited?"

"Yes, the information is all there." Xanos tapped the image on the screen and replaced it with lines of statistical information.

"But did you keep measuring them over time?" Adam said.

Xanos shook her head. "We had only just begun mapping the Void when..." she trailed off and glanced at Elyssa. "When the war began. Most of the data is static."

Adam examined the dates and other information. "These measurements were taken over a year ago. It's possible something changed."

"Perhaps." Xanos held out her hands helplessly. "Anything is possible."

"How were you able to study the Void for a year?" Adam said. "You didn't even have your powers."

Xanos pushed herself off the wall. "We had portal generator technology."

Adam's eyebrows arched. "The same as the device you used to get into the Abyss?"

She nodded. "The earlier prototypes lacked the power to punch through the Abyssal fringe."

I cleared my throat. "We need to talk about what just happened." I'd calmed down and was no longer considering tossing Xanos into the Void. "Something on the other side fought me. It didn't want me to close the portal."

Xanos nodded. "Most likely the Beast or one of his creatures."

"I've unintentionally opened portals to the Void when I messed up with omniarches." I shook my head. "Nothing on the other side ever fought back to keep it open."

Adam raised a hand. "In all the times we've opened an accidental portal to the Void, what are the three things that usually happen?"

I gave it some thought. "Uh, the Beast growls, we freak out, and then we close the portal."

He nodded. "Exactly. Shelton, Cinder, and I were experimenting with portals with Emily one day to figure out how they work. If she used the symbols to open a portal to another realm without first envisioning where to go, the portal would open in a seemingly random location in that realm."

I'd learned a lot about portals from Emily. "Correct."

Adam continued. "But if you attempt to open a portal within the same realm without envisioning a destination you get the Void."

I tapped a finger on my chin. "Because for whatever reason, it's the default place?"

"Cinder and I hypothesized that the quantum tunnels linking the realms have an absolute zero axis." Adam projected an image from his arcphone, several crisscrossing lines spanning not just the X and Y axis, but multiple dimensions as well. Small orbs representing the realms were mapped out at various coordinates.

"This looks like the same diagram Cinder showed us when we were trapped in Utopia." I stepped closer and used my fingers to rotate the image. "But you didn't have coordinates mapped out."

"Yeah, we only recently added them."

"This is amazing work." Xanos peered at the image. "How were you able to map it so precisely?"

"We went to the Glimmer and used the realms orbiting the Anchor Stone as a reference." Adam shrugged. "It wasn't that hard once we figured out how to get a drone up there."

I zoomed in to a small black orb that sat precisely at the zero position on all axis. "This is the Void?"

Adam nodded. "That's the working theory. We don't know how to prove it."

"Why wouldn't the Anchor Stone be absolute zero?" Elyssa said. "It's literally the only thing binding all the realms together."

Adam shook his head. "The realms were created in an act of pure destruction and chaos. The Sirens bound it all together the best they could, by destroying a realm and creating the Anchor Stone. It took all their collective power just to do that because they're not gods."

"No, they are not." A note of respect sounded in Xanos's voice. "I suppose that makes their feat even more impressive."

"You're damned right it does." Elyssa shook her head.

Adam blew out a long breath. "I believe that the reason this portal opened to the lair is because this oasis no longer exists."

Elyssa sucked in a breath. "Well, shit. You're saying the Beast has a way of eliminating the oases?"

"I can't say for sure, but that's my working hypothesis." Adam chewed on the inside of his cheek. "On the upside, maybe Unmaker is in the Beast's lair."

I scoffed. "Wow, that's tremendous news. The best news ever. I was hoping we'd run into the Beast while trying to steal the sword from the Void."

Adam closed the stats window for the failed oasis and picked another one another hundred miles west. "Let's give this one a try."

"I'm a little scared to try." I examined the image. "I don't think I can fight off another attack."

"Maybe we should take a break." Elyssa put a hand on my shoulder. "Resting for a few hours won't hurt."

I closed my eyes and assessed my current state. I was tired, but not exhausted. The battle had been one of willpower, not magical power, so I hadn't had to overextend my Apocryphan powers. I'd been tested in a battle of wills before but something about this one felt different—alien.

"I'm fine," I said at last. "As long as Elyssa is here to help me again, we'll be fine."

She grinned and clapped me on the shoulder. "I've always got your back, babe." Elyssa cast a glare at Xanos. "Unlike others."

Xanos looked away.

I focused on the image and with bated breath, opened the portal. A narrow strip of forest appeared on the other side and we let out a collective sigh of relief.

"Thank god." Adam activated his helmet and stepped through.

Bushes and trees impeded our progress, but we found the veil about fifty feet from the portal.

Adam held out his arcphone and waved it around. "This oasis is three inches less in width and length than the measurements taken a year ago."

"Is that significant?" I asked.

He shrugged. "Maybe, I don't know. Without collecting more data, I'm just taking wild guesses at this point."

Xanos paused at the veil. "Are you coming?"

Adam nodded. "Yeah. Let's go." He and Xanos vanished across the barrier.

Elyssa and I followed right behind. We stood on a mountain over-looking gray valleys and a mountain range. There was no vegetation, just an ash-covered world beneath a sky of gray, swirling vapors. I wished the vapors would clear, if only for a moment, so I could see if the sun matched the one inside the oases.

Xanos turned in a circle until she detected the magical signature of the sword. Her eyes flared.

I turned around and my eyes widened too. The mountain descended into a valley of darkness. Not even the gray light from the sky penetrated the pitch black. I went cold to the very core of my soul.

Xanos shivered. "I feel it staring back at me."

"Is that where the sword is?" I asked.

She nodded. "Almost certainly."

Adam rubbed his arms as if warding off the cold. "I think we're looking at the zero point. The heart of darkness."

I gulped. "Um, let's go back." I didn't see anything coming from the darkness, and only a few locusts drifted lazily around our periphery, but I didn't want to take any chances. "Move it, people!"

The others snapped out of their dazes and quickly passed through the veil to the oasis. We didn't waste any time getting back into the lab where I instantly closed the portal.

I sat down in a chair at the lab table and began questioning all my life choices. "I say we leave the sword. Let Baal take his chances with it."

"And what if the Beast remembers it was once part of Baal?" Xanos said. "What if it willingly gives him the sword?"

"Then we're fucked, okay?" I threw up my hands. "But going into that place is a death sentence. There are obviously creatures that are bigger than the locusts, and big enough to rip us out of our suits."

Elyssa turned to Xanos. "What do you know about the big bugs?"

"Not much," Xanos said. "We lost people to them, but they only seemed to appear after we'd been there for a while. We suspected the locusts detect movement and eventually draw the larger creatures if the movement persists."

"What if the wind moves them around?" I said.

"That probably won't trigger them." Adam shook his head. "I don't even know how much wind is possible given the lack of vegetation."

Elyssa scoffed. "I don't even know how wind works in the first place."

Adam chuckled. "Either way, the entire surface is like a giant spider web."

"Let's take an army." Elyssa pursed her lips. "We'll fight our way in."

"We don't know that any of our weapons will even remotely affect those things." Adam tapped a finger on the front of his helmet. "I need Shelton and Cinder. We need to run some experiments."

"Contact them. I'll portal them here." I looked at the severed limbs still lying on the floor. "We've already got some specimens to test."

"Those will be useful." Adam pressed his lips into a flat line. "But we need a couple of the big bugs alive."

"Is that all?" I scoffed. "I'll be sure to invite a couple over for dinner."

Adam turned to Xanos. "How much data do you have on those things?"

"Very little." She tapped a few keys on the laptop and displayed half a page of text below the sketch of one of the bugs. The vague outline resembled a roach, much like the silhouette I'd seen previously.

Adam set his phone on the table and projected a holographic call.

Shelton's face flickered into view a moment later. He shook his head and snorted. "Can't survive without me, can you?"

"We've hit a snag," Adam said.

"Yeah? Well, so have we." Shelton blew out a breath. "We've hit a dead end trying to find Conrad and Ambria."

I didn't like pulling him off that assignment, but we really didn't have a choice. "We need to capture some specimens from the Void."

His eyebrows rose. "Well, ain't that a tall order? Why don't I just get my fairy godmother on that? Maybe she can get us into the Prince's ball while we're at it."

I fluttered my eyelashes. "Shelton, you're our fairy godmother."

"Don't I know it?" He groaned. "How are we supposed to catch freaking monsters from the Void?"

I shrugged. "That's what we need you, Adam, and Cinder to figure out."

"Man, I'm gonna need extra tacos for this one." Shelton sighed. "Yeah, all right. Meet you at the Ranch?"

I shook my head. "We're using a Razor lab. It's a more controlled environment. The swarm can't escape and destroy the world if something goes wrong."

Shelton stared at Xanos. "I hope you're right." He ended the call and texted Adam a picture of his location. I opened a portal and he stepped through.

I spread my hands in greeting. "Welcome to Italy."

Shelton took in our confines. "Just the vacation I always wanted."

I chuckled. "I've got a timeshare in the Void I think you'll love."

He snorted. "Can't wait."

"Where's Max?" Adam asked.

"He's in the Glimmer." Shelton knelt next to the severed limbs on the floor. "Cora and Evadora are searching everywhere to make sure Conrad and Ambria didn't somehow get in without them knowing."

It made me feel better knowing they were still looking even without Shelton.

Adam contacted Cinder and I portaled him over a few minutes later.

Our golem friend wasted no time examining the insectile limbs on the floor. "Studying the specimens of the Void will be fascinating. However, if we're to bring any of them here, we'll need a containment unit."

"Somehow I doubt that'll be a problem with this place." Elyssa cast some side glare at Xanos.

Xanos nodded. "We have rooms set aside for that."

"Then we're in business, folks." Shelton didn't look or sound excited.

I couldn't blame him. Once again, we were about to experiment with forces that could annihilate entire worlds.

CHAPTER 11

Xanos led us to a holding cell that resembled the ones we'd been held in while prisoners in one of her other facilities. A wall with an observation window split the room. A table in the confinement area could be configured to hold a variety of subjects.

Elyssa's jaw tightened when she saw it, but she bit her tongue. Flashbacks of my time in a similar chair sent nasty chills down my spine. I'd been poked and prodded in ways I wished I could forget. The scientist working on me had been ready to cut off my arm to see if it regenerated.

I'd escaped with the help of a hellhound and made every scientist in that forsaken place pay for their crimes. It made me realize more and more that Xanos hadn't paid a high enough price for her crimes. She'd suffered the loss of her powers and physical strength, but maybe she needed to suffer as she'd made others suffer.

Elyssa shoved past Xanos when we left the holding cell. Xanos stumbled backward and would have fallen, but Adam caught her at the last minute. Shelton raised an eyebrow and shook his head.

Xanos said nothing. Her face contorted with anger and shame. She was powerless to protect herself, and once again I felt guilty about wanting to punish her. She'd trampled the powerless during her climb to power. She'd looked down on us like ants to be trampled underfoot. I, on the other hand, felt the instinctual need to protect those without power, even Xanos.

Sometimes I didn't like being the good guy.

Cinder, Adam, and Shelton went to the lab and began poring over Xanos's research. Xanos hovered behind them but remained quiet unless asked a direct question.

"We can't send a drone into the darkness." Adam leaned back in his chair and stared at the laptop screen. The swarm will drain the power supply in seconds."

"How does the Beast and its bugs survive without a food source?" Shelton spun in his office chair, stopped with his feet, then spun again. "You'd think it would've died a long time ago."

"Perhaps sunlight is enough to feed it," Cinder suggested. "Perhaps it requires little to no energy when it lays dormant."

Shelton blew out a breath. "I say we skip all this conjecture and just capture one of the big ones."

Cinder nodded. "Do you think I require a suit? I might look organic, but I am not."

Adam turned to Xanos. "What do you think?"

"His spark is a power source," she said. "His body would not be enough to shield it."

"Suit up, buddy." Shelton clapped Cinder on the shoulder. "Ain't no reason to risk your precious little soul."

"I do not possess a soul," Cinder said. "My spark is nothing more than magical code and energy."

Adam snorted. "Well, whatever it is, we don't want it devoured."

"Then I will wear a suit." Cinder stood and turned to Xanos. "Please lead the way."

Half an hour later we gathered back in the lab, ready to embark on our quest to capture a live specimen from the Void. Just the thought of grappling with a giant roach was enough to make my flesh crawl. I'd faced off against some pretty nasty creatures in the past, but giant bugs gave me the heebie-jeebies.

Despite my disgust, I volunteered to be the bait and opened a portal to the oasis with the playground.

Shelton groaned when he saw the twisting constructs. "What the hell is wrong with this place? It makes my brain hurt just looking at it."

Cinder studied the shapes. "The irregular geometry has form and function but only from a perspective completely opposite of our own. It's not only non-Euclidean, but intentionally chaotic."

Xanos's eyes lit up at the geek talk. "Precisely. I can only describe it as ordered chaos."

"Yes, that is a good term for it." Cinder touched one of the twisted structures. "It would indicate that a completely different method of thinking once existed here."

"Might be awful to say, but maybe it's best that civilization got wiped out." Shelton activated his helmet. "Let's go catch us a bug."

I took a deep breath because the next part was risky as hell. Since we couldn't bring anything from the Void through the veil guarding the oasis, I'd have to close this portal and open a new one on the other side. I'd memorized every detail of the prison cell so I could quickly open a portal when we were ready to return.

"Everyone ready?" I asked.

The others nodded. I closed the portal and headed for the rippling veil. "Hopefully, we can find a bug quickly and get the hell out of here."

Adam nodded. "Yeah, maybe we'll get lucky." He and the others followed me through the barrier.

The instant we stepped foot on the other side, I realized that wouldn't be a problem. Dozens of monstrous roach creatures skittered to a halt no more than fifty feet away from us and rose on their hind legs. They had thick black abdomens, six spiky legs, and long roach wings. But it was their heads that roiled my stomach with disgust.

The heads were human, but with glossy black bug eyes and antennae. Antennae twitching, one of them opened its twisted mouth and seemed to speak to the others in a language that sounded like a cross between a cricket chirping and a dog gagging on the vomit it had just licked up from the sidewalk.

"Holy farting fairies!" Shelton stumbled backward.

The creatures toppled back onto all six legs and skittered toward us. Elyssa nocked an arrow on her light bow and fired it. The arrow struck the nearest bug in the eye. It shrieked hideously and fell onto its back, legs twitching.

I was in disbelief but didn't have time to question the results. I channeled Brilliance and unleashed a sizzling beam of white-hot energy at the next creature. It slashed the creature in half. Gray guts oozed out. Shelton and Adam began firing spells from their arcphones.

We'd mowed down five of the monsters when the entire ground came to life. Clouds of locusts swarmed the fallen bugs. At first, I thought they meant to eat them, but instead they pulled dismembered creatures together, buzzing into their insides and healing them. The formerly dead bugs twitched back to life and rejoined their comrades.

Elyssa fired another arrow. The locusts intercepted it, soaking up the energy discharge. A few of the locusts fell to the ground, but the majority seemed unaffected. I fired another blast into the swarm. The cloud drank it greedily, losing only a few of its number.

"Plan B!" Shelton shouted over the buzz of thousands of locusts.

"What the hell is Plan B?" Adam said.

"Run away!" Shelton backed toward the veil, but the swarm of locusts formed a barrier between us and freedom.

I tried to push through, but the sheer mass of bodies was like solid steel. "Son of a bitch!"

Xanos screamed as a roach leapt on top of her. Adam fired a spell from his arcphone, severing the head. Green goop spilled out, covering Xanos's helmet. She thrashed blindly beneath the corpse.

In the space of a few seconds, we'd be completely swarmed. The locusts might not be able to penetrate our suits, but the big bugs could.

There was only one way out. "Plan C!"

"How come no one told me about these other plans?" Adam shouted.

I channeled a shield of Murk between us and the big bugs. But the locusts swarmed it and began draining it. I felt the drain reaching down the stream and back into me. There was no way I could keep this up for long. "Someone put up a shield so I can make a portal!"

Shelton cast a shield from his arcphone, but the locusts tore through it like paper. Two more roaches skittered toward us. I dipped into my Apocryphan powers and fired a green blast of energy at the locusts blocking our retreat. It was too much power for even them to handle. A huge swath of them vaporized, but the swarm closed in the hole too quickly for us to slip through.

Adam tapped on his phone and another shield replaced Shelton's, but it wasn't fast enough to block the giant roaches. Elyssa grappled with one of the creatures while Shelton wrestled with the other one. Spiked mandibles sprouted from the human mouths and clamped onto the helmets. The material began to crack under the strain.

The locusts swarmed Adam's shield. Blue sparks flew like moths in a bug zapper. Locusts fell to the ground. Miraculously, it was keeping them out. But the shield wasn't wide enough to keep us covered for long. I pictured the lab and slashed open a portal to the containment cell. I tore the giant roach off Shelton and flung it through the portal. Elyssa rolled backward and flipped her bug through after its buddy.

Adam grabbed Xanos and dragged her through. Elyssa and Shelton ran after them. That was when I noticed Cinder was missing. I spun in a circle and saw a writhing mass of giant bugs ten feet away. Locusts began swarming around Adam's shield and poured through the portal. I channeled a sword of Brilliance and slashed through heads and limbs of the giant roaches.

I spotted Cinder's suit through the morass of spiked legs and grabbed his arm. I yanked him mostly free, but the roaches clung to him, mandibles cracking at his helmet. I dragged him to the portal at a run, slashing at the roaches still clinging to him. His helmet was broken. Locusts swarmed his face.

"Cinder!" I shouted. With a roar of desperation, I flung him ahead of me and through the portal. The containment room was so full of locusts, I couldn't even see the others. I dove in after Cinder and willed the portal to close. It winked away and the swarming insects fell to the floor like a cloud of ashes.

The pair of roaches continued to struggle. I punched one in the face and it toppled onto its back. Elyssa and I gripped the other one and strapped it to one of the tables. Shelton and Adam hefted the other one onto the other table and secured it. Even though I was covered from head to toe in crystal armor, I shuddered when I touched one of the disgusting creatures.

I dropped to my knees next to Cinder. "Cinder!" He remained unmoving, his face covered by dead locusts. "God damn it, no!"

Shelton knelt next to him. "How do you remove the fucking helmet?"

I gripped both sides, twisting and pulling. The crystal didn't come free, but it finally shattered. I brushed the unmoving bugs and shards off Cinder's face. His eyes were closed, but the eyelids twitched.

Adam held his arcphone up to him. "His energy level is critically low."

"How do you recharge a golem?" Shelton said. "I thought they charged on ambient aether."

"They do, so maybe he just needs time to recuperate." Adam shook his head. "I don't know enough about golem construction."

Xanos's helmet dematerialized and green goop splattered on her face. She rolled over onto her hands and knees and threw up.

Elyssa looked at the writhing bugs. "Can we get out of here? I've had enough of these things for the day."

"Me too." I cradled Cinder in my arms and carried him out of the room.

Groaning, Xanos climbed to her feet and shuffled out after the rest of us, closing the door behind us.

"We can't just hope that Cinder recharges," Shelton said. "We need to talk to Fjoeruss and get him to fix him."

"Hell no," Adam said. "Fjoeruss would love to get his hands on Cinder and experiment on him while he's unconscious."

Gagging, Xanos wiped bug guts off her face. "I can help."

Elyssa wheeled on her. "How?"

"We captured some of Fjoeruss's grays to study." She exited the cube. "We engineered a power source compatible with the spark matrix because we considered making our own golem soldiers. It should recharge your golem."

Elyssa bared her teeth. "He's our friend, not our golem."

Xanos stared blankly at her for a moment. "Do you want my help or not?"

Elyssa turned away. "Yes."

Shelton nudged Xanos. "Well, hurry it up!"

The Apocryphan put a finger to her lips and looked left and right, as if figuring out where to go. She eventually went right, walked past several cubes, and checked the fourth one. "Wrong one." She checked the next two before motioning us into the last one in the row. "In here."

Inside was a table lined with an array of aether gems just like the ones the Mzodi fished from the giant aether vortexes in Seraphina. Shelton lay Cinder on the table.

"We need to remove the armor." Xanos pressed the sides of the collar and the armor split open. Shelton lifted Cinder out of the way and Adam tugged the armor off the table. It landed on the floor with a thud.

Once Cinder was back on the table, Xanos turned to me. "You'll need to channel into this gem." She put a hand on a black one just above Cinder's head. "Once it's sufficiently primed, the black aetherite will activate and power the charge cycle."

I did as requested, channeling a trickle of Brilliance into the black gem. The gem glowed and energy coursed down the channels in the table to the other gems. I stopped channeling, but the primed aetherite continued generating.

"How long will it take?" Shelton said.

"At least an hour." Xanos looked at Cinder's still form. "If he were organic, he would have been reduced to nothing before you could save him."

"No need to remind me." I tried to wipe the sweat from my forehead, but the armored gloves weren't designed for the task. "Well, we got our bugs."

Shelton sighed and shook his head. "There's no way in hell we're going to pull this off. The roaches die, but the locusts just swarm in and heal them." He tapped the armor with a fist. "Once the roaches swarm you, they crack open the armor like eggs and it's game over."

Adam shook his head sadly. "Justin, I hate to say it, but maybe we should just leave the sword where it is."

I dredged my mind for something positive to say, for a sliver of hope that might propel us to victory, but they were right. Cinder had nearly died, and we'd only been in the Void for a few minutes. The locusts proved they could block us in while the roaches tore us to pieces.

I thought coming back from the dead was the biggest challenge I'd ever faced, but I was wrong—dead wrong.

CHAPTER 12

"Let's take a break. Get something to eat." My stomach growled and the fading adrenaline rush from the battle left my knees weak.

Shelton's ears perked at the thought of eating. "Man, I'd love some authentic Italian."

"Good luck getting anything," Elyssa said. "The noms are on lockdown due to a pandemic."

"Say what?" Shelton frowned. "Is it swine flu?"

She shrugged. "I don't know. I haven't exactly been paying attention to the nom world lately."

"All the restaurants are closed?" Shelton looked ready to cry. "No lasagna?"

"I'm sorry, man." I put a hand on his shoulder. "There's no lasagna."

"Well, shit." He threw up his hands. "What are we even saving the world for if a growing boy can't get a heaping dish of lasagna?" His mouth fell open. "I can't even get tacos, can I? Or burgers?"

"There's plenty of food back at the Ranch," Elyssa said.

Adam walked toward the door. "I need to get out of this armor."

"Yeah, me too." I followed him and the others formed a procession behind us. We went back to the armory cube to shed our crystalline skins.

"Unless you want to see my hairy, white ass, give me a minute," Shelton said as he walked inside the room.

Adam chuckled. "He can have all the time he needs."

Elyssa and I changed next and then went to the lab. I was bone-tired from making so many portals and my palms were blackened from channeling destructive Apocryphan power through the armor. I healed from physical damage pretty quickly, but this was magic damage and would probably have to heal overnight.

Elyssa looked disapprovingly at the wounds. "Do I need to talk to Emily and have her turn off your powers again?"

"I'm fine." I hated the constant reminders that I wasn't strong enough to channel Apocryphan powers. "I won't kill myself again. Promise."

"Wish I could believe that, but when your friends are in trouble, your sense of self-preservation goes right out the window."

"I need an upgrade." I slumped into a chair. "There's gotta be some way for me to handle Apocryphan powers."

"Brute force is rarely the answer, and you know that." Elyssa stroked my hair. "Cunning and perseverance are your strengths. We'll figure this out somehow."

Shelton and Adam waltzed inside with Xanos in tow.

"Man, I don't want cafeteria food at the Ranch." Shelton huffed. "When did this lockdown start anyway?"

"I don't know." Elyssa shrugged. "We could go to Queens Gate."

Xanos tapped some keys on the laptop. "There are restaurants with takeout available, even here. I can order the food online if you would like."

"Say what?" Shelton sat next to her and stared at the screen. "I can't read anything."

Adam snorted. "Because it's in Italian, stupid."

Shelton rattled off an order. "I want beef lasagna, tiramisu, limoncello, and a bottle of house wine."

"I'll have the same," Adam said. "I have a nom credit card you can use to pay for the order."

"Not necessary." Xanos typed in the order and looked at me and Elyssa. "Shall I order you something?"

"No." Elyssa stared coldly at her. "Fulfilling Shelton's culinary dreams doesn't forgive the slaughter of thousands."

"Jesus H. Christ on a moped, Elyssa." Shelton huffed. "Lighten up for a damned minute and enjoy the food. Just because Xanos is a purple piece of shit doesn't mean she can't be useful and order us food."

Xanos swallowed hard but kept silent.

Elyssa narrowed her eyes. "Fine. I want spaghetti with meat sauce and a salad."

"I'll have the same." I turned to Shelton. "What's limoncello?"

"It's a lemon liqueur. Kind of nice as a dessert." Shelton projected the image of a yellow liquid from his arcphone.

"It's tart, but tasty," Adam said.

Xanos put in our food order, then she, Adam, and Shelton left to go pick it up.

I slid my arm around Elyssa's shoulder and pulled her against me.

"Never thought we'd be ordering takeout from a super-secret under-ground base that used to belong to our enemies."

She leaned her head on my chest. "I wish I could enjoy it more."

"I mean, you can, but you're just thinking about it the wrong way."

She raised an eyebrow. "How so?"

"We're bossing around a former demigoddess." I grinned. "This experi-ence must be pure torture for her, but there's nothing she can do about it."

"Unless it's all a ploy." Elyssa shook her head. "The moment I think she's up to something, I will end her."

"That's fine and dandy but remember that Xanos is in a living hell right now." I waved a hand at the room. "She's nothing more than a servant in her former kingdom. I think you should get a little sadistic pleasure out of that."

The tension in Elyssa's shoulders eased. "You're right. I should enjoy putting her through hell."

"That's the spirit!" I kissed her cheek. "And no matter how bad it is, she totally deserves it."

"Like that face full of bug guts." A mirthless grin spread her lips. "Hearing her puke was music to my ears."

"Um, maybe you're already enjoying it too much." I nibbled her ear. "Dial it back a notch."

Elyssa kissed me long and hard. "You always make me see things in a positive light. I'm going to enjoy this a lot."

I suspected that I was going to regret giving this pep talk.

Shelton and the others brought back bags full of Italian yumminess. Xanos led us to what was formerly the employee cafeteria for her evil empire, and we laid out the spread. Elyssa and I shared a delicious bottle of red wine with our spaghetti while Adam and Shelton chowed down on lasagna. Xanos tried to move to the end of the table, but Adam asked her to sit next to him.

Elyssa and I exchanged concerned looks. Adam's girlfriend, Meghan Andretti had broken up with him just before we went on an adventure to find Emily and Tyler for the fight against Xanos. Now it looked like he was interested in turning our former enemy into his girlfriend.

"Please tell me I'm reading this wrong," Elyssa said to me in a soft voice. "Adam is smarter than this, right?"

I snorted. "He's way smarter in many ways, but definitely not when it comes to women."

"Yeah, well Xanos isn't a woman." Elyssa twirled strands of spaghetti around her fork. "Maybe we need an intervention."

I winced. "I think it's better if Shelton and I talk with him. No need to get overly dramatic."

She nodded. "Better do it soon. If he catches feelings, it'll be even rougher."

"No doubt." I turned my attention back to the meal, but it was hard not to notice the way Adam kept looking at Xanos. Admittedly, she was super cute in her current form, and the purple skin was exotic. But there was no way this former demigoddess would ever love a human or anyone she deemed lesser, despite her current status as a mere mortal.

It was more likely Xanos would die of old age before ever changing her mindset.

After eating, we checked on Cinder.

His eyes blinked open when we entered the room. He tried to move an arm but seemed unable to do so.

Shelton hovered over him. "Cinder, buddy, how you feeling?"

"I...am surprised." It was a struggle for him to speak. "To be alive."

"Justin dragged you out from under a pile of roaches and locusts." Adam stood opposite of Shelton. "We've got you on a spark regenerator, so you should be good to go in a few hours."

Cinder managed a nod and turned his eyes on me. "Thank you."

"We're not done with you yet." I felt a little misty-eyed seeing him like this but covered with a grin. "We'll check up on you later, okay?"

Cinder nodded again and closed his eyes.

The rest of us went back to the lab to plot our next moves.

As normal, Shelton voiced his thoughts before our asses even hit the chairs. "All I gotta say is if those roaches break your helmet, you'll probably die of asphyxiation if the locusts don't eat you first. That atmosphere looks toxic as hell."

"Surprisingly, it's not that bad," Adam said. "The oxygen levels are too low to support us for more than a few minutes. What's most surprising is that there's oxygen at all without vegetation."

"Those oases are everywhere." Elyssa tapped a finger on her chin. "Maybe the oxygen they produce travels through the veil."

"Still wouldn't be enough." Adam shook his head. "I know that magic can account for some things, but I don't know how it would maintain the atmosphere over an entire world."

I leaned back in my chair. "So much for Xanos's research saving us time."

"Oh, it's saved us months already." Adam projected the map of the Void. "We have a topographic view with knowledge of the oases which is a huge advantage." He frowned and pointed to two areas shaded blue. "What does that mean?"

"Uncharted territory," Xanos said. "Our drones died before they could fly over those areas."

Adam pursed his lips. "Can I see the footage from their flights?"

Xanos leaned over him and tapped on the laptop, practically rubbing her boobs against his shoulder. It almost looked calculated, which didn't surprise me. Xanos had to know Adam was interested and what better way to manipulate someone than by cashing in on their feelings?

A folder of videos appeared on the holographic display above the laptop. The file names consisted of long numbers. Adam stopped on one, consulted the map and opened the file.

Xanos raised an eyebrow. "How did you know?"

"Easy." Adam pointed to the map. "Your people were smart to label them with x-y-z coordinates."

"Well, slap my ass and call me Sally," Shelton said. "Those numbers are longitude, latitude, and altitude."

Adam nodded and played the file. The drone recorded everything in three-hundred and sixty degrees. Adam fast forwarded to the final few minutes of recorded flight. The drone was flying fifty feet off the ground, leaving a rising cloud of agitated locusts in its wake. But with its miniature jet engines, it was too fast for the swarm to catch it.

Elyssa and I had narrowly escaped death from similar drones. Judging from the grimace on Elyssa's face, she hadn't forgotten that either.

About a minute from the end of the video, Adam paused it.

"What is that?" Elyssa pointed at the skyline ahead of the drone.

"That's what I was wondering." Adam peered at the projection.

I stared at the image, rubbed my eyes, and looked again. "What am I looking at?"

Elyssa traced a finger around the orange clouds ahead of the drone. "Notice the big clear area in the middle?"

"Sure." I hadn't, but it didn't seem important. "What's the big deal?"

"The clouds are bending around something." Adam jotted down some numbers on the laptop, then continued the playback. As the drone neared the clouds, even I began to notice the slight ripple in the air. It wasn't as pronounced as the other oases, but it was there. The drone reached the anomaly and the video went black.

"So, it's another oasis?" I said.

Adam tapped away on the laptop and leaned back. "If that's an oasis, then it's easily the largest one in the realm." He switched to another video, this one of the drone approaching the other blue-shaded area. We noticed the same anomalies in this one as well.

Shelton grunted. "I ain't no expert on Razor drones, but they didn't have any problems when they flew through the smaller oases, right?"

Xanos shook her head. "Some drones crashed into trees because they couldn't detect what was on the others side of the veil, but otherwise there were no problems."

"Whatever is going on in those areas isn't the same." Shelton turned to Adam. "Maybe they're shields."

Adam nodded. "Possibly, but we're talking about shields that cover hundreds of miles."

"Maybe we should check them out," I said.

"I'd love to." Adam's eyes lit up. "Maybe there's another kind of oasis we don't know about."

"I haven't seen him get this excited since we went into Voltis." Shelton chuckled. "Talk about a journey through hell."

"I'm not even remotely excited about exploring the Void," Elyssa said. "Wouldn't it be better to direct all our attention to getting the sword?"

"We tried that, and it didn't work." Shelton crossed his arms. "We can't even take a short stroll without stirring up the hornets' nest. Once those roaches swarm us, we're toast."

"We need stronger armor." I turned to Xanos. "Something that can withstand the roaches."

Xanos shook her head. "The armor is as strong as we could make it while still allowing flexibility." She touched her elbow. "The flexibility of the alloy prevents it from achieving maximum strength."

Adam nodded. "The armor has to be airtight, so no joints. But what if we took a layered approach?"

She pursed her lips. "That could work, but it would be very bulky."

I blinked. "You mean armor for the armor?"

"Yep." Patted his arm. "If we build an outer shell, it could be strong enough to withstand the roaches. But we'd also have to power it to offset the added weight for those of us who don't have super strength."

"We need every advantage we can get against the bugs." Shelton frowned. "But can we shield the power sources for the exoskeletons?"

"The engineering for such an endeavor is no easy feat." Xanos shook her head. "It could take months."

"Doesn't have to." Shelton grinned. "Science Academy is open for business again. I'll bet they've got something we could adapt."

"How about an army of robots?" Elyssa suggested. "If we shield their power supplies, we could march into the Void, take what we want, and leave."

"It wouldn't be that simple," Adam said. "You saw how the locusts were able to form a barrier from the sheer mass of their bodies. Even an army of robots would have a tough time penetrating that."

Elyssa raised an eyebrow. "Only if we took the direct approach. The locusts act like a spider web, detection motion and reacting to anything in their vicinity. I'll bet that anytime they're triggered, the hive mind sends out roaches to investigate."

Xanos nodded. "That was our observation as well. But the roaches only come if there is continuous triggering of the web."

"Then we need to test response times and calculate how many of those creatures the hive holds in reserve." Elyssa tapped several oases on the map. "We'll send robots to several locations one at a time and measure how long it takes for roaches to appear and in what numbers."

"I think I see where you're going with this," I said. "Maybe if we throw enough disturbances against the web, the hive will deploy all its troops, then we can sneak in behind enemy lines and steal the sword."

Elyssa snapped her fingers. "Exactly. What we need next are robots with protected power supplies that can last long enough to cause the distraction we need."

"Then it's time to hit up Science Academy," Shelton said. "This time we won't take no for an answer."

"Yeah, they weren't exactly helpful during the Second Seraphim War." Adam pushed a finger up the bridge of his nose. "I just hope they have what we need."

Shelton looked down at Xanos. "Do you still have the capacity to build more armor?"

She nodded silently.

He posed another question. "Can we leverage that to produce shielded power supplies?"

Xanos shook her head. "The suits are of single-piece design by necessity, and I suspect the robots would be incompatible with an aetherite power supply. There is no way this plan will work."

CHAPTER 13

I groaned. "Damn, Xanos. Don't be such a Debbie Downer."

Elyssa shook her head. "Even with unshielded power supplies, I think we can make this work."

Xanos didn't look convinced.

I shrugged. "It can't hurt to check out Science Academy."

Shelton clapped me on the back. "Road trip?"

I nodded. "Road trip."

"Can you send me back to the Ranch?" Elyssa bit her lower lip. "I want to consult with my father and see what we can come up with."

"Sure." A yawn caught me off guard. "Maybe we should all get some shuteye first and hit the ground running tomorrow."

Shelton checked his arcphone. "It's the middle of the night in Queens Gate anyway."

"I can't wait until the new Mansion is done." Adam sighed. "The bunks at the Ranch aren't very comfortable."

"And the cafeteria folk get pissed if I try to cook breakfast." Shelton scowled.

Cinder wasn't quite ready to be up and about, so we told him where we were going and left him to recuperate. I opened a portal to the underground transit room at the Templar compound.

When we arrived, Elyssa took Xanos by the arm. "I've got a special room for you."

"A cell, no doubt." Xanos tensed but didn't resist.

"Is that really necessary?" Adam said. "Where's she gonna go?"

"I'm not leaving her free to roam." Elyssa towed Xanos out of sight around a corner.

I decided it was time for a very awkward conversation with Adam.

Shelton sensed what was coming and rolled his eyes. "It is too late for this shit."

Adam raised an eyebrow. "For what?"

I jumped in before Shelton distracted me. "Adam, are you catching feelings for Xanos? Because if you are, it's a really bad idea."

Adam flinched as if caught completely off guard. "You think I'm falling for Xanos?" He burst into laughter then abruptly stopped. "Okay, maybe I do think she's hot with her incredible intellect, purple skin, and cute little nose, but I have no illusions about entering a relationship with her."

Shelton pursed his lips. "You do you, buddy. More power to you if you get to bang a former demigoddess. Just know that she killed a lot of our people directly and indirectly and ran labs that committed atrocities."

Adam grimaced. "Well, when you put it like that, I don't think you meant the first part."

Shelton shrugged. "Bad girls are hot, you're lonely, and it's okay to blow off some steam."

I shook my head. "Shelton, you're the worst interventionist ever."

Adam chuckled. "Is that what this is? An intervention?"

"Mostly." I sighed. "Xanos is in a vulnerable state now and that might make her seem like a different person than the one who committed all the war crimes Shelton mentioned. I know she's smart and cute, but if she ever got her powers back, she wouldn't hesitate to kill us all."

"She's like the bunny in *The Holy Grail*," Shelton said. "Innocent looking, but she'll rip out your throat."

Adam held up his hands in surrender. "Look, I get it. But I'm not going to be an ass to her. Remember, honey catches more flies than vinegar."

Shelton snorted. "She's got you stuck in her honey, that's for sure."

"I mean, that's the best way to keep her cooperating." Adam clapped Shelton on the shoulder. "Now, why don't you go get some honey from Bella and stop bugging me about this?"

"Man, I wish." Shelton scuffed his foot across the floor. "She went back to Colombia to help setup operations at the Razor facility in El Dorado."

It was yet another reminder of how widespread Razor Echelon had been. They'd created prison facilities at several of the Alabaster Arch sites like Thunder Rock and El Dorado. On the upside, we'd inherited all their hard work.

"Well, there's always internet porn." Adam smirked. "Thanks for the intervention."

"Any time." I headed down the hallway. "Good night."

Elyssa joined me in our small room about fifteen minutes later. "I'll sleep better knowing that bitch is locked up."

I nodded. "Shelton and I spoke to Adam."

She raised an eyebrow. "And?"

"He said he'll keep being nice to her, but he's not trying to bang her or anything."

Elyssa pressed her lips together. "He can bang her. He just can't fall in love."

"I don't think Adam is capable of sex without love." I shrugged. "I could be wrong."

"No, he's a hopeless romantic like you." Elyssa pushed me on the bed and straddled me, slowly sliding her shirt up and off.

I tried to speak, but words failed me. "Justin like so much!"

Elyssa slid the bra straps off her shoulders. "Are you my caveman?"

I nodded. "Oh, yeah!"

She frowned. "Or my Kool-Aid man?"

I pulled her down for a long delicious kiss. "Whatever works."

My bones ached when I woke the next morning. Overusing Apocryphan abilities had that side effect. Hopefully, I wouldn't need them too much today. Elyssa was already up and gone, probably doing her morning routines. I tried to do them most days but waking up at a decent hour was already hard enough.

Elyssa was waiting at the cafeteria entrance when I arrived. She checked the time. "You're ten minutes later than usual."

"Sorry." I cracked a yawn. "Tired from fighting the forces of evil."

She peered at my eyes. "Your eyes are bloodshot, and you have bags beneath them. You need to take a break from Apocryphan powers."

"Today shouldn't be too strenuous."

Elyssa shook her head. "We're going to use the omniarch to travel today. No Apocryphan powers at all."

We were halfway into eating a delicious meal of turkey sausages and scrambled eggs when Adam and Shelton appeared.

"Still no bacon?" Shelton threw up his hands. "What is it with Templars and no freaking bacon?"

His declaration drew the eyes of just about everyone in the room. Many Templars nodded in silent support, but they were too disciplined to start cheering for tasty pork products.

After breakfast, we retrieved Xanos. A tray with a mostly uneaten breakfast sat on the table in her small cell.

Shelton's jaw dropped open. "Is that—" he walked in and inspected it. "This bitch got bacon?"

The Templar on guard duty nodded. "Prisoners are not subject to the nutritional requirements of Templars."

"Nutritional requirement can bite my hairy white ass!" Shelton snagged an uneaten piece of bacon and held it up to Xanos's face. "I can't believe you'd just let a perfectly good piece of bacon go to waste."

Xanos looked at him uncertainly. "You may have it if you wish."

"Darned tootin'!" Shelton took a bite and moaned in extasy. "Oh, man this is good."

Adam snorted. "Shelton just jizzed in his pants."

I snorted. "Someone get Shelton some wet wipes so we can go."

The Templar guard produced a wipe from a cabinet on the wall. "Here you go, sir."

Shelton and Adam burst into laughter.

I awkwardly took the proffered wet wipe. "I was just joking."

Without cracking a smile, the Templar said, "I know, sir." Then he resumed patrolling without another word.

"That look on your face is priceless!" Elyssa giggled. "That man deservers a promotion."

Eyes wide, forehead scrunched, Xanos looked absolutely perplexed. "This is considered funny?"

"Yeah, but inhuman murderous assholes wouldn't understand." Elyssa's smile faded. "Let's go."

Adam grimaced. "That got awkward fast."

I pressed the wet wipe into Shelton's hand. "Don't say I never gave you anything."

He snorted, wiped the bacon grease from his hands, and tossed the used wipe on Xanos's tray.

We took a levitator up to the underground parking garage. Yellow squares of varying sizes were painted on the concrete floor about a hundred feet to the right of the levitator doors. There had only been one for a long while until Thomas began stationing Templars at multiple omniarch locations.

Even with multiple stations open, there were long lines to all the transit zones.

Shelton started grumbling almost immediately. "Can't you just zap us there, Justin?"

"He needs a break," Elyssa said.

"It's gonna take thirty minutes just to get a portal." Shelton tapped the shoulder of the Templar ahead of us. "You on a mission to save the world?"

She looked uncertainly at him, then saw Elyssa and saluted. "Commander Borathen, I'm sorry I didn't realize you were here."

"It's fine." Elyssa shook her head at Shelton. "Our friend is impatient."

"Clear the way for Commander Borathen," the Templar shouted to those ahead of us in line. "Emergency business."

Not everyone in line was a Templar, but everyone stepped out of the way to let us proceed.

Elyssa's cheeks flushed. "Shelton, I'm going to kick your ass."

He grinned. "Can't be waiting in long lines if we're trying to save the world."

"He does have a point." I nodded thankfully at those who stepped aside, and we moved to the front of the line.

"I don't like calling rank," Elyssa hissed to me. "It looks bad."

"It's necessary." Shelton shook his head. "We've got to get Cinder then head to Science Academy, and if we stood in line, it'd be lunchtime before we got there."

The Templar on duty at the transit zone tapped a finger on his arcphone. "Sir, the omniarch is still in use and won't be available for another fifteen minutes."

Elyssa sighed. "I'm sorry, but we're on emergency business." She took out her arcphone and showed him a priority status document signed by Thomas.

The Templar saluted. "Yes, commander." He made a call on his arcphone and a moment later, a portal opened.

"I thought you didn't like pulling rank," I whispered in Elyssa's ear.

"I don't, but you were right. We don't have time to wait in lines."

We stepped through the portal and found ourselves in a vast cavern filled with rows upon rows of arches. A massive map of the world as it might have been eons ago covered the wall at the far end of the control room. Beneath it was a pedestal with a large orb that controlled the Obsidian Arch in another cavern adjacent to this one.

Long lines of small black arches occupied the middle of the control room. Most of them were numbered in accordance with a specific destination. We stood in an alcove to the side where the omniarches had been built long after the initial construction of the facility. Most arches required a corresponding arch at the destination, but omniarches could create a portal anywhere.

Three of the omniarches in the control room were tagged green, meaning they functioned. Those with red tags didn't work at all, or they might simply transport someone to a horrible death. Long lines of people waited at each omniarch.

We stepped out of the portal in the omniarch that had brought us here, and the portal winked away.

The Templar in command of the station pressed a hand over his chest in salute. "What are your orders, sir?"

Elyssa saluted back. "We need to retrieve additional personnel, so I'll take over control of the arch for a moment."

"Yes, sir." He backed away.

Elyssa knelt at the thick silver band encircling the omniarch and sealed the circuit with a focus of willpower. Then she stared at a picture of the Razor lab in Italy. A portal slashed open in the arch, a window mirroring the exact view in the picture.

Cinder stepped into view. "Ah, you have come to retrieve me."

"What, did you think we'd just leave you there all alone?" Shelton motioned him over. "Come on. We're in a hurry."

"One moment, please." Cinder vanished and returned a moment later. He stepped through the portal and Elyssa turned it off.

"After intense scrutiny of the data and videos in the Razor archive, I have arrived at some interesting conclusions." Cinder consulted his arctablet. "It would seem that—"

"Save it for later." Shelton dragged Cinder out of the silver circle. "We're headed to Science Academy."

Elyssa opened a portal just outside a large chrome building shaped like a giant flying saucer. She turned to the Templar. "I'll close it behind us, and you can resume regular duties."

"Yes, sir."

We stepped through and Elyssa closed the portal. A group of students in lab coats glanced at us curiously as they passed by.

Shelton looked up at the newly redesigned administration center for Science Academy. "Leave it to them to demolish the old structure and build a new one just because of a little damage."

"The damage was extensive," Adam said. "Besides, with robots doing all the work, it's probably just as easy to rebuild."

Shelton grunted. "I guess."

The old building resembled a seashell, but this time they'd gone pure retro with a giant chrome flying saucer that closely resembled something I'd seen in a vintage movie from the fifties. Four thick legs supported the building around the circumference. A ramp leading up into the saucer completed the effect.

Shelton spat on the ground. "Bastards redesigned it to look just like Frankenberg's Antarctica base."

"It does have a passing resemblance." Former Chancellor Frankenberg had been part of the crystoid plot, helping Cephus seed our realm with the aether-draining meteors so Science Academy could rule supreme.

We took the ramp up into the saucer and reached a security desk in the lobby. A pair of thin men rose from their seats, hands resting threateningly on the laser blasters holstered at their sides. The only discernable things about them were their name tags and one sported a thick porn mustache.

Naturally, Porn Stache spoke first. "You're not students here."

I looked at his nametag. "Officer Hicks, we're here to speak to the administrator on urgent Overworld business."

"Do you have an appointment?" he asked.

Elyssa bared her teeth. "I'm Commander Borathen of the Templars. Please connect us to the administrator."

Hicks shook his head. "You magic people keep trying to drag us into wars we don't want. I've been given authority to kick you out."

Elyssa raised an eyebrow. "Oh? Please try."

Hicks looked at his partner, Officer Sims. "Help me escort them out."

Sims drew his blaster and pointed it at us. "Get out."

Hicks smirked and looked at Elyssa. "That's a mark eight plasma blaster. It'll take down a lycan or a vampire, so I don't think it'll have much of a problem with a Templar."

Elyssa blurred across the room. Sims doubled over as the air exploded from his lungs. Hicks suddenly found himself pressed against the wall, his feet dangling slightly off the ground. Elyssa squeezed her hand around his throat. "Impressive."

Hicks's eyes filled with terror. He squealed something inarticulate and struggled uselessly in the iron grasp of my ninja girlfriend. Elyssa dropped him to his feet and tossed the blasters she'd liberated from him and his pal across the floor.

"Take us to the administrator or I'll test one of those plasma blasters on your balls."

Hicks gulped. "Y-yes, at once!" He hit a button and the door behind the desk buzzed open.

Elyssa grabbed Sims by the collar and dragged him through the door after us so he wouldn't sound an alarm that might start a clash we didn't want. Hicks led us into an elevator that took us to the top level of the saucer. We disembarked in a room with a clear domed roof. A flashback of my final showdown with Frankenberg flashed through my mind.

A secretary seated at a chrome desk looked at us in alarm. "What's the meaning of this?"

Hicks nodded at the woman. "Madeline, these Overworlders are here to see Administrator Perkins."

Shelton scoffed. "You realize that Science Academy is part of the Over-world, right?"

Hicks looked as if he took exception to the comment, but a glare from Elyssa quieted him instantly.

"The administrator will not see Overworlders." Madeline straightened her shoulders. "Please leave."

Elyssa sighed. "Maybe it's just time to end Science Academy once and for all." She crossed her arms over her chest. "I think Victus left too much of a taint to leave this institution standing."

A door to the left slid open and a squad of guards rushed out, blasters drawn.

Shit was about to get real.

CHAPTER 14

M adeline raised her chin. "Who are you to make such preposterous threats?"

"I'm Commander Borathen of the Templars." Elyssa's violet eyes flickered with inner light. "And I'll tear this place to the ground if you people don't get it in gear!"

Hicks flinched away, a startled shriek escaping his throat.

Shelton leaned close to me. "Hot damn, your woman is scary when she wants to be."

I nodded. "We should've brought her with us when we tried to convince the academy to fight Daelissa with us."

Adam snickered. "Dude, they would've signed up in five minutes."

"In case you hadn't noticed, you're outnumbered and outgunned," Madeline said.

Hicks cowered, because he knew what was coming next.

I channeled a thick Murk shield between us and the guards, then used it to shove them against the wall. "Drop your blasters or I'll crush you!"

They struggled uselessly for a moment before the weapons clattered to the floor.

Adam and Shelton grabbed the weapons and tossed them in a pile on the other side of the room. I dropped the shield. "Now get back in your room and stay in there."

Elyssa turned to Hicks and Sims. "You too."

The guards cleared the room. Channeling a thin beam of Brilliance, I welded the door shut.

Elyssa stared daggers at the secretary. "Now let us in or else."

Madeline shrank away from us. "I'll have you know I don't appreciate being threatened."

"Then shut up and keep out of my way," Elyssa growled. She shoved through tall double-doors behind the desk.

A group of old men sat around a table on the other side. They looked annoyed at the interruption. That annoyance quickly morphed to confusion as Elyssa stormed inside.

I caught a glimpse of a holographic projection in the center of the table before someone hurriedly turned it off. I was almost positive the title had Victus Edison in it. That man had banished us to Seraphina and then proceeded to take over the Overworld with battle bots and monstrous mutants he created in his labs.

Conrad had killed his father, but the legacy of the man's inventions and creations lived on.

A portly man with a thick gray beard and a funky silver cone hat rose from the table. "Madeline, what is the meaning of this?"

Madeline sighed. "I'm sorry, Administrator Mason—"

Elyssa cut her off. "I'm Commander Borathen of the Templars, here to enlist the help of the academy."

"Absolutely not." Administrator Mason stepped from behind the table. "You brought destruction upon us when that—" His eyes widened when Xanos stepped out from behind Adam. "It's the Apocryphan! Run!"

I'd never seen fat old men run so fast. Even so, it was like watching three-legged turtles climb a hill. I blurred to the doors and shut them. "Not so fast, old man Withers."

Xanos's eyes gleamed with delight at the fear she instilled in the men. The gleam died when Elyssa cast a glare at her.

That's the Xanos I know, I thought to myself. The old Xanos is just lurking beneath the surface of that innocent façade.

Elyssa pounded a fist on the table loud enough to wake the dead three planets over. "Please have a seat."

The men huffed and puffed to comply. Once they were seated, Elyssa prowled around the table, a predator sizing up a meal.

Mason looked fearfully at Xanos. "Is that truly the Apocryphan?"

"It is." Elyssa took Xanos by the arm. "But her powers are gone, and she has been reduced to human size. Now she's helping us fight Baal."

"Baal?" Mason said. "What does he have to do with anything?"

Elyssa groaned. "We send daily briefings here and to Arcane University and post them on the aethernet. Haven't you been reading them?"

"No." Mason cleared his throat. "We voted unanimously to remove ourselves from the Overworld Conclave. There is no reason for us to involve ourselves in your affairs."

"How is it possible I lost to such idiots?" Xanos hissed under her breath.

Shelton chuckled. "You didn't lose to those idiots. You lost to us."

"I will summarize for you." Elyssa laid out a brief history, including the part where Xanos nearly took over the world with Razor Echelon and their advanced anti-magic technology. The scientists were indignant to learn how advanced Razor's weapons were, especially the auto-destruct mechanisms that prevented supers from using them. Then Elyssa explained how Baal planned to recombine the realms by piecing together the relics of Jura.

"We saw what that woman did," one of the other men said. "What do we have that could possibly stop the Grand Overlord of Haedaemos from doing what he wants?"

Elyssa turned to him. "We need an army of battle bots to help us remove something from the Void."

"The Void?" Mason looked ready to keel over. "The Beast devours all. It's impossible to enter the Void."

"We've entered the Void, caught some of its denizens, and brought them back for study," Adam said. "Nothing is impossible."

They returned dumbfounded looks.

"Impossible," Mason said. "You've entered the Void and returned alive?"

"Thanks to Xanos's arcnology," Adam said.

"We have very few battle bots available," another man said. "Victus Edison took most of them. Given the turmoil of the Overworld in the last decade, it's been very difficult to rebuild."

"Speaking of which." I stepped up to their table and tapped a finger on the arctablet in front of Mason. The hologram flickered back on.

The title at the top told me all I needed to know. *Leveraging the assets of Victus Edison for a new tomorrow.*

Mason harrumphed. "I can explain."

Elyssa glared at him. "Please do."

He tried to hide a tremble in his hand. "Victus was not a good man, but his inventions were brilliant. Unfortunately, someone broke into our vault and stole some of his more insidious designs. We, of course, retained copies, but there is a concern that whoever took the designs will sell them on the black market."

"And you didn't think to report this to the Templars?" Elyssa held up a finger. "Oh, that's right. You're not part of the Overworld."

"Guess what, fools?" Shelton stomped a foot on the ground. "You've got responsibilities whether you think you're in the Overworld or not!"

"Whoever took them most likely doesn't have the resources to construct them," Mason said. "We hired trackers to hunt down the culprit."

Shelton opened his mouth to say something when his eyes locked onto something in the holographic presentation. He marched over to the table and scrolled down to the first blueprint, labeled, *Anti-magic Staff.*

The staff looked like a shiny curtain rod. A pair of Tesla coils protruded like horns from a knob on the top.

Shelton turned to me. "This thing looks exactly like the residual energy signature I found at the site where Conrad and Ambria vanished." His jaw tightened. "Dollars to dog nuts Serena Thain is the one who stole the designs, and she damned sure has the resources to manufacture them."

Serena had been on Team Daelissa, then Team Victus, and was now on Team Baal. The woman knew how to consistently make Santa's naughty list. Her primary concern was being able to do her experiments with zero rules and regulations, making her a perfect fit for the bad guys.

"Serena Thain?" Mason's eyes went wide. "That woman gives science a bad name."

"Yeah, well so do you." Shelton frowned. "We can't let these jokers have free reign anymore. The academy needs a real director. Not these guys."

"I agree." Elyssa tapped a finger on her chin. "I know the person perfect for whipping this place into shape, but she'll probably hate me for it."

I didn't have the faintest idea who she was talking about, but I took a wild stab anyway. "Your mom?"

"Close." Elyssa turned a cold gaze on the scientists. "My sister, Phoebe."

"Oh." I pursed my lips. "Um, why her?"

"Because she's a brilliant tactician and she understands how to oil and maintain the cogs of a war machine."

Mason pounded a fist on the table. "This is an outrage. We will not allow this fine institution to be commandeered for war-mongering Templars."

Shelton scoffed. "Time for the old farts to get out of the way."

"You people don't care about making things better." Elyssa looked around at the expensive high-tech furniture in the room. "All you care about is making money off of Victus's inventions instead of innovating yourself."

"You can take your slanderous accusations and leave this instant." Mason's face turned purple with rage. "Science Academy belongs to us, not outsiders."

Elyssa ignored the outburst. "Justin, I hate to ask, but can you get Phoebe and possibly my father up here ASAP?"

"As you wish." I winked and left the room so I could make a few calls in private.

Phoebe's face appeared on my screen after the second ring. With her fair skin, black hair, and violet eyes, she could have been Elyssa's twin sister, except for the fact they'd been born over a hundred years apart.

She raised a dark eyebrow. "To what do I owe this pleasure, Justin? I haven't talked to you in nearly a month."

"Well, I was dead for a while and all that." I shrugged. "You know, the normal stuff."

She grinned. "Totally normal for you."

I got straight to the point. "Elyssa thinks you'd be the perfect person for a tough job. It involves turning around an organization that shit the bed and still hasn't managed to clean up the mess."

Phoebe's violet eyes gleamed with amusement. "Whose diapers do I have to change?"

"Science Academy." I explained the situation, including our forays into the Void. "We need this place up and running so we can raid the Void and steal the sword of Jura."

She blew out a breath and shook her head. "Do you wake up in the morning and ask yourself what's the most outrageous thing you can do? Because I never in a million years would have considered casually strolling into the Void for any reason."

"It's not what I planned on doing." I shrugged. "It just happened."

"I see." Phoebe's gaze grew serious. "We don't have the manpower to fight Baal in any of the realms, so our war plans are on hold. Thomas has focused all our efforts on strengthening the defenses of Eden and uprooting Baal's infernus."

It sounded like she was convincing herself to take the job, so I nodded.

"I'm not a scientist, but I can identify the real experts and leaders and put them where they need to be." She bit her lower lip. "The admins in charge of most institutions are the last people who need to have any kind of authority."

"I agree wholeheartedly."

Phoebe nodded. "I'm in. I'll organize an entourage and call you when I'm ready."

"Will that include Thomas?" I asked.

"Depends on if he's free." Phoebe shrugged. "He's out at Thunder Rock today."

"Sounds good. We're engaged in conversation with the admins of the academy right now, so the sooner the better."

"Don't worry. I'll be quick." She winked and the call ended.

I went back into the conference room. Shelton, Adam, and Cinder were poring over the information on the holographic display while Elyssa lectured the admins about responsibility.

"Well ain't this interesting?" Shelton highlighted a paragraph of text on the display. "Most of these clowns were on Xander's payroll."

"How interesting." Elyssa slowly arched an eyebrow. "That explains a lot."

The faces of the men around the table turned various shades of green. Their top-secret meeting had turned into their worst nightmare.

Phoebe called me about twenty minutes later. I sent her a picture of the receptionist area. A portal formed a moment later, and she and her entourage poured through.

A towering hulk of a man strolled in at the end. Michael Borathen kept a straight face but managed to look amused at the same time. "I see you organized a little excitement for us today, Justin."

I grinned. "I know how bored you get at the Ranch."

Phoebe hugged me and kissed my cheek. "Where's my little sister?"

"Bossing around a bunch of old men in the other room." I shrugged. "The usual."

She snickered. "Sometimes I wonder if she isn't really the one who's a couple hundred years old."

Madeline looked ready to shoot herself. "Why are you people doing this to the academy?"

I felt bad for her. She was just a receptionist doing her job without a clue that her bosses were former sympathizers of Xander Tiberius. That bastard had turned away refugees from other Overworld cities and cost countless lives by refusing to listen to reason.

"Madeline, things are going to get better, okay?" I sat on the edge of her desk. "The men in there aren't doing what's best for the academy. We will."

She put her face in her hands and began sobbing. "That's what Administrator Mason told me. All I've seen are a long line of people with promises and none of them deliver."

Phoebe put a hand on the woman's shoulder. "Madeline, I need someone to be my right-hand around here. Someone who knows the ins and outs of this place and is a skilled organizer. Can you be that person?"

Madeline wiped away her tears and nodded. "Yes."

"You can call me Phoebe, okay?"

"Okay." Madeline didn't look convinced, but her shoulders straightened a bit. "How can I help, Phoebe?"

"I need to call a general assembly. I need to know who the best and brightest are so we can form a real science council." Phoebe handed Madeline an arctablet. "Perform all your duties with this, please. I want to keep all data off the academy servers."

"At once." Madeline looked at her academy tablet. "I'll need to transfer the school roster and other information over to this tablet, but I don't have the credentials for that."

Phoebe nodded. "Get whoever is in charge of that over here so we can get them on board."

They continued talking and my eyes started to glaze over. Administration and organization were not my areas of expertise. I looked at Michael. "This isn't as exciting as I thought it'd be."

He nodded. "Phoebe loves reorganizations. Hell, she really whipped Daelissa's forces into shape. Gave us a run for our money."

Phoebe glanced up from her conversation with Madeline, a troubled look in her eyes. "Why do you have to bring that up again? Do you know how many good people died because of me?"

"A lot." Michael shrugged. "But you redeemed yourself. Plus, you were brainwashed."

Phoebe sighed. "If you never bring that up again, it'll be too soon."

Madeline looked pleased to already have fresh office gossip on her plate. "You were brainwashed and were on Daelissa's side?"

"Enough." Phoebe slashed a hand through the air. "We've got enough work to do without worrying about the past."

The conversation struck a nerve in me. Phoebe was a brilliant strategist and her war plans had led to the deaths of hundreds, maybe thousands of our people. She'd been convinced that her parents, Thomas and Leia, had left her and her brother to die during a skirmish with vampires in the American Civil War. Daelissa's brainwashing had reinforced that belief, making Phoebe think her parents were monsters and the real enemy.

When all was said and done, we'd welcomed Phoebe with open arms. Maybe she hadn't committed the same atrocities as Daelissa and Xanos but forgiving her for all those deaths because she was family seemed like favoritism. Daelissa was working to redeem herself. Was it possible Xanos could do the same?

I wanted to believe, I truly did. Death might be too easy a sentence on Xanos. Maybe it was better to guide her along a path to redemption in life instead.

"Deep thoughts?" Michael watched me carefully.

"Maybe too deep." I led him away from the others and told him my thoughts. "Can someone like Xanos redeem herself despite all the horrors committed by her and in her name?"

He pressed his lips into a thin line. "I don't have a good answer for you, but I think if someone wants to redeem themselves, you need to make sure they're being genuine first."

I nodded. "That's my main worry. That we gave Xanos power by letting her help us and she'll somehow manipulate events to put her back in power."

"What are the key elements to putting her back in power?" Michael asked. "What does she need to regain her Apocryphan powers?"

I knew the answer already. "Emily or Eve would have to strip the powers from me and give them to Xanos since Emily allowed Xanos's powers to dissimilate. Eve would probably have to upgrade Xanos's body so it could handle the power again."

Michael nodded. "How would Xanos convince either of them to help her?"

I shrugged. "Emily would never do it unless it was our last hope. Eve is insane and unpredictable, but I don't think she'd help Xanos, especially not after what she did to her body."

"What you've described are nearly impossible odds for Xanos to over-come." Michael pinched his chin between thumb and forefinger while he considered it. "Unless Xanos knows something we don't, there isn't much of a chance she can pull that off."

"I hope you're right."

The door to the admin office opened and Elyssa stepped out. "Hey, sis! You ready to take over?"

Phoebe nodded. "Let's get this wagon on the trail."

Michael shook his head. "Her sayings are so eighteen-hundreds."

I snorted. "Yeah, I don't think Phoebe cares about updating her idioms."

"She's stubborn." He followed the others into the conference room.

Shelton and Adam motioned me over excitedly when I stepped in.

"Bad news, man." Shelton bared his teeth. "I think Serena Thain used that anti-magic staff to capture Conrad and Ambria."

Adam nodded. "I have a really bad feeling about this, Justin. There's no telling what she'll do to them."

Shelton took off his wide-brimmed hat and slumped. "They might be dead already."

CHAPTER 15

While Phoebe delivered a speech to the academy admins, Shelton, Adam, Cinder, and I left the room and plotted how to find out what happened to Conrad and Ambria.

"Oh no." Shelton stopped, eyes wide.

Adam looked around as if expecting a robot attack. "What's wrong?"

Shelton sniffed his armpits. "I think I forgot to put on deodorant this morning."

Adam groaned. "No, that's just your usual odor."

"I am thankful I can ignore odors while around Shelton," Cinder said. "Especially after he has a beef and onion taco."

Adam gagged.

I snorted and rolled my eyes. "Worry about the stench later, okay? For now, can someone explain how that anti-magic staff works?"

"When you use magic in its vicinity, it creates an equal and opposite backlash." Adam held up a fist and simulated firing a blast of magic. "If you channeled a pulse of Brilliance within the vicinity of the staff, it would absorb the energy and zap you with an equal charge of malaether. The reverse polarity might be enough to knock you unconscious."

"And that's what happened to Conrad?" I said. "Serena challenged him, he tried to fight, and the staff knocked them out?"

"Probably." Shelton took out his arcphone and showed everyone the pictures he'd taken of the scene. The outline of the residual magic looked nearly identical to the blueprints of the anti-magic staff.

Cinder projected another image from his arctablet, this one of a vault door. "I discovered some interesting information on the admin arctablet. Apparently, Victus created a secret vault with prototypes of his inventions. The vault is somewhere on the academy grounds and can only be opened with Victus's DNA."

"Now how would they know all that if it's a secret?" Shelton said.

"Because this information was gathered by Xander Tiberius while Victus was still alive." Adam flipped to the first page of the document and zoomed in on a paragraph that read, *Property of Tiberius Industries*. "Xander's company made planes, trains, and automobiles packed with arcnology. He owned majority stock in MagicSoft and tried to buy out Orange several times."

"In other words, he made bank by selling other people's intellectual property," I said.

Adam nodded. "Victus didn't care about money, just power."

"Usually the two go hand in hand." I shook my head. "We can't leave a brother behind. We're going to have to drop what we're doing and pool all our resources into finding Conrad and Ambria."

"He'd do the same for us." Shelton reached out and mimicked choking someone. "Plus, it's time to choke a bitch. I'm sick and tired of Serena throwing a monkey wrench in our plans."

"Finding Conrad might also be advantageous to our efforts in the Void," Cinder said.

Shelton frowned. "Yeah? How's that?"

"Conrad's DNA might open his father's vault." Cinder shrugged. "Perhaps there is something inside that will help us."

I nodded. "Let's get on it then." I turned to Shelton. "You saw Serena in Queens Gate. Do you think she's still there?"

"Maybe." He shook his head. "Max and I followed her, but she went into a magical prank shop and never came out. We looked everywhere inside, but she was gone."

"Then that's where we start." Phoebe was still talking to the admins, so I motioned Elyssa over and told her our plan.

She nodded. "I agree. We need to find Conrad and Ambria and hope they're still alive."

"We need someone to find Victus's hidden vault." I glanced at Phoebe. "Can she organize Templars to scour the academy grounds?"

"I'll head that effort," Elyssa said. "Phoebe wants me around while they start the reorganization, and if we're not going back to the Void until we find Conrad, then it's best if I help here."

"What about Xanos?" The Apocryphan had been paraded before the academy admins and then seated on a nearby couch.

"We can put her in a cell for the time being," Elyssa said.

"Please don't." Xanos bolted to her feet. "I can be useful."

She wasn't wrong, but I let her sweat it for a moment before answering. "Okay, you can come."

With that settled, I kissed Elyssa goodbye and left with the crew. The moment we left the building Shelton whooped.

"Boys day out!" He pumped a fist. "Let's get that bitch, Serena Thain."

"Agreed," Cinder said calmly. "We will rail her ass."

We burst into laughter.

"You mean nail her ass." Shelton wiped tears of mirth from his eyes.

Cinder frowned. "Apologies. Some of these idioms are nonsensical and hard to use properly."

"Agreed." Xanos shook her head. "I know many languages, but idioms are the most difficult."

"Yeah, whatever." Shelton bared his teeth. "I can't wait to see Serena in a cell."

Adam smirked. "You really don't like her do you, Shelton?"

"Back when I was in the bounty hunting business, she tried to financially ruin me." He scowled. "She said my style of bounty hunting was inhumane and should be outlawed."

I raised an eyebrow. "I didn't realize you two went that far back."

"Not by choice." He grunted. "Her husband at the time ran his own bounty hunting company. Turned out she just wanted to ruin me so they could make bank. Then her husband vanished after he got rich. I'm convinced she fed him to their pet tigers."

Cinder tilted his head. "It would take several tigers to consume a fully grown man."

Adam blinked a few times. "You're telling me Serena was married to a rich bounty hunter and she killed him for his money by feeding him to a tiger?"

"I'm just shitting you, man." Shelton burst into laughter. "That look on your face is priceless!"

"You liar." Adam rolled his eyes. "I should've known something like that could never happen."

I chuckled. "Where do you even come up with a story like that?"

"Shelton's got an endless reservoir of crap like that." Adam shook his head.

Queens Gate sprawled across the valley between the cliffs where Arcane University and Science Academy were located. Back in the day, we'd carried brooms or flying carpets everywhere. I kind of wished we could fly down there. It had been a while since I'd felt the rush of diving off a thousand-foot cliff.

Since Elyssa wasn't around to police me, I decided not to contact the Templars at the transit hub and opened a portal directly into town. We stepped through the gateway and onto a side street near the Copper Goose. Designed like its namesake, it was one of the most popular restaurants in town.

Curious gazes immediately settled on Xanos. Purple people weren't exactly common, not even in the Overworld.

"She went this way." Shelton led us through the winding streets until we reached the prank shop he'd mentioned. Younger kids crowded the shop while their weary parents watched and wondered what sorts of shenanigans they'd have to suffer through should they actually purchase anything.

"Was it this busy when you were here, Shelton?" Adam asked.

Shelton nodded. "Yeah."

There were several clothing shops, an ice cream parlor, and a magical toy store in the nearby vicinity, but none of them were nearly as crowded as this place.

Shelton pointed into the store. "She went inside and must have left through the back door. I didn't risk following her inside because I didn't want her to notice us."

"Are you certain she didn't realize you were tailing her?" I asked.

Shelton nodded. "She kept her nose buried in a notebook. You know how she likes to write."

Adam leaned back against the building next to us. "How long was she in the Copper Goose?"

"Maybe ten minutes," Shelton said. "She was picking up a takeout order."

Cinder tilted his head as he stared at the people in the prank shop. "Some of those people are repeating the same behavior over and over again."

I watched an excited child pick up a brown packet and wave it in front of his father. The father frowned and shook his head, then resumed looking miserable. The child returned to browsing the aisles, occasionally bringing something for his father to look at and returning it to the shelf after he shook his head. This went on for ten minutes. "Man, that kid is relentless."

"How does his dad not yank his ass out of there?" Shelton said.

"After observing the crowd as a whole, I believe only a few of the people in there are real." Cinder stepped across the road and walked up to one of the bored parents. He started talking. The father looked blankly at him for a moment, smiled, and said something back.

The smile was stiff and precise. It reminded me of the way Cinder's expressions used to look before he finally improved. "I think he might be onto something." Shelton looked ready to walk over, but I held him back. "Hang on a moment."

Cinder spoke with a few more people then returned to us. "As I suspected, many people in the crowd are actually golems."

"They're pretty damned lifelike," Shelton said.

"That is because they are using integrated illusions to cover synthetic bodies." Cinder shook his head. "I touched one and discovered wood beneath the illusion."

"What the hell?" Shelton frowned. "I guess Max and I were in too much of a hurry to notice something like that."

Adam pursed his lips. "What's the purpose of making fake customers out of golems?"

"I detected eight fake people and five real ones," Cinder said. "Perhaps the golems are meant to be pranks themselves."

Shelton shook his head. "Something doesn't add up."

"I think it's to make this place a convincing cover for a hideout." I headed across the street and into the store. The golems didn't even glance at me, but a couple of the real people did. If I continued walking straight through, another door would take me to the street behind the store. There were shelves to my left, and a counter to my right where a young man worked the register. He smiled when I looked his way, so I pegged him as a real person.

I walked over to him. "Are you the owner of this store?"

He shook his head. "No, that would be Miss Tree."

"Did you say mystery?"

He chuckled. "No, the owner's name is Miss Tree." He enunciated each word with a clear pause in between.

"Ah." I grinned to show I appreciated the clarification. "Is she in?"

"Are you with the paper? She doesn't like to advertise."

"No." I pointed to one of the golems. "I want to know how much those are."

He tilted his head. "What do you mean?"

"Those are golems, right?"

His eyes widened. "How did you know?"

"I just notice things."

"We use them to make us look busier than we are." He smiled sheepishly. "Miss Tree thinks it's good for business."

"So, they're not for sale?"

He shook his head. "I don't think so. I'd have to ask her."

I glanced at the door behind him. "Can I speak with her?"

"She doesn't like to be disturbed." His smile faltered. "I can leave the question for her and if you come by tomorrow, perhaps she'll have answered it."

I didn't want to barge past him and into the office only to find out Miss Tree was someone wholly unrelated to Serena, but the way this guy was stonewalling made me even more suspicious.

"But I'd really like to purchase one now." I tapped my pocket. "I've got plenty of tinsel. Price is no object."

That gave him pause. He bit his lower lip and looked at the door behind him. "I'll ask. Please wait."

Finally! I thought.

He opened the door a crack, slipped inside, and shut it behind him. I was tempted to cross behind the counter so I could take a peek, but he returned less than a minute later.

"She's not in at the moment." He slid a piece of parchment and a quill to me. "Leave your name and symbols and I'll get back to you the moment I have an answer."

"When was the last time you saw her?" I asked.

"She came in this morning, but I haven't seen her since."

I trusted his sincerity, but if Serena owned this place, then it was likely she had a secret lair on the premises. It was clear I'd have to force my way through the door behind him. We didn't have time to mess around.

With a reassuring smile, I nodded. "Thanks for your help."

"You're welcome."

I headed to the end of the counter. The moment he looked away, I'd rush him, grab him, and shove him through the office door before he knew what hit him. Hopefully, the customers wouldn't even realize it had happened.

I reached the end of the counter, tensed, and—

A teenaged girl grabbed my arm and whispered, "This is a dead end. Come with me."

"Huh?" I looked from her to the cashier in confusion.

She pointed toward the back door. "Out there, please."

I was curious enough to comply. I turned to ask her a question, but she'd vanished. "Just what I need, another mystery." I went through the back door and reached a nearly empty alleyway. Shelton, Adam, Cinder, and Xanos appeared around the corner a moment later and joined us.

I held out my hands. "What's going on?"

"I happened, sir!" A young lad who couldn't possibly still be young after so many years emerged from the shadows, a bright grin on his face. "It's been a long while, guvnah!"

"Oliver?" I rubbed my eyes and looked at him again. The pooper-scooper kid from the stables in the Grotto hadn't changed a bit. "How in the hell are you still a kid?"

"Well, sir, it's a bit hard to explain." He shrugged. "I find it easier to just keep it a mystery."

"Oh." I frowned. "I like solving mysteries."

"They are interesting." He looked at Xanos. "It that the twit who nearly ended the Overworld?"

I nodded. "That's the twit, all right."

Xanos stiffened, but kept her mouth shut.

"Bloody hell." He frowned. "She looks different than the pictures."

"She lost her mojo," Shelton said.

Oliver chuckled. "That's good or we'd all be dead."

"What are you doing in Queens Gate?" I asked.

"I needed a change, so I slipped on over this way for a bit." He rocked back and forth on his heels. "My network of informers saw you appear in Queens Gate and I thought it'd be wise to contact you."

Shelton mussed his hair. "Good to see you again, kid."

"You as well, Harry." Oliver leaned against the alley wall. He'd grown slightly over the last decade, but not by much.

Oliver had provided Shelton vital information way back in the day, and even put a tracker on a car so we could follow Jeremiah Conroy back to one of his secret lairs and rescue my mother from Daelissa.

Ah, those were the days.

"What do you have for us?" I asked.

"As you may know, I make a few quid here and there by selling information. I also provide eyes and ears for Underborn." Oliver shrugged. "It's a living."

"Ain't no surprise to me," Shelton said. "Underborn would be stupid not to pay for your help."

Adam nodded. "Where is Underborn?"

"That's the unfortunate part." Oliver frowned. "Baal's bloody minions have been searching for Underborn relentlessly. Baal uses these creatures called infernus and, of course, people possessed by demons."

"We're familiar with them," I said.

"Hardly surprising, sir." Oliver rubbed his forehead. "Underborn asked me to plant false leads so he could go into hiding."

"Underborn has a relic that Baal needs." I felt uneasy knowing spies were everywhere and glanced around just in case. I turned back to Oliver. "Any idea where Underborn is now?"

He shook his head. "Phissilinth was visiting me from time to time for updates and to let me know Underborn was still on the move."

Adam nodded. "Underborn has the map and key of Jura so he can travel just about anywhere in an instant. I imagine he's giving Baal fits."

"Hang on, back up a minute." Shelton frowned. "You said Phissilinth *was* visiting you from time to time, past tense."

Oliver sighed. "I haven't heard from him in a while and there are hardly any infernus around anymore. I think the search for Underborn has ended."

Shelton scowled. "Because Baal found him."

CHAPTER 16

I f Baal really had located and captured Underborn, that was horrible news. What was even worse, was that we had no way to confirm it.

Xanos slumped. "We're doomed."

"Well, that's just wonderful." Shelton threw up his hands. "I wonder if Serena had anything to do with it."

Oliver frowned. "Serena Thain?"

"The one and only." Shelton groaned. "We're know she's in Queens Gate, but not exactly where."

Oliver perked up. "I know where she might be."

"Oh yeah?" Shelton's expression brightened. "Where?"

"Right here." Oliver jabbed a thumb at a building behind him. "There's a stairwell hidden by illusion."

"Well, what do you know?" Shelton grinned. "I was within spitting distance and didn't even realize it."

I turned to Oliver. "You've been tracking Serena?"

"We track all sorts of people," he said. "She was new to town a few weeks ago. When I found out who she was, I made sure to keep tabs on her regularly."

"I've been waiting a long time to wrap my hands around Serena's neck." Shelton cracked his knuckles. "Let's bust a cap in her ass."

Cinder tilted his head. "Is that another sexual term, Shelton? I seem to recall you saying something about busting a nut—"

"Dude, stop!" Shelton's face turned red. "Not another word."

Cinder frowned. "Is there a difference between busting a cap or a nut?"

Adam and I burst into laughter. Oliver doubled over, howling. He might look like a kid, but he probably knew as much as most adults.

"I know way too much about Shelton's love life." Adam tried to catch his breath from laughing so hard. "God, I can't get the visual out of my mind."

Shelton elbowed him. "Hey, you're welcome."

Xanos shook her head. "You joke and laugh though an enemy might lurk beneath your very feet."

I rolled my eyes. "Way to ruin it."

Oliver looked her up and down. "Why is she with you? Isn't she dangerous?"

"Nah, we stripped her powers." I shrugged. "Now she's helping us prevent the end of the world."

"Really?" Oliver looked doubtful. "The enemy of my enemy is my friend and all that?"

"In theory." I shook my head. "Only time will tell."

Shelton scoffed. "Oh, she's our friend until she figures out her next move. Then all bets are off."

"I have no reason to betray you." Xanos met his eyes. "If I can prevent the end of the realms, then I will do my part."

"I hope that's true." I nodded at the area with the hidden stairwell. "All right folks, let's get inside."

Adam tapped his phone to activate a spell that scanned for wards while I switched to demon view for a look. The ground was webbed with tiny glowing leylines, magical power conduits carrying aether. A massive leyline ran directly beneath the building, making it the perfect place for someone like Serena to set up shop.

"Couple of alarm wards, but nothing major," Adam said a moment later. "I'll have to scan again once we're inside to make sure she didn't sneak in anything deadly."

"Wouldn't put it past her," Shelton said.

Using a decryption program on his phone, Adam defused the alarm wards and found the stairwell Oliver had mentioned. He seemed to sink into the cobblestones as he walked down them and vanished.

"Give us a minute." Shelton followed him down.

I let the pros do their thing.

"Ah." Cinder nodded. "Now I understand." He turned his phone screen toward me, allowing me to read the graphic definition of "busting a nut" he'd found on Urban Dictionary.

I grimaced. "Shelton really needs to watch what he says around you."

"Sometimes I overhear conversations between Harry and Bella." Cinder put his phone away. "I believe they are rather experimental in their love-making. I hope to one day find someone with whom I can also be exper-imental."

I put a hand on his shoulder. "Cinder, there is such a thing as too much information. You know that, right?"

He frowned. "On the contrary. You can never have too much information."

"Agreed," Xanos said. "For a golem, this one is quite intelligent."

Cinder nodded at her. "Thank you."

"No, you're wrong." I shook my head. "You'll understand the concept of TMI one day—I hope."

Shelton's head poked up from the illusory cobblestones. "It's clear."

"Good to proceed?" I asked.

Shelton nodded. "Adam breached the magical door locks and scanned the interior. Looks clear."

Oliver watched us with a grin. "I wish you good luck. I'll notify Harry if I discover anything else useful."

"Thanks, Oliver." I had a lot of questions for the kid, but they'd have to wait. I turned and followed Shelton into the stairwell.

The illusion hiding the stairwell was only one-sided. Once beneath it, I could see the outside area like normal. Adam stood just inside an open metal door. On the other side was a small landing and another descending stairway.

"I scanned the area at the bottom and didn't find anything," Adam whispered.

I gave him a thumbs up and took the lead. The room at the bottom of the stairs gave me flashbacks to my time in the Gloom. Contraptions of all shapes and sizes occupied the basement. They'd been haphazardly placed with little semblance of order as if hurriedly dumped by impatient movers.

One device on the far right was composed of rings within progressively smaller rings. A silver orb the size of a cantaloupe rested in the center. Each ring had an independent axis, presumably so they could spin in different directions. A Tesla coil hung from the ceiling above, a thick metal rod with a pyramid of discs spaced down its length with the smallest at the top. I noticed several more of the coils arranged in a hexagonal shape on the floor around the ring device. None looked active.

We passed a silver box a little larger than an old-school phone booth, something that looked like a seesaw with circular saw blades along its length, and even an iron coffin filled with metal coils. This was definitely the lair of a mad scientist.

Adam held his phone out scanning for wards. Shelton dragged a finger along the top of a nearby apparatus and showed me a thick accumulation of dust.

"This stuff's been here for a while." He wiped his finger off on his jeans. "Unused."

The floor was dusty too, except for a faint trail wending between the machines to the left. I sniffed the air and detected a faint whiff of lavender. I followed the scuff marks in the dust until we reached another metal door in the back.

Adam checked it out. "No wards." He gingerly tapped the door handle as if making sure it wouldn't shock him.

"Better let me do that." I flexed my fingers. "I could probably survive anything nasty."

"Good point." Adam backed away and let me open the door.

When nothing exploded in my face, I peeked into the next room. What lay on the other side was the polar opposite of the room we'd just passed through. The floor and walls were polished white. Hovering glowballs cast brilliant light from every angle, eliminating shadows.

A holographic blueprint rotated slowly in the middle of the room.

Victus's signature in the lower right corner left no doubt as to who had stolen his files from the academy. Standing before the blueprint was the subject of the hunt itself: Serena Thain.

Shelton flicked his staff out to full length. "I'm going old school on that bitch."

A green bolt of lightning speared from a rod in the ceiling and struck the end of Shelton's staff. He cursed and threw it to the ground.

Serena turned toward us, a smirk on her face. "Clever boys, but not clever enough by half. Do you really think you could just sneak into my lab without me knowing?"

Shelton snatched his smoking staff off the ground. "What the hell was that?"

"It's anti-magic arcnology, or antima for short." She produced a metallic rod, this one a smaller version of the four I only now realized hung from the ceiling. "I took Victus's original work and have improved upon it tenfold."

Xanos seemed entranced. "It truly punishes the use of all magic?"

Serena blinked. "Xanos?"

"I am, or rather was." The Apocryphan shook her head. "I possess powers no longer."

Serena nodded. "I am disappointed. Testing my invention against Apocryphan powers would have been interesting. I am quite interested to see how the Slade boy performs."

I stepped past Shelton and into the room. "What did you do to Conrad and Ambria?"

"Now that is an interesting story." Serena stepped away from the holographic blueprint, her rod tapping the floor as she walked. "You see, what I took from Science Academy is only a fraction of what Victus left behind. His secret vault contains resources I need to continue my research. But only his DNA can open it."

I calculated how quickly I could cross the space between us. "You went after Conrad so he could open it."

"I did." She twirled the slim rod. "He tried to fight, but the antima turned his own magic against him. I believe he tried to escape with a blink stone. A tremendous backlash blinded me and turned the antima blisteringly hot. When I could see clearly again, he and his little girl were gone."

"You fucking killed them!" Shelton roared and stomped across the room. "I don't need magic to choke the life out of you!"

Serena didn't look the least bit worried. "I'm not certain they're dead."

Shelton smacked into an invisible barrier and bounced back. "Shit!" Blood trickled from his nostrils. "You almost broke my nose!"

I held up a hand. "What do you mean, Serena?"

"I mean, there was evidence a portal opened." She shrugged. "I believe the interaction between the antima and an object of extreme power like a blink stone created an unforeseen event."

Shelton dug in the pockets of his leather duster and stuffed tissue into his nostrils. "Daelissa is dead. Victus is dead. When are you going to get it through your thick skull that everyone you back ends up taking the eternal dirt nap?"

"If at first you don't succeed, try, try again." Serena leaned her staff against a table and jotted notes on a pad of paper. "My dear Daelissa deserved to rule. She promised to unveil the very secrets of the universe to me." Her eyes threw daggers at me. "And then you killed her."

I scoffed. "I hate to break it to you, but Daelissa didn't know squat back then."

"Unlike the fools at Arcane University and Science Academy, Victus believed in pure research, whether based in magic, science, or both." Serena shook her head. "We discovered so much together. Traveled to so many realms. And yet we barely scratched the surface of all there is to know."

I shook my head. "You want to know the secrets of the universe? Join our team. I'm not the ignorant kid you held prisoner in the Gloom fortress all those years ago."

Serena smiled sweetly, a mother presenting a calm face before whipping her child for his insolence. "You would place unacceptable restrictions on me. I cannot have that."

Shelton huffed. "Don't even bother trying to negotiate with her. She's as much of a monster as Xanos was."

"I greatly respected your approach to world domination, Xanos." Serena's voice sounded reverent. "But even if you'd succeeded against this boy and his little friends, I'm afraid you'd have stood no chance against Elohim."

Xanos's eyes flared. "You would have lost such a wager."

I flicked my gaze toward her, surprised at the regal tone. "Um, girl, you lost to us and we're losing to Baal. I'm pretty sure he could have mopped the floor with Razor whenever he wanted." I turned back to Serena. "I have no idea why you support Baal. If he succeeds, he'll destroy the realms."

"And open other interesting avenues." Serena giggled maniacally. "There are other dimensions and worlds to explore. When Elohim is restored to his former glory, his powers will allow me unlimited latitude."

"You really think he'll have time for a lowly scientist once he's back in his body?" I scoffed. "You'll be left behind and forgotten."

She shrugged. "I suppose we shall see. Either way, I will witness one of the most incredible events since creation."

"This is pointless." Shelton pressed a hand against the invisible shield protecting Serena from our wrath. "Let's break this down and take her in."

"How do you propose to do that without magic?" Serena sat in a chair and watched us in amusement. "This shall be interesting."

I looked at the antima rods hanging from the ceiling far above. If I could reach them, I could disable them. But not even my supernatural strength could propel me that high.

Cinder knew what I was thinking. "Perhaps if you get a running start, I can give you a boost." He laced his fingers together to provide a foothold.

Serena looked from us to the rod, probably calculating the distance. She didn't look the least bit concerned, which concerned me greatly. I almost used magic out of force of habit but restrained myself at the last minute. Instead, I reached into a pocket, found a penny, and flicked it toward the rod.

The penny wasn't on target, but it didn't need to be. It pinged off another invisible shield about two feet from the rod.

Serena shook her head sadly. "I was so looking forward to seeing you attempt to leap to the rod. It appears you've grown marginally wiser with time."

"Yeah, marginally." I whispered in Shelton's ear. "Hang tight. I'll be right back."

"Say what?" He tried to grab my arm, but I was already gone.

I left through the door and entered the dusty basement, then ran to the opposite side of the room, putting as much distance between me and those rods as possible. From there I opened a portal to Cinder's lab. I found what I needed in the back of the room, grabbed it, and pocketed some backup options just in case. I went back through the portal, closed it, and rejoined my comrades in Serena's lab.

"For a moment, I thought you gave up." Serena shrugged. "As much as

I'm enjoying this reunion, I think it's best to settle matters once and for all." She produced an arctablet and tapped on the screen. The door shut behind us.

I instinctively tried to open it, but a new barrier blocked it. Another set of rods descended from the ceiling. These began to hum and vibrate at a low but quickly rising frequency like an Obsidian Arch charging to open a portal. I didn't need to know what was happening to realize it wasn't good for our collective health.

"What the hell is going on?" Shelton said.

"An experiment," Serena said. "I've tested it on lycans and vampires, but you represent the strongest sample of specimens yet." She stood and pressed her face against the shield between us and her. "They say it's like being microwaved."

Shelton scowled. "What the hell is microwaving?"

"It's a nom food heating box," Adam said. "It'll be like having your insides cooked."

"A most unpleasant death." Cinder tilted his head. "But I do not have real flesh."

"Well ain't that lovely." Shelton thrust his staff toward the shielded door. "I don't plan on dying today." A blast of energy fired from the end. The nearest antima rod hummed, and the magical energy vanished. In the very same instant, green lightning crackled from the tip of the rod and blasted the staff. Shelton cried out and fell over backward, his hand blackened and burned.

"Shelton!" Adam tried to help up his wounded friend, but Shelton gripped his hand and howled in pain.

I unslung our ace in the hole from my back and aimed it at the shield. It was a Razor anti-magic rifle, the kind they'd used to disintegrate our shields. And now it was my turn to smile.

"Is that Razor tech?" Serena's eyes flared.

"Hell yeah."

Serena gulped and backed away. "You little bastard."

"*Hasta la vista*, baby." I pulled the trigger and grinned like a madman.

The trigger clicked. Nothing happened. I frowned, looked down at it and clicked the trigger several more times to no avail. It looked like we were going to die after all.

CHAPTER 17

Serena cackled with glee. "You fool. Supers can't use Razor tech."

Someone tapped my shoulder. "Justin."

I turned to face Cinder. "We're dead."

He tilted his head. "You did not activate the power pack." He reached out a finger and depressed a tiny button on the stock of the rifle. "Try it now."

I spun and pulled the trigger. Gray rings of energy rippled out. The shield cracked like glass and shattered.

Serena shrieked in anger, grabbed her rod, and ran.

"Not so fast, you asshole!" I blurred after her. She made it through a metal door and slammed it shut behind her before I could reach her. I yanked on the handle and rammed my shoulder against it, but it was built to withstand even my demon strength.

Adam searched the table and surrounding area. "This apparatus must be controlled by her arc tablet. I don't know how to turn it off.

And just like that, we were still going to die. Electrical currents prickled my skin and my insides began to feel warm. It wasn't unlike the time I'd overused my Apocryphan powers. Xanos stumbled and her knees gave out. Adam caught her before she hit the floor.

Shelton clung to his staff. "Feeling...awfully...warm." Sweat beaded on his forehead and he began to gag.

The humming rose higher, nearing a fever pitch that would herald our painful deaths. I aimed the anti-magic gun toward the ceiling and fired. The shield crackled and fell apart. I blasted the rods, but the rifle didn't have any effect.

Cinder was the only other one still on his feet, so I motioned him over. "Cinder, give me a boost!"

"My head feels fuzzy, Justin." He seemed disoriented but positioned himself beneath the rods and laced his hands together.

I dropped the rifle, got a running start, and ran at him. When my foot landed in his hands, he threw me upward with such force that I nearly impaled myself on one of the rods. I reached out and grabbed one. It was like touching a hot stovetop. I shouted in pain but letting go meant everyone died, so I hung on for dear life.

Hand over hand, I climbed higher, turned upside down, and braced my feet on the ceiling. A solid yank broke the rod free of the metal brace beneath it. I grabbed the neighboring rod just before I fell. My hands were numb from pain. The muscles began to weaken, and my grasp slipped.

I tore off the next rod just as my hands lost all sensation and refused to respond. I vainly reached for the next rod, but my numb flesh merely slapped it. I plummeted toward the hard concrete. The painful impact never came because Cinder caught me.

"You did it, Justin." He cradled me like a baby for a moment before setting me on my feet.

"What do you mean?" I looked up at the remaining rods. "I didn't destroy it."

"The humming stopped when you tore off the first one." Cinder put a hand to his chest. "I am already feeling better."

"It did?" I turned my trembling hands palms up. The skin was red and blistering. If I'd actually touched a hot stove, the wounds would start healing immediately, but magic damage took longer. The nerve endings in my hand were too damaged to tell me how much pain I was in, but that was the only blessing. I still couldn't wiggle my fingers no matter how hard I tried.

Adam lay on the floor, Xanos slumped over him. Shelton had fallen against the table while cradling his staff. I rushed over to him but could only gently slap his face with my useless hands.

"Mmm, tacos." Shelton blinked open and gazed blankly at me. "Bacon?"

My forehead scrunched. "Say what?"

He flinched. "Oh, shit. What happened?"

"Justin disabled the apparatus," Cinder said from behind me. "But he severely injured his hands." He knelt next to Adam and shook him.

Shelton climbed woozily to his feet. "You're not gonna die again, are you?"

I shook my head. "I hope not, but my hands feel like rubber."

He looked at the burn marks. "Just great. Bottom of the fourth quarter and the heavy hitter is down and out."

"Football has quarters, not baseball."

"Oh." He scratched his head. "I thought that was a hockey analogy."

"Dude, your brain is still scrambled." I sat heavily on a chair. "We need medical treatment now."

Adam grunted and jerked awake. He seemed surprised to see Xanos sprawled across him. "Can you get her off me, Cinder? I feel really weak right now."

"Of course." Cinder plucked Xanos off Adam and lay her on the floor a few feet away.

"Cinder, call a healer." I shook my hands, but they were lifeless lumps of flesh. "I can't even use Nookli right now."

Cinder looked at his phone. "Something is impeding the signal. I will need to go aboveground." He walked across the room toward the rifle then used it to break the shield over the other door. He pushed on the handle and it opened.

Shelton grunted a few times but didn't seem to have the energy to say anything. That told me everything I needed to know. Adam pressed his fingers to Xanos's neck then staggered over to the table.

"We've got to stop Serena." He looked at the broken rods on the floor. "That woman is a menace to society."

I closed my eyes to rest them and apparently fell asleep. When I woke up, Cinder was just returning with three people in tow. The first one gave me a look of disapproval and shook her head.

"We should devote an entire medical wing to you people." Meghan Andretti directed the other two healers to Adam and Shelton then examined my hands and grimaced.

Adam blinked awake. He flinched and shouted when he saw Meghan just a few feet away. "Who—what?" He swallowed. "Where did they come from?"

"You've been asleep." Meghan raised an eyebrow. "And you're extremely disoriented."

Adam looked away from his ex-girlfriend and nodded. "Yeah. Maybe permanent drain bamage."

"It's worse than I thought." Meghan, as usual, didn't laugh at the obvious joke. She poked and prodded my hands with a wand. "Do you feel that? How about that? This right here?"

"I feel nothing." I tried not to panic. What if I'd screwed up my hands for good?

She dug in her medical bag. "Tell me exactly what happened."

I did.

Meghan glanced at the rods, then turned to me and cast a spell. Chemical symbols and numbers appeared in the air above my hand. Meghan studied them for a moment then nodded. "You've suffered severe burns, but the underlying cause is physical, not magical. It seems the magic running through the metal caused them to heat."

I dared to hope. "What does that mean?"

She rubbed blue salve on my hands. "It means you're going to be in serious pain in a little while as your nerve endings regenerate. Otherwise, you'll be good as new."

I sighed in relief. "Oh, thank god."

Meghan turned to the man treating Adam. "What did you find?"

"General disorientation and some cellular damage that will heal," the man said. "Nothing permanent."

"Same here," said the woman treating Shelton. "But I suggest they take malaether meds because there is some residual radiation in the cells."

"Malaether radiation?" Adam shook his head. "It's no wonder."

Meghan moved over to Xanos. "This one has much higher levels of residual radiation." She waved her wand under Xanos's nose and the Apocryphan jerked awake with a scream.

"What? Where am I?"

Meghan gently patted her cheeks. "You're okay. You suffered some injuries but we're here to help."

"No need to be gentle with her," Shelton mumbled. "Xanos deserves a lot more pain than this."

Meghan ignored him and gave Xanos a potion to drink. "I will not mistreat a patient no matter who she is."

I wanted to remind her how she'd reacted when she discovered I was Daemos. She'd changed a lot since then.

Before much longer, the healers were done, leaving us with the malaether meds and stern warnings to lay off the adventures.

Adam and Meghan did a good job ignoring each other. I was pretty sure by now neither of them still had feelings for the other. Then again, I questioned if Meghan really ever had feelings for Adam or much of anything. She was kind of a cold fish.

Cinder studied Serena's contraption while we received our care, and a squad of Templars arrived to secure the location within the hour. By then, my hands felt as if they were being constantly pricked by hundreds of needles. I wasn't about to complain despite the constant pain. Meghan had given me an anesthetic, but I refrained from using it. My hands had been uncomfortably numb for too long already.

Using voice to text, I sent Elyssa a report instead of calling her because she was probably busy helping Phoebe set Science Academy straight.

Though Shelton and Adam were still a bit scrambled, Cinder didn't miss a beat.

"Interesting." Cinder entered information on his arcphone. "The malaether device converts aether to malaether then emits it as a high-frequency wave that can disorient, disable, and kill in minutes. The only shortcoming is the limited effective range."

"What about power requirements?" Adam asked.

"This one uses an aether generator." Cinder shook his head. "Aside from killing, I can see no use for such a device. It is a shame Serena chooses to be evil."

"It's a shame anyone chooses to be bad." I shot a look at Xanos. "Think of all the death and destruction that could be avoided if people just weren't assholes."

"Amen," Shelton said. "I don't care that Serena is a woman. I'm going to punch her lights out the next time I see her."

I nodded. "Maybe Oliver can track her down. The Templars have the Queens Gate exit under heavy guard, so hopefully she can't escape that way."

"In the meantime, I have an idea," Cinder said. "If what Serena said is true, then Conrad and Ambria are alive, but trapped in another realm or pocket dimension."

"Man, I hope so." Shelton shook his head. "Otherwise, that blink stone might have disintegrated them on the spot."

I didn't even want to think about it. "What's your idea?"

"We use the same method that helped us track Emily Glass across multiple realms." Cinder folded his arms. "Using Clarity and Stasis, you may be able to reveal a portal scar, should one exist."

"And if it doesn't?" I asked.

Shelton sighed. "It means they're toast."

"Man, I hope there's a scar." Adam pinched the bridge of his nose. "After everything they survived, it'd be a real kick in the nuts to die by Serena's hand."

"That's for damned sure." Shelton pushed to his feet. "Let's get this show on the road."

Adam nodded wearily. "Yeah, let's do it."

The sensations in my hands had grown from pin pricks to burning. My nerves were regenerating with a vengeance. "I may not be able to channel just yet."

"Then we should call in reinforcements." Cinder tapped on his phone and made a call. "Nightliss, can you join us in Queens Gate? We need your help."

Her voice emitted from the speaker. "What has Justin gotten you into this time?"

Cinder smiled. "Another quest."

She laughed. "I will be there soon." The call ended.

"Talk about someone I haven't seen much lately." Shelton took off his wide-brimmed hat and ran fingers through his hair. "Is she really spending a lot of time in Nowhere?"

"Yeah." I winced at the unrelenting pain and decided now was a good time to take the pain potion Meghan had given me. "She's reconnecting with Daelissa."

Adam grimaced. "I know Daelissa nearly lost her soul to save you and all, but that's just weird."

"It's a bitter pill for damned sure." Shelton glanced at Xanos and shook his head. "Maybe Dark Helmet was right. Evil wins because good is dumb."

"That's ludicrous." I winked and gulped the pain potion. "Daelissa wouldn't have made it to paradise if she hadn't selflessly sacrificed herself."

Xanos shook her head. "You people spend more time worrying that you're making the right decisions than actually making decisions."

I opened my mouth to contradict her but couldn't. On the other hand, was it a bad thing? "That doesn't make it wrong."

"You obviously didn't spend enough time questioning your decisions." Shelton grunted. "My guess is you don't even have a moral compass."

"Xanos is a survivor," Adam said. "Beings like that don't have the luxury of morals."

I didn't know if that was true or not, and I didn't feel like debating it. The pain potion was doing its job. The burning sensation was still there but muted.

A Templar entered the room and saluted. "Commander Slade, we have people sweeping the area. Would you like us to expand our search?"

I nodded. "You won't find Serena, but keeping her on the run for now is the best option."

He pressed a hand to his chest. "Yes, sir."

Nightliss appeared a few minutes later. She looked happier than I'd seen her in years. I supposed seeing her once-evil sister turn good had everything to do with it. "Justin!" She stood on tiptoes and kissed my cheek. "You do not waste any time finding trouble, do you?"

"I mean it's been a couple of weeks or so." I shrugged. "Guess I needed a vacation."

"Being dead will do that to you." She looked at my hands and winced. "What happened?"

I gave her a brief rundown of recent events. "We need to find out what happened to Conrad and Ambria, but I'm not up to channeling just yet."

Nightliss nodded. "I will gladly help, just lead the way." She glanced at Xanos, eyes narrowed, but said nothing.

I still couldn't use my hands, so Shelton called the transit hub and arranged a portal for us. Since we were on the priority list, it took less than five minutes for us to portal to an arch control room and then to the destroyed mansion in the Fairy Gardens near Arcane University.

Shelton took us to the spot where he'd found the blink stone. "If they were sent to another realm or dimension, the scar will be around here somewhere."

Nightliss cupped her hands. A white orb of Brilliance formed in her right hand while an ultraviolet sphere of Murk blossomed in her left.

She pressed the orbs together, twisting her palms this way and that. When she pulled them apart, a large orb of gray Stasis dangled between her hands from silver threads of power.

I grunted thoughtfully. "That's an interesting way to do it."

"A new trick I learned from Fjoeruss." Nightliss smiled. "And with my contacts in the afterlife I have access to knowledge he can only dream of."

Beams of Murk and Brilliance speared from her eyes into the Stasis orb. Translucent Clarity rippled through the air on the other side. Nightliss swept the air back and forth, high and low, searching for the invisible scar left by a portal. But after a thorough search, she found nothing.

Shelton took off his hat and held it over his chest. "Fuck me. They're dead."

CHAPTER 18

"**N**o, this can't be true." Adam put a hand on his forehead and walked in a circle. "We're missing something. Maybe the blink stone didn't leave a scar. Maybe we can use Serena's equipment to replicate the process."

Nightliss raked the beam of Clarity around the area once more but found nothing. Her shoulders slumped and tears pooled in her eyes. "I can't believe they're gone."

Something caught my eye where the beam struck the ground. "Wait!" I dropped to my knees at the spot. "Aim the clarity here."

She did. It looked like almost nothing, a thread of spider web on the ground. I tried to dig with my hands, but the fingers were stiff and unresponsive. Shelton knelt next to me and clawed at the dirt. We found it just beneath the top layer, a long, ragged scar.

"Yes!" Adam raised a hand.

Xanos watched us with a furrowed brow, obviously confused by the feelings we had for other people. This was a foreign language to someone who'd never loved anyone except herself.

The panicked pounding of my heart slowed even though I knew this didn't mean Conrad and Ambria were still alive. There was no telling what waited on the other side of the portal scar. During a blink, there was a single heartbeat of absolute nothingness. They might be trapped there, dead in a vacuum.

It didn't matter. We had to open it and get them out. But we had a problem. Opening a portal scar required two people. One revealed the scar with Clarity while the other froze it with Stasis so it could be pried open with Murk. Powerful as she was, Nightliss couldn't manage it all on her own. Once it was opened, it had to be held open or it would shut immediately.

Nightliss stopped channeling Clarity and the scar vanished. She wiped sweat from her forehead. "I had forgotten how taxing that is."

I looked down at my hands. "I'm useless right now. We need help."

Nightliss nodded. "Alysea, perhaps?"

"Yeah, your mom could do it," Adam said. "And it'd be nice to have some powerful backup in case things go to hell."

"Amen to that." Shelton plopped his hat back on his head. "I've had enough of almost dying for one day."

Adam chuckled. "Nearly dying is one of those things that doesn't get old no matter how many times it happens."

"That's why I keep a fresh pair of underwear handy when I'm on an adventure with Justin." Shelton patted his pocket. "Shitting your pants is just another Tuesday with him."

Everyone burst into laughter except Xanos, whose forehead pinched into a confused V.

Shelton noted her expression. "Hey, Apocryphan take dumps, right?"

Xanos frowned. "If by that you mean defecate, then yes, we do. We eat, we expel waste."

"I'll bet they were some mongo sized craps," Shelton said.

"At my normal size, an ordinary defecation would be about your size."

Adam snickered. "I think she just called you a piece of crap, Shelton."

Xanos blinked. "I meant no such thing. Each one of you is close in size to—"

"One of your turds?" Shelton guffawed. "Apocryphan assholes must be huge."

She sighed. "At no point in my considerably long existence have I understood why bodily functions are such a source of amusement for human males."

"I did not find it funny at first either," Nightliss said. "But if you spend enough time with Justin, Shelton, and Adam, the humor grows on you."

Cinder appeared from around the corner. "I put the moment of levity to use and called your mother, Justin. She will be here shortly."

Xanos turned to him. "You do not find this form of humor funny, golem?"

"It is rather hilarious," Cinder said in a deadpan tone. "I simply have not developed a true appreciation for it."

That only made Adam and Shelton laugh harder.

A portal opened moments later. Ivy skipped through, her long blond hair bouncing. "Bro!" She leapt ten feet and slammed into me with a bone-crushing hug.

"Oof." I nearly fell over backward, but Ivy held me up. I returned the hug awkwardly with my injured hands. "Hey, sis."

"Justin, what happened to your hands?" Mom gently took my wrists and examined the injuries.

Dad came through the portal last, wearing his standard amused smirk. "What trouble are we getting into today, son?"

I freed myself from Mom and Ivy and showed him my red, blistered hands. "Nothing that's too hot to handle."

He snorted. "That's my boy. Everything's a joke if you laugh hard enough about it."

"I fail to see how terrible injuries are humorous." Xanos pressed her hands to her temples. "You people are exhausting."

Dad raised an eyebrow. "Is this your idea of punishment for the Apocryphan?"

I shrugged. "It didn't start out that way, but at this point Xanos has to be wondering what's more torturous—being with us or being stuck at her mom's house."

"This is not torture," Xanos said. "The mystery of your companions intrigues me."

Dad put an arm around her shoulder like a guy talking to his kid about something. "I'll bet not having your powers makes it even more of a challenge, am I right?"

She nodded unsurely. "I am working with limited capacity."

"Isn't that better than ruling the world?" Dad waved a hand across the horizon. What's the point of controlling all that garbage anyway? Now you've got limitless mysteries to solve."

Xanos pressed her lips together. "I suppose I looked at ruling the world as revenge for banishment. It was to show Eve that I could best anyone."

"Mommy issues." Dad nodded. "Usually it's a guy thing, but in your case, I totally get it. At least now, you have nothing to prove." He slid his arm off her shoulder and took a position next to Mom. "I just want to make sure we're on the same page here—no ideas of double-crossing anyone to regain your powers."

"Ah." Xanos nodded. "As you can see, I'm powerless to do such a thing."

Dad shrugged. "Maybe. I guess we'll see."

"First you forgive Daelissa and now Xanos?" Ivy summoned a sizzling orb of Brilliance. "This is stupid!"

Xanos's eyes flared in alarm.

"I should blast her right now." Ivy's eyes narrowed to slits. "Destroy her utterly." Her voice deepened and tiny horns sprouted from her forehead.

Mom gripped Ivy's wrists and stepped in front of her. "Deep breaths, honey. Control the demon."

Blue flames flickered in Ivy's eyes. "Destroy the Apocryphan!"

Mom slapped Ivy with a resounding smack. Ivy reeled back. The Brilliance flickered out and the horns fell from her forehead.

My mouth dropped open. "What in the hell is going on?"

Dad smirked. "Ivy just hit demon puberty. Seems she's a late bloomer like her brother."

"Wow, congrats." Shelton frowned. "I think."

"Uh, Ivy going through demon puberty is the most frightening thing I've heard today," Adam said. "Remember the time Justin destroyed the Darkling government?"

"Hey now, I was set up!"

Adam winced. "Yeah, I know, but it's still scary considering your upbringing."

Shelton snorted. "What he's trying to say is, Daelissa didn't train you to be a killer."

"Yeah, I got it, Shelton." I couldn't refute Adam's point. Ivy had issues. Being trained at a young age by Daelissa would mess up anyone.

Ivy rubbed her eyes. "Oh, crap. Did I go demonic again?"

"Yes, dear." Mom stroked her hair. "But you didn't kill anyone, so that's good."

Uh, has she killed anyone?" I asked

Dad chuckled. "Let's just say she gave Colin McCloud a run for his money."

I winced. "She fought the freaking leader of the lycans?"

"It was an accident. Colin got a few scrapes and bruises, but he was impressed." Dad shrugged. "Ivy is a real scrapper."

"Channeling Brilliance really triggers her inner demon," Mom said. "Much like it used to do with you."

Ivy was technically older than I'd been when I hit demon puberty, but having spent years inside a preservation chamber, her body hadn't aged much, meaning she was actually way ahead of my curve. Plus, she hadn't even been a tween by the time she'd learned her Seraphim powers whereas it had taken me a while just to learn a bit of Arcane magic. Then again, she'd had real training. Mom and Dad had left me to my own devices.

I tried not to feel a little jealous about that and steered the conversation back on topic. I brought my family up to date on the situation. "We need to open that portal scar as soon as possible. Every moment we wait could mean life or death for Conrad and Ambria."

Mom nodded. "Then let's do it."

"I want to help!" Ivy said.

Mom shook her head. "No Brilliance, only Murk."

Ivy nodded. "Okay, I promise."

Nightliss wove Clarity and revealed the scar. Mom channeled Stasis onto the crack until it phased into solidity. Ivy channeled two thin beams of Murk and rammed them into the scar. Biting her bottom lip, she pried it open like an elevator door. Thunder boomed. A gust of cold wind whipped through my hair and sent a flurry of dust into our faces.

I crept to the edge of the portal. The surface rippled like water, but it wasn't reflective. There was nothing but a white void on the other side. I dreaded to think what that might mean for Conrad and Ambria.

Ivy tied off the weave to hold open the portal and wiped sweat off her face. "Wow, that's hard."

I turned to Mom. "Can you tether me? I'm going in."

Mom shook her head. "You're injured. Someone else should check."

"No." I held up a hand. "I'll go first."

Ivy gripped my hand. "Hold on, bro!" Then she jumped feet-first into the portal.

"Ivy!" I still didn't have much control over my fingers, so Ivy's grip was the only one that kept her from slipping inside.

Instead of falling into an endless nothingness, Ivy landed on her bottom with a loud grunt. "Ow!" She patted around with her free hand. "This is a floor."

"A what?" I tried to drag her back through, but she let go of my hand and stood. It was mind-bending watching her stand sideways beneath me. I rubbed my eyes and looked again, but that didn't change anything.

"I'm in a room!" Ivy ran out of sight.

"Wait!" I jumped into the portal and slid across a slick surface. I glanced back and saw Mom and the others looking down at me from the gateway. Ivy stood at a window, jaw gaping at the view outside the window. I pushed to my feet and joined her.

The view was extraordinary.

A golden street ran through a city of buildings so diverse I hardly knew what to make of it. There were towers of multi-hued crystal even more ornately designed than those I'd seen in the Darkling capitol of Pjurna. One building resembled a giant conch shell. A cluster of towers swayed gently like a sea anemone. Crystalline abodes drifted above the ground on clouds.

Seraphim soared on blazing wings overhead while Sirens swam through sparkling canals that paralleled the roads. Drakes flitted through the air, screeching as a young white dragon pursued them. Other dragons congregated atop a rugged mountain of basalt amid other buildings.

At the far end of the golden avenue sat the gem atop the crown of this amazing city—a palace so immense it looked as if it could hold an entire army. Five pillars rose in the courtyard before the palace. A statue stood atop each one. They weren't the same statues I'd seen from Baal's palace, but I recognized the figures.

Kathazal held a fist skyward. Zon stood to his left, hands clasped behind his back, shoulders square and at attention. Posthanied stood to the right, a helmet covering his oval head, and diagonally behind him was the curvy form of Couriondral, chin up, eyes gazing to the right. Araxos crouched diagonally behind Zon, eight legs bent as if ready to pounce.

At first, I thought Xanos was missing, but then I spotted the lone figure without a pillar, kneeling in subservience to the others, head bowed, eyes on the ground.

"Holy crap, this is Juranthemon." I looked around the stark white room and finally noticed a slight indentation to the right of the window. I pushed it and the wall swung open to the outside. I took in a breath and smelled a mélange of odors I'd never experienced before. Or maybe I had, but not all at once like this.

"Wow, we can step outside?" Ivy looked up and around. "It's like being outside the lost room of Jura."

I took her hand clumsily in my still recovering hand and pulled her back inside the door. "Don't go jumping into strange portals, okay? What if this had been an endless void and your hand slipped?"

"I knew you'd catch me." She grinned and turned in a circle. "Dude, we travelled back in time! Maybe we can save the world before it gets Sundered!"

"And then we'll cease to exist." I shook my head. "Or we might create a paradox that makes things even worse." I couldn't believe we'd really travelled back in time. We'd have to be careful not to do anything to upset the balance or it could lead to world-ending consequences.

Conrad and Ambria were out there somewhere and we had to find them and hope they hadn't done anything that might upset the balance. I fumbled with my phone and managed to tap in Conrad's symbols. But since there were no arcphone companies servicing whatever year this was, the call didn't go through.

I should have known it wouldn't be that easy.

Finding our lost comrades was going to require extremely careful planning. Anything we said or did could change the future. I was frankly surprised Conrad and Ambria's presence here hadn't erased our timeline. Then again, we might not even change the timeline but create an alternate branch.

There were too many possibilities to consider. I needed Adam and Cinder to help me understand the possibilities before I jumped to too many conclusions.

Ivy gasped. "Uh oh."

"What?" I looked around but didn't see any nearby dangers.

"The portal!" She pointed into the room. "It's gone!"

"Maybe it's not visible from this side." I walked around to face it and found only empty air.

The portal was gone, and we were trapped in the past.

CHAPTER 19

"This isn't good." For all I knew, the Sundering was going to happen in ten minutes, and we'd be blasted to bits. I tried to channel Clarity so I could find the scar, but my body wasn't ready yet. I didn't dare ask Ivy to do it for fear channeling Brilliance would bring out her demon again. One surefire way to alter the past was to let a rampaging demon run amok through the city. That also reminded me—Daemos didn't even exist yet. They weren't created by Baal until the First Seraphim War. Haedaemos also didn't exist.

My skin went cold when I thought about what that meant. Could I even contact Kalesh? I concentrated and wasn't surprised when I found him absent. I gulped and tried not to panic. I smiled reassuringly at Ivy. "Hang on a minute while I think, okay?"

She smiled brightly and rocked on her heels. "Sure thing, bro! I'm gonna watch the dragons." Ivy went to the window and watched the white dragon chase drakes between the buildings.

I sat on the floor, closed my eyes, and went inside my mind. The small apartment room Kalesh used was still furnished the same as before—a small bed, a chest of drawers, and a vintage television on the dresser.

The only difference was the number of video game consoles on the table next to it had multiplied.

The window in my soul was a literal window in this place, but now it was closed, and the glass was frosted over. I pounded on it, but it was like striking bricks. I'd been unable to summon Kalesh while dead, but at least I'd been able to talk to him through the window.

An entire part of me didn't even exist in this time and place and it was terrifying. On the other hand, it meant Ivy could safely channel Brilliance without fear of awakening her demon. But even if she could reveal the scar, she couldn't freeze it with Stasis and then open it all by herself.

"Justin!" Ivy's voice filled the room.

I jerked from my trance and flinched back because Ivy was right up in my face. "What is it?"

She flourished a hand as if presenting something. The gateway was open again.

"We've got to go through." Ivy gripped my arm and yanked me to my feet. Before I had a chance to process the moment, Ivy and I went through the portal and gravity abruptly shifted ninety degrees, threatening to drag us back into the past.

Dad reached down and jerked us back to solid ground. Nightliss and Mom gasped in relief and the portal winked shut.

I staggered dizzily, my mind still in shock. "What happened?"

"Ivy's weave didn't hold long," Mom said. "The gateway snapped shut before we knew what happened."

"Opening it was difficult." Nightliss flexed her fingers. "It felt much harder than opening the scars we used to find Emily."

I had a hunch as to why. "We've got bigger problems than I imagined." I ran a hand through my hair. "Conrad and Ambria are probably alive, but they might accidentally destroy the world as we know it if we don't find them."

Adam's brow furrowed. "What do you mean?"

"Accidentally destroy the world?" Shelton snorted. "How?"

"Because they're in the past." I shook my head. "They're in Juranthemon before the Sundering."

Dad whistled. "Are you kidding me? We could stop the Sundering from ever happening?"

"Dad, Daemos don't even exist back then." I reached inside and felt the reassuring presence of Kalesh. "Oh, thank god, you're there."

You were gone. Kalesh said in my head. *I was suddenly alone.*

Yeah. I went to the past. I notice the others staring at me with concerned looks. "What?"

"You went away for a moment," Shelton said. "Talking to your demon?"

I nodded. "Yeah. He said I vanished, and he was alone."

"Because you traveled eons in the past." Adam shook his head. "That should be impossible. Time doesn't work that way."

Cinder tapped a finger on his chin. "Travelling in time would require the quantum fabric of the universe to reset precisely the way it previously existed."

"It's like saving a video game," Adam said. "Except every variable in existence would need to be saved and restored."

"There are theories that every moment leaves an imprint in the fabric of space." Cinder tilted his head. "Perhaps it is possible to open a gateway to such imprints. As such, it would be akin to travelling in time."

Shelton scoffed. "I totally believe in time travel. How do you think Kirk saved humpback whales?"

Adam rolled his eyes. "If time travel exists, it's nothing like the movies. Regardless, if it's even remotely possible that Conrad and Ambria are in the past, we need to recover them immediately."

"Agreed." I flexed my fingers and was pleased that they responded a little better this time. "We need to keep the portal open somehow so I can keep in touch with my demon."

"Son, I think you should sit this one out." Dad motioned to the others. "There are plenty of us who can search for Conrad and Ambria. You need to rest."

I raised an eyebrow. "You're just saying that to sound concerned, right?"

He shrugged. "I mean, it's what any good father would say, right?"

"Yes, of course he means it…in his own way." Mom took Dad's hand. "But you're going to go anyway, aren't you?"

I nodded. "Yep."

Ivy frowned. "But how are we supposed to keep the portal open?"

"Perhaps we can recruit more Seraphim," Cinder said.

Mom shook her head. "We'd need a constant rotation but there aren't enough Seraphim in Eden to help."

"My portal generator might work."

All eyes turned toward the voice in the back.

Xanos met our gazes. "It would need to be adapted to hold open an existing portal instead of creating one."

I automatically ran through a checklist of ways she could double-cross us and get her powers back. Or perhaps she could alter the timeline enough to prevent her from being trapped in the Abyss along with the other Apocryphan. With time travel, the possibilities were endless.

But there were no two ways about it. We needed her tech. "Whatever happens, you won't be allowed to enter that gateway. I don't need you running off to warn your old self about what's to come."

Xanos nodded. "I understand."

I knew she had ulterior motives. Someone like Xanos wouldn't just help us out of the kindness of her heart. All we could do was remain vigilant and accept the help.

"What do we need to do?" I asked.

"The portal generator prototypes are in the lab in Italy." She turned to Adam. "Perhaps you could help me make the modifications."

Adam's eyes brightened. "Sure, I'd love to."

Shelton groaned. "Not by yourself, you aren't."

"Let's request an arch." I tried to use my phone, but Shelton shook his head and dialed the omniarch operator himself.

"Dude, you need some rest." He looked at my hands. "I guarantee you that modifying the portal generator will take some time. We need you operating on all cylinders when we go back through the gateway."

I couldn't argue with him on that. At the same time, I didn't think Shelton and Adam were enough to keep an eye on Xanos. I turned to Dad. "Hey, could you go with them? You're one of the most conniving people I know."

Dad chuckled. "But in a good way, right?"

I nodded. "Of course."

"I'll go too." Mom cast a distrustful look at Xanos. "Better to be safe than sorry."

"Amen to that," Shelton said.

"I will go as well." Nightliss gently touched my hand. "We will ensure the Apocryphan behaves."

A portal back to the Ranch opened moments later and everyone filed through. I bid adieu to the others as they portaled to Italy. Then I took a levitator down to the barracks and went to the room I shared with Elyssa. My mind raced with the events of the day, but the moment my head hit the pillow, the lights went out.

WHEN I WOKE UP, I heard the gentle breathing of Elyssa next to me. I wiggled my fingers and was delighted to find the numbness mostly gone. It was four in the morning according to my arcphone, but I couldn't go back to sleep.

I reached over and gently stroked Elyssa's thigh. She instantly jerked awake, gripped my finger, and bent it back. I rarely woke her for hanky panky in the middle of the night, and this was a fresh reminder why.

"Ow!" I shouted.

"Sorry!" Elyssa released her grip. "I'm just glad you didn't touch me with something else."

I winced. "That hurts just thinking about it."

She turned on the glow lamp next to the bed and propped her head on a hand. "Did I ruin the moment?"

I leaned over and gently kissed her lovely lips. "That would be impossible." There was a lot to tell her, but I wanted my dessert first.

Sometime later—longer than thirty seconds, but less than thirty minutes —I held her in my arms and told her about our troubling discovery.

"Time travel?" Elyssa rolled onto her chest and propped her elbows. "You can't be serious."

"Huh?"

Elyssa put a finger under my chin and brought my gaze up from her breasts. "My eyes are up here."

"Yeah, but your boobs are down there."

She rolled her eyes. "Concentrate, Justin."

I sighed. "Yes, I'm serious about time travel."

"I hate to say it, but I hope Xanos can help." Elyssa brushed a lock of black hair from her eyes. "After hearing this, I really want to come with you, but I also can't just abandon Phoebe. Reorganizing Science Academy is a tall task." She yawned. "Speaking of which, I really need some rest."

I yawned too, suddenly tired again. Apparently, our energetic romp had convinced my mind that more sleep was good. Elyssa turned off the light and we returned to dreamland.

A text from Adam waited on me when I woke a few hours later. *I feel good about this. Let me know when you're awake.*

I texted him back and hopped in the shower. He hadn't responded when I finished, so I went to the mess hall and got some grub.

Shelton phoned me just when I was leaving. "Hey man, you feeling better?"

"Ninety percent," I said. "What's the dealio with the thingamabob?"

"Running some final calibrations now. We're already here working on the scar, so come on over when you're ready."

I ended the call and made haste to the parking garage. I felt the weight of disgruntled glares from people waiting in long lines for an omniarch portal. Even under the dire circumstances, I felt guilty using my priority status to cut the line. On the other hand, it was really nice to make it to the destination in five minutes instead of an hour.

Most of the gang was assembled behind the burned-out mansion when I arrived, watching Xanos and Adam fuss over a large metal ring anchored to a floating platform.

"Doesn't it have to face down?" Shelton said. "How's it supposed to work if it's not facing down?"

"It only needs to angle down." Xanos gripped the bottom edge of the ring and pulled it about seventy degrees. "This will be sufficient."

Adam nodded. "Yeah, I think so."

I walked up behind the others. "Have you guys been up all night?"

"Nah, we got a few hours of shuteye." Shelton nodded at Xanos. "We locked her in one of her own cells for good measure."

Cinder looked up from his arcphone. "Justin, are you able to channel again?"

I test-fired a few flares of Murk and Brilliance. There was no pain, no numbness. "Yeah."

"Good. We still need the scar opened by conventional means, then we can use the portal generator to keep it open."

"Have you actually tested it on the scar?" I asked.

"Not yet." Cinder put away his phone. "I believe we are ready to try."

My parents weren't there, leaving me and Nightliss as the only ones able to open a scar. I cracked my knuckles. "Ready to go?"

Nightliss mustered a fierce but adorable scowl. "Let's do it!"

I grinned. "You look so cute when you're determined."

She sighed. "No one is ever afraid of me."

"Just dye your hair blonde." Shelton snorted. "That'd make some people shit their pants."

I doubted even dressing her up like Daelissa would make her look scary. Nightliss just didn't have any evil mojo in her.

Nightliss frowned at the joke. Her sister was still a tender subject despite their ongoing reconciliation. "Perhaps we should get to work."

Shelton cleared his throat uneasily. "Sorry."

I let the awkward moment linger a little longer just to enjoy the look on Shelton's face, then wove Clarity and revealed the scar. Nightliss suffused it with Stasis, slowing the quantum vibrations until it phased into equilibrium with our plane.

Xanos tapped the screen of an arctablet and the portal generator hummed to life. Crystals on the outer lip of the ring glowed. Thin beams of blue energy speared into the scar, covering it from one end to the other.

Adam held his arcphone toward the beams and shook his head. "There's some slippage in the flux. It's not holding steady."

Xanos nodded and dragged her finger along the screen. The beams shifted color, becoming darker and the hum of the machine shifted lower. "How is that?"

"Better." Adam scanned the other beams. "I'm getting signal degradation. Must be a bad crystal." He held his phone up to the ring. "Power down for a second."

"I believe one of the crystals is not making proper contact with the ring," Cinder said.

Xanos dragged her fingers down across the tablet and the ring went dead.

Sweat trickled into my eyes. "Will this take long?"

Adam held up a finger. "Hold on." He hovered his phone over a crystal, frowned, and banged on it with the bottom of his fist. The crystal snapped into place. "It was just loose. Power up again."

Xanos did her thing and power thrummed through the crystals. Power speared into the scar. "Calibrating." The energy shifted colors, growing darker, looking more like Murk as it did.

Cinder looked at his arcphone. "The power matrix is stable."

Adam raised a thumb. "Agreed. Engage the pry beams."

Xanos tapped the tablet and the beams pulsated. The ring separated from the floating platform, now hovering under its own power. It rotated until it faced straight down at the scar. Power pulsed faster along the beams. Slowly but surely, the crack widened. The next minute felt like an eternity as I held Clarity along the length of the scar.

The scar cracked as if speeding icebergs collided. Thunder rumbled, and the scar was torn wide open. The ring dropped lower until it touched the ground. Crystals along the lip facing up glowed green.

"Seal achieved," Xanos said. "The lock is stable."

Cinder looked over her shoulder at the tablet. "The numbers are optimal."

My knees were starting to wobble. "Can I stop channeling?"

Adam held up a finger and knelt next to the ring. He took his sweet time scanning the circumference with his arcphone. A moment later, he nodded. "The scar is locked open."

I released the Clarity weave and sagged. Nightliss didn't look the least bit tired, probably because Stasis wasn't nearly as difficult to maintain as Clarity.

Xanos knelt next to a small cube near the ring. "The aether converter is operating nominally."

"Converter?" I hadn't heard of those.

"Yeah, it's the neatest thing." Adam's eyes lit up as he looked down at the ordinary looking cube. "It condenses the aether and converts it into liquid form which allows the portal generator to exert more powerful energy."

"Liquid aether?" I'd seen solid and gaseous aether on Seraphina, but liquid form was new to me.

Adam nodded. "The only downside is that it needs at least an hour to fill up in advance so it can keep up with the energy demand."

That was a bit concerning. "How long can it power the portal device?"

"At least twenty-four hours." Adam glanced at the tablet in Xanos's hand. "If the numbers hold steady, we might be able to squeeze thirty-two hours from it before we need to shut down the portal device for an hour."

A portal opened a few feet away and my family stepped through.

"Sorry we're late to the party." Dad pursed his lips and looked down at the portal device. "Neato."

"Wow!" Ivy skipped around it and peered over the edge. "Now we can time travel all we want!"

I just hoped we could find Conrad and Ambria before they destroyed the timeline.

CHAPTER 20

I held up a hand. "We can cover more ground if we split into groups. Asking questions about Conrad and Ambria might be okay, but you need to minimize contact so we don't inadvertently screw up the timeline."

"About that." Dad didn't look concerned, but he wasn't smiling either. "The Sundering is a massive event orchestrated by Xanos. I don't think any amount of tinkering by us will stop it."

Xanos looked down but remained silent.

"I mean, he's not wrong," Shelton said. "I hate to say it, but most of the people we talk to will be dead after it happens."

"But what if this point in time is centuries before it happens?" Adam shrugged. "That far out from the event, even a tiny nudge in the timeline could affect something."

"The butterfly effect," Xanos said softly.

"Do we even know what year it happened?" Mom turned to Xanos. "Would you be able to tell us how much time remains?"

"Perhaps." Xanos shook her head. "I did not track time since it held very little meaning for me. I only know of events that occurred preceding it."

"I hate to say it, but Xanos will need to come with us," Shelton said. "She knows the lay of the land and could probably help us find Conrad and Ambria faster."

It was a good point. "Well, I guess she's coming."

"Ah, that reminds me." Adam dug into a nearby backpack and removed several metal tabs. "I need everyone to stick one of these on their arcphones so I can network them together. That way, we'll have a way to communicate with each other."

I took one of the tabs and stuck it on Nookli's backside. Adam came around to each of us and tapped his phone to ours.

Shelton grinned. "Hey, you're not downloading my pics, are you?"

Adam shuddered. "Last thing I want are your dick pics, Shelton."

Ivy's eyebrows rose. "What pics?"

Adam grimaced. "Oops."

Shelton gave my parents a disgusted look. "You haven't talked to her about the birds and the bees yet?"

Even Dad looked a bit uncomfortable fielding that question. "It's not that simple with her."

"What isn't?" Ivy said.

Mom groaned. "I'd rather risk destroying the timeline than talk about this in front of everyone."

Shelton snorted. "Prudes."

While Adam finished networking the phones I tried to figure out the best way to group people. Someone had to keep an eye on Xanos, but it would be optimal to divide us into as many groups as possible. Ivy also needed a firm hand to guide her, further limiting options.

"Ivy, you're with Mom. Shelton, you're with me." I turned to Dad. "You're with Nightliss and Xanos."

Adam glanced at Xanos and then to me. "Why can't I go with Nightliss and Xanos?"

"Whoa, stud." Shelton grinned. "Save some women for the rest of us."

"Actually, I'd like to go with Cinder," Dad said. "Besides, I'm a one-woman kind of guy."

Mom rolled her eyes. "And a smooth talker."

I didn't like pairing Adam with Xanos, but at least he'd have Nightliss around to keep him from doing too much thinking with his other head. "Fine, Adam. Just keep it in your pants, okay?"

"Keep what in his pants?" Ivy scratched her head. "His wiener dog?"

"Oh, man, that's just sad." Shelton looked at my mother in disbelief. "How's she supposed to appreciate humor if she doesn't understand the punchline?"

"How are you going to appreciate humor in a coma, Shelton?" Mom's tone was cold enough to freeze the air between them.

Shelton gulped. "Just joking, I swear."

Ivy shook her head. "Do you really think I don't understand? Ambria told me all about sex stuff." She threw up her hands. "You guys are so easy to play."

Mom's mouth dropped open.

Shelton clamped a hand over his mouth but couldn't repress his laughter.

Dad smirked. "Well, with that settled, let's get on with saving the universe, okay?"

Mom gripped Ivy's hand. "Yes, let's." She looked at her daughter. "We've got a lot to talk about once we find Ambria."

"Oh, do we?" Ivy batted her eyelashes innocently.

"Knowing Ambria, she ain't gonna apologize," Shelton whispered to me. "Bet that'll be a hell of an argument to witness."

Adam overheard him and shook his head. "I don't want to be anywhere near that mess."

After a few more delays, everyone grouped up and entered the portal. Once we adjusted to the reorientation of gravity, I took a moment to reach out to Kalesh. He was still there. So long as the portal remained open, I could hopefully connect to him. With that done, I considered some what-if scenarios.

Even if the portal device failed, we could still open the scar from this side. But there was another even more serious concern. "Can we set some wards? I want to make sure Serena doesn't follow us."

"She can't." Adam tapped the metal tab on his phone. "The portal device is attuned to only allow people with these through. Without one that's been networked to my phone, she'll be stuck outside."

"Oh, well that's good to know." I felt much better knowing that. "I just hate leaving our back unguarded."

Shelton grunted. "I'm the same way. That's why I set wards around the perimeter of the device while Adam was messing around." He gave me an amused look. "This isn't our first rodeo, cowboy."

"Yeah, Justin. You act like we're total noobs or something." Adam patted my back. "We've got our bases covered."

"We've just never gone back in time before so I'm nervous." I looked out the window at the incredible city vista and took a deep breath to calm the jitters. "I hope we can find Conrad and Ambria."

"Well, it ain't gonna happen if we stay here all day." Shelton pushed on the wall until he found the door. "Somebody needs to decorate this place, though. Why is it all white?"

"It's a self-generating domicile." Nightliss rubbed her finger over a small bump in the wall. "This appears to be an aether gem." She channeled a trickle of Murk into it and a table materialized in the middle of the room.

"Whoa, just like the buildings in Pjurna." I tapped a finger on the table. "I guess this type of magic has been around for a while."

"But where do they get the aetherite?" Adam scratched his head. "Seraphina doesn't exist yet and neither do the aether vortexes or Mzodi."

"Earth is most likely completely different from the Eden we know today," Mom said. "For all we know there are aether vortexes and more."

"Man, I'd like to take some time to travel this time period," Shelton said. "Once we find Conrad and Ambria, of course."

I shook my head. "I don't know if that's a good idea."

Xanos stepped outside and stared at the palace in the distance. I followed her just in case she thought she could run away. But she just stood there, tears trickling down her cheeks.

"What is that place?" I asked.

"Unity." She wiped her cheeks. "Juranthemon was a neutral zone, ruled by a council of all races and headed by Saila."

I recalled what I could about her. "She's the daughter of Kathazal, right?"

"Yes." Xanos stepped into the small courtyard outside the house. The odd mix of smaller homes side-by-side towers was a bit unsettling, but it didn't seem to bother her. "Saila dreamt of a united world. Kathazal so loved her that he gave her this entire region and autonomy to do as she wished. It took her centuries to see this dream come to fruition."

"And you caused its destruction."

Her shoulders shook. "I actually liked Saila. She was always kind to me and asked that I guide her and expand upon her vision. But I had a vision of my own. Little did I know it would lead to such destruction."

"I don't know," I said. "You seemed kind of pleased about it before."

Xanos nodded. "I was pleased by my success, but also saddened at the cost."

I wished I had the ASE Elyssa had sent to Hell because having one of those would make mapping the city a whole lot easier. "The first thing is to locate a map. Whoever gets one first, text it to the rest of us. Then we can coordinate the search better." The mix of canals, skyways, and streets presented quite a challenge. There was just as much to search vertically as there was horizontally.

A wave of hopelessness washed over me. This was going to be a major pain in the ass. I put on a confident smile. "Well, split up and let's get this started."

Dad and Cinder went left. Mom and Ivy followed them a short way before splitting off. Adam, Nightliss, and Xanos went right.

Shelton pursed his lips and looked around. "Dollars to donuts the kids made a beeline for that place."

"Unity?" I looked at the distant structure. "Why there?"

"Because it's impressive as hell." He shrugged. "After that, who knows? At least it's a place to start."

I looked up at the towers. "How are we supposed to search all the buildings? They could be anywhere."

"Just start walking." Shelton adjust his wide-brimmed hat. "We'll figure it out along the way."

Street traffic was minimal. There were no cars, but there were a few horse-drawn carts and carriages along with creatures that looked like they ate horses for breakfast. A dozen drakes towed a long, sleek carriage. Some vehicles had no visible forms of propulsion at all.

The citizens wore colorful tunics and cloaks. Nearly all who passed by gave us strange looks, probably because of our alien attire. Shelton tried to wave down a couple of people, but they continued without stopping.

"Not very friendly," Shelton muttered. "I need to show people pictures if we're going to find anyone."

"You think it's safe showing them arcphones?" I said.

He shrugged. "This city looks more futuristic than the ones in the actual future."

"True." I stared back at a pair of females who were eyeing us from the patio of a small café. It was hard to believe this was at least a hundred-thousand years in the past. Civilization literally devolved after the Sundering, sending humans back to the stone ages. I doubted this city would be so magnificent if not for the other races helping them.

Shelton made a beeline for them and didn't look the least bit embarrassed disturbing their meal. The tables and everything else looked crystalline, meaning they'd probably been made on the spot from gems like the ones in the house. As for the women, their sea-green hair led me to believe they were Sirens.

A mix of fruits and berries in cream sat in bowls fashioned from woven leaves. The women intently watched us as we approached.

Shelton took out his phone and asked in Cyrinthian. "Have you seen these people?"

The women blinked. One replied in the same language, but the accent was so heavy as to be almost incomprehensible. "Who are you? What are those clothes?"

"We are visitors." I had no idea what else to say. "Our friends came to this city a couple of days ago. We need to find them." I pointed to the picture of Conrad and Ambria on Shelton's phone. "Have you seen them?"

"What is this…thing?" One woman reached out and touched the screen.

"Yeah, touch it all you like." Shelton snorted. "It ain't gonna bite."

"I do not like these beings." The other woman rose. "They are strange and intrude upon our repast."

"Sit down, sister." The other woman put a hand on her arm. "They are strangers in a strange land. They have lost their friend."

"We have not seen them," the other woman announced. "I would remember if I saw someone in such strange garb."

"Check with the overwatch." The friendlier of the pair pointed down the street. "They will know if any strangers have come through."

"Thank you." I bowed and backed away because I wasn't sure what else to do.

Shelton wasn't so quick to leave and looked down the street. "Which building is overwatch?"

"The dark one shaped like a tree," the woman replied.

It was hard to miss the giant crystal tree even though it was at the far end of the avenue near the palace.

"Thanks." Shelton tipped his hat and we left the pair to enjoy their meal. We started walking, pausing occasionally to soak in the strange sights and take pictures like ordinary tourists. We waved down anyone we could during our walk and showed them pictures of our friends, but no one remembered seeing them.

A pair of Sirens leapt from one of the canals paralleling the street, their finned lower halves morphing to human legs. At first I thought they were coming for us, but they ignored us and crossed the street to a building shaped like a giant conch shell.

"That Seraphim has been following us." Shelton pointed up.

I put a hand over my eyes to guard against the glare of the sun and spotted the seraph atop a small puff of cloud. He crouched and looked down at me for a moment before sprouting silvery wings and gliding to the ground.

"What the hell?" I'd never seen wings that color before. They were usually white or ultraviolet, depending on whether the Seraphim was a Brightling or Darkling.

His wings puffed to vapor as he landed lightly before us. "I have not seen your kind before. What are you?"

Shelton and I stared in open-jawed amazement.

My vocal chords were paralyzed. I was petrified to say a single word, because I knew for a fact that this being survived the Sundering. And saying a single word to him could change the course of history.

CHAPTER 21

This man, this seraph, was Ussor, one of the original Seraphim. In our day and age, we knew him as Fjoeruss, Mr. Gray. The being behind these eyes was much younger, but certainly still quite old.

"Speak, boy." Ussor folded his arms over his chest. "Your apparel is unlike any I have seen before. And what are those things in your hands?"

"Uh, we're looking for missing friends," Shelton stammered. He held up his phone. These are simply carved and polished crystals that allow us to show images."

Ussor pursed his lips. "Ah, yes. They look quite different from the ones I have seen."

"We mixed metals in with the crystal for a unique appearance." Shelton displayed an image of our missing friends. "Have you seen either of these people?"

The seraph nodded. "Indeed. I was not entirely honest when I said I had never seen this apparel or your devices before." He raised a hand and the cloud he'd ridden on earlier dropped to the ground. "Come."

I paused. "I don't know…"

"Come." Authority resonated in his voice.

Shelton stepped onto the cloud. "You're not gonna kill us, are you?"

Ussor raised an eyebrow. "Murder is a crime in Juranthemon."

"Yeah, but that doesn't deter everyone." I reached for Kalesh and felt his reassuring presence. I couldn't fight Ussor, but I could toss Shelton over my shoulder and make a run for it if things went south.

Ussor stepped onto the cloud and it rose into the air. Within minutes, the city of Jura stretched out beneath us, a sparkling jewel in the midst of a vast desert.

I glanced up at the low-hanging clouds. "Where are we going?"

He regarded me for a moment. "There is something strange about you. I sense an otherness about you."

"Otherness?" I had no idea what that meant. "We're just a couple of strangers passing through."

"Your accent is different from any I've heard." Ussor pressed his lips together. "Are you one of the new ones?"

"New ones?" I shook my head. "I have no idea what you're talking about."

"How high are we going?" A gust of wind blew Shelton's hat off his head, but the stampede string kept it from flying away.

We entered the cloud. My skin tingled from the chilly, moist air. I could barely see anything for several seconds and suddenly we broke through. Shelton and I synchronized another jaw drop at the next view. Pearl gates and a golden wall guarded a crystal mansion perched atop the cloud.

"Holy shit," Shelton exclaimed in English.

Ussor tilted his head. "What language is that?"

I grimaced. So far, we were doing a terrible job at protecting the timeline.

"Those are words he made up," I said. "Just gibberish."

"I make up curse words." Shelton shrugged. "It's what I do."

Ussor didn't seem to buy it. The pearly gates opened when he approached. We followed him through and into the mansion. Like many Seraphim structures, there were no doors. The front wall turned to mist and let us through, then solidified behind us. That would make escaping tricky if not impossible.

Despite the cold crystalline exterior, the inside was warm and rustic, with wooden beams, stone walls, and a wild assortment of furniture. Giant clam shells with cushions, trees and vines grown into the shapes of tables and chairs, and a few constructs I didn't recognize. The Fjoeruss I knew was cold and minimalistic, a complete departure from his origin as Ussor.

A woman stepped into the corridor to meet us. I froze in place. "Mom?"

She blinked. "What an odd thing to say in greeting." Her brow furrowed. "Ussor, you found more of them?"

"I found them wandering the avenue," he replied. "Perhaps they will tell us what the others would not."

The woman who looked just like my mother turned to me. "Who do you think I am?"

I knew exactly who she was but was afraid to reveal it. She was Seaa, the matriarch of my mother's bloodline.

Shelton cleared his throat. "Where are our friends?"

"Strange accents like the others." Seaa stared at us for a long moment. "Could they be related to the dark omens?"

"Perhaps." Ussor pursed his lips. "Elohim is playing a dangerous game if he truly plans on reclaiming power. The Apocryphan will not go peacefully."

"Once again, he and Eve threaten to destroy all they have made." Seaa sighed. "I believe the end is closer than we fear."

Ussor turned to me. "I see it plain on your face that you know something about the darkness ahead. Tell me what you're hiding."

I relaxed my face. "Please take us to our friends. It's very important we find them and leave."

"Because of what is coming?" Ussor stepped closer until he was nearly in my face. "Tell me, boy. Do not make me force the information from your lips."

"I don't know anything."

He gripped my shirt and pushed me against the wall. "I take no pleasure in using force, but I will if I must."

My heart beat faster. "Please don't do this."

Silver energy gathered around his other fist. "I will dig into the depths of your mind if I must. Answer me and spare yourself the pain."

"Please answer him," Seaa said. "Are you of Elohim's tribe?"

"I can't tell you anything." I tried to push Ussor away from me but didn't have any leverage. I struggled uselessly in his grasp.

"Speak your mind." Ussor's glowing hand grew closer. "Or I will open it for my own viewing."

I didn't know of any Seraphim abilities that allowed mind reading, but the OG angels were something else. I gripped the hand against my chest and tried to push it off me, but he was just too strong.

"Lay off of him!" Shelton reached for Ussor's other arm, but Seaa threw out her hand and a barrier of sparkling Murk pressed him against the wall.

"Last chance," Ussor said, his glowing fist inches from my face.

I panicked. My inner demon surged. Muscles coiled around my arms and legs. Ussor stared in amazement at my forehead, presumably due to the horns sprouting. Seraphim were physically strong, but my infernal strength and his shock gave me the opening I needed. I gripped his wrist and wrenched his hand off my chest, then used my foot to shove him away. His feet skidded across the floor.

Seaa cried out in surprise.

I tried to free Shelton, but Ussor aimed a fist and silver energy flashed toward me. I threw up a shield of Murk at the last instant. The energy crackled against the surface. I strained to hold it off, but my shield cracked and shattered within seconds. I blurred to the left, narrowly avoiding the attack, then fired a shot of Brilliance.

What in the hell am I doing? Fighting Ussor was the worst choice possible. If I won and accidentally killed him, I'd completely rewrite the history books. This was pure insanity.

"What manner of creature are you?" Seaa shouted. "I have never seen anything like it."

"He is an abomination." Ussor clapped his hands together and a shock-wave of silver flashed toward me. I countered it with a blast of Murk, but his attack shredded through it, sending ultraviolet shards spraying into the air.

I dove and rolled out of the way. His Seraphim magic was completely different. I'd never seen him use it like this as Fjoeruss. Whatever it was, it was much stronger than anything I had to offer.

Before I rose to my feet, another blast caught me in the shoulder and sent me spinning across the floor. I slammed into the wall and looked up as he leveled another blast. My shoulder felt charbroiled and dislo-cated. My demonic regeneration was already helping snap the bone back into the socket, but the magic damage was going to take a lot longer.

There was no way I could move in time. I had no choice but to counter him with whatever I had. I drew upon the Apocryphan powers and thrust a green shield between us. His attack splashed harmlessly across it.

Ussor's mouth dropped open and he stepped back. "Apocryphan!"

"By the Goddess!" Seaa released Shelton bowed low. "Our humblest apologies."

I released the shield and staggered to my feet. The burn on my shoulder didn't look quite as bad as I'd feared, but it hurt like a bitch. I bared my teeth and glared at Ussor. "Return my people this instant!"

He nodded. "Fetch them, Seaa."

She vanished and returned a moment later with two groggy teenagers in her wake. "My apologies, but they have been in preservation chambers."

Shelton crossed the room and took Ambria and Conrad by the hands, then pulled them close to us. He patted Conrad on the cheeks. "Hey, man, you okay?"

Ussor straightened his shoulders. "You know of my investigations. You are here because you intend to stop me from discovering the truth."

I shook my head. "No. I have nothing to do with the Apocryphan. It is important that you continue doing whatever you were doing and pretend as if you never met us."

"Why?" Seaa shook her head. "How do you have such powers if you are not one of them?"

"Your body transformed into that of a hellion." Ussor narrowed his eyes. "I did not realize the denizens of Hell could morph."

Though Haedaemos didn't exist, Hell did. The physical demons that lived there were nothing like the ones that would exist after the Sundering. This world was so alien from the Eden that existed now, it was practically a different planet. I released my demon and let my body shrink back to normal.

"Perhaps he is an outsider," Seaa said. "One of the gods from the outer dimensions Saila spoke of."

"I'm not an outsider god or an Apocryphan." I looked for the exit. "If you'll open the exit, we will leave."

Conrad gasped and flinched back from Shelton. "Where am I?"

"We're here to get you out of here," Shelton said.

Ambria shrieked and held out her hand as if holding a wand. "Watch out, Conrad!"

I put my hand on hers. "Ambria, you're okay."

She blinked. "Justin? Y-you're here?"

I nodded. "No time to explain. We have to leave."

Conrad leaned against a wall. "You're too late. It's all about to happen again."

"What's about to happen?" Ussor's brow furrowed. "What are you hiding?"

"Nothing!" Conrad slashed a hand through the air. "Not like it matters anyway."

"Uh, I don't like the sound of that." Shelton looked back and forth from Conrad to Ambria. "What's going on?"

Ambria slumped to the floor and put her hands over her eyes. "The end."

"Say what?" Shelton yanked her off the floor. "What the hell is that supposed to mean?"

Conrad groaned and shivered. "We've been trapped here for three cycles. The worst part is the end. It seems to go on forever. Just when you feel your mind slipping away, it finally starts over."

"You sound like you've already lost your mind." Shelton turned to me. "I have a really bad feeling about this."

"Yeah, you and me both." I turned to Ussor. "Take us back to the city, now."

"No, not until you tell me what's going on."

Conrad shoved me away and staggered to Ussor. "You want to know what's going on?" He grabbed the seraph's tunic. "The end of the world! Everything is about to blow up and there's nothing you can do to stop it!"

Ambria screamed at the top of her lungs and I knew right then and there that our friends were definitely not all right. In all the time we thought they'd been off doing their own thing, they'd been trapped in the past, probably tortured by Ussor for information they couldn't risk giving him.

"They're mad!" Seaa put hands over her ears. "Get them out of our home, Ussor."

Jaw set into a grim frown, he nodded. "Very well. Come with me."

I scooped Ambria into my arms while Shelton dragged Conrad along behind him. Ussor summoned a cloud from the smaller cloud and we hopped on. The descent was fast enough to make my stomach feel like the bottom had dropped out. I desperately wanted to call the others but didn't want to risk it in front of the seraph.

"The end is nigh," Conrad mumbled. "Again and again."

"I can't take it anymore," Ambria sobbed.

Shelton scowled at Ussor. "Did you torture them?"

He shook his head. "They were already like this when I found them. Unfortunately, much of what they say is nonsense."

It was good that they hadn't spilled the beans, but what in the hell had driven them crazy like this?

"I will end it!" Conrad leapt over the side of the cloud.

"Conrad!" I grasped for his hand, but it was too late. I dove off the cloud and pressed my hands to my side to fall faster. He plummeted past the top of the tallest tower and I passed it a second later.

I thrust out a hand and channeled a thread of Murk. It wound around his ankle and leg. Concentrating on my back, I channeled my wings and spread them. I wasn't very good at flying, but I could glide like a mofo. The strand of Murk went taut in my hand as it supported Conrad's weight. His weight was more than my wings could handle. We were still falling, but not quite as fast.

At this rate we probably wouldn't die, but we'd suffer a lot of broken bones. Ambria's screaming drew my attention skyward. Her face repeatedly appeared over the edge of the Ussor's cloud as if she were trying to jump off but couldn't. The cloud seemed to be catching up to me, albeit too slowly for it to make a difference.

We were only a few hundred feet above the ground. Pedestrians looked up in shock, their attention probably drawn by the incessant screaming of Ambria. This was going to be painful, embarrassing, and would probably lead to a break in the space-time continuum.

The Sirens we'd spoken with at the café ran until they were almost directly beneath us. They opened their mouths inhumanly wide and a haunting song filled my ears. The air felt thicker and our descent slowed. Conrad gently touched down. I released the tether and rotated so my feet hit the ground first.

"Thank you." I put a hand over my chest. My heart was pounding so hard, I thought it might break free.

Ussor's cloud landed a moment later and a wailing Ambria launched herself at Conrad.

"Don't leave me like that!" she shouted. "Take me with you!"

"What is the meaning of this, Ussor?" one of the Sirens asked.

"These beings, whatever they are, know something about the plot to destroy the city." His shoulders stiffened. "I tell you Elohim is up to something and it will not end well for us."

"Elohim is long gone from the Earth." The first Siren shook her head. "Your conspiracy theories will do this city more harm than anything else."

"It is said Elohim has returned." Ussor thrust a finger toward the palace. "That even now he comes to Unity to announce his reign over all creation. The Apocryphan will not stand for it."

I followed his finger and noticed a crowd gathering in the plaza outside the palace. A tall woman with light purple skin stood on a stone pillar, hands outraised as if trying to calm a crowd. The crowd's eyes raised skyward. I looked up and saw a purple giant upon a massive white dragon.

"Tell me it is not true, daughter." Kathazal's voice boomed throughout the city. "Has your allegiance shifted?"

I gasped so hard I nearly crapped myself.

Conrad laughed maniacally. "It's the end again," he sang. "The end again!"

Today was the day of the Sundering.

CHAPTER 22

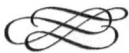

"Holy shit, we've got to get out of here!" I snatched Conrad off the ground like a sack of potatoes.

"The end is nigh!" Ambria cried.

"By the Goddess." Ussor backed up a step. "We are doomed."

Shelton was trying to talk, but only crazy sounds emanated from his mouth.

I yanked him around. "Call the others and tell them to get back to the house now!" While Shelton shouted orders into his phone, I manifested into larger demon form, stretching my clothes to the max without shredding them. I tucked Conrad under one arm and Ambria under another, then turned my back to Shelton. "Climb on!"

He latched himself to my back like his life depended on it.

I blurred down the street toward the house even as Kathazal's discussion with his daughter echoed in my ears as if I were standing right next to them. Other citizens screamed and ran into their abodes. More shadows crossed the sun. I looked up and saw Posthanied and Zon ride in on their dragons. The Sundering might happen at any minute.

I reached the house a couple of minutes later and ran inside. I ran through the portal and dumped everyone, then ran back through the gateway. I called my father first. "Where are you?"

"Hauling ass to the house with Cinder," he panted. "Alysea and Ivy are running back too."

"Hurry, or we're freaking dead!" I ended the call and dialed Adam. He didn't answer. "Son of a bitch." I was about to dial him again when I saw Nightliss, Xanos and Adam emerged from one of the towers and start running toward the house. I blurred down the street to meet them and tossed Adam over my shoulder. "Nightliss, get Xanos!"

Xanos looked up into the sky with awe. "This is what it felt like for the others? This is pure terror?" Her next words vanished in an "Oof" as Nightliss grabbed her and began to run with me.

Posthanied began shouting threats at Saila as the rest of the Apocryphan gathered in the sky above Unity Palace.

"There he is!" another voice cried out. "Elohim himself come to reclaim the world!"

I shot into the house and sent Adam and Nightliss through.

Nightliss paused on the other side of the gateway. "Justin, what are you doing?"

"My parents aren't back yet!" I ran back into the street and looked all around.

"Saila has betrayed us!" Couriondral roared. "Destroy Elohim and raze this city to the ground!"

Saila thrust out her hands and grew to double her size. A shield dome covered the plaza. Massive beams of green energy crashed against her shield. The ground rumbled and the shield collapsed. Saila fell to the ground and all attention turned toward another figure.

My eyesight was superhuman, but I couldn't make out the face. Even so,

I knew who it was. The Apocryphan did too and unleashed their wrath. This was it, the final moment of Earth before it was shattered into countless realms. Mom and Ivy blurred out of a side street. Dad and Cinder appeared a second later.

"Go, go, go!" I shouted, motioning them all inside.

We raced into the house just as a deafening roar rumbled in the distance and the ground began to shake. The others made it through. The ground burst upward, slamming me into the ceiling. I hit the floor hard enough to lose my breath for a moment. I desperately climbed to my feet. A dome of brilliant white destruction grew in the plaza and raced down the street. Before I could move, the shockwave passed over me and all went silent.

"Not again!" I shouted. There was nothing around me but a white void. "I can't afford to be dead right now!"

A hand reached out and grabbed me. The next instant, I fell to solid ground.

Dad grinned down at me. "Trying to die again, son?"

"Close that portal!" Adam shouted.

"What the hell happened?" Shelton stood next to me gazing into the whiteness on the other side. "How did that not explode out of the portal and kill everyone?"

Conrad sat up next to me, eyes wide. "I'm back?" He looked around. "I'm back?"

"There seems to be no harm in keeping the gateway open," Xanos said. "I detect no energy emerging from the other side."

I sat up and rubbed my head. "What in the hell is going on?"

"Another cycle." Conrad climbed to his feet. "And another. And another."

"What's wrong with Conrad?" Ivy asked. "He's talking like a crazy person."

"I think I know." Shelton shuddered. "That wasn't the real past, but a time remnant—a constantly repeating loop. And these poor kids have lived through it three times."

Adam hissed a breath between his teeth. "Meaning they were stuck in that white void."

"How long does it last?" Nightliss stared into the gateway as if the void might vanish at any second.

It didn't.

Shelton got some takeout pizza from a nom restaurant and used a portal to pick it up while we waited.

Xanos looked suspiciously at the veggie lover's pizza when Nightliss opened the box. "This looks unappetizing."

"It's right up there with burgers and tacos for the best food in the world." Shelton chomped down on a slice of the meat-lovers pizza. "Eat it or don't. I don't care."

Xanos nibbled on the end. "The texture is strange, but it does have a pleasant taste."

"Pizza?" Conrad wandered aimlessly until Cinder redirected him back to us. "I-I remember it."

"Queens Gate!" Ambria raised a fist and promptly slumped to the ground, sobbing.

"Man, this ain't good." Shelton shook his head. "Whatever happened to them in there broke their brains."

"I wish I knew more about repairing mental schisms," Nightliss said, "but I'm afraid all the experts are on Utopia."

I nodded. "Flava is there, right?"

"Yes." Nightliss raised an eyebrow. "Why?"

"We've got to do everything possible to help them." I polished off another slice of pizza, then rose and brushed off my jeans. The seams were stretched and worn from my earlier transformation, but I'd learned to buy jeans a little larger so I wouldn't go through so many pairs.

"You going to Utopia?" Shelton said.

I nodded. "I need to pick up someone. I'll be back soon." I took out Nookli and selected an image outside a village where the Seraphim had begun rebuilding their lives since Baal took over Seraphina. Travelling to Utopia in the past had required us to wait for Voltis to come into alignment with Eden. With the Apocryphan powers, it was so much more convenient.

I slashed open a portal and the village appeared on the other side. I stepped through and closed it behind me. The area bustled with activity. Darklings worked side-by-side with their former enemies, Brightlings, to construct a tower in the center of the village with the help of a large construction gem provided by the Mzodi.

Further to the east sat a small fleet of Mzodi warships—all that had been saved from destruction during the exodus from Seraphina. Other groups of Seraphim worked with Mzodi to build a new shipyard so we could eventually take the fight back to Seraphina and defeat Baal's dragon army.

It felt like I hadn't seen these people in ages, though it hadn't been all that long ago when we helped them resettle here. Flava and I hadn't exactly left on the best of terms. As the governor of the Darklings, she'd been devastated to leave her homeland behind especially after having worked so hard to rebuild after the destruction caused by Cephus.

I tried to make my way into the village before anyone noticed.

"Commander Slade!" A seraph I didn't recognize pressed a hand to his chest, eyes wide with excitement. "I heard you died!"

"At ease." I held up a hand. "I need to speak with Flava."

"Yes, at once!" He grinned. "She will be ecstatic to learn you live. She is meeting with the Trivectus in the common room. I will take you." He turned and led me between the domed buildings that served as homes and storage buildings.

Like most Seraphim buildings, they were made of crystallized Murk and Brilliance and utilized aether gems for power and interior decorating. The experience in the time fragment taught me that this kind of magic had been around for eons, but it seemed more powerful back then. It seemed as if Murk and Brilliance operated on a different level.

The seraph took me to a large dome on the western side of town. He channeled a trickle of Murk into a gem on the outside and a section of the wall misted away to leave an entrance. The auditorium on the inside looked capable of holding a couple hundred people, maybe more, but there were only a scattered few citizens in attendance. Flava sat at a table much like the one used by Utopians in their meetings. It seemed they'd copied a lot from their hosts.

It was a bit awkward just walking in on a meeting like this, but I didn't feel like waiting around until it was over. A female in a white tunic was droning on in a monotone voice while a third sera in rich blue robes watched with a bored expression. Judging from the necklace of aether gems and the tattoos on her wrist, she was one of the Mzodi. That meant they had one from each of the Seraphim factions represented at the table.

I was pleasantly surprised to see unity among the Seraphim. The Darklings and Brightlings had been at each other's throats for millennia while the Mzodi remained a neutral party.

Flava's gaze flicked sharply toward me. She leapt from her seat and rushed down the aisle. "Justin, you are alive!"

I felt even more awkward because apparently no one had told her that I'd recovered. She'd tried to save me, but not even her healing powers had been up to the task. "Yeah, it's kind of a long story—"

"I have time." She gripped my hand and raised it. "Justin Slade lives!"

Scattered clapping echoed in the mostly empty chamber.

The Mzodi representative rose. "We thought you died, and with it, our hopes for reclaiming the homeland."

"This is wonderful news," the Brightling ambassador said. "Utopia is a nice place to visit, but I don't like living in the wilderness."

It was still so strange seeing the three factions just hanging out peacefully like this. It seemed the orderliness from the Utopians had rubbed off on their guests. Or was it something else? My mind wandered back to the discussion about the Void. Maybe the best parts of Elohim really had ended up here.

I smiled reassuringly at the others. "I am actually here because I desperately need Flava's skills to help our friends."

Flava nodded. "I would be happy to. But first, I would like to know how you survived. Did you find another healer?"

Conrad and Ambria probably weren't in immediate danger so I decided it was best to bring the Trivectus up to date on the current happenings. I told them how I'd died, encountered Daelissa, and eventually allied with her to start saving souls in the afterlife. I feared an argument might break out about Daelissa, but everyone seemed content to listen in awe about my adventures as a dead man.

After that, I brought them up to date on our current mission—rounding up the remaining relics and keeping them safe from Baal. I told them about our visit to the Void and the time fragment where Conrad and Ambria had been trapped.

Flava's eyes widened. "You met Ussor? You've seen the fabled city of Juranthemon?"

I nodded. "You're all welcome to come see for yourself if you'd like."

"Yes, we would." The Mzodi raised a hand. "Thira of the Mzodi hereby votes to adjourn this meeting."

The Brightling raised her hand. "Galena of the Brightlings votes in favor."

Flava raised her hand. "Flava of the Darklings also votes in favor. The meeting is adjourned."

The attendees gathered nearby, apparently planning to tag along. I held up a hand. "I hate to be a party pooper, but I need to limit the tour to the Trivectus for now. This is sort of an emergency."

A chorus of sighs and sagging shoulders let me know they were plenty disappointed, but that couldn't be helped. Once outside, I opened a portal back to the others and we stepped through.

Shelton snorted when he saw us. "I thought you went to get one person, not three."

"We are here to see history," Galena said, rubbing her hands in excitement. She walked up to the portal and looked into the white void. "Is this it?"

"It's the end!" Conrad shouted. "The end of everything!"

Adam restrained him from lunging at the sera.

"Goodness, I see what you mean." Flava put her hands to Conrad's temples. "Rest, child."

His eyelids grew heavy and he slumped. Adam and Flava eased him to the ground. Ambria was already asleep. It seemed someone had put sleeper cuffs on her to keep her quiet.

Flava knelt next to Conrad and pressed her fingers to his head. "This will take a while."

I was still hungry, so I had more pizza.

"We've got a working theory," Adam announced a short time later.

"Indeed." Cinder tapped on his arcphone. "We believe the blink stone Conrad and Ambria possessed was a part of a building in Juranthemon."

"Namely, the building that the portal leads to," Adam said. "When Serena's antima device turned the power of the blink stone back upon itself, it somehow sent Conrad and Ambria into a time echo."

"Did you just make that up?" Shelton said. "Because it sounds made up."

Adam shrugged. "Call it what you will—a time remnant, an echo, or whatever. We believe that portal leads to a window of the actual past just before the destruction of Juranthemon. But this window is stuck on loop and our actions seem to have no effect on it."

It sounded plausible to me. "So, it's like going back to an old save in a game, but the game crashes and restarts instead of letting you finish and change the outcome?"

"Yeah, exactly," Adam said. "It recreated the precise state of a small part of the universe back at that time but not the entire universe."

I grunted. "And we definitely can't affect the future by playing in it?"

Adam nodded. "Exactly."

"Man, you sound awfully sure of yourself." Shelton shook his head. "How can you say for sure after one trial run?"

"Because I called Fjoeruss," Cinder said. "I asked him if he remembered seeing you back then and he did not."

I raised an eyebrow. "Did you tell him about the time remnant?"

"I invited him to see for himself." Cinder clasped his hands. "It might be interesting for him to see himself in the past."

Shelton scoffed. "Or it might cause the space-time continuum to implode."

"We're somewhat certain it'll have no effect," Adam said.

"Somewhat?" I didn't like the sound of that.

Cinder nodded. "It is like *Groundhog Day*. The rest of the world proceeds as normal, but the interaction between the blink stone and the antima device created a pocket dimension with an immutable replica of the past."

"*Groundhog Day*, huh?" Shelton snorted. "I wouldn't rely on nom movies for your hypotheses."

"I think it's apt," Adam said. "We have a precise working model of a time shortly before the world was destroyed, and I think we can use it to our advantage."

I blinked. "If it doesn't affect the future, then how can it help us?"

Adam grinned. "Because it gives us a chance to get to know the man, the myth, the legend, Elohim."

CHAPTER 23

"Your idea is to befriend Elohim?" I looked from Adam to Cinder. "How in the world is that going to help us?"

"Actually, it's not so much getting to know him personally as physically." Adam turned his arcphone screen toward me to display lines of code. "I'm working on a spell that will try to measure what happened to Elohim at the moment of the Sundering. We might be able to understand how the realms came into existence and figure out a way to keep them from collapsing even if Baal completes his master plan."

"We must conduct a number of experiments to find out precisely what is happening." Cinder tucked his phone into a pocket. "For instance, you were injured by Ussor and yet the Sundering did nothing to harm you."

I glanced down at the blistered skin on my shoulder. "This is no holodeck game, that's for sure. There's nothing keeping you from dying, especially if you start screwing around with Elohim. My guess is the time echo ends with the Sundering, so it can't harm you."

"Actually, we believe the white void is a part of the Sundering," Adam said. "Right now, the world is splitting apart into realms."

Ivy looked through the gateway. "Then why don't we see anything?"

"The quantum plane once occupied by Earth is empty," Cinder said. "Atlantis is the only part that remains here."

"We don't have eyes that can see interdimensional shifts." Adam held his arcphone toward the gateway. "What looks like pure white to us is actually the absence of everything, because Earth no longer exists at the same dimensional coordinates. Eden, Seraphina, and all the realms occupy the same space but on different frequencies."

"Like radio waves?" Ivy said.

Cinder nodded. "An apt analogy. Unfortunately, I don't know how to view what is happening right now."

"Earth as it was, is completely gone, leaving behind a void." I walked to the gateway and put my hand into the whiteness. "This is the space between the realms." I traced the symbols for Eden inside the void and slashed open a gateway.

Golden desert sands baked beneath a yellow sun on the other side. There was no ground, no up or down in the void, so I had to leap the distance from the portal in our world to the portal leading to Eden of the past.

Heat beat down on my head. I channeled a barrier of Murk overhead to create some shade, and then used Apocryphan powers to rise into the air for a look around. I rose higher and higher but there was nothing to be seen. No destroyed cities, no signs of life.

Using the symbols without a precise visual of the destination opened a gateway to a random place in the target realm. Since none of my points of reference existed in the past, I'd have to open portal after portal and look through to see what I found. I dropped back to the ground and looked back through the portal. Everyone else was huddled around the gateway to the time remnant.

"Coming through!" I jumped the void. Shelton grabbed my outstretched hand and pulled me up and out of the portal in the ground.

"Dude, this is epic!" Adam looked like he'd jizzed in his pants a dozen times already. "We need some way to record everything!"

"Mom, I want to go back to the past again," Ivy said. "Can I, huh?"

"Not now." Mom turned to my father. "What do you think of all this?"

He shrugged. "It's unbelievable. When the cycle restarts, I'd like to take you out for dinner in Juranthemon."

"Ooh, that would be neato!" Ivy clapped her hands. "I want to try their ice cream."

That brought up another point. "What happens if we bring matter from the time echo back with us?"

Adam raised an eyebrow and looked at Cinder. Cinder looked back at him and raised both eyebrows.

I snorted. "You don't know, do you?"

They shook their heads in unison.

"I'll tell you what happens." Shelton dug a white fragment from the coat of his leather duster. "I found this on the street near that café where the Sirens were having brunch or whatever."

I plucked it from his fingers and rubbed it in my hand. It matched the color of the cups the Sirens had been drinking from. Tiny ridges in the surface confirmed my suspicions. "I gotta admit, this is really freaky."

"Yeah, it is." Shelton grimaced. "The more I think about this stuff, the more confused I get. I could use some tacos right about now."

"Dude, we just ate pizza." Adam took the cup fragment from me. "If we can take items from the time remnant, then this opens up all sorts of possibilities."

While he and Cinder nerded out on that, I checked in on Flava and her patients. She hadn't moved from the last time I'd spoken to her, eyes closed, hands on Conrad's head. I figured it was best to not disturb her.

Shelton sidled up next to me. "What are you thinking?"

"About our next steps." I stepped away from Flava so as not to disturb her. "I hoped to ask Conrad about the dagger, but it doesn't look like he'll be able to anytime soon. We still don't have a plan for retrieving Unmaker from the Void, and there's no telling where Underborn is."

"Not to mention the mystery relic in the Abyss." Shelton glanced at the gateway to the past and his eyes lit up. "Holy farting fairies, I think I got it."

"What, gas pains?"

He shook his head. "The perfect hiding place for the relics."

I turned my attention to the gateway and gave it some thought. "If we dropped each of the relics inside a realm in the past, then they'd be virtually unreachable and unfindable."

"That's what I'm thinking." Shelton grinned. "And we're the only ones who know the way to open the portal scar."

He was right. But there was one glitch in the plan and her name was Xanos. I could trust everyone except for her to keep the secret.

Shelton followed my gaze. "Ah, shit, I forgot about her."

"I think we can work around the problem."

He grunted. "Drop her in the Void and let the Beast eat her?"

I snorted. "No. We use your plan but don't tell her about it. Even though she knows about the scar, she wouldn't know we're using it to hide relics."

"Yeah, I think that'd work." Shelton rubbed his hands together. "Now all we gotta do is get the damned relics."

I motioned him to follow me and we approached Adam and Cinder who were discussing sciencey stuff. "I need to talk to you."

"Yeah sure," Adam said.

He and Cinder followed us a distance from the others and I told them the plan to dump the relics into the time remnant.

"That is a very sound plan," Cinder said. "Perhaps we should place a blink stone inside the portal with a tracker and see if it maintains a relative position or moves during the void phase of the cycle."

"Yeah, good idea." Adam turned to Shelton. "Do you still have the blink stone Conrad and Ambria were using?"

He checked his pockets. "Nah, I think it's back at the Ranch."

"Be faster just to go to the vault." I didn't want Xanos to see what we were up to, so I led them around the corner of the burned-out mansion. My memory was a bit fuzzy since I hadn't been to Jeremiah's secret vault in a while, so I looked up an image on my phone and opened a portal.

We stepped through and into a sprawling warehouse that looked as if it went on forever. I closed the portal and looked around. Jeremiah had been storing things here since the dawn of man, or at least the dawn of man in Eden. I wondered how much history needed revising after visiting Jura.

Rows of giant shelves held everything from mundane books to artifacts that could probably end civilizations. Thankfully, it was all neatly organized, so we waltzed down to the J section where Jeremiah had dumped all the relics of Jura he'd collected over the centuries. According to Conrad, the key and map of Jura had once been here, but Underborn had somehow broken in and stolen them. We reached the Jura section. Several crates of debris sat on the bottom shelf. A display case above them held what looked like a nose broken from a stone statue. The rest of the case was empty.

Though many relics had unique properties, the vast majority were just rubble that we called blink stones. Using them could instantly transport a person from one place to another within a hundred feet or so. They might be handy if not for the unfortunate side-effects, namely dizziness and nausea.

"Hey, is that what I think it is?" Shelton reached into the glass case and took the stone nose.

Adam's eyes widened. "Is that the nose of Jura?"

"I mean, what else would it be?" Shelton held it closer, examining it. In the blink of an eye it flowed like putty onto his face and molded itself over his nose. Shelton sputtered and stumbled backward, arms flailing. "What the hell?"

"That is normal," Cinder said calmly. "Conrad and Ambria told me how the nose works. You should now have a greatly enhanced sense of smell."

Shelton grimaced. "Oh, god, did someone fart?"

"Like five minutes ago," Adam said.

"Lay off the kale smoothies, you sick bastard." Shelton shuddered. "There's this really acrid, burning odor too." He spun toward the crates of blink stones. "Those smell like they came from a cave and I could just about tell you there are two-thousand, four hundred and eighty-two of them."

"Just about?" Adam snorted. "Could you be more specific?"

Shelton's mouth dropped open. "Whoa, this is crazy." He turned in a circle. "This thing is like a tracker for relics."

"Indeed." Cinder leaned closer to examine the nose. "The nose went missing some time ago, supposedly taken by Underborn. Perhaps he returned it here for a reason."

Adam tapped a finger on his chin. "If Underborn was close to being caught by Baal's agents, perhaps he thought it would be prudent to have a backup plan."

I saw where he was going with this. "He left the nose here so we could track him."

Cinder nodded. "The nose is not considered vital to rebuilding the statue of Saila, so Baal would not be hunting it."

Shelton pinched the nose between thumb and forefinger, and it popped off, resuming its stone form once again. "Oh, man, that was brutal. It was like having a super sense of smell."

"I'll take any advantage we can get." I took the nose and pocketed it, then picked up a couple of blink stones to test in the time remnant.

"Do you know how many times I unleashed a silent but deadly around lycans?" Shelton shook his head. "They must smell farts on a whole new level."

I rolled my eyes. "Dude, you make me suffer all the time."

"Yeah, but it's funny because we're friends." He grinned.

"Oh, super funny." I slashed open a portal back to the Fairy Gardens and we stepped through. No one seemed to have noticed our brief absence, so we casually walked back to the time remnant portal.

Adam used his arcphone to put a tracking spell on one of the blink stones I'd brought back. "I think I'll just put it right inside and see if it maintains relative position. We'll place the others once the cycle resets."

I shrugged. "Sounds good to me."

He held the blink stone over the portal and dropped it. Blue sparks crackled and popped along the surface of the portal as the blink stone hopped around like water on a hot kettle. Adam yanked the stone back and dropped it on the ground. "What in the hell was that?"

Cinder recovered the blink stone and attempted the same thing, but try as he might, the stone wouldn't go through the portal.

"Wow, it's like fireworks!" Ivy tried to grab some of the sparks out of the air.

Cinder withdrew the blink stone and studied it. "This would explain why the stone didn't go into the remnant with Conrad and Ambria."

Shelton picked up a rock and tossed it into the portal. It flew through without incident and continued drifting through the white void until it was out of sight. "Well, that settles that."

I stood with my back to Xanos so she couldn't see the nose of Jura and tried to slip it through the portal. It encountered the same problem. I tucked it away. "That sucks."

"Yeah, you could say that." Shelton bit his lower lip. "Let's put tracker spells on regular rocks and use them for now."

Cinder nodded. "That would seem to be our only choice."

While they worked on that, I ducked around the corner and held the nose up to my face. Like an alien face hugger, it latched on before I knew what happened. Thankfully, it wouldn't implant an alien embryo in my belly.

An overwhelming acrid odor caused my eyes to water and then faded just as quickly. I smelled the blink stones we'd brought with us, counting five distinct signatures. My nose pulled me south, facing the exit out of Queens Gate. The odors were faint, but I sensed dozens of relics far, far away. They were most likely the ones in Baal's possession.

There was nothing else aside from those—no separate scent indicating Underborn was still on the loose with the heart. Unless he'd gone off-world to another realm, Baal had the relic and quite possibly Underborn. I pinched the nose and it popped off. It was a relief to have my own sense of smell back again.

"Hey everybody!" A young girl with silvery skin leapt from the copse of trees hiding the crack in the world. Evadora leapt like a kangaroo and landed in front of Ivy. "I'm so happy to see you!"

"Evadora!" Ivy and Evadora held hands and hopped up and down in place, squealing as if they hadn't seen each other in years.

A woman with bright orange hair appeared a moment later with Max Tiberius in tow. Her orange eyebrows rose. "I was not expecting such a crowd here."

I bowed slightly at the Glimmer Queen. "Good to see you, Cora. We've made some startling discoveries."

Max saw his friends and gasped. "You found them!" Tears trickled down his cheeks. "I knew you could do it, Shelton! I just knew it!" He rushed to their sides. "What's wrong with them?"

I hated to dash his good spirits. "Give me a minute and I'll explain."

Cora walked around the portal in the ground. "Why is it white on the other side?"

Max approached me. "Where were Conrad and Ambria?"

I looked at her and Max. "Probably better if I start from the beginning."

"Very well." She began to sit down on nothing. Black vines sprouted from the ground, weaving themselves into a chair an instant before her bottom reached them.

Max went over to his friends and knelt next to them, remaining quiet while Flava continued treatment.

I told Cora everything and was beginning to think it might be better just to record myself telling the story since it was getting longer with every telling.

Cora whacked me upside the head with bad news the moment I finished. "I regret to tell you that the dagger is gone. Somehow, agents of

Baal slipped into the Glimmer unseen. If not for the Soul Tree, I would never have known they were there."

"How could anyone get in without you knowing?" My chest tightened. "This is bad—really bad."

Baal had the dagger and quite possibly the heart. He was only one relic away from ending the world as we knew it.

CHAPTER 24

I leaned heavily against the crumbling mansion wall. "This can't be happening. How in the hell could Baal's people slip in and out without you knowing?"

"An excellent question." She sighed. "I had my creatures and plants search the Glimmer for Conrad and Ambria. It was then that the Soul Tree told me the dagger was missing from its roots. It vanished around the time you died, Justin."

"Baal probably saw my death and the aftermath of Emily's wedding as the perfect time to steal the dagger." I shook my head. "Everyone was distracted, and you weren't in the Glimmer."

She nodded. "The Glimmer was left undefended. The Soul Tree saw Cain and Olivia searching the roots of the tree with the aid of a black cube."

I sucked in a breath. "One of Razor's magic detectors."

"Is that what it was?" Cora pressed her lips into a thin line. "It did not take them long to find it and leave."

"They already knew where to start looking because Baal read my mind when I was mostly dead." I ran a hand down my face. "Thank goodness I didn't know where the other relics were."

"This is terrible news." Mom shook her head. "Doesn't that mean Baal only needs the heart and sword to complete the statue?"

I decided it was time to break the other bad news to them. "I think Baal already has the heart." I showed them the nose. From what I can tell, either Underborn isn't on Eden, or Baal got to him."

"This is disastrous." Cora turned to me. "And you plan to retrieve the sword from the Void?"

I nodded. "We had another plan to keep it out of Baal's hands forever, but it's not going to work."

Mom gave me a curious look. "What plan was that?"

"We were gonna toss them into the time remnant," Shelton said. "Scatter them in the past realms. But the relics won't go through the portal."

"A most unfortunate discovery." Cinder pressed his lips together. "It seems we are between a hard place and another hard place."

"A rock and a hard place," Adam said.

Cinder nodded. "Two very hard places."

Shelton snorted. "So, what now, glorious leader?"

Mom made a thoughtful noise. "Isn't there a mystery relic in the Abyss?"

"Yeah, but we have no idea what it looks like." I suddenly stopped talking because I realized we had the answer to finding out what it was, but I didn't want Xanos to know.

Flava entered the circle of people standing around the portal. She looked exhausted. "We need to take Conrad and Ambria somewhere they can rest and recover."

I nodded. "Let's get you settled at the Ranch." Since Elyssa wasn't around to scold me, I made a portal to the traveling room in the underground complex beneath the Ranch.

"I will return to the Ranch for now as well." Nightliss cradled an unconscious Ambria in her arms. "I have many more recruits to bless so we can replenish the Templar ranks."

Max trailed behind Nightliss. "I'm going with them."

Flava picked up Conrad. "I will let you know the moment they're awake."

I touched her shoulder. "Thank you, Flava. I know they're in good hands."

Dad watched them go. "What's next, son?"

I only had one move left, but I wasn't going to announce it in front of Xanos. "I think we should all rest."

He nodded. "This isn't the first time we've been caught in a tight spot. We'll figure it out."

"Yeah, I hope so." I turned to Adam and Cinder. "Do you want to stay here and keep experimenting on the time echo?"

"I think that would be best," Cinder said. "Perhaps we can discover something useful."

Unless learning history was important, I doubted it.

"What can we do?" Cora asked.

I had no answer for her. "Emily told me that you still haven't been able to revive your people. Is it a lost cause?"

"Naeve used magic unknown to me to put them to sleep." Cora shook her head. "I'm afraid they may be like that until the end of time."

"Yeah, well that ain't so far off," Shelton said.

Evadora twirled and began singing, "Go to sleep tonight, and you will surely die. The evil queen has cursed your kin, and you will never wake."

Shelton shuddered. "Jesus, that kid gives me the willies."

Evadora blurred over and hugged him. "I like you too, stinky!" Then she dashed into the trees, presumably returning to the Glimmer.

Cora clasped my hands. "Please let me know if I can help." Then she followed Evadora.

I turned to Xanos and nodded at the portal leading to the Ranch. "Let's go."

She stood and made her way through. Everyone except for Adam and Cinder filed through the portal. I closed it behind me and took Xanos straight to the holding cells so I could put her away for the time being. Shoulders slumped, she entered the empty cell and dropped onto the bunk. I couldn't help feeling bad at first but remembering the awful things she'd done made me feel better about it in a hurry.

"What now?" Shelton said. "Tacos?"

I snorted. "We just freaking ate, man."

He shrugged. "I'm a growing boy."

I led him out of the room and went back to the travelling room. "I've only got one more idea left right now, and I don't even know if it's a good one."

"Yeah?" he raised an eyebrow. "What's that?"

"I have the nose so I can track relics, right?"

He nodded.

"That means I can find the mystery relic in the Abyss. Baal wouldn't be looking for it so hard if it weren't important."

Shelton pursed his lips. "Hot damn, maybe you're onto something. When do we leave?"

"Soon." I'd learned the hard way that jumping straight into action without a plan would only land me in trouble. "We need to talk to Elyssa first."

He grinned. "Good idea."

Elyssa was still at Science Academy, so I opened a portal there. The weight of leaning on the Apocryphan powers was growing heavier, like stacking another boulder on already weary shoulders. If I didn't pace myself, I'd be hard pressed to get into and out of the Abyss in one piece.

We stepped through the portal and onto the front lawn of the administration building at the academy. Crowds of students were filing out of the building, most of them talking excitedly. It was hard to miss the heavy Templar presence, grim-faced people in black uniforms evenly spaced around the building perimeter.

I stopped one of the students. "What's going on?"

He flinched, apparently so caught up in the conversation with his companions that he hadn't seen me approach. "Oh, they're finally dumping the current admins and putting some real scientists in charge."

The woman next to him nodded vigorously. "And we'll finally be able to fully integrate arcnology into our designs instead of it being a fringe college of study."

"Yeah, arcnology is where it's at!" another student said. "I just hope Arcane University finally enters this century instead of teaching pure magic."

I let them go on their way.

Shelton grinned. "Sounds like Phoebe and Elyssa are shaking things up."

"Yeah. I just hope we can get some robots to help with the Void problem."

He grunted. "I don't think there's enough time."

We backtracked the exodus of students to an auditorium where Phoebe and Elyssa were conversing with a group of professors. I got Elyssa's attention and she excused herself.

Elyssa put a hand on my cheek and shook her head. "Justin, you've got dark marks under your eyes. Have you been overusing your Apocryphan powers again?"

"Just for portals." I held up a hand to ward off further conversation along those lines. "I think we can find the mystery relic in the Abyss." I pulled the nose of Jura from my pocket and gave her a glimpse before tucking it back in.

Her eyes widened. "Where did you get that?"

"Found it in Jeremiah's vault." I gave her the bad news about the relics.

Her face paled. "We're nearly out of time then."

I nodded. "Our only hope is that Baal needs the relic from the Abyss. If we can beat him to it, we can figure out how to hide it."

"Too bad that idea about hiding them in the time remnant didn't pan out." Shelton pulled off his hat and scratched his head. "There's got to be some way to keep Baal's grubby hands off them."

Elyssa bit her lower lip and nodded as if coming to an internal decision. "Let's go to the Abyss. Once we find the mystery relic, we'll get it out of there. Maybe I can retrieve the ASE I sent to Hell."

Shelton snorted then sobered once he realized she was serious. "Dude, you sent an ASE to Hell?"

Elyssa nodded. "We know nothing about Baal's physical base of operations."

"Hopefully, the ASE survived the journey." I leaned against the wall. "You ready to go now?"

She peered into my eyes. "I am, but are you? Maybe you should get some rest first."

It was getting late, but I didn't think I'd sleep well knowing Baal might find the mystery relic while I slept. I shook my head. "We're running out of time. We should go now."

Elyssa glanced at Shelton.

He shrugged.

She sighed. "Fine. Let's go."

Using omniarch portals, we made a pit stop at the Ranch to slip into Templar gear. Even Shelton ditched his standard outfit for the black uniform. Unfortunately, nightingale armor was still in short supply, but this would do.

Elyssa left to update Thomas while Shelton and I made our way down to the travelling room. Templars bustled up and down the corridors, every last one of them hurrying as if on an urgent mission.

"Are there more Templars down here than normal?" Shelton asked me.

I nodded. "Sure seems like it."

He twisted his lips. "They only get like this when a major mobilization is under way."

We picked up three brooms then went to the travel room and waited. Elyssa showed up twenty minutes later, her face set in the grim lines of battle mode.

"Is Thomas mobilizing troops?" I asked.

Elyssa waggled a hand. "He recalled several squadrons to prepare for a major offensive if the need arises."

I raised an eyebrow. "A major offensive where?"

She bit her lower lips and seemed to consider telling me. "I don't want you to think about it right now."

"Well, now I'm guaranteed to do nothing but think about it." I narrowed my eyes. "What's going on?"

Elyssa blew out a breath. "When I told my father about the portal to Hell, he thought it might be a good time to carry out a surprise attack on Hell and steal the relics."

I staggered back a foot. "Baal has an army of demons in Hell. There's no way an attack like that would work."

"It's just an option," Elyssa said. "It may be our last resort."

I hated to admit it, but she was right. Baal was only two relics away from victory and if we didn't do everything in our power to stop him, then the staggering death toll would be on our hands.

Provided we survived, of course.

I nodded. "Then let's hope it doesn't come down to that." I traced the symbols for the Abyss and slashed open the portal. The vertical line spread open slowly revealing a bubbling pool that resembled tar. I hated this part. I stepped into the portal and my forward momentum slowed to a crawl. Freezing cold climbed up my limbs as I slowly sank into the darkness. For an instant, there was nothing and then I stumbled forward onto the rocky surface of the Abyssal plain.

Elyssa and Shelton emerged seconds later.

Shelton hugged himself and shivered. "I feel so violated."

I took out the nose and let it mold onto my face. The odor of brimstone nearly overwhelmed my senses. My demon side found brimstone pleasant, but there was such a thing as too much of it. I resisted the urge to remove the nose and gave my senses a moment to recover. After a short while I was able to filter out the sulfurous odor.

There were other smells, but the nose zeroed in on the acrid burning odor that signified a relic of Jura. It was hard to tell how far away it was but it was somewhere ahead to the right. Beyond it I sensed a varying mélange of similar odors that had to be the relics Baal kept in Hell. They felt much further away than the one in the Abyss, but still tantalizingly close, just on the other side of the infernal fount.

Elyssa laced her arm in mine. "What is it, Justin?"

"I smell the relics in Hell." I shook my head. "But I also smell the one here in the Abyss." I pointed the way. "Let's go."

We climbed on our brooms and set out across the rocky terrain while keeping a vigilant watch in case any of Baal's minions were nearby. The Abyss was shaped like a shallow bowl, surrounded by towering mountains tens of thousands of feet high. Craggy cliffs bisected the bowl, forming a maze of canyons around the crater where the underside of the infernal fount bubbled and boiled.

Dark shadows flitted around the periphery, trapped spirits and wraiths stalking, waiting to pounce. We had defenses against such creatures, but the humans Baal tossed in here were like chum in a sea of sharks. I wondered how many more had been possessed since mine and Elyssa's last visit.

We flew low and fast, dodging between boulders. Elyssa halted us on occasion to check the area for infernus, then we resumed our flight. The nose pulled me toward the right, a direction I arbitrarily assigned as east since there were no magnetic poles in the prison. It soon became evident that the scent from the relic was higher than it had been earlier. It had moved from the abyssal canyons and was steadily moving upward.

"Hold up." I drifted to a stop behind a boulder and focused on the scent.

Elyssa stopped next to me. "What is it?"

"The relic is moving." I fixed my vision on the general area and saw a silhouette against the mountain wall.

Elyssa held a pair of spectacles to her eyes. "It's too dark to make out at this distance, but I think it's a giant rock crab."

"Great." Shelton rubbed his hands together. "I was expecting to fight infernus, not Abyssal monsters."

"Don't forget about the cliff worms." Elyssa scanned the mountain. "Maybe one of the monsters ate the relic."

I chuckled. "Stranger things have happened."

"Guess we'll be shoveling monster shit to find it." Shelton leaned back in his broom saddle. "That'll be a fun story to tell everyone."

The hairs on the back of my neck prickled. Elyssa must have sensed it way before I did because she was already drawing her light bow and nocking an arrow.

Shelton looked confused. "What's going on?"

We didn't have to answer because Baal's infernus were nearly on top of us by then, a cloud of camouflage fading away to reveal them floating low on flying carpets.

CHAPTER 25

Baal's personal infernus were thick and meaty specimens, created from the DNA and soul shards of the heartiest supers. They were the only beings that could reasonably hold a fragment of the demon lord's essence for long. This particular group looked especially frightening with their blazing curved sabers and barbed whips.

Shelton gulped. "Holy farting fairies! Where the hell did they come from?"

Elyssa unloaded a slew of energy arrows at the nearest flying carpet. The infernus in the front blocked two arrows with his saber, but the third caught him in the eye. Screaming as his demon flesh fried, he fell to the ground twitching violently. But he was just one of at least twenty infernus.

One leapt twenty feet in a single bound, sword raised to slice me right down the center when he landed. Our brooms weren't fast enough to evade, so I jumped off and manifested, swelling to seven feet in height, thick muscles bulging up and down my body. The Templar uniform easily accommodated the extra bulk, ensuring there'd be no embarrassing nudity.

I caught his mighty blow on a shield of Murk. The next instant, I channeled a sword of Brilliance and slashed off his weapon arm. His cries of agony went silent when I separated his head from his shoulders. I spun and ducked as a barbed whip whistled over my head.

Shelton's staff rammed into the ground. The earth buckled beneath two attackers, sending them stumbling away. "I beat an archangel. I sure as hell can beat you little hell bitches!" He whirled his staff, firing head-sized fireballs in all directions. One plowed through the chest of an infernus, leaving a charred, gaping hole in its wake.

A heap of bodies lay at Elyssa's feet as she hacked her way through the group assailing her. That was when I noticed there were way more than twenty attackers. I'd only seen the first group arrive while the others circled around behind us. They were on foot bearing automatic rifles and other nom weapons. The individuals in this group were smaller, probably normal infernus thrown into battle.

One of them hefted a rocket launcher and aimed it at Elyssa as she faced off against four infernus.

"You've got to be kidding me!" I slashed another attacker in half, then blurred toward Rocket Man. He pulled the trigger before I even got close. "Incoming!" I roared. Time seemed to slow as I increased my speed. I aimed my fist and fired a blast of Brilliance on an intercept trajectory.

It missed.

The rocket hissed through the air, leaving a black trail of smoke behind it. It was way too fast for me to catch.

Shelton slammed his staff against the ground and a shockwave rippled through the air, ripping through the rocket with a violet explosion fifty feet from its target. I slashed a beam of destruction at Rocket Man, cutting him from his shoulder down to his waist. As his body slid into pieces, another infernus picked up the rocket launcher and aimed it.

A barbed whip wrapped around my wrist before I could end Rocket Man Jr. Jagged barbs cut deep into my blue skin, drawing bright red blood. I roared in pain and jerked on the whip. But the massive infernus on the other end dug in his heels and held on tight. A razor whip wrapped around my throat, the sharp edges digging deep into my flesh. Blood bubbled in my mouth and I began to choke.

Elyssa and Shelton were too busy fighting off their own hordes to help me. I tried to channel a shield of Murk around my skin, but the whip had already buried itself deep in my flesh and was slowly tightening like a garrote. Another whip arrested my free hand.

Unless I used Apocryphan powers, I would die.

Another option occurred to me. I released my demon and let myself shrink as quickly as possible. My monstrously thick neck and arms became skinny by comparison. I slipped out of the grasp of the whips, the cruel razors and barbs slashing my face and arms as I did. Hot blood poured down my chest. My vision blurred. I stumbled forward grasping at my slashed throat in a vain effort to staunch the bleeding so my supernatural healing could kick in.

A vicious kick sent me to my knees. Another kick rolled me onto my back. The massive infernus leered down at me. "Well, boy, seems you get to die a second time." Baal was in the infernus.

I tried to make a smart remark, but blood bubbled in my throat.

He raised an eyebrow. "No parting remarks? What a shame." Baal raised a saber and brought it down.

Something huge and black flashed past. A terrified scream cut off an instant later. A monster roared and more screams filled the air. I grinned, tried to say something, and passed out. I woke up an instant later but was too weak to move. Swords clanged. Elyssa sang a battle cry. Men screamed. Another roar sent shivers down my spine.

I felt so warm. So tired. Despite the raging battle, I felt so peaceful. A part of me knew it was probably because I was about to die.

"Fuck, more reinforcements," Shelton shouted. "We gotta get out of here."

"How?" Elyssa said. "Justin can't open a portal."

Growls and strange yips seemed to answer them.

"Might work," Shelton said. "Let's do it."

I tried to talk. "Ungh."

"He's not bleeding anymore." Elyssa kissed my forehead and lifted me. She placed me on something warm and furry and strapped me down. "We'll follow."

A deep voice filled my head. *I will save you, master.*

Whatever I was on began to gallop. My head lolled side to side as scenery blurred past. Then the world tilted, and I was looking down. Claws scraped against rock. Rubble fell, and we began a vertical ascent.

I must have blacked out because I was in an enclosed space when I opened my eyes again. I felt weak but alert. The acrid odor of a relic filled my nostrils because the nose of Jura was still attached. The odor seemed to be coming from the massive purple hound staring down at me.

"Holy shit." I pulled off the nose and stared at the creature. I didn't recognize the body, but the way it looked at me reminded me of someone I'd lost long ago. "Cutsauce?"

He yipped as if he were a ten-pound chihuahua and not some monstrous creature of the underworld. *I found you!*

I blinked in confusion. "You never talked before."

I have grown over the past years.

"That's putting it mildly." I looked around and saw Shelton and Elyssa crouched outside the mouth of a cave. A dim glowball drifted a few feet overhead.

Elyssa came back inside. "Justin!" She kissed my forehead. "If it hadn't been for this hellhound or whatever he is, we'd be dead by now."

"Yeah, he really saved our asses." Shelton crouched next to me. "I thought for sure he was another one of Baal's minions."

I grinned. "You're not going to believe it, but this is Cutsauce."

Their mouths dropped open.

"Cutsauce was smaller than a cat." Shelton looked the hound up and down. "And he sure as hell wasn't purple."

I put the nose of Jura back on to confirm the earlier odor, then pulled it off. "Cutsauce, why do you smell like a relic of Jura?"

He gave me a doggy grin, tongue sticking out. *I made a friend.*

"A friend?" I held up a hand. "Hang on. Back up and tell me how you got into the Abyss in the first place."

Shelton sighed. "You mind telling us what he's saying? Not everyone here can hear hellhounds speak."

I am sorry. Is this better?

Shelton flinched. "Holy ass burgers. I can hear him in my head now."

"Me too," Elyssa said.

My friend helps me. He flopped down on the floor. *But I will start at the beginning. My memory is not as good because my mind was puny then.*

"Uh, yeah, you weren't the brightest bulb in the bunch," Shelton said. "You were Justin's first attempt to make a hellhound."

Yes. I was a great disappointment.

"Hey, you were my fave hellhound," I said. "Why do you think I kept you around instead of banishing you back to Haedaemos?"

He whined. *I was a good boy?*

"A very good boy." Elyssa reached out tentatively and touched his fur. "We're glad to see you again, Cutsauce. Thanks for saving us."

You are welcome. He licked her hand. *My humans—you—vanished many years ago. Some men came to the Mansion. I tried to drive them away with my fierce barks, but they laughed at me. One of them knew I was Justin's. Instead of sending my spirit to Haedaemos, he sent me away. I went through many hands and ended up in a hot and scary place underground. A man there was very happy to learn I was Justin's pet. I barked ferociously at him, but he only laughed. Then he tossed me into a lake of fire. The fire vanished before I hit it and I ended up in this place.*

I took a moment to process his rapid-fire explanation, but it was clear what happened. "The last man you saw was Baal in an infernus. He opened the doorway from Hell to the Abyss and dumped you in here."

Yes, the Abyss. He paned happily. *My friend told me about it.*

"Who in the blazes is your friend?" Shelton said.

Cutsauce paused and tilted his head. *She never told me. She said it was dangerous. But she joined my spirit in this body and has been with me for a long time.*

"She's been in there the entire time you've been in the Abyss?" I said.

He yipped. *Yes. Sometimes she leaves for alone time, but she likes having a body.* His hound body smoothly morphed into a thin human male. "She likes body." He speech was stilted and uncertain. *Sorry. I have not mastered talking with a human mouth.*

Shelton shuddered. "I forgot how creepy hellhounds look when they morph into human form."

Elyssa looked him up and down. "Your friend is Apocryphan."

The light purple skin of Cutsauce's human form made it all too evident. Eve had released the souls of the slain Apocryphan from the Abyss, meaning this entity wasn't one of the originals. There was only one Apocryphan child I knew of, but it seemed impossible for her to be here.

I shifted to demon vision and looked at Cutsauce's aura. Tinges of green power lurked at the periphery. "Saila, is that you?"

There was a long pause. Cutsauce answered, but this time the voice spoke in smooth Cyrinthian. "How did you know?"

"The nose of Jura knew." I held up the stone nose. It was hard to believe she was here, but at the same time made all the sense in the world. "The relic Baal seeks isn't physical. It's the spirit of Saila."

Shelton whistled. "Well, slap my ass and call me Karen. How in the hell did her spirit end up in the Abyss? This place wasn't even around back when the Sundering happened."

"May I borrow your body?" Cutsauce said.

Shelton backed up a step. "Hey, hold on now."

Yes, my friend! Cutsauce replied to himself.

The male body morphed into a female who resembled the figure I'd seen in the time echo. "Thank you."

Anything for my good friend!

Shelton breathed a sigh of relief. "Man, I thought she was going to possess me."

Saila sat cross-legged on the cave floor. "After the Sundering, I found myself adrift in a world of endless forests. I, of course, did not know the world had split into realms. I thought I had died and entered the after-life. I found humans lost in the wilderness. When I could not speak with them, I realized I was a spirit drifting in the physical world."

"Crazy." I shook my head. "Were you in Eden?"

"The place had no name. I eventually discovered how to merge with the humans and speak with them." She clasped her hands together. "I did not reveal who I was, but I taught them how I had created Jura. I hoped they could build another utopian city and rebuild what the Apocryphan destroyed. I remained among them for many generations. They were unlike any humans I had met before. They were strong and independent but worked together for the betterment of the whole."

Elyssa and I exchanged a look.

Shelton blew out a breath. "We were wrong about Utopia. It wasn't the good part of Elohim that made it that way, it was the guidance of Saila."

"We've been to that realm," I said. "It's the best example of human evolution I've ever seen."

Saila beamed. "I am so happy to hear they are doing well."

"Why'd you leave?" Elyssa asked.

"It was an accident." Saila's smile faded. "I began to experiment, hoping to use my powers again through a human. I accidentally opened a micro portal and was sucked through. This time I was on a world of insects and reptiles. Their forms were alien to me, but I managed to eventually merge with one of the reptilian overlords. Using him, I made another portal."

"Reptilian overlords?" Shelton's eyes brightened. "Cool!"

I whistled. "You drifted from realm to realm for thousands of years?"

She nodded. "I eventually made it to Eden and met Vitania, the former queen of the Sirens. When she discovered Baal was hunting relics of Jura, she decided it was safer for me to hide in the Abyss. She would come visit on occasion and even take me in her body to other worlds. But then she simply stopped coming and I don't know why."

"Somehow Baal knows you're here," I said. "And he's hunting for you."

"You speak of Elohim," Saila said.

I nodded. "Baal is technically a part of Elohim."

She nodded. "He was sundered like the realms, his physical form shorn from the spirit."

Shelton grunted. "But he ended up in a newly created spiritual plane called Haedaemos. I wonder why you didn't end up there."

Saila shrugged. "Despite my long existence, there is still much I don't know."

"How can a spirit be a relic?" Elyssa said. "Does that mean Baal is a relic?"

I gave it some thought. "Maybe."

Shelton made a thoughtful grunt. "Is the Beast really a part of Elohim after all?"

"What I do know is this," Saila said. "A part of Elohim exists in the Void, for I have been there and have seen and felt the corruption."

"How in the hell did you survive the Beast?" I said. "I thought it consumed souls."

"It was young, a fledgling when I found that realm." She shivered. "You say Baal is searching the Abyss for me, but I have seen what he is building in Hell and I can tell you it has little to do with me."

My forehead scrunched. "What do you mean? Rebuilding your body will undo the Sundering."

She shook her head. "The focus of the Apocryphan's wrath was not on me. The killing blow for the world landed on Elohim himself."

Shelton's jaw dropped open. "Then that means—"

Elyssa hissed. "The relics aren't parts of Saila. They're pieces of Elohim."

"Which means Unmaker is not the only other relic he needs." I shook my head in disbelief. "The Beast is."

CHAPTER 26

I couldn't wrap my head around it, but the Beast was somehow a part of Elohim.

"Riddle me this," Shelton said. "If the Beast is a relic spirit like Saila here, then why is Baal so busy searching the Abyss?"

"Baal may not know the Beast is something he needs." Saila shrugged. "His minions only know they need Unmaker and talk about it incessantly."

"I thought Baal knew Unmaker was in the Void." I frowned. "Something is off about this."

Elyssa pursed her lips. "Baal must not realize he needs the Beast. He also doesn't know what relic is hidden here and probably thinks it's the final part of the puzzle."

I bit my bottom lip and started nodding at the thoughts circulating in my head. "We're fine, then. Baal will continue searching the Abyss while not even knowing he needs the Beast."

Saila flinched and looked toward the cave mouth.

Elyssa was already up on her feet, swords in hand. She flitted to the opening and looked out. "Shit!"

"What?" I tried to run but my legs didn't have quite enough blood to respond. I reached her side and saw the silhouette of a flying carpet diving toward the ground below.

Elyssa's eyes widened. "Baal's minions must have seen us go in here."

Shelton shook his head. "No, I camouflaged us."

"Then they've been searching this area for us." Elyssa huffed. "They weren't there a moment ago, so they must have just found us."

Shelton grimaced. "You think they heard us?"

Elyssa nodded. "Safe to say Baal knows about the Beast now."

I clenched a fist and groaned. "We've got to get to the Ranch. There's no time to waste."

Elyssa gripped my arm. "Justin, you couldn't poke a hole in a sheet of paper, much less open a portal."

"Great." Shelton face-palmed. "What now?"

Saila stood. "I can open a portal."

I blinked a few times before remembering what she'd just told us about wandering the realms. I knew from being dead that spirits still had their powers, so it made sense that Saila could use them through another being's body. "How is Cutsauce strong enough to handle Apocryphan powers?"

"I've molded his physical form to be more robust," she said. "His spirit is now so deeply rooted in this body, that he can no longer be banished like an ordinary demon."

I took a moment to process that. "His body is real now?"

She nodded. "He is fully functional, though his morphing abilities are limited to only a few forms."

I couldn't help but feel nostalgic. "Can he be teeny tiny again like he was?"

Saila smiled. "Yes, that is his primary form."

Shelton whooped. "Dude, Cutsauce is the first Apocryphan dog."

I nodded. "Yeah, I guess you're right."

"My powers are not nearly as great as those of my father's, so it took me years to evolve him." Saila shrugged. "But he has been a worthy and faithful companion."

Her comment shifted my line of thought. "Did you talk to the other Apocryphan?"

She shook her head. "I was disgusted at what they had done to our beautiful world, so I simply observed them. I found it amusing, as did Vitania, that had the Apocryphan understood how the Sirens built the arches, they could have left the Abyss at any time."

"Irony." I shook my head. "The slaves were smarter than the masters."

"They relied too heavily on their powers for everything." Saila sighed. "Eve thought to make new gods, but instead she created monsters."

Elyssa clapped her hands together. "Maybe we should get back to Eden and brainstorm how to keep Baal from invading the Void and taking the relics."

"Yeah." I turned to Saila. "Will you do the honors?"

Saila bit her lower lip. "I must admit I am conflicted."

"Uh-oh, here it comes." Shelton braced as if waiting on a physical blow.

"I miss the old Earth. These realms feel alien to me." Saila looked out the cave. "What if unbreaking the world is the right decision?"

I felt sick to my stomach. "You seriously think it's okay to snuff out billions of lives just to go back to the good old days?"

She shook her head. "Of course not. But would it not be wonderful to have Earth whole once again? I would perhaps even have my body returned."

Elyssa nodded. "Saila, that would be wonderful. But the cost would be too high. And if you're whole again, then so is Elohim, and there's no telling what he'll do once he's elevated back to godhood. His eons as the grand overlord of Haedaemos have not made him a better person at all."

She slumped. "My father and half-siblings are responsible. Had they not attacked Elohim, this world would be a paradise."

"Maybe, but it's more likely the Apocryphan would still rule most of it with an iron fist." I hesitantly patted her back. "You were the only benevolent one, the only truly wise one. I've seen Juranthemon in person and it was an amazing city."

Her eyes flared. "How did you see it?"

"I'd rather not discuss that here." I held my breath for a moment and asked her once again. "Will you take us home?"

She nodded. "Yes. Where do you wish to go?"

"The Ranch." I showed her a picture of the travel room. "It's in Eden."

Saila flicked her fingers and a portal of bubbling pitch appeared.

"Damn, you make that look so easy."

"It is only possible to portal from the Abyss when I am in this body." She shook her head. "Even so, it is very difficult and draining."

"Well, it's still impressive." I entered the portal, let the freezing darkness suck me in and spit me out in the travel room on the other side.

Saila wasn't far behind and stepped aside for the others. "I sense a great power in you, Justin. Not many have the strength to open portals."

Another story time was coming up and I still hadn't put my memoirs to paper. "There's a lot to talk about."

This is exciting! Cutsauce said in my head. *I'm finally home!*

"You didn't take him to Eden in all this time?" I asked Saila.

"As a spirit, I couldn't easily create a portal out of the Abyss." She shrugged. "It wasn't until recently that his body could handle the strain of making portals. He asked that I take him to the Mansion, but I'm afraid his unevolved mind simply couldn't remember where it was or what it looked like."

Elyssa slowly emerged from the portal, a tar pit birthing a perfectly preserved specimen. Shelton emerged last.

"I'm calling a meeting ASAP." Elyssa kissed my cheek. "Find Flava and get patched up. We'll need you."

"Can someone give Saila an update for the past decade?" I said. "I just don't have it in me to talk that much right now."

Shelton nodded. "I got you, fam."

I walked with the others for a while then split off to go to the healing ward. Flava was inside with the slumbering forms of Conrad and Ambria on nearby beds.

Her eyes flared. "Justin, you're covered in blood!"

I shrugged and told her what happened. "Can you get me back to a hundred percent?"

Flava sighed. "I cannot magically create blood, so we will have to resort to something I learned during my time here." She patted a bed and headed for the door. "Lay down."

I followed her instructions.

She returned moments later with an IV and a blood bag. "This is called a transfusion. It will help you recover faster."

"Um…" I looked at the bag dubiously. "Is that the right kind of blood?"

"It's your blood," she said. "You regularly donate so vampires and dhampyrs have a steady supply."

"Oh." I hadn't even thought of that. She flashed a smile. "I came with you when you were near death and they gave me a complete tour of the facility in the hopes I could find another way to save you. That was when I discovered how much blood you've donated."

"Yeah, I was pretty screwed up." I shrugged. "At least this time I won't be as much of a challenge."

Flava rolled her eyes. "You are a never-ending source of challenges." She poked the IV into a vein without even looking down. "And if we're to ever drive the dragon army from Seraphina, then we need you alive and healthy."

I didn't want to think about how far Baal had pushed us. Just when we'd nearly united a realm that had been at war almost since its inception, Baal had turned the denizens of Seraphina into refugees. There was no telling how many other realms he'd conquered in his quest to find relics of Juranthemon.

With the endgame right around the corner, I didn't know how we were going to pull this off. If the Beast really was a soul relic like Saila, how could we possibly prevent Baal from claiming it? Our only hope was that the Beast would fight him as it fought us. Because if it recognized him and identified with him, then there was nothing we could do to stop Baal.

I dozed off during the transfusion and didn't wake up until the ass crack of dawn. Three empty blood bags lay on the table next to me and the fourth on the IV was low. I'd apparently been running on almost empty after getting my throat cut. The transfusion must have worked because I felt pretty damned good.

Old blood crusted my clothes and skin so the first thing I did was go to the showers and clean off. I texted Elyssa on the way back to the room for fresh clothes.

She replied a moment later. *In the war room. Bad news.*

Icy dread gripped my chest. I threw on another Templar uniform and raced to the war room. Thomas and Elyssa were poring over a map of the Void while Xanos observed from a nearby chair.

Tiny paws clicked on the stone floors. Cutsauce trotted into the room and yipped. He was back to his dainty size, but his black fur had a discernible purple tint to it.

Justin! He pranced around my feet yipping and growling happily.

I picked him up and scratched his ears. He licked my face. His breath reeked of brimstone, but I didn't mind. "Is Saila still in there?"

No, she is resting. Shelton told us all about everything since you vanished. He glanced at Xanos. *She is the one who almost took over the world?*

"Yeah."

He bared his teeth and growled at her. *Bad Apocryphan! She is not a good girl.*

"No, she's not."

Xanos watched me curiously, unaware I was talking to the teacup hellhound.

"Cutsauce says you're not a good girl." I petted him. "But you're a good boy."

I am?

"You're the best. You saved me!" I scratched behind his ears and he whined in pleasure.

I always tried to be a good boy even when I was sad and alone in the Abyss.

"Why is that hellhound purple?" Xanos said.

I shrugged. "Some of them come out that way."

She tilted her head. "Do they?"

I turned to Elyssa. "What's this bad news you texted me about?"

Elyssa blew out a breath. "Saila took us back to the Abyss while you were asleep. We recovered the ASE I sent to Hell. It captured very little useful information, but it did overhear a conversation between Baal's infernus and Olivia. He's going to send an infernus with a fragment of him into the Void to see if he can reason with the Beast. The only good thing is that we killed his personal infernus in the Abyss so he's generating a new one. We've got maybe twenty-four hours before he's ready."

I hissed. "If he does this, it's game over."

"I'm afraid so." Elyssa sighed. "Phoebe says they haven't found any robots that could withstand the energy drain of the swarm."

"And I have no armor that would fit on robots," `Xanos said. "Nor do I have enough to outfit an army."

"Shit!" I put Cutsauce down and started pacing. "There's got to be something we can do."

"Adam and Cinder have been up all night experimenting on the bugs from the Void." Elyssa bit her lower lip. "I hope they've come up with something."

"We haven't come up with anything," Adam said the second we stepped into the Razor lab.

One of the giant roaches squirmed in restraints inside the specimen room. The juxtaposition of the human face and body parts with the bug body sent shivers up and down my spine.

"The creatures are quite resilient," Cinder said. "Even when cut to pieces, the parts are still alive and can be reconstituted by the swarm."

"What about giant cans of bug spray?" I was only half-joking.

"We acquired boric acid, roach spray, and several other chemicals the noms use to fight insects, but these creatures have a mixture of human and insect biology." Cinder shook his head. "The only way to kill these creatures permanently is to either burn them to ash or somehow prevent the Void swarm from regenerating them."

"They're nearly impossible to burn." I'd learned that firsthand from our last venture. "The swarm soaks up most of my energy when I attack them."

"The swarm can block us, heal the soldier insects, and devour our power," Cinder said. "I'm afraid we have no good weapon against them."

Our last encounter had nearly proven fatal for Cinder. If it hadn't been for—I flicked my gaze to Adam. "Why did your shield work so well against the swarm?"

Adam blinked. "Oh, um, it's the same one I used against the Razor weapons." His brow furrowed. "When they tried to soak up the energy from the shield, the malaether matrix zapped them."

Cinder tilted his head. "Malaether is toxic to most living creatures. It seems the swarm is no exception."

I pursed my lips. "The swarm can be killed with regular magic, but it takes so much energy that I can't sustain it. How much power does it take to generate your malaether shield?"

"Not much," Adam said. "The size and power are limited on purpose due to the volatility of malaether."

"What about the Razor weapons?" I said. "They break down magic, so could they be used to fight the swarm?"

"We'd have to build them or disable the self-destruct mechanisms that prevent supers from touching them." Adam shook his head. "The malaether shield idea might be better, but I don't know how to scale it."

Cinder nodded. "Too much power would be as dangerous to us as it would be to the swarm."

"And an arcphone or arctablet are the only ways to use the spell," Adam said. "I guess we could copy the spell to dozens of phones and tablets and overlap them, but it would be extremely dangerous."

"Overlapping the shields would likely cause an explosion." Cinder pressed his lips into a grim line. "We will have to study the idea and come up with a feasible way to utilize it."

I had another thought. "What about something like Serena's antima weapon?"

Adam grimaced. "It's possible we could rig weapons with that arcnology, but it would take time."

"Adapting her weapon to a mass scale would require extensive research and experimentation." Cinder tilted his head. "Perhaps magic interdictors would achieve a similar effect."

Magic interdictors had been used by Daelissa's people during the war. Special pendants allowed them to use magic while our side was nearly helpless. "Interdictors corrupt aether within a radius around them, right?"

Cinder nodded. "It creates a less volatile form of malaether, but it might also prove toxic to the swarm."

Adam shook his head. "We don't have any working interdictors. Most of our equipment was stolen or destroyed while we were gone." He slumped. "I'm sorry, but there's no way we can come up with something in time to fight the swarm before Baal creates a new infernus."

"No." I shook my head and grinned. "You're wrong." Because I had an idea that was amazing.

CHAPTER 27

Adam's jaw dropped open after I explained my wonderful idea. "Dude, that's an awful idea. It'll never work."

"It'll totally work." I jabbed a finger at the bug monster. "We'll kill the swarm and then it'll be down to us and the giant roaches."

Elyssa tapped a finger on her chin. "Your plan is pure madness, but at this point I'm willing to try anything."

"Then let's get to it." I rubbed my hands together. "There's no time to waste."

She nodded. "Let's do it."

Elyssa and I returned to the Ranch and told Thomas the plan.

He didn't even blink when I told him what I needed. "I'll assemble a team immediately."

On our way to Cinder's lab I sent a group text to everyone I needed for this to work. The lab was still a horrendous mess, but we managed to locate the supplies we needed without too much delay. By the time we made our way up to the parking garage and the travelling area, forty-two Templars, Ivy, Mom, Dad, and Nightliss were filing through a portal leading directly to the Razor facility.

I looked around. "Where's Shelton?"

"He went through already," Dad said.

Ivy clapped her hands and danced in place. "I can't wait to blast some baddies!"

"Don't get too excited just yet," I said. "This might not work."

"Some of the best plans never do," Dad replied. "Which is why yours usually work."

I snorted. "I'm not sure how to take that."

"It just means your plans aren't orthodox." He shrugged. "No one even sees them coming."

"Half the time I don't see them coming." I shook my head. "They just hit me out of nowhere."

He clapped my shoulder. "How do you think the enemy feels?"

Elyssa checked the time on her phone. "Baal will have an infernus within the next two hours. We need to get in and get out ASAP."

Dad peered down the line of Templars entering the portal. "It might have been better to assemble Daemos. We can summon an army if need be"

Elyssa shook her head. "We simply didn't have time or resources to organize the factions into a massive attack. If this works, we won't need them anyway."

Cutsauce trotted up to us. *We are ready to save the world!*

I bent down and scooped him up. "You always sound so excited."

Everything is exciting! And I got sausages. I have not had them in a long time.

"Who gave you sausages?" I asked.

Friendly people in the eating place.

I snorted. "Not even back a day and you're already begging for food?"

Life is not worth living without treats.

I couldn't disagree.

The Templars picked up the pace and marched through the portal within minutes. The reason for the earlier traffic jam was on the other side. Apparently, Adam had tried coordinating the handing out of Void armor before the Templars relieved him of that duty.

Nightliss stood to the side with Shelton and Adam, watching as a lieutenant quickly and efficiently handled the allotment. Nightliss hurried over when we stepped through the portal. "Justin, this seems terribly dangerous."

I sighed. "If we had any other way to do this, I would. But this is our last chance to stop Baal."

Shelton brandished one of the Razor rifles Adam had modified so it wouldn't self-destruct when supers touched it. "I'm ready to go in guns blazing."

"Then let's get suited up." The last of the Templars were already emerging from the armory, having suited up in minutes, and equipped themselves with shields and swords.

It took a lot longer to instruct my family and Nightliss how to put on the armor.

Once everyone was equipped with weapons, it was time to put the plan into action. We went into the room with the portal device.

Cutsauce morphed into Saila. She wiggled her fingers as if getting used to the abrupt change in body shape. "I am ready to help."

Adam took out his arcphone and showed her a picture taken from one of Xanos's drones. The image had been taken just beneath the cloud cover, thousands of feet above the ground. Saila concentrated on the image and slashed open a portal. I opened a null cube and tossed through one of our secret weapons.

It was a weapon that had been used against us and nearly destroyed all magic on Eden. Now it was our last hope for weakening the Beast enough that we might recover Unmaker from the Void and play keep away from Baal long enough for us to defeat him and break up the relics of Jura once and for all.

The crystoid began to swell larger as it streaked toward the ground below. Saila closed the portal and Adam showed her another image. She opened another gateway and I deployed another crystoid. We repeated the pattern twenty-four times, saving the last crystoid for the heart of darkness, the supposed home address of the Beast himself.

Once the last one was out, Saila wobbled on her feet. "I'm afraid that took everything I had."

I nodded. "It's okay. Rest up and hope for the best."

She paused to take in the line of Templars running out of the door. "It is no wonder Baal hasn't succeeded. You never give up, do you?"

I shook my head. "We have to be as relentless as the enemy."

Saila yipped and growled, throwing me off for a moment before I realized Cutsauce had taken back the reigns. He shifted back to his diminutive size. *I want to go.*

I shook my head. "We don't have a set of armor for you. If the crystoids diminish the Void swarm, then maybe you can help. Until then, stay here and guard the portal."

He pranced in a circle and yipped. *I will guard it with my life.*

I scratched his ears. "Good boy."

Everyone was suited up and armed. It was go time. I opened a portal to the oasis near the darkness and we filed through. Steeling myself, I stepped through the barrier and into the wasteland outside. A glowing ember flickered in a crater not far down the hill from the oasis. The crystoid had already swollen to the size of a small car as it sucked up the ambient aether.

The nearby ground was remarkably bare, devoid of the swarm. It was soon clear why. A dark cloud swirled overhead, twisting into a funnel toward the crystoid. It seemed the Beast was sending his creatures to investigate.

"Holy hell in a handbasket." Shelton stood next to me. "How are they still flying?"

"There must still be enough ambient aether or..." I trailed off as I thought of the other possibility.

Shelton nudged me. "Or what?"

"Or the swarm doesn't rely on magic to fly or communicate with the Beast." I met his concerned gaze. "We need to wait and see."

Even though the swarm had left the area, shadows flitting through the broken structures nearby told me the bigger bugs were still close.

Adam joined us, a Razor rifle at the ready.

Shelton pointed to the swarm. "Dude, the bugs are still flying."

Adam nodded. "The swarm is comprised of insect-like creatures with wings, so I'm not surprised they can still fly. It's possible they also use other means to stay in communication with the Beast."

"The whole purpose of the crystoids was to disable the swarm." Shelton shook his head. "This ain't good."

Adam shrugged. "I told Justin it wasn't a good idea."

Mom looked around. "I never thought I'd visit the Void. Now I'm sure I never want to see it again."

"Creepy," Dad said. "We're being watched."

Ivy made a fist. "Wish I could blast them."

"The crystoids are sucking up all the aether," Adam said. "You won't be blasting anything with magic."

Nightliss held a sword at the ready. "Then I am glad my Templar training prepared me for this."

"Oh, I don't think anything prepares you for fighting giant bugs." Shelton shuddered. "What are they waiting for? They should've attacked by now."

"I don't know." I switched to demon vision. The beam of aether shooting into the sky from the distant crystoid looked like a spotlight. There was no ambient aether and the leylines in the ground flickered off and on as they struggled to keep up with the drain.

My enhanced sight didn't pick up any enemies in the shadows of the broken buildings. Where had they gone?

Elyssa led the Templars from the oasis and held up a fist to halt them. She looked out at the swarm and turned to me. "I thought the crystoid would disable the swarm."

I shook my head. "I was wrong." That was the last thing out of my mouth before the ground buckled beneath our feet.

"Holy shitballs!" Shelton stumbled backward.

"They're beneath us!" Elyssa shouted. "Find solid ground!"

A hole opened beneath a Templar and he fell in without so much as a shout of alarm. One of his comrades caught his arm. Two more Templars reached into the hole from the other side and they pulled him out to safety. Outraged screeches rose from the hole. More cracks formed in the hard-packed earth and the ground heaved.

A Templar raised her hand. "Over here!"

Everyone scrambled to her position, a slab of granite, and formed up. The next few moments were straight out of a horror movie. Countless giant black roach people crawled from holes in the ground, mandibles clacking, antennae twitching. They outnumbered us three to one. To make matters worse, the Void swarm was turning away from the crystoid and back toward us.

"Templars, phalanx formation!" Elyssa raised a hand and held it flat.

With silent precision, the Templars formed a tight circle, shields up, swords protruding, placing me, Shelton, Adam, Elyssa, and my family in the center. Nightliss joined the formation with the others. The roaches attacked from all sides, scurrying forward on six legs before rearing up and striking. The Templars thrust their swords into soft underbellies and slashed upward for maximum damage, sending incapacitated enemies falling back into their own ranks.

They repelled wave after wave until the ground was slick with bug guts. Squirming roaches screeched and hissed, unable to stand and rejoin the fight. But no matter how many we killed, more crawled from the ground. It wouldn't be long before the pile of bodies grew higher than the Templars.

I looked to the sky. The swarm was rapidly approaching and would be here in minutes. "How many freaking roach soldiers does the Beast have?"

"Too many." Elyssa gripped my arm. "Give me a boost."

I knelt and she stepped onto my shoulders. My physical strength was unaffected by the lack of aether, so I lifted her easily. "What now?"

"Pray this works." She reached into the pouch at her side and threw scorchers left, right, and behind us. The grenades burst into flames. Roaches screeched. Bug flesh sizzled. The stench filled the air. Elyssa pointed toward the oasis. "Diamond formation!"

The Templars shifted and those of us in the center moved to adjust.

Elyssa hopped off my shoulders. "Forward!"

Using the shields, the formation shoved through the carcasses. Elyssa had set fire to everything around us except the path she wanted us to take. Unfortunately, the aether fueling the flames was rapidly running out thanks to the crystoid. We were nearly back to the oasis when the next problem presented itself.

The Void swarm funneled out of the sky like a tornado, blocking our retreat. Part of the swarm broke off and settled over the fallen roaches. In no time at all they'd be back on their six feet and tear us to pieces. My plan had failed spectacularly, and we were all going to die because of it.

I turned to the others. "I'm sorry."

Adam shook his head. "It's okay. We tried."

Shelton grinned wryly and brandished the Razor rifle. "We ain't done yet." He leveled it at the wall of locusts and pulled the trigger. Gray rings pulsated from the end and struck the bugs—to absolutely no effect. He raked the beams up and down the wall to no effect then turned back to me. "Okay, maybe we are done."

"I want to blast them so bad!" Ivy bared her teeth. "I'm so angry right now!"

Elyssa flung scorchers and icers at the wall. Locusts burst into flames or froze, falling to the ground in droves. But no matter how many she took down, there were countless more to replace them.

Adam peered over the heads of the Templars behind us. "Hey, look at that."

I watched as the locusts swarmed over the bodies. "What am I looking at?"

"The swarm!" His brow furrowed. "They can't revive the dead roaches!"

I watched for a moment and realized he was right. The swarm couldn't reconstitute the dismembered bodies like they had the last time. The lack of aether was affecting them after all. It was a silver lining, but I didn't think it was enough to save us. More roaches were climbing out of the ground and we couldn't break through the swarming wall before us.

Then again, maybe we didn't have to. I looked toward the crystoid about a quarter of a mile in the distance. I shifted to demon vision. The air and sky were devoid of free-floating aether as every last bit was being vacuumed into the meteor. But just like the crystoid in Cinder's lab, a brilliant beam of aether was shooting up into the sky at an angle.

If I could reach the crystoid and somehow get myself into the beam, I'd have all the power I needed to burn the swarm to dust. There were two major problems with that plan. First, I'd need a boost to get into the aether beam, and second, the swarm had to follow me, or it'd be out of range of my attacks.

Elyssa narrowed her eyes. "Justin, you've got that look like you're about to do something crazy."

She was right. What I had in mind wasn't just crazy, it was suicide.

CHAPTER 28

Suicide or not, I had to try. Otherwise we were never getting out of here. "Get me to the crystoid and we can use magic to destroy the swarm."

She blinked and looked up. "In case you hadn't noticed, the swarm is monstrous. It would take massive amounts of energy to wipe it all out."

"Me and my bro can blast anything!" Ivy said defiantly.

Nightliss turned from her position in the formation. "I can help."

"So can I," Mom said.

Dad grinned. "Race you to the crystoid?"

Whoa, what about us?" Shelton said. "We can't run like you guys."

"You're not coming." I put a hand on his shoulders. "If the swarm follows us, I want you and Adam to get back to the oasis."

Elyssa frowned. "What about us?"

"If this works, then we have a shot at getting the sword. If it doesn't, get out of here."

"I'm not leaving you." She gripped my gloved hand. "I'm not leaving this hellhole unless you're with me."

"I knew you'd say that." I grinned. "Wish us luck."

Elyssa snorted. "Our luck can't get any worse." She grimaced. "I hope."

Shelton grabbed my shoulder. "I'd kind of hoped we could all die together, so keep alive until Baal does the honors, okay?"

I nodded. "I'll do my best."

Dad, Mom, Ivy, and Nightliss huddled together in the middle of the formation.

"Everyone ready?"

They nodded.

"God, I can't wait to incinerate these bugs," Ivy growled in demonic undertones.

Elyssa held up a hand to signal the Templars to open a hole for us.

I held up a hand. "Wait." I shook my head. "Ivy, we can't risk you going full demon. Maybe you should stay behind."

Ivy clenched her fists and sucked in a breath. "I can do it, bro. I can control it."

I shook my head. "Sorry, sis, but we can't take the chance."

Tears pooled in her eyes. "Please don't leave me behind."

It tore at my heart. "Crying isn't fair."

"Well, the Void isn't fair either." Ivy bit her lower lip. "If I feel like I'm slipping, I'll stop, okay?"

I turned to Mom and Dad. "What do you think?"

"We've got a fifty-fifty chance of her going full demon." Dad shrugged.

"Leaving her behind might be wise, but we're going to need all the fire-power we can get."

I hated to admit it, but he was right. I turned to Ivy. "You need to control yourself like you've never controlled yourself before."

She nodded. "I will."

"One thing's for certain," Shelton said with a grin. "We're going out with a bang."

Ivy pumped a fist. "Boy and how!"

I nodded at Elyssa. "We're ready."

She tapped the shoulders of two Templars. "Make a hole and close it up."

They shifted slightly to the side even as another roach soldier tried to break through the lines. I bulled forward, knocking the giant insect away and plowing through two more before I cleared the enemy lines. The rest of the team followed in my wake.

Roaches screeched. Some gave chase. Others continued fighting the Templars. We ran. At first it seemed the swarm was going to ignore us, but the Beast must have decided we were a greater threat than the Templars. Roaches skittered down the hill after us and the swarm shifted away from guarding the oasis and came after us.

Dad and I were easily the fastest with Ivy a close third, thanks to our demonic strength, but we maintained pace with Mom and Nightliss. We left the roaches in the dust, but the swarm wasn't far behind. It didn't take long for us to cross the quarter mile between us and the target. When we got there, Dad wasted no time flinging Mom up into the air.

She caught the aether beam and channeled wings, hovering in place. I tossed Ivy up while Dad boosted Nightliss. He turned to me and grinned. "Give 'em hell, son."

"We're in angel mode now." I grinned. "So, we'll give 'em heaven."

Dad knelt and cupped my foot. "If bad jokes could kill, we would've just won the war." Then he tossed me into the air.

Mom, Ivy, and Nightliss had spread out to give each other room to levitate. I channeled my wings and positioned myself slightly higher than the others. Aether flowed into me and my veins hummed with magic.

"Let's burn the swarm to the ground." Channeling through the gems in the palms of the armor, I summoned twin orbs of Brilliance in my hands and waited for the swarm to close within range. Even at max power, a hundred yards was a stretch for my Seraphim abilities. For maximum effectiveness while still maintaining a safe distance, we'd have to hold fire until the swarm was fifty yards away. The armor would protect us to a certain degree, but the sheer mass of the swarm could force us out of the aether beam and back to the ground where we'd be powerless.

The Beast might not even realize we were getting aether from the crystoid. I hoped it was as much in the dark about it as we'd been when the crystoids first struck Eden. The swarm veered up and dove at us and it suddenly seemed quite clear that the Beast knew exactly what we were up to.

"Oh, shit." I watched the funnel of death rapidly descend. "It's going to knock us out of the sky."

Mom drifted higher next to me. "Then we'll have to give it everything we've got."

Ivy joined us, orbs of Brilliance dancing in her hands. Blue flames flickered in her eyes, but she seemed to be holding it together. "They shall not pass."

Nightliss came to my other side. "What if we formed a cloud of Stasis?"

Mom pursed her lips. "It might work, but I think we'd be better off just burning the swarm outright."

I nodded. "A Stasis cloud might protect us better, but the bugs will still be alive."

"Very well." Nightliss balled her fists and charged them with destructive energy. "Let's give them heaven." She winked at me.

I snorted. "You liked that joke, didn't you?"

She nodded. "You make me smile even when we're about to die."

I looked down at Dad. "You hear that? She thought my joke was funny."

Dad shook his head. "There's no accounting for taste."

"They're in range." Mom thrust out her fists and the rest of us followed suit. "Fire."

Eight sizzling beams of Brilliance speared into the swarm. Countless bodies were instantly incinerated, filling the sky with a cloud of ash. But the sheer bulk of the swarm pushed forward relentlessly, growing steadily closer and closer. Before long, I could barely see anything except ash and a sky black with locusts.

I had no choice. I had to use my Apocryphan powers. Before I could concentrate and make the switch, the swarm slammed into us. Ivy screamed. Mom and Nightliss vanished. And I plummeted toward the ground, propelled by countless bodies. Slashing with my wings, I managed to spin myself around. An instant later, my wings vanished. The swarm had carried me out of the aether beam.

The ground rushed to meet me. I hit the hard-packed earth and rolled to a stop a few feet from the crystoid. Ivy slammed next to me. Mom and Nightliss dropped nearly a hundred yards away. I sensed movement coming from the darkness and peered into it as if I might be able to make out shapes.

The movement reached the light, revealing another roach army, this one heading straight for us. Mom and Nightliss were in their path, pinned down by attacks from the swarm. I turned in a circle, looking for Dad and saw him fighting off a pair of roaches. There was no way for me to get back into the aether beam. No way for me to save them.

Ivy struggled to her feet. "Those bastards!" Her voice deepened demonically. "I will tear them from this world!"

I gripped her arm. "Ivy, calm down."

"I will feast on their blood!" she roared.

"They don't have blood, and that's just gross." I looked up the hill and prayed Elyssa and the others had escaped. They would at least have time to plan for the end. There really was nothing else to do at this point.

The crystoid hummed and glowed malevolently as it sucked the Void dry of magic. I'd thought it would automatically kill the swarm. I'd hoped the Beast relied on magic to control his minions. Apparently, he did not. I wished I'd brought explosives with me. Detonating a crystoid would unleash an explosion of malaether not unlike a magical nuke, but I didn't even have that option.

Going out with a bang would be preferable to being dismembered by roaches, but I might as well wish for rainbows and lollipops at this point. Then another idea occurred to me. The possibility of death was only slightly less, but at least we'd take as many nasties with us as we could.

I hauled Ivy back as she tried to run toward the others again. "I know how we can destroy them."

She turned to me, eyes burning. "How?"

I pointed toward the spikes jutting from the crystoid. "We each grab one of those. It'll overload us and we won't have much control, but if we aim right, we can take out most of the swarm."

Ivy nodded and the flames in her eyes flickered out. "Let's kill them, bro."

I marched to the crystoid and hesitantly reached a hand for one of the long spikes. The last time I'd done this, I'd blown a hole in a hillside and nearly burned myself to a husk. I'd managed to let go back then. This time I planned to hold on until I was dead.

I aimed one armored hand toward the swarm and gripped the spike with my other. The effect was instantaneous. Power surged into me, the sickly sweet poison of malaether. It thrummed through the armor, through my body and exploded from my other hand. Somewhere distantly, I heard screaming and realized it was me. Ivy's screams soon joined my own. Crackling yellow energy surged from our hands and into the swarm. It was like killing flies with a baseball bat.

Massive swaths of locusts turned to dust. My body was locked into place like a kid who'd just stuck a fork into an electrical outlet. I tried to adjust my aim, but my muscles were rigid. The swarm came for us. Gritting my teeth, I managed to adjust my arm slightly. Ivy did the same and the once infinite swarm was suddenly reduced to a smaller cloud.

Nightliss appeared next to me. She locked her hand around my wrist. The overload of energy lessened ever so slightly as her body acted like an extra circuit breaker, taking some of the load off me. I aimed my fist at the roach army coming from the darkness and slashed hundreds to burning chunks in one swipe.

Nightliss yanked me free from the crystoid. Ivy lay gasping on the ground, her head in Mom's lap. I felt like an overdone steak, but if memory served, I didn't feel nearly as bad as the last time this had happened.

Dad hefted me and threw me over a shoulder. I grunted as his long strides carried me across the wasteland. Moments later, we were back in the oasis and through the portal into the Razor lab.

"Let me down." My throat was rough from screaming so much.

He set me on my feet. Surprisingly, I didn't keel over.

Shelton got right in my face. "Dude, that was epic! You and Ivy looked like freaking Ghostbusters!"

I grabbed his shoulders. "Get me a rocket launcher."

"Say what?" He looked around. "Elyssa, Justin's asking for a rocket launcher."

Elyssa shoved Shelton to the side. "Justin, we don't have rocket launchers."

"Not true." Adam fit himself in between Elyssa and Shelton. "There's a crate full of missiles used by Razor drones, but we don't have a drone to use them with."

"Get me one." I said.

Adam dashed away.

"Justin, what in the hell are you going to do?" Elyssa gripped my shoulders. "We escaped. We lived to fight another day."

I shook my head. "We killed most of the local swarm. We've got to finish the mission."

Adam returned a moment later with four missiles. They weren't much bigger than his index finger, but they were extremely powerful. "We don't have anything to fire them from."

"Can I set them to detonate?" I asked.

"I thought you might ask that." He produced an electro grenade. "Just pull the pin and it should set them off."

I managed a weak smile. "Got any duct tape?"

Elyssa sighed and plucked a small roll of gray tape from her side satchel. "You want to blow up the crystoid, don't you?"

I nodded.

"Let me do it." She looked me up and down. "You can't run."

Cutsauce yipped. *I can run like the wind!* He morphed into a hound the size of a small horse with a long mane along his neck. *Let me carry you, Justin.*

"Now that's what I'm talking about." I tried to climb on.

"Are you insane?" Elyssa grabbed my arm and pulled me off. "You nearly burned yourself out less than five minutes ago."

"The armor protected me." I flexed my fingers. "It wasn't nearly as bad as the last time."

Adam finished taping together the makeshift bomb. "It's ready."

I blew Elyssa a kiss through the bubble helmet. "I'll be back."

Shelton grimaced. "That was a horrible Schwarzenegger impression."

I climbed onto Cutsauce. "Get to the choppah, Billy!"

Okay, Justin! He trotted back through the portal and into the oasis. *Will the swarm eat me?*

"I don't think there's enough left of it right now." I gripped his mane. "Just run fast."

I'm very fast. He emerged from the oasis and into the wasteland. *It smells like brimstone and rock crab farts out here. I'm glad I can breathe anything.*

I nudged his sides with my feet and turned him downhill. "Let's go."

Cutsauce surged forward so fast I nearly fell over backward, and would have if not for my death grip on his mane. I leaned forward, putting my head against his neck as we sped across the land. Darkness crept up the horizon as if someone were pulling a black curtain over the world. It took a moment to process what it was—a swarm so large it dwarfed the one we'd faced earlier.

The Beast's creatures covered this realm. It seemed he was recalling the entire freaking swarm to crush me like an insect.

I think there is more than enough swarm to eat me, Cutsauce said. *But they will not catch us*. He picked up speed, hurtling toward the crystoid so fast, I didn't think we could possibly stop in time. The roach army skittered from among the bodies of those I'd killed moments ago and rushed to intercept us.

Cutsauce put on the brakes, skidding sideways to a stop. I held on for dear life as the crystoid spikes grew alarmingly close. We stopped scant inches from one. That was when I realized I hadn't asked Adam one crucial question.

"I don't know how long we'll have from the time I pull the pin to detonation."

Then this will be very exciting. Cutsauce turned away from the crystoid. *I am ready.*

The swarm began to blot out the dim sunlight and the roaches were nearly upon us. One way or the other, we were out of time. I pulled the pin on the electro-grenade and tossed the duct-taped missile bomb to the top of the crystoid. I wrapped my arms around Cutsauce's neck as the roaches blocked our path.

"Go!" I shouted.

Growling and baring his fangs, Cutsauce plowed through the roach soldiers, sending them flying left and right. Mandibles clacked, narrowly missing my arms and legs. A roach leapt onto my back and started chomping at my bubble helmet. I elbowed it hard in its soft underside, but it wouldn't let go.

I reached over my shoulder and grabbed the bug's head, pulling as hard as I could. With a terrible pop, it tore free and the lifeless corpse fell away. I tossed the head away. "Looks like we're gonna—"

The missiles exploded.

I winced. "—make it?"

Is it okay to look back? Cutsauce asked. *Shelton said that action heroes don't look back at things they blow up.*

I looked back. A shockwave of superheated energy rushed behind us, sweeping up the roaches and obliterating everything in its path. "Don't look back, just run!"

Panting like the bellows of a forge, he surged even faster. But there was no outrunning a shockwave of pure energy. We were about to be flash-fried.

CHAPTER 29

I felt the approaching heat even through my armor. At the last
instant, Cutsauce leapt. We soared up the last few feet of hillside
and flew into the oasis. He stumbled through the portal and we
skidded across the floor.

"Close it!" Elyssa shouted.

The portal generator clicked off and the deafening roar of the explosion
cut off. Shelton and Adam pulled me to my feet. I deactivated the helmet
and was instantly overwhelmed by the odor of burnt doghair.

Cutsauce limped on singed hind legs. *Having a real body is painful
sometimes.*

I scratched behind his huge ears. "Are you okay, boy?"

I will heal.

I flopped his ears back and forth. "We did it!"

He gave me a puppy-dog grin. *Yes, we did.*

But we weren't done yet. "Adam, I need twenty-five more bombs."

He grinned. "I'm on it."

I turned to Cutsauce. "Can you ask Saila if she's up for opening more portals?"

Cutsauce paused panting for a moment. *She can, but it will be slow.*

"Just ask her to do what she can." It was going to take Adam a while to construct the bombs, plus we were out of duct tape. In the meantime, it was probably safe to go back into the Void. I turned to Elyssa. "Let's go see what it looks like in there."

She grabbed my head and pulled me in for a kiss. "You're crazy."

I chuckled. "I'm not the only one."

Ivy gave me a thumb's up from across the room. "We blasted 'em good, didn't we, bro?"

"It was a blasting of epic proportions." I traced the symbols for the Void and concentrated on the image of the oasis, then slashed open the portal. Surprisingly, the oasis was still intact. I activated my helmet and Elyssa did the same.

Mom, Dad, Ivy, and others turned theirs on and followed us into the portal. I peered hesitantly through the barrier. The wasteland looked a bit more singed, but no worse for the wear. The bug bodies that had once littered the area were gone, bits of ash and burnt limbs the only evidence they'd ever been there.

We walked to the hillside and looked down at the plains. A blackened crater sat at the epicenter of charred, baked earth. The heart of darkness was gone, revealing the ruins of a conical building with spikes protruding irregularly from the sides. As for the swarm, there wasn't a single bug to be seen. Since the swarm covered the realm, I imagined there were still plenty more bugs to go, but they were too far away to get here anytime soon. Adam's bombs would detonate the other crystoids and hopefully wipe out most of the rest.

For now, it seemed safe to take a walk and see who or what resided inside the strange building. Like the other structures I'd seen in the Void, I felt nauseated staring at it for too long. The insanity of the people who'd built it was evident in every irregular angle and twist.

We'd just reached the outskirts of the area when a figure emerged from the building. He was hunched over and walked with a shambling gait. Thick tumors sprouted from his back, pulsating with dark energy. Infected scabs covered his skin. The face was twisted and horrific, the eyes wide, black and glassy. But the general shape of the face looked too similar to be coincidence.

This creature could have been the stunted misshapen brother of Baal himself. He opened his mouth, moaning like a cow in pain. Then the noises escalated to screeches. I tried to put my hands over my ears, but the helmet prevented it.

"It's awful!" Ivy said.

I knew the answer but asked anyway. "Are you the Beast?"

Black liquid dribbled from the corner of its mouth. It moaned and screeched again, its gaze searching the sky. Without warning, it lunged for us, flickering and blurring like something out of a nightmare.

Ivy unleashed a torrent of Brilliance, slashing the creature to burning chunks. Black liquid exploded from the tumors and the Beast cried out horrifically as if a thousand donkey-monkey-bear-cows were tossed into a blender at once.

"Get me out of here!" Shelton danced backward, shuddering. "This place is bizarro world!"

I looked down at the smoldering heap of the Beast. "Is it really dead?"

Shelton gagged. "I ain't touching it to find out."

I tried not to look at the building, but it was like trying to look away from a train wreck. Dread filled me at what came next. "I have to go inside and find the sword."

Ivy made a sour face. "I really don't want to go near that place, but I guess if we have to."

"Yeah, we kind of have to." Elyssa seemed to gather herself. "Be extremely careful. There's no telling what horrors might be inside."

Dad snorted. "The outside is horror enough."

I forced myself to walk toward the building, but every step became progressively harder, as if the building projected a negative aura. "It's like forcing myself to walk into the grossest place in the world."

"You mean like a place that was home to giant roaches and a tumorous hunchback?" Elyssa grimaced as if she'd just smelled raw sewage. "Because that's what we're doing."

"Stop it!" Shelton shivered and shouted like a man who'd just walked into a giant spider web. "Don't make me think about it."

Summoning all my courage didn't help. I wasn't afraid of the building, but it filled me with dread and confusion. The structure defied logic. It toyed with the rational mind like looking at a puzzle that was too abstract to solve. Whatever this thing did, it defied all my attempts to make sense of it. There was only one way to deal with it.

I looked down at the ground and kept my attention there. Surprisingly, it worked. "Don't look at the building. Keep your eyes down."

"Hey, that's a lot better," Shelton said.

Ivy chimed in. "Ooh, my brain doesn't hurt as much anymore."

The next few minutes passed painfully slowly, but we finally reached the orifice that passed as a doorway. Rusted hunks of metal with misshapen gears and bellows sat just inside. I couldn't tell what purpose the machinery once served, but there was a wide belt connected to one end that might have once been an automated walkway.

Dark trails climbed the walls, grooves worn into the concrete by the massive number of roaches. The center was wide open, though I would hardly call it an atrium. Irregular patterns of dark holes spotted the walls, probably where the roaches nested.

I threw up a little in my mouth.

"Is that a sword?" Ivy pointed toward a tall green mound that might be dirt, or possibly a mound of roach poop. The hilt of a sword protruded from the side.

"Oh, thank god," Shelton said. "Let's grab it and get out."

"I'll get it." Keeping her eyes on the floor, Ivy jogged across the atrium. She reached the mound and slowed down to navigate the slope. The armored boots slipped but she managed to keep her balance. A few feet later, she reached out and yanked the sword. It came free with a wet sucking sound.

Black ichor spurted. Ivy screamed and tumbled backward. The mound rumbled. Ivy rolled out of the way and ran from the quivering mound. Like an overripe melon, it split open, releasing a wave of black liquid. We jumped back. Despite being in armor, the disgust factor was off the scale.

A lump in the center of the space where the mound had been caught my eye. It jerked spasmodically unfolding four limbs and a head. It crawled an all fours, unnaturally twisted like a contortionist. Its mouth opened horrifically wide and a black blob dropped out. A membrane burst. Brown ooze spread across the floor revealing an infant covered in tumors.

The newborn screeched horrifically, unfolding and growing at an incredible pace.

My cries of horror were echoed by all those around me. By the time our screams died down, the infant was a toddler, its body misshapen, a tumorous hump growing on its back. Ivy sped past me in her rush to get outside.

"Run for your life!" Shelton shouted.

He didn't have to tell me twice. I turned around and beat him out of the building. I stopped before I reached the corpse of the last tumor dude and turned around. I wasn't physically tired, but my heart raced as if it were about to burst.

Shelton stopped and leaned on his knees, panting. "That thing we killed wasn't the Beast."

I shook my head. "No, it wasn't."

He jammed a thumb over his shoulder. "Was that other thing inside the Beast?"

Mom and the others flew past us and stopped next to Ivy.

I nodded. "I think so."

The tumor toddler emerged from the building, already grown to nearly a tumor tween. I was tempted to burn it with fire, but the contorted nightmare that was possibly the Beast jerkily walked its way outside right behind him. I tried to make sense of the twisted shape and how it was possible to walk on all fours with its head turned a hundred and eighty degrees too far.

The new tumor kid stopped and stared, moaning and screeching. In jerky, imprecise spasms, the Beast twisted and unfolded until it stood its legs like a normal biped, its black eyes gazing dully at us.

Then it spoke in Cyrinthian. "Beings taste delighted fear essence drain kill living eternal of mine."

I blinked a few times, trying to make sense of it.

Then it spoke again. "Renew thrive will collective not eternal of mine forever gone."

Its voice seemed to rasp against my very soul, but I managed a response. "What?"

The tumor creature moaned and screeched. A scab on its arm peeled open and a locust crawled out and flew away.

"Jesus Christ on a hippity hop!" Shelton gagged. "I'm going to be even sicker."

"I think it's saying that it will regenerate the swarm, but the eternal creatures are gone forever." Nightliss looked around and found the husk of a burned roach. She pointed to it. "Eternal of yours?"

The Beast's head tilted so far sideways that its neck cracked and popped. "Eternal of mine forever gone."

Another scab popped open on the tumor kid and another locust buzzed away.

A distant explosion told me that Adam and Saila were dropping bombs on the remaining crystoids. But even if we wiped out the current swarm, it was evident that given enough time, the Beast's horrific children would replenish his stock.

"Why?" I said. "Why devour everything?"

The Beast's head tilted back the other way, causing the bones to press horrifically against the skin. "Not always past the same." Then the tumor kid turned and hobbled toward the building, its body flickering and blurring in and out of vision until it was gone.

"I think it means it was not always so," Nightliss said.

The Beast trembled. "Past gone never not always."

Nightliss made a face. "I didn't understand that."

"Children create. Children control." It said. "Never I."

Nightliss gasped. "I think the tumor babies make the swarm and control it, not the Beast."

Dad stepped closer to us. "It probably hasn't spoken in eons, and if its mind is as twisted as the Void, then it'll be hard, if not impossible, to understand."

The black eyes twitched, but the Beast said nothing.

One long, awkward silence later, the tumor kid reappeared, but now he was nearing adulthood. Another locust emerged from a scab in his head and took flight. With a screech, the kid threw a black stone the size of an apple at Nightliss. She gasped and caught it with two hands.

I expected something horrible to happen, but the stone didn't explode.

"Past and now," the Beast said. "Past and now."

Nightliss examined the stone. "I don't understand."

The stone cracked and unfurled into a giant slimy slug. Nightliss shrieked and dropped it.

The Beast slapped his arm. "It puts the past on the skin."

"Now that I understood," Shelton said. "And it'll be a cold day in hell before I'd put something the Beast gave me on my bare skin."

The slug curled up until it once again resembled a stone. Nightliss picked it up and nodded. "Yes, thank you."

Still clenching Unmaker, Ivy came closer. "What now? Do we leave with the sword?"

Knowing what little I knew, we didn't dare take the Beast out of here. It'd keep birthing tumor babies until it repopulated the swarm. So long as we had Unmaker, Baal couldn't complete his project. I doubted he'd want anything to do with the Beast until it was the last piece of the puzzle.

Or maybe...I looked at Unmaker and wondered if it could kill the Beast. That would permanently prevent Baal from succeeding. Then again, if he were truly a relic, nothing could kill him. It also seemed incredibly rude to kill someone after they just gave you a giant slug as a gift.

"Let's go." I didn't want to spend another moment here. I looked at the slug and considered leaving it, but what if it held useful information? Either way, it couldn't pass the barrier to the oasis, so I'd have to make another portal. But first, I wanted to be far away from the tumor kid. Allowing one of those in another realm would spell disaster.

"Thank you," I told the Beast. It was always best to be polite if possible, even to world-ending monsters. Then I led my people a good distance from him and his child.

I tapped the screen on the arm of my suit and pulled up the picture of an isolation room in the Razor facility, then traced the symbols for Eden and slashed open a portal. We stepped through, took one last look at the Beast, and then I closed it. The sooner I got that place out of my sight the better.

A table with a transparent containment unit sat against the wall. Nightliss put the slug inside and sealed it. The creature unfurled, eyestalks taking in its new environment, then it rolled back into a ball.

"I hope to god none of you are considering putting that thing on your skin," Shelton said. "It might eat you alive."

"Even if the Beast meant well, its mind is so twisted that it might not even know if it's compatible with our physiology," Nightliss said. "But I must admit I'm curious."

"The strange thing is that the Beast didn't seem evil." Ivy shook her head. "It was just gross and awful."

"A living horror," Mom said. "The darkest part of a soul, stunted and confused by everything others deem normal."

Dad scoffed. "I've seen some disturbing stuff in my life, but that thing and its entire world take the cake."

"We literally nuked its home and it didn't even seem to care." Shelton shook his head. "I thought for sure we'd have another fight on our hands."

I regarded the slug for a moment. "Or else it gave us a Trojan horse."

"We'll need to be extremely careful with it." Mom pressed her lips together. "This might be a horrible idea, but what if we tested it on the people in the time echo? Even if it hurts them, they'll just be back for the next cycle."

I grunted thoughtfully. "That's an excellent idea."

Ivy looked uneasily at the sword. "I feel like it's tugging in a direction. Is it supposed to do that?"

"It's trying to rejoin the other relics," I said. "Baal has nearly rebuilt his original body, and the sword is one of the final pieces."

Ivy held the sword out to me. "What now?"

"Good question." I gingerly took Unmaker by the handle since a cut from the blade was deadly. "And I haven't a clue."

The world, it seemed, was once again safe. Now we'd simply have to play keep away from Baal for the rest of eternity.

The end.

CHAPTER 30

"Well, this definitely ain't the end." Shelton shook his head. "We've one got one relic—one—and Baal's got almost all the others. He's got the full deck of cards and all we've got is a joker."

We'd gathered back at the Ranch to discuss options, but so far hadn't come up with a single one.

Adam shook his head. "The reason Baal has had so much success lately is because the more relics you gather in one place, the more the others gravitate toward them. No matter where we put the sword, it will try to reunite with the others."

"We can't put it in the time echo and putting it in another realm will only delay the inevitable." Cinder clasped his hands on the conference table. "Perhaps it is best to place it under heavy guard."

I'd been rolling around ideas in my head and there was only one that might solve the problem for the foreseeable future. "We have to attack Hell."

All eyes shifted toward me.

"You heard me right." I leaned my elbows on the table. "We need to take the relics and disperse them all over creation again."

Mom shook her head. "Son, I don't think we can pull that off."

"Sure, we can!" Ivy pumped her fist. "Let's go to Hell!"

Dad grinned but said nothing.

Thomas pursed his lips. "That might be a bit ambitious."

I projected an image of Eden and rotated it to the location the ASE had pinpointed as Hell. Unsurprisingly, it was in Australia. "We know where it is. All we have to do is portal in with an army and take it by surprise."

"No wonder everything in Australia can kill you," Shelton said. "It's literally Hell on earth."

"It's not the worst idea." Elyssa quirked her lips. "But we have no idea how many demons are there. Olivia is almost certainly there, and we don't have Emily around to fight her."

"We just fought a small part of Baal's demon army at Emily's wedding." Shelton shook his head. "Lest you forget, good buddy, old pal, you ended up dying."

"Mostly dying," I reminded him. I grinned. "Besides, we have a secret weapon this time."

Adam's eyes brightened. "Saila."

I nodded. "Saila."

Shelton grunted. "The ghost possessing your dog."

Cutsauce yipped and hopped up on the table. He spun in a circle and growled at Shelton.

Shelton looked at me. "What's he saying?"

"Uh, he hasn't said anything to me yet." I watched for another moment. "I think he's just showboating."

Cutsauce leapt off the table and morphed into Saila. "Apologies," she said. "Cutsauce and I were having an argument."

Shelton shook his head like a wet dog. "About what?"

"I think it would be unwise for me to go anywhere near the other relics." Saila looked downcast. "I fear my presence near Baal's collection may have unintended consequences."

Thomas nodded. "Do you feel pulled toward them?"

Saila nodded. "It feels like a riptide trying to suck me under."

I grimaced. "Then the Beast must feel the same thing."

"Yeah, but there's no way Baal is gonna get the Beast before he gets the sword," Shelton said. "Even he doesn't want that nasty creature walking around Hell puking up tumor kids."

"I don't think the Beast has any control over his children," Nightliss said. "It's almost as if he's a prisoner in the Void."

Elyssa nodded. "I can't believe I'm saying this, but hopefully the Beast regenerates the swarm so Baal can't get to him very easily."

"Agreed," Mom said.

I stared at the tiny red dot on the map. Without Saila, I'd have to rely heavily on my Apocryphan powers to fight Olivia and the demons. We'd be fighting on Baal's home turf against unknown odds. "We need Emily."

"That brings up another issue." Thomas pressed his lips into a line. "Emily still hasn't checked in."

I threw up my hands. "Do we need to go to Aquilis and find out what happened?"

Thomas paused before answering. "It's possible. So long as Baal has Olivia, we will be at an extreme disadvantage without Emily."

"Great." Shelton threw up his hands. "Does this mean we have to go on another adventure searching for Emily again?"

I sighed and ran my hands through my hair. "No, it just means we're going nowhere fast."

Elyssa patted my back. "Hey, we stopped Baal from getting Unmaker and that's not nothing."

I nodded. "I know, but the stress of wondering when and how he'll try to steal it is killing me."

"You and me both." Shelton patted his chest. "Feels like a knot right there."

Adam stood. "Since we have some free time, Cinder and I are going to go into the time echo and try to find Elohim. It's a long shot, but we want to see if there's a way to track the creation of relics at the moment of the Sundering."

I stood. "I want to meet Elohim and punch him in the face."

"Not a good idea," Adam said. "He can still kill you."

"We plan to covertly observe." Cinder clasped his hands behind his back. "We will be dressing in accordance to the styles of the time to avoid incidents like our first visit."

"Good idea." I motioned them toward the door. "Let's go dress up."

"I'm coming too." Elyssa hopped out of her seat. "Are there enough clothes for all of us?"

Cinder nodded. "The fashion is much like the styles in Zbura before we toppled the Brightling Empire."

"I might as well join you." Shelton tipped his wide-brimmed hat back. "I ain't no fan of robes, but I don't feel like sitting around either."

"I would like to see this time remnant," Saila said.

"You probably won't be able to enter it." Adam pushed a finger up his nose. "Relics can't seem to enter the portal."

"And I am a relic." Saila nodded. "May I at least try?"

He shrugged. "Sure."

"Oh, to see the world when it was young and whole." Saila sighed. "Sometimes I wish I had died instead of continuing this pale existence."

"Can I come?" Ivy asked.

Mom shook her head. "You need to rest and then it's training time for you, young lady."

Dad mussed her hair. "Real proud how you handled yourself today, kiddo, but we need to work on that demon temper of yours."

Ivy sagged. "Aw, okay. It sucks still being a kid even though I'm supposed to be an adult."

I felt her pain. "Hey, you were amazing today, Ivy. I can't wait for you to get control over your demon powers." I'd gone through hell and high water to get training from my father, namely being trapped in the Gloom with him where he had no choice.

Ah, the good old days.

I bid my family adieu and turned to Nightliss. "What about you?"

She rubbed her eyes. "I want nothing but sleep right now. I do not understand how you keep going."

"You're not getting enough tacos in your diet." Shelton patted his belly. "I'm chock full of energy."

"And farts," Adam said.

Nightliss smiled. "I can certainly attest to that." She stretched languidly like a cat. "I will see you later."

The rest of us left and followed Adam to one of the storage rooms where we kept all the odds and ends we accumulated during our travels. Clothing from Seraphina filled several racks along the center of the warehouse. "Find something that fits and meet back in the hallway."

Elyssa and I found suitable attire, then went to our room and changed. The others were waiting when we returned.

I noticed another set of robes draped over Adam's arm. "What are those for?"

"Xanos." He started walking toward the prison. "She knows the lay of the land and will increase our odds of finding Elohim."

"Xanos?" Saila scowled.

I realized that Saila had been resting when Cutsauce saw Xanos and hadn't had a chance to see her yet. "We're making do with what we can."

A growl rose in her throat and Cutsauce spoke. *Xanos is a bad girl.*

I nodded. "Yeah, she's a bad girl."

That comment drew confused looks from my friends.

Elyssa snorted. "Did Cutsauce say that?"

"Yep." I shrugged. "He isn't wrong."

We waited in the hall while Adam retrieved the prisoner. When Xanos joined us, she did a double-take of Saila. "You look familiar."

"I should." Saila scowled. "Though you're barely a shadow of your former self."

Xanos's eyes widened. "Saila?"

"Yes." Saila gripped Xanos by the throat and pinned her to the wall. "Your trickery led to the destruction of a beautiful world!"

Xanos struggled uselessly, slapping at Saila's hands.

Saila flinched and dropped her. "I have committed violence against someone who cannot defend herself." A tear trickled down her cheek. "I apologize for my rage."

Shelton snorted. "Hey, I don't blame you one bit."

Xanos fell to her knees. "How?" she gasped. "How do you consider that world beautiful when my siblings ruled it mercilessly?"

Saila gently lifted Xanos to her feet. "They grew weary and bored of Earth. I had nearly convinced them to seek ventures elsewhere, out among the stars. Then I could have healed the Earth and the ideals of Juranthemon would have bonded together all life."

Xanos rubbed her throat. "Wishful thinking. My plan was to let them destroy each other and leave me the sole heir to the Earth."

"Even if that had come to pass, Juranthemon would have paid the price." Saila shook her head. "Cutsauce is right. You are a bad girl."

Xanos sagged and looked down. "I was an arrogant fool."

Shelton cleared his throat. "Can we get the show on the road? I've had enough of Xanos and her worthless apologies."

"Just one more stop," Adam said.

We dropped by Cinder's lab and retrieved the portal generator, then went to the travel room. I showed Saila a picture of the area and she opened a portal to the area behind the burned down mansion. Adam and Cinder began setting up with help from Xanos, who occasionally cast wary glances at Saila.

Shelton turned to me. "Hey, what about the slug?"

I'd nearly forgotten about it. I showed Saila an image of the containment room we'd stored it in. "Mind opening another portal?"

"Of course." She slashed one open and I hopped through. I found a pair of gloves and gingerly removed the slug from the large container. Since carrying it around with a glove would look odd to the citizens of Juranthemon, I found a smaller black container and dropped the slug inside. Then I hopped back through the portal and rejoined the others.

Since Nightliss and my parents were with us, I began explaining to Saila how to open a portal scar.

She frowned. "That is quite a convoluted method."

I shrugged. "It's the only way we know."

"Ah." Saila rubbed her fingers together like a chef sprinkling ingredients onto a pizza. Droplets of water seemingly appeared from nowhere, dripping onto the soil. Where they fell, the scar faded into view and crystalized into solidity.

My mouth dropped open. "How are you doing that?"

"I'm simply weaving Stasis and Clarity into liquid form," she said. "Even Seraphim can do it."

"Liquid?" My voice rose. "Tell me how, please!"

"Uh, can it wait until later?" Adam said. "I'd rather open the portal first."

I turned to Xanos. "Did you know about this?"

She shook her head. "We were not given much instruction with our powers."

Saila scoffed. "You only had to listen. The Sirens and Seraphim were wonderful teachers. Thankfully, my father allowed me to grow up among those he considered lesser. My Lyrolai mother made sure I had instruction from all different races."

I snapped my fingers. "That's right. I'd forgotten your mother was one of the Glimmer folk."

"The Glimmer did not exist then," Saila said. "In my eons of travel, I was unable to reach the Glimmer to see if my mother survived."

"Yeah, well most of the Glimmer folk are asleep." Adam shook his head. "If she's alive, she's probably still slumbering."

"Uh, you guys gonna open that portal scar, or what?" Shelton said.

I looked down at the solidified scar. "Oh, yeah." I looked at Saila. "Any tips for opening it?"

She examined it for a moment. "I believe prying it open is the most effective way." Hands glowing green, she put her fingers against the thin line. With one solid jerk, the portal ripped open. The clap of thunder and shockwave rocked me back on my heels.

Adam turned on the portal generator to stabilize the gateway. The room from yesterday was once again on the other side. Saila reached down but an invisible barrier stopped her hand from going through the portal. She sighed and stood. "I'm nothing more than a ghost of a relic."

"I'm sorry." Adam awkwardly patted her back. "Dude, this is so strange. I'm petting Cutsauce and comforting Saila at the same time."

Shelton snorted. "I don't think you're comforting anyone, buddy. You're just making it awkward."

Adam grinned sheepishly. "That's my specialty."

"Amen to that," Shelton said.

Adam stepped next to the portal, reached inside, and withdrew an arctablet from the other side. He stood and stared silently at the screen, once again making things awkward.

Cinder answered the unspoken question. "We placed an arctablet in the void to measure how long it took for the next cycle to begin."

Adam tapped the screen and nodded. "The total cycle is fifty-two hours, three minutes, eleven seconds." He tapped the screen again. "I'm only extrapolating since I don't have a complete cycle recorded, but I think we have about thirty-six hours until the Sundering."

"So, Conrad and Ambria were spending sixteen hours in the void each cycle?" I shuddered. "No wonder they went loco."

"I totally forgot to check in on them while we were at the Ranch." Shelton shook his head. "Max wasn't taking it very well."

"I checked on them," Cinder said. "They were conscious and appeared to have mostly recovered their facilities, though it will be some time before they are back to normal."

Adam chuckled. "At least one of us is a good friend."

Saila regarded the portal. "I dearly wish to see my city again. Perhaps you could use your device to record it for me?"

Adam nodded. "Sure. I'll bring you some pictures."

One by one we slipped into the portal in the ground and pushed ourselves off the floor in the room on the other side. Saila watched from the other side, regret heavy on her face, then walked out of sight.

Adam took out his phone. "I activated a beacon on an arctablet that will guide us back to the portal in case anyone gets lost or stuck in the void."

Shelton frowned. "That's smart and all, but how are we supposed to move in a void?"

"The tablet tracks your arcphones, so maybe we can toss you a rope?" Adam shrugged. "We'll figure out something."

"Let's just try to get out in time, okay?" I checked the timer on my phone. "Unless something goes horribly wrong, we've got plenty of time to explore."

"You know something is gonna go wrong," Shelton said dryly. "It always does."

CHAPTER 31

S helton scoffed. "Maybe we should've brought brooms so we can fly through the void in case we get caught."

Adam snapped his fingers. "Why didn't I think of that?"

"Because they don't have flying brooms in this time." I pointed out the window. "Or flying carpets, for that matter."

"Let's stick together." Elyssa looked at the slug container. "I feel bad saying this, but let's test that out on some unsuspecting citizen first, then we'll look for Elohim."

Xanos looked curiously at the cube. "What is in there?"

We hadn't told her about our recent venture into the Void and I didn't see a good reason to fully inform her now. "You'll see."

"Aren't most of the citizens Seraphim and Sirens?" Shelton said. "Might be hard to force one of them to use it."

"We'll trick them into it." Elyssa shrugged. "Easy."

"So you say." Shelton shook his head. "Nothing is ever easy with us."

Cinder tapped Adam on the shoulder. "Perhaps it would be best to hide Xanos's purple skin?"

"Oh, good point." Adam took out his arcphone and aimed it at Xanos. "The robes cover most of her skin, but that face would stand out." He tapped the screen and an illusion gave her an olive complexion.

Shelton grunted. "Glad Cinder is here for the small details, or we'd end up fighting Ussor again."

With all our ducks in a row, we left the building, took some narrow side streets, and started hunting for a victim. Elyssa pointed to a Siren who was painting the cityscape with watercolors. I shook my head. A little further on we found a woman weaving flower-covered vines into the shape of a giant unicorn. I shook my head again.

We finally found a café with a lone man drinking from an ornate seashell. This time I nodded my head.

"Ain't that sweet." Shelton chuckled. "Justin won't experiment on females, but men are fair game."

"Justin, these people don't even exist," Adam reminded me. "At least not in the conventional sense."

I shrugged. "Whatever. Let's test the slug on the man."

I gave Elyssa the cube. "You're up."

She rolled her eyes. "Gee, thanks."

We sat at a nearby table while Elyssa approached the mark.

The man looked up from a parchment he was reading and smiled. "May I help you?"

Elyssa sat at the table and opened the cube. "I found this strange rock and don't know what it is. Have you ever seen anything like it?" She tilted the box and the chunky black rock rolled out."

The man's brow furrowed. "Well, it's not from the ocean, I can tell you that." He reached for it and rolled it around in his hand. The slug unfurled and he gasped in surprise. "Why, it's not a rock at all!" He grimaced as the slug crawled covered his hand. "This thing is monstrous."

Elyssa gagged, but managed to speak. "It's huge and gross."

He nodded. "I'm a trident, so I can confidently say it's not from the Siren domain. But I met some Lyrolai a few years ago who mentioned creatures like this wandering the midwest regions of Stygia."

"Stygia?" Elyssa tilted her head. "I'm not familiar with that."

"The dark lands." He frowned. "It's the one place not even the Apocryphan venture."

"I led a very sheltered life," Elyssa said. "Can you tell me more about it?"

He chuckled. "Anything for a beautiful woman." He pointed to himself. "I'm Tritain."

Elyssa blushed. "I'm Elyssa."

Shelton snorted. "I think she likes him."

I elbowed him. "Shut up."

Tritain rubbed a seashell bracelet on his left wrist and a holographic image of the world appeared. It looked nearly identical to Eden, but the labels were different. Juranthemon was highlighted by a glowing dot right at the southern tip of where Portugal would be in Eden.

The Stygia he'd mentioned was Australia. The continent was larger and roughly the same shape. Tritain rotated the image and zoomed in. The land was black, dotted by craggy trees and brambles.

"The region is covered in hell founts, so demons of all shapes and sizes will sometimes climb to the surface." He continued zooming in until tiny moving shapes on the ground resolved into bizarre monsters shambling over the awful terrain.

That was when I noticed the buildings. They were conical, irregularly shaped, and with spikes protruding at all angles.

Elyssa gasped. "It's awful!"

Tritain removed the slug from his hand and set it on the table. "It's said the lands of the infernal lord can drive even gods mad. Ironically enough, I've heard rumors that one of the original gods himself is in Juranthemon."

"I've heard such rumors as well," Elyssa said.

He leaned forward conspiratorially. "Some even say he comes to overthrow the Apocryphan and reclaim the world."

A sudden tremble from Xanos caught my eye. "What's wrong?"

"Where did you get that slug?" She looked at me.

I decided to tell her. "The Void. Why?"

"I knew I had seen such a creature before." Xanos trembled again. "Elohim created his own demigod, Apollyon, sometime after Eve birthed Kathazal. But his creation was sick and twisted, so Eve banished him to the bottom of the world where he became known as the infernal lord."

Adam pursed his lips. "The god of Hell?"

Xanos nodded. "I wondered what happened to him after the Sundering. Now I know."

Shelton blinked. "You mean the Beast isn't part of Elohim after all?"

"Yes and no." Xanos's gaze went distant. "Baal is Elohim and Baal is Apollyon." Her eyes focused on me. "The world was sundered, but parts of Elohim and Apollyon became one."

Now I was really confused. "Baal is a combination of two gods?"

She nodded. "I'm almost certain. Apollyon long sought to confront his father for making him such a monstrosity. Perhaps the rumors I spread of Elohim in Jura also drew him here."

"The law of unintended consequences." Adam folded his arms across his chest. "If Apollyon is anything like the Beast, he'll be easy to pick out of a crowd."

A brief shriek yanked my attention away from Xanos. Eyestalks extended, the slug and Elyssa seemed to be in a staring contest. The look of horror faded from Elyssa's face, slowly relaxing to numbness.

"Are you okay, milady?" Tritain snapped his fingers, but Elyssa didn't so much as flinch.

I jumped from my seat and put my hand between Elyssa's eyes and the slugs. She blinked, shivered, and gasped. I rubbed her cheek. "Are you okay?"

She nodded. "Yes. I-I was somewhere else."

"The slug!" Tritain raised a fist as if to crush it.

I put a hand on his wrist. "Wait!"

He frowned and withdrew his hand. "Why do I get the feeling you know this woman and this slug?"

I sighed. "I'm sorry. We thought a pretty woman would get more answers than us."

Tritain narrowed his eyes. "Good manners get more cooperation than trickery." He gulped the last of his tea, turned his back, and left in a huff.

Shelton gave me a slow clap. "Nice work, man. You're a real trickster."

"Yeah, yeah." The slug's eyestalks had retracted, and it looked ready to curl into a ball again. Holding my breath, I reached out and poked the slimy flesh. It had the consistency of boogers and moldy gelatin. My gorge rose out of disgust, but I didn't feel otherwise sick or infected. Apparently, touching the slug wasn't dangerous, but that didn't mean I wanted to do it.

"Its eyestalks stretched out and it stared at me for a moment, then I was suddenly in the middle of a forest." Elyssa rubbed her eyes. "It felt like I was someone else."

I took Tritain's abandoned seat and turned the slug toward me. "That must be how it works."

The slug's eyestalks rose slightly, and it watched me for a moment, as if making sure I was serious about what was about to happen. When I maintained eye contact, the stalks stretched out. I suddenly dove forward, falling into blackness.

I stand in a sunlit meadow filled with life. Colorful birds sing in the trees. Deer and their fawns dance in the grass. The beauty of this moment fills me with joy. I laugh and spin in a circle. The joy wells up inside me until I am full to bursting. I speak, but the words are garbled, like a toddler trying to form a coherent sentence.

Silence settles over the meadow. The grass withers, the trees wilt, and birds fall to the ground. The deer writhe and buck before slumping to the ground. The belly of a fawn swells and bursts. A swarm of flies buzzes out, falling upon the other corpses and feasting.

"What is this?" A deep voice booms. Elohim drops from the sky like a meteor and lands before me. "In all this time you have learned nothing?" He slashes a hand and flames consume the flies, the animal corpses, and the dead grass. "Your power is corrupted."

"Make life," I say. "Want more life."

Elohim shakes his head. "I have protected you as long as I can. Confined you to this island to keep you from tainting the world. You were supposed to counter Kathazal and maintain balance, but I wish I had never made you." He thrusts a hand against my head and the world seems to dim. "I will not kill you, but I have muted your powers. You will remain here until I decide how to deal with you." He leaps into the sky and is gone.

The world continues to dim, and sadness overwhelms me until I cannot even move.

MUCH TIME HAS PASSED. The barren patch where the meadow was has never healed, but the rest of the land thrives. I have survived like a wild animal, eating what I can. Sometimes it makes me deathly ill. I vomit until it seems death is certain, but I do not die. The veil Father placed on me has slowly lifted and I feel my powers returning.

IT IS FURTHER in the future and the island is a desolate wasteland, covered in flies and misshapen beasts that rise from the corpses of other animals. Where once there was the scent of flowers, trees, and grass, there is now only a rotten stench from the boiling sores in the ground. I miss the beauty that was once here, but I am slowly coming to love these creations of mine.

A bright star descends from the sky, lighting the darkness of night until it is like day. A beautiful woman appears and regards me silently. She is not smiling.

"So, you are the abomination Elohim hid from me." She spits on the ground. "You are a taint upon my creation. A destroyer."

"I...love beauty." The words are so difficult to form because I have not made them in so long. "You beautiful."

A sad smile crosses her lips. "It is not your fault, child." She puts a hand on my forehead. "I cannot take your powers, nor can I kill you. Elohim succeeded in making something truly eternal but failed in every other way."

I sigh with pleasure at the touch of another person. "Lonely. So lonely."

Tears fill her eyes. "What has he done but condemn a soul to an eternity of this?" She sighs. "You cannot remain here, but I have prepared a place which will suit you well. It is a deadly land, filled with monsters and isolated from the rest of Earth. It will be your home forevermore."

"Who are you?" I ask.

She stroked my hair. "I am Eve, child. If I can ever free you from this curse of a life, then I will do so. For now, let us get you to your new home." Eve slashes a hand in the air and a new world is revealed on the other side of a gateway. We step through and my new journey begins.

The first-person view receded, and I found myself sitting on a stone in the middle of nowhere. A perfectly proportioned young man sat on a neighboring stone, a broad smile on his face. He was the most beautiful human I'd ever seen, perfectly proportioned with flawless dark green skin. It hurt just looking at him.

I sucked in a ragged breath. "Apollyon?"

He nodded. "I am memories of before. Want show life." His words were slow and slurred. "What want see?"

I could barely stand to look at his beauty, so I diverted my eyes. There was so much I wanted to know, but at this moment, only one critical time period came to mind. "Show me how you found Elohim in Juranthemon."

"Father." A tear trickled down his cheek. "I show."

"Wait." I held up a hand. "How do I wake up?"

He clapped his hands twice in rapid succession, then flicked his nose.

I waited for more, but that seemed to be it. "Okay, thanks."

Apollyon grinned. "Welcome, friend."

I hesitated with my next question. "You're not mad that I killed the Void swarm?"

He shook his head. "I am monster. Bad."

"Damn." I felt awful for him. He wanted beauty but killed everything around him. It had to be the most horrific existence ever. "I'm ready to see your father."

I must find Father. Only he can kill me and end this misery. I escape Hell and wander the world for many years to find him. As long as I do not stay still for long, I will not corrupt the world or leave many dead in my wake. I hurry and search, then leave. Many have heard a rumor that Father is going to Juranthe-mon. I go there next.

I AM at last in the fabled city of Jura. It is so beautiful I cannot keep tears from my eyes. I pray Father is here for there is no other place I would rather die than this paradise. I am sad for my demons because they will miss me. But all life will be better when I am dead.

DAYS HAVE PASSED, but finally, I sense my father. He is disguised in colorful striped robes, but his smell is unlike the others. I believe he is the man ahead of me. I hurry to catch up. Seraphim and Sirens watch me in wonder, and I realize my head covering has slipped.

"Who are you?" A female stops me. "You are so beautiful I can hardly stand it."

"Perfection," a seraph says. "Please, may I touch you?"

"No!" I shout and cover my head before ducking into a narrow alley. I run from the throng until I am alone. But the scent of Father is fading. I make my way back to the main thoroughfare leading to Unity. Shadows flit across the sky as angels soar on clouds and wings. They called me beautiful, but I am not. They are the perfect ones.

Overcome by a strange feeling, I clap my hands twice and flick my nose.

I GASPED and jerked back from the gaze of the slug. The others were crowded around me, concern and confusion plain on their faces.

"Dude, you're crying." Adam shook his head. "What did you see?"

Elyssa wiped my cheeks with her thumb. "What happened, babe?"

I tried to speak, but the sharp pain of sadness choked my words. Having seen Apollyon was unlike anything I'd ever experienced. Seeing his sad existence through his eyes weighed heavy as lead in my chest. It took everything I had not to burst into tears. I held up a hand and took deep breaths to recover.

I knew how to find Apollyon, but if my experience in his memories was any indication, finding him might be more dangerous than locating Elohim.

CHAPTER 32

"**M**ust have been awful." Shelton shuddered. "If the Void fucked with our minds, I can't even imagine what this slug does."

My voice finally returned. "I know where Apollyon is." I looked up at the sky. The sun was nearly in the same position it had been in the memory. "He's in an orange cloak that covers his head."

"Orange?" Shelton looked like he'd eaten a lemon. "Who the hell wears an orange cloak?"

"Someone with zero sense of fashion." I sighed. "Someone who's known nothing but eternal loneliness." My body felt heavy as I pushed to my feet.

Elyssa slipped a hand around my waist. "What else did you see?"

"We can talk about it later." I leaned my head on her shoulder. "All I can say is, I feel terrible for Apollyon."

Cinder picked up the slug and put it in the box. "I am most curious to see if I can also connect with the slug."

"I wouldn't recommend anyone do that." I swallowed a lump in my throat. "Also, avoid looking at Apollyon's face if you can."

"That horrific?" Shelton said.

I shook my head. "He's so beautiful it hurts. Believe me when I say it will fuck you up harder than anything you saw in the Void."

Adam grunted. "Now I really want to see what he looks like."

I gripped his robes and stopped him. "Believe me, you don't."

Adam flinched and held up his hands. "Not even for science?"

"There's nothing scientific about this entity." The weight slowly lifted from my shoulders as we walked, and I was finally able to stop leaning on Elyssa. "You'll regret it if you see his face."

"I ain't taking chances," Shelton said. "Seeing Justin bawling his eyes out was more than enough to convince me."

Adam chuckled. "True."

Xanos watched me as we walked. "May I view his memories some time?"

I nodded. "Knock yourself out." If Xanos had an ounce of humanity in her it would certainly change her perspective on life.

I looked around for a good vantage point over the main thoroughfare. Sometime over the next hour, Apollyon would walk right past here. A serpentine building with multiple balconies seemed to be the best spot, but before we got there, a disturbance a few hundred yards back drew my attention.

A figure in an orange robe burst from a crowd and ducked into an alley. I hadn't seen another robe even remotely as ugly on anyone else, meaning it had to be our quarry. Before I could point it out, a man in a striped robe shoved past me, nearly bowling me over. I stumbled against Elyssa and caught my balance.

I got one good look at the man's back as he vanished into the crowd ahead. "That was Elohim!"

Shelton did a double-take. "Who? Where?"

"He just shoved past me." I held up a hand. "But I also saw Apollyon behind us."

Elyssa nodded. "I saw him, too. I think we can head him off if we go this way."

I shook my head. "No, I know where he'll go next." I led them back down the thoroughfare and onto a side street with the silver conch house I'd seen in the memory. "Just wait here."

"This is freaky." Shelton touched the glossy silver house. "We're in a time echo tracking down the devil by using his own memories."

Adam shrugged. "Stranger things have happened."

I tilted my head. "Have they, though?"

Cinder tilted his head the other way. "I am not a qualified judge on strangeness, but this is quite unusual, even for us."

"In all my life, this is the strangest thing to ever happen to me." Xanos clasped her hands and looked up at the buildings. "It fills me with profound regret."

Shelton scoffed. "Too little, too late."

Elyssa scoffed along with him. "Amen."

Xanos nodded. Her gaze caught on something behind us and she gasped. Tears welled in her eyes and her lips trembled. "Perfection."

Adam's eyes widened and his mouth worked as if trying to speak.

I groaned. "Apollyon is behind us. Don't look into his face." I turned and saw the hooded figure in orange coming our way. His hood had slipped back so I looked down at his chest to avoid direct eye contact. "Apollyon, I would speak with you."

He gasped and stopped. "Know me?"

I nodded. "Pull your hood over your face, please."

"I cannot bear such perfection," Xanos wailed.

Adam slumped to the ground.

"Holy farting devils," Shelton said. "Glad I didn't look."

"He is objectively quite perfect," Cinder said, apparently unaffected. "This is fascinating."

I looked up and was relieved to see Apollyon's face was covered. "Your father is nearby."

"He is?" Apollyon reached into the robe and pulled out a thin, rusty chain hanging around his neck. A large but perfect diamond hung at the end. "I will finally die."

The jewel sparkled not from the sun striking it, but from a light within.

Elyssa's eyes filled with concern. "You want to die?"

He nodded vigorously. "I am bad for world. I want to die." He held up the diamond as if it were the key to his wish.

It was heart-wrenching to hear that. "We must find your father too. Please take us to him and we can all get what we want."

"You help?" he said.

I nodded. "We help, my friend." I put a hand on his shoulder. "We help."

He sniffled. "Thankful."

Elyssa wiped her eyes. "God, now I'm going to cry. This is awful."

"Necessary." Apollyon pointed down the street "I smell him that way."

"Let's find Elohim." I flourished a hand and let him pass.

Cinder picked up the dazed Adam from the ground. Shelton took Xanos by the hand and led her even as she silently cried.

317

It felt almost too easy to earn Apollyon's trust. Being confined to Stygia for most of his existence had left him innocent even as the aura of his dark magic twisted the land and creatures around him. It explained why the Beast had been so easy to deal with. It was hard to believe Baal was a combination of this demigod and Elohim, but it explained how he'd come to control Hell and why the demons of Haedaemos were so twisted.

I checked the time. The Sundering wasn't due for another two hours. I was eager to find Elohim and put a tracker on him so we could see what happened at the moment of destruction. A cloud passed overhead, and I recognized Ussor. The urgent expression on his face told me he knew something was coming and was determined to stop it.

Now that we had the sword and the end of the world wasn't nigh, I wanted to spend more time studying this day and experiencing the wonder of Juranthemon. Saila's plans for a Utopian world might be applicable even today. Maybe it was time to consider bringing the noms into the light and showing them the world that could exist.

"Father!" Apollyon leapt twenty feet through the air, clearing several people, and landing before the man in the striped robes.

No one seemed surprised by the sudden display of affection or strength which made sense in a city populated mostly by Seraphim, Sirens, and Lyrolai. The crowd simply walked around the now-stopped figure.

Adam shook his head as if clearing it of cobwebs. "Oh, man, you weren't kidding about not looking at him." He wiped tears from his face. "He's painfully beautiful to look at."

"Too beautiful." Xanos looked wistfully at Apollyon. "I never knew such a being could exist."

"Apollyon?" Elohim stopped in his tracks. "How did you get here?"

"I am happy to see you, Father." Apollyon tried to hug Elohim, but the man pushed him back.

"You should not have left." Elohim sighed. "I would take you back this instant, but rumor has it the Apocryphan mean to destroy this city and I want to witness it." He chuckled. "Eve's monstrous children have done nothing but wreak havoc on this world. Perhaps today is the day all life ends, and I can recreate the world in my image."

Apollyon's shoulders slumped. "No. Life is pretty, Father. Life is gift."

Elohim groaned. "Eve helped me create the Seraphim, the Sirens, and the others. But they are simply too weak to deal with what is to come. It might be ten years or ten thousand before the outsider gods set their sights on this universe. When that day comes, we must have beings as powerful as me guarding this existence." He swiped a hand through the air. "But you are too dense to understand."

Apollyon shook his head. "I sorry, Father." He looked down. "I bad."

Elohim sighed and embraced his son. "No, son, it's my fault. My pursuit of perfection came at too high a cost. I lack something that allows me to create beings as perfect as myself."

"Talk about arrogant," Shelton muttered.

Elohim released his son and turned. "Who eavesdrops on our private conversation?"

"We do, Elohim." I prayed to him he didn't blast me on the spot and continued. "We are here to discuss an urgent matter."

Elohim narrowed his eyes. "You are not of this world." He took my hand and inspected it. "You are connected to something outside this world." His eyes flared. "You are an outsider god."

I held up my hands defensively to keep him from disintegrating me. "Nope, no way. I'm from this universe, promise."

"You are human, and yet you are not." He walked around me. "There is something connected to you that does not exist in this world."

The connection to my demon was apparently giving me away.

Nightliss stepped forward. "I am of this universe."

Elohim frowned. "Your auras are similar but wrong." He reached out and it felt as if my soul were being gripped. His eyes widened. "What is this world I see through your eyes?"

Apparently, it was nearly impossible to trick a god. I saw no choice but to admit where we came from. "What you see is the future. We have come here to see the past."

He abruptly released my aura and backed up a step. "Impossible. Time is change, and the universe is constantly changing. There is no way to return the universe to its identical state even ten seconds ago."

"That's because this isn't really the past," Adam said. "A relic in our time that has remained completely unchanged was used to create a time remnant of Juranthemon. As far as we know, it didn't recreate the entire universe."

Elohim tapped a finger on his chin. "I will put that to the test." He grabbed my hand and we launched into the air without warning.

I screamed like a little boy and hung on for dear life. We soared at high speeds for miles, me flopping like a caught fish behind a speedboat. Elohim gasped and slowed, hovering in the air while I dangled beneath him. I twisted around and saw what he saw. Beyond the edge of desert hills was nothing but white. He continued to the white area and reached out a hand. Something solid stopped it.

"It is as you say." Elohim pulled me up as if I weighed nothing and looked me in the eye. "How did this relic remain unchanged? Everything changes."

I wasn't sure I wanted to tell him.

He looked back toward the city in the distance. "I must go."

The next thing I knew we were speeding back toward the city. "Why are we going back?"

"Don't you feel it?" he said. "The Apocryphan come."

I wondered what would happen if Elohim didn't go there. Would the Sundering still happen? I decided to throw caution to the wind and find out. "This is a trap set for you by Xanos."

He scoffed and looked down at me. "You think an Apocryphan could trick me into something?"

"Yes. I'm from the future, remember? I know what's going to happen."

Elohim shook his head. "I am eager to see the Apocryphan destroy all that Eve has built. Then I will be justified rebuilding as I see fit."

"No, you don't understand." I managed to grab his arm with my other hand to stabilize myself. "Xanos is jealous of her siblings. She drew them here with rumors that you want to, once again, rule the world. They are coming to stop you. When they do, they'll attack. When you fight back, the sheer power will demolish the world and split it into realms."

Elohim shook his arm and flung me off like a pesky mosquito. I channeled wings just in time to avoid pancaking into a building and used the forward momentum to glide back toward Unity. The sky was already darkening with the approach of the Apocryphan by the time I landed. Shelton and the others were still waiting where I'd left them, but Apollyon was gone.

"Where'd Apollyon go?" I said.

Adam shrugged. "He said he had to go and started walking toward Unity."

I told them what happened with Elohim. "It's like he stopped being rational and went to meet the Apocryphan no matter what."

Cinder pursed his lips. "It seems that the time echo is somewhat malleable, but the closer we come to the Sundering, the more rigid it becomes."

Adam nodded. "In other words, it's impossible to change the timeline even here."

Shelton started walking toward Unity. "Well, we've got another forty minutes. Might as well check out the main event."

Elyssa shook her head. "Uh, I think heading back to the room is the better idea."

I gauged the distance back to the room. "We're almost to the plaza. I think we can hop down for a peek and get back in time."

Elyssa held up an ASE. "How about I just leave this here and we can watch it later?"

Shelton grunted. "Leave it to Elyssa to be the logical one."

"She is a brilliant tactician and understands risks," Cinder said. "In my experience it is better to listen to her than to you, Harry."

Adam burst into laughter. "Oh, man, what a burn!"

Elyssa made a hashtag symbol with her fingers. "Truth."

I snorted. "Cinder stating it how it is, as usual."

Xanos's forehead scrunched. "I do not understand why insults are amusing."

"Just take my word for it." Adam patted her back. "They're hilarious."

She looked longingly down the thoroughfare. "I would like to stay and see it in person."

"But why?" Adam said. "I guess we could retrieve you afterward, but there's no guarantee. You might be stuck in the void for a while."

"I want to find myself." Xanos sighed. "I want to talk to myself."

"Well, if your current version is locked into the main event coming up, I doubt there will be much to talk about." Shelton checked the time. "T-minus thirty-five minutes. We'd better get back to the portal."

Xanos gazed longingly at Unity. "Very well."

I shrugged. "You can go if you want." It wasn't like she could go anywhere else while in here. This was as much a prison as the holding cell back at the Ranch. "We'll try to fish you out later, but no promises."

She nodded. "I understand."

Adam looked from her and back to us, then seemed to reluctantly come to a decision. "Be careful. You can still be killed in here."

"I know." She touched his hand. "Thank you."

He blinked. "For what?"

"For being nice even when you had no cause to do so."

"Oh." Adam scratched the back of his head. "You did awful things. Killed a lot of people. Maybe you don't deserve to live, but then you'd just go on to the afterlife without learning anything. Humanity is crappy and imperfect, but dictatorships by godlike beings didn't work in the past and won't work in the future. I just hope you can see that and understand that perfection lies in imperfection."

Xanos's eyes widened. "I never thought of it that way." She shook her head. "Perfection lies in imperfection. Is that not like saying chaos lies in order?"

Adam nodded. "Without opposing sides, boredom and stagnation will grind life to a halt."

She rubbed her forehead as if the idea gave her a headache, then turned and walked down the thoroughfare toward unity.

"Wow, Adam." Elyssa clapped. "Well said."

Cinder nodded. "Surprisingly eloquent."

"Nice pep talk." Shelton clapped his shoulder. "Too bad it was wasted on her."

Adam shrugged. "I just remember what Justin went through when he had to choose between the light and the dark. He realized that extremes cause nothing but problems. It's best to look for balance while understanding that the tug of war between opposing sides is healthy."

It seemed like forever ago that I'd made the decision between Murk and Brilliance. I felt a little guilty that Adam remembered the lesson better than I did. "Maybe one day Xanos will learn to embrace humanity."

Shelton snorted. "Doubtful."

We made it back to the portal with five minutes to spare and paused at the window to watch the Apocryphan gathering in the sky. Elyssa watched the live feed sent from the ASE to her phone, panning around until she found Elohim and Apollyon at the edge of the plaza while Saila strode boldly into the center to confront her half-siblings.

Other citizens began to scatter, though a few brave ones remained. I couldn't imagine how ballsy someone had to be to stand at the epicenter of this showdown.

Elyssa frowned and zoomed in on Elohim. "Oh, shit."

"What?" I peered at the screen.

"The sword." Elyssa pointed at the holographic image. "Where's the sword?"

Elohim was no longer wearing the sword. It was now strapped to Apollyon's back. The meaning of that stabbed me in the heart.

Baal didn't need Unmaker.

CHAPTER 33

"Unmaker is part of Apollyon!" Shelton shouted.

Adam hissed. "Which means Baal only needs the Beast to complete his collection."

We stumbled over each other in our haste to get through the portal and out of the time echo.

"What now?" Shelton shouted.

I rapidly considered the options. "We have to take the Beast out of the Void."

"Insanity." Nightliss shook her head. "But it is the only way."

"A null cube might work," Adam said. "It'll put the Beast into stasis and keep him from replicating."

I nodded. "Let's get back to Cinder's lab and get a cube. Then we'll go straight to the Void."

Cutsauce trotted up. *You are back!*

He morphed into Saila and she spoke. "Did you discover anything useful?"

"No, in fact we realized something horrible." I told her about our discovery.

Her eyes flared. "This is disastrous."

I slashed open a portal to Cinder's lab, ran inside, and grabbed the largest null cube. It was just big enough for a grown man to curl up inside, but since anything inside would be in stasis, that would work just fine. I closed the portal to the lab and prepared to make one to the Void.

Saila beat me to it, opening a portal just outside the Beast's lair.

"We're not wearing armor," Shelton said. "What if we can't breathe?"

I poked my head through the portal and took a sniff. The air reeked of brimstone. "It's breathable, but not by much."

Shelton put his head through and gagged. "Holy stank-ass fairies. I can't deal with that."

Adam gave it a try and tears filled his eyes. "It burns like a thousand farts."

"I'll go. The rest of you wait."

Saila nodded. "I will come as well."

Elyssa touched my arm. "Be careful. There might be enough of the swarm to eat you again."

I kissed her cheek. "I'll run away if things look bad."

Saila and I went through and marched toward the lair. The dismembered body of a young tumor man lay outside the opening. Pools of black liquid seeped into the hard-baked earth. I ran inside and saw a sight that sent ice into my chest.

An infernus turned and smirked at me. "Hello, grandson."

A pair of bulky rock demons flanking him turned to look at me.

"Baal." I bared my teeth. "You knew!"

He chuckled. "Young man, I'm the one who convinced Eve to throw Unmaker into the Void. You and your associates erroneously thought I needed it, but it was bait to see if you could do the heavy lifting for me and clear a path to the Beast." He chuckled. "As usual, you delivered."

I shook my head. "How in the hell did you trick Eve?"

Baal smirked. "Eve is so mental right now that Olivia was able to pass as Emily and talk her into it."

An orange-haired woman stepped from behind the rock demons. "I'm super impressed. I thought you guys would storm in here with your army and fight the swarm head-on. I told Baal you'd sacrifice most of your forces clearing a path to Unmaker and the Beast. Then we'd swoop in and take him right out from under your noses."

"Your solution was brilliant, Justin." Baal clasped his hands together. "You knew the Beast was too dangerous to take from the Void, so you took Unmaker, determining it was all you needed to keep me from finishing my plan."

"You gave your sword to Apollyon the day of the Sundering." I scowled. "Yours and his souls somehow combined to make the entity called Baal while the leftovers ended up in this realm."

Baal's eyebrows rose. "How do you know about Apollyon?"

"He gave us his memories." I'd left the slug behind or I would have thrown it in his face. "I saw what you did to him. How you tried to create perfection to counter the Apocryphan and instead made a pure, innocent being, perfect in appearance, but with an aura that corrupts everything he touches."

"I am so sick of the gods!" Saila raised a fist. "They think they know best, but all they do is destroy."

Baal blinked and shook his head. "Saila? So that was you Justin found in the Abyss."

"Yes, it is me." Energy glowed around her fist. "I will not allow you to take Apollyon. I will not allow you to destroy the world again."

The Beast looked from us to Baal. His current form was a shadow of the beautiful form of Apollyon, but I saw traces of him in the features. "Father want me. Me for Father."

Baal shrugged. "He wants to come with us, Saila. Would you deny the boy a visit with his father?"

"I will deny you existence itself." Saila unleashed a beam of green energy.

Olivia leapt into the air and met the attack with a shield. "You're not the only demigod in here, bitch."

Saila bared her teeth and power surged through the green pulse. Olivia's shield cracked, but she snarled and reinforced the barrier.

Baal pursed his lips. "Fascinating. Saila has transformed a hellhound into her own personal vessel."

Saila relented and Olivia lowered her barrier. The pair of powerful women glared at each other with the hatred of a thousand suns.

I resisted calling upon my own Apocryphan powers to break the stalemate between Olivia and Saila because I had no idea what the rock demons were capable of. Elyssa had taught me that brute force wasn't always the answer.

Baal wasn't one to make idle conversation. If he saw something he wanted, he took it. If he was still talking to the Beast, did that mean he couldn't physically haul him out of the Void against his will? I was willing to bet that was a possibility.

Instead of fighting Olivia and escalating the situation, I held out a hand toward the Beast. "You don't really believe your father wants you, or you would have gone with him already. If you go with him, he will end billions of lives."

The Beast's head tilted to a horrific ninety-degree angle. "World me kill." His head straightened and turned three-hundred and sixty degrees. "All eternal I keep."

"You will return the world to its natural state, son." Baal smiled reassuringly at him. "Earth will once again be whole."

"Billions of living creatures in the other realms will die, Apollyon." I held my hands wide and approached him. "Please don't go with your father. He is only using you to make himself whole again."

The Beast walked in his jerky, spasmodic way, not quite approaching me, but not standing in place. "Apollyon again?"

I nodded. "You will be Apollyon again. You will be banished to Hell again."

"Not true." Baal scoffed. "I have the only cure for your condition."

The Beast spun toward him. "Kill me?"

Baal faltered and his grin faded. "Yes, son. That is the only cure."

The Beast fell to his knees. "Yes. Kill. Apollyon bad."

Baal's lip trembled and his Adam's apple bobbed as if he'd just swallowed a very bitter pill. It was but the briefest flicker of humanity, something I had never seen in the ruler of Haedaemos. He nodded. "Yes, son. I will end your existence and give you peace."

The Beast slumped, shoulders shaking with sobs. In that instant, I knew the battle was lost. "Please, Apollyon, don't go with him. We will find a way to end you if that's what you want. Just please don't help Baal end the world."

"So long as you are a relic, you cannot die." Baal put a hand on the Beast's head. "I will help you find peace, son."

The Beast gripped his father's hand and cried. "Thankful." He rose to his feet. "Ready."

Baal nodded. "Let's go."

"Baal, stop!" I ran across the divide between us. "If you have even a trace of humanity in you, please don't do this."

Olivia blurred in front of me. "Don't make me kill you again, kiddo."

I ignored her. "Baal, maybe there's another way to give you back your body without destroying the realms in the process. Can't you at least give us a chance to find a way?"

He sighed and turned to face me. "Grandson, you have been a worthy adversary. Even though you're not technically my flesh and blood, it's obvious you've inherited some of my stronger traits. You will survive the Mending and be stronger for it. My work will be done, and a beautiful new existence will begin."

I shook my head. "That won't be the end of it. Your entire purpose for creating Apollyon was to counter the Apocryphan. But your hatred of Eve spawned corruption inside your perfect son. When you heard of the Apocryphan descending on Juranthemon, all you wanted was for them to wipe out each other so you could remake the world as you saw fit."

Baal's eyebrows rose. "How could you possibly know what I wanted?"

"Because I spoke to you the day it happened!" I was breathing heavily, fear snaking through my insides, coiling around my heart. "We found a time echo that takes us back to the day of the Sundering. I found you and Apollyon walking toward Unity, drawn by Xanos's trap. You told Apollyon what you wanted."

For the first time in a long while, Baal looked shocked. "Time is not malleable, nor can one visit the past. If that were possible, I would have undone everything."

"You're doing this for the wrong reasons." I held out my hands. "If not for you, the realms would not exist. In the moment you were attacked by Eve's monsters, you created an entire realmverse full of wondrous creatures. Instead of one world, you created hundreds."

Baal pursed his lips. "But this creation is meaningless if I cannot physically see it in my own body." He put a hand to his chest. "I am trapped in a hell of my own making whether in Haedaemos or in an infernus." His voice rose. "This is not living!"

Olivia flinched and backed away from him, as did the rock demons. Only the Beast remained steadfast.

"We can find a way to restore your body, Elohim." I held out a hand. "I promise we will figure this out. If Saila can mold a hellhound to her needs, then surely Elohim can do the same."

Baal's gaze turned inward. A hand went to his chin, and for a long moment, he went still. "I have tried many times to make a body that can hold all I am. But I have grown greater over the eons." He looked at the Beast. "Part of Apollyon is trapped within me, and part of me within the Beast."

"We can figure out how to separate the pieces." I didn't dare suggest asking for Eve's help. "Olivia is powerful enough to untangle those parts."

"Then I die?" the Beast asked.

I nodded. "Then he can end you, Apollyon."

Baal blew out a breath and looked at me. "You are perhaps the first mortal I truly respect, Justin Slade."

You have a real funny way of showing it, I thought.

He continued speaking. "I truly believe you would help your enemies if it meant saving lives." A sad smile crossed his face. "Did you know Eve discovered how to spark sentience before I did and refused to share the secret?"

Of course I hadn't known something dating back to the dawn of mankind, but I stated it anyway. "No, I didn't know that."

"I designed Seraphim and Nazdal while she was granting life to Sirens and Lyrolai." Baal scoffed. "She refused to give my creations the spark of sentience unless I altered them to fit her expectations. But what choice did I have?"

I wasn't surprised in the least that Elohim had designed Nazdal, but kept my mouth shut.

He shook his head. "Unless and until Eve told me the secret to granting sentience, I was at her mercy. We built the world with the help of other old gods. I created some animals, a few insects, and even a plant or two. But Eve held the greatest secret and refused to share with the others."

"That explains why you despise her," I said.

Baal nodded. "I planted a spy with her, but Eve was done creating sentient beings. It wasn't until eons later when the other old gods left that Eve decided to create her first god. It was then that I learned the secret and began laboring to create perfection."

The Beast shook its head. "Not perfect."

A long sigh escaped Baal. He patted the Beast on the head. "I was too impatient to show Eve perfection. Now I know better."

I risked interrupting his monologue. "Does this mean you'll let me help you?"

"No, Justin." Baal sighed again. I respect what you're trying to do, but in the end, saving the lives of inferior creations is of no interest to me." He spread his hands. "Even the realms in all their glory are imperfect. I will undo the mistakes of the past and wipe the slate clean."

"I had the perfect city and you ruined it." Saila began to weep. "You and the Apocryphan and Eve think you are the alpha and omega, but your interference has done nothing but wreak havoc!"

"Not this time." Baal nodded as if agreeing with himself. "This time it will be different." He turned to Olivia. "Let's go."

"No!" Saila unleashed an attack. The rock demons leapt between her and Olivia, their massive forms soaking up the attack as if it were nothing.

Baal smirked and vanished behind them. I blurred after them, my mind blank with the horror of what was going to happen if I didn't stop them. The rock demons watched me impassively as I streaked around them. Baal and Olivia stood on the other side of a gateway.

The Beast looked back at me. "Sorry." Then he stepped through.

Olivia slashed her hand down and the portal began to close. All rational thought left my mind and I leaped for the opening. I expected to be cut in half, or at the very least, lose a few toes. Instead, I hit rough stone and rolled to a stop at Baal's feet in an underground cave. We were in Hell.

He grinned. "This is actually perfect." He hefted me without effort. "I think it's good that you're here for this."

Olivia pressed her hand to my chest. It was as if she'd reached into my soul and flipped a switch. I struggled against her godlike power, but I was a ninety-pound weakling wrestling a football player. My Seraphim and Apocryphan powers vanished.

I was powerless.

CHAPTER 34

S he giggled. "I've wanted to do that for a long time." Her hand closed around my throat. "Especially after you took Cain from me."

I choked as her hand squeezed tighter. My demon strength was still intact, but it was barely enough to resist her. "You stole my father from me first."

She shrugged. "Doesn't matter. You'll be my little bitch."

Baal put his hand on her arm. "Save that for later. I don't want to wait another minute."

Olivia kissed me, then bit my neck and ears just hard enough to draw pain. "I'm glad you look like Cain." Then she shoved me to the side and started walking behind Baal and the Beast.

I reached inside and tried to find my powers. They were there, but muted, unavailable. She hadn't removed the auras, but she'd turned them off. "Baal, please—"

Baal spun and backhanded me against the tunnel wall. "Remain quiet or you won't get to see the fireworks."

I staggered away from the wall, barely able to keep my feet. The time for verbal appeals was over. I had to find a way to sabotage him at the last minute. How I'd do that without powers, I didn't know, but I was willing to try anything.

The Beast took Baal's hand and limped next to him, a frightening smile on his face. Baal managed an uneasy smile back at his son. "I'm glad we're spending quality time together. It'll be even better when we have our bodies back."

We stepped into a large levitator and shot up at a frightening pace. The Beast lost his footing and fell to the floor where he hugged Baal's ankle for dear life.

Olivia giggled, shook her head, and put an arm around my waist. "I hope you're as good in bed as Cain." She licked my ear and brushed her eyelashes against my cheek. "Do you like my butterfly kisses, sweetie?"

"No." I tried to move, but she held me in her steel grasp.

"I hope you struggle this much later." She nipped my ear. "I love it when they struggle."

"How in the hell did you end up so damned evil, Olivia?" I gave her a disgusted look. "You're a demigod, for god's sake. Act like one."

"I can't tell if you're joking or serious, love."

"Are you like this just to spite Emily?" I raised my eyebrows in challenge. "Or just because you like being used by Eve's arch enemy?"

Olivia gently slapped my face. "He's not using me, but I will be using you later."

I laughed. "You're letting some has-been god use you to get his body back. You're a next-gen goddess. Why are you letting this old coot back into the game?"

"Much as I admire your tenacity, grandson, you're barking up the wrong tree." Baal smirked. "Olivia understands the power I wield even without full access to a physical body. She couldn't turn on me if she wanted to."

A scowl flashed across Olivia's face, but she recovered quickly. "Elohim will teach me how to be a real god. I'll ascend to my rightful place, and Emily won't be able to hang with my power."

I rolled my eyes, but before I could talk, the levitator stopped, and Olivia shoved me out. We walked onto an ornate marbled floor. The ceiling was a vast dome artfully painted with the *Creation of Adam*, much like the room I'd seen in Juranthemon just before I died. Sitting in the center of the floor was the statue of a man, hands upraised as if defending himself. Some of the pieces were in full living color. Others were black or off-white. The robe was striped just as I'd seen it in the time echo, and the face was that of Elohim.

This was it—the moment the world ended—and I was powerless as a babe.

But Baal didn't send the Beast to the statue. "Open the way, Olivia."

Okay, so maybe this wasn't the moment just yet.

She slashed a hand and a portal ripped open. Warm, salty air carried the scent of the ocean to my nose. Seagulls cried and a car hummed past on a road perhaps thirty feet from the gateway. Olivia opened her hand and a giant flaming hand appeared. It lifted the statue and carried it through. Baal stepped through after her, the Beast in tow. They didn't seem to care whether I stayed or not, but I figured it was better to get out of Hell.

The portal closed just as I cleared it. Olivia giggled when I flinched in surprise. "Careful not to lose anything vital, boy toy."

"Where are we?" I asked.

Olivia ignored the question and continued carrying the statue across a plain of scrubby weeds and grass. The ocean shore was perhaps fifty yards away, guarded by a white lighthouse. That meant we had to be in

Eden. I slid Nookli out of my pocket and checked the location. We were in the southern region of Portugal—the same location as Juranthemon on old Earth.

Olivia carefully placed the statue on a clearing marked by burned vegetation and rotated it precisely. She stood back, apparently lining it up with another marker in the distance. "This is it."

Baal consulted a tablet with images of Juranthemon taken from Haedaemos. "Yes, it is. The exact spot."

Now we'd reached the moment the world would end.

A group of noms out for a walk to the beach stared in horror and surprise at the giant flaming hand Olivia used to position the statue. Olivia gave them the giant, flaming middle finger and they ran screaming.

There was nothing I could do, but I wasn't going to just stand here and do nothing. I ran for the Beast, determined to grab his other hand, and try to whisk him away. My demon speed might be enough to outrun Olivia. Then again, she could fly pretty fast. It didn't matter. I had to stop this.

The thunderous roar of water drew my attention back to the ocean. Water dragons leapt from the ocean. Sirens rode the magnificent creatures. Vitania, former queen of the Sirens, rode the lead dragon. I didn't recognize her other two companions. Their mouths opened and a haunting melody froze me in place.

I couldn't so much as turn my head, but frustrated growling told me Baal was right behind me.

"We knew you would eventually come here," Vitania said, somehow still singing with the others. "We have lain in wait for the perfect moment to undo all that you have done, Elohim." She pointed to something behind me, presumably the statue. "Sisters, take it quickly."

Their dragons dove. An orange beam slashed into the lead dragon, severing its head and cutting the Siren in half. The other Siren screamed in anguish. The music ceased and suddenly, I could move again.

Olivia burst into laughter. "Do you really think your Siren bullshit works on me?" Another orange beam slashed at the other dragon, but it dodged out of the way.

Funnels of water rose from the ocean, arching overhead and slamming into Olivia. I dove out of the way as tons of sand and broken seashells rained down from the watery mass. A massive burst of energy turned the water to steam, burning my lungs. I stumbled to my feet and made another run at the Beast, but Baal stiff-armed me and slammed me to the ground.

He turned to the Beast. "Go, son. Touch the statue."

The Beast grunted happily. "Yes!" He flickered toward the statue in an erratic pattern just as he'd done when moving in the Void.

I tried to move, but Baal yanked me off the ground and spun me toward the statue even as Olivia flew into the air, battling Vitania and the water dragons.

"Watch it, grandson. Watch the world be reborn."

"We're all going to die here," I gasped. "This is the epicenter."

"The safest place to be." He patted my back. "I almost wish I'd brought popcorn."

I reached for my inner demon, but something blocked me, kept me from manifesting.

Baal's grip tightened on my shoulder. "Patience, child."

"No!" Vitania cried. "You will destroy everything!"

Baal roared with laughter. "That's the point, little mermaid."

Time seemed to slow as the Beast closed to within ten feet of the goal. He flickered closer. Five feet. Four, three, two, one.

"No!" I roared. But there was nothing I could do. Nothing any of us could do.

The Beast touched the statue.

The ground shuddered. The Beast split open from the crown of his head to his crotch, but there were no guts, no blood, nothing inside. Baal's grip on my shoulder vanished. The infernus stumbled drunkenly. I punched him with everything I had, sending him flying ten feet to land in a crumpled heap.

A portal ripped open. Sparkling light all colors of the rainbow streamed into the statue. It had to be the spirit form of Baal. One half of the beast began to mold around the statue, the flesh molding like putty to perfectly fit the contours. The other half of the Beast changed shape, the diseased green skin turning lighter. It fell into a kneeling position and froze.

The ground shook more violently. Olivia grinned maniacally at me. "Ooh, this is gonna be fun!"

I barely managed to keep my feet. "Destroying the world isn't fun, you bitch!"

The last of Baal's spirit form poured into the statue and the portal vanished. One of the hands flexed, and then the other. The trembling earth grew still as a newborn Elohim slowly turned and smiled. "God is back." He raised a fist and the earth buckled as if by his command.

I looked around, confused. "Why hasn't everything blown up yet?"

He pursed his lips. "It would seem the Mending won't happen all at once." He shrugged. "What has drifted apart for so long may take some time to find its way home."

Olivia giggled. "In the meantime, you're mine."

I felt the presence of Kalesh again and drew upon all the strength and speed I had. Then I turned tail and ran. A shadow swooped down behind me. I screamed like a frightened kid as giant talons plucked me from the ground. A portal ripped open and we flew through. I squirmed and looked up to see Vitania looked sadly down at me.

"We failed." My voice trembled.

Tears filled her eyes. "Yes."

The dragon circled over rolling hills. It swooped low and hovered in place where it released me from its talons, and then landed nearby. The dragon bearing the other Siren landed. She leaned against the dragon's neck and sobbed, mourning the loss of their fallen companion and perhaps the world.

With the immediate threat of death over, I asked the most obvious question. "How did you know Baal would be there?"

Vitania slid off her dragon and leaned against it. "The short answer is that I knew Baal would eventually have to take the relics to the original location of Juranthemon."

"We needed your help sooner, not at the last minute." I threw up my hands. "Where have you been, and where's Emily?"

"Queen Dactia took me prisoner when I sought her help." She shook her head. "Dactia recalled all Sirens so they could take refuge somewhere and wait for the collapse of the realms. Emily came to my rescue, but by then, I sensed the gravity of the relics upon the quantum threads between the realms." She shrugged. "I was only able to escape with my two companions."

I clenched a fist. "We really needed Emily today. I don't understand why she didn't return right after saving you."

"That was her intention." Vitania frowned. "She has not returned yet?"

I shook my head. "No one's seen or heard from her and Tyler since she left to find you."

"She did say that she wanted to make one more appeal to Eve for help." Vitania's eyes flared. "Perhaps Eve detained her."

I huffed angrily. "The way things have been going, I wouldn't be surprised." My mind raced. "Since the world hasn't ended yet, maybe there's still time. Maybe breaking the statue apart will stop it."

Vitania shook her head. "Elohim has risen. The gravity of the relics has reached critical mass, causing all the realms to drift back to the center. I believe the only reason collapse wasn't instantaneous is because the dark rift of the Abyss counters it from one side while the Anchor Stone resists from the other."

I snapped my fingers. "It all boils down to gravity."

Vitania nodded. "Yes. The completion of an entire relic has created a tug-of-war on the quantum fabric."

"We need to rejoin my friends." I traced a symbol to open a portal and ran into the wall Olivia had placed between me and my powers. I showed Vitania a picture of the Razor lab. "Can you take us there?"

"I cannot fit the dragons inside."

I threw up my hands. "Can you leave the dragons here with your friend for a minute?"

Vitania nodded. "Yes." She slashed open a portal to a room full of shouting people.

"I don't give two shits on a hamburger bun," Shelton yelled over the others. "Let's go kick Baal's ass!"

Elyssa, ever the perceptive ninja, had already seen me and plowed through the others to get to me. "Justin!"

I met her enthusiastic hug with a sigh of relief. "Hey, babe."

"Dude, is that Vitania?" Adam said.

Elyssa kissed me long and hard, then looked from Vitania to me. "Tell me what happened."

I gave her the rundown. "Baal is gone. Long live Elohim."

"Let me get this straight." Adam pursed his lips. "The realms are being drawn back together much more slowly than anticipated because of two artificially created sources of gravity?"

Vitania nodded. "The Anchor Stone and the Abyss were created after the spawning of the realms. Both are strong sources of quantum gravity, tasked with creating a stable orbit of the realms."

Cutsauce morphed into Saila. "Vitania, my old friend, it is good to see you again."

Vitania gasped. "Saila?" She hugged the other woman then held her at arm's length. "Are you in a hellhound body?"

"Yes." Saila shivered. "But even now, I feel an invisible force trying to rip me away and drag me somewhere."

Vitania sighed. "I had long thought Saila was the epicenter of the Sundering, but now I see it was Elohim. Piecing his sundered body back together not only restored him to life but has created a powerful gravitational well that will draw all the other fragments together. The more pieces that are assembled, the stronger the pull upon the realms. Every piece will hasten the collapse."

"We're fucked!" Shelton face-palmed. "After everything we've been through, that rat bastard Baal got his wish."

"I'm powerless and Emily is missing." I pinched the bridge of my nose. "If there's any chance of stopping the collapse, we'll need her."

But if Eve had taken her, then it was truly game over.

CHAPTER 35

Vitania nodded. "Emily will be key, but if Eve has her, I'll need help recovering her."

"I'm in." I didn't know what I could do, but I was willing to try anything.

"First, I must go to Pangaea and find Lumia." She clasped her hands at her waist. "We are Eve's oldest friends. Perhaps together we can convince her to help us or at the very least, release Emily."

Shelton shook his head. "Without Justin able to open portals, we're screwed."

"With a few modifications, Xanos's portal generator would suffice for the task." Cinder turned to Adam. "Perhaps we should recover it from the time echo."

Adam nodded. "Yeah, let's do that."

I turned to Vitania. "Can you open a portal there so we can get it?"

She nodded. "Show me where it is."

I showed her a picture and she opened a gateway.

Adam stepped through and looked down at the gateway into the time echo. "We need to get Xanos out first."

Shelton scoffed. "Do we, though?"

Vitania flinched. "Xanos?"

"Dude, it's cruel to leave her in there." Adam took out his arcphone and activated the tracker. He stared at it for a moment, then tapped the screen a few times. "This can't be right."

Shelton frowned. "Maybe the tracker broke during the Sundering."

Vitania frowned and shook her head. "Is this an elaborate new prison for Xanos?"

"It's a gateway to an echo of the past." I told her about the time echo and how Xanos came to be there. "Xanos wanted to stay inside for the Sundering."

Vitania's eyes widened. "This is an incredible discovery. There is so much I'd forgotten about that day and now I can once again see it first-hand!"

"Uh, except the world is ending?" Shelton said.

Adam's phone began beeping. "Hey, Xanos's signal is back."

"Great." Shelton acted as if he were holding a fishing pole. "Let's fish her out."

I went stepped inside the burned-out mansion where we'd stored flying brooms and grabbed one. "I'll go get her. We need to make this fast."

Adam made a confused noise. "What in the hell?" He hit the side of his phone a few times as if that would fix his confusion. "She's getting closer really fast."

"How?" Shelton leaned over and looked at the phone. "She didn't have a broom."

Adam leaned his head into the white void on the other side and gasped. "Oh, shit."

"What?" Shelton tried to lean inside, but Adam grabbed him and pulled him away.

Adam stumbled to his feet. "Cinder, turn off the generator right now!"

Cinder hesitated, then took out the arctablet with the controls and tapped on it. The device powered down with a low hum and the portal winked off. An instant later, a thin green beam of light pierced the scar, and the portal burst open.

Xanos flew through the opening and hovered in the air. Her eyes glowed green and her purple skin was flush with power. She'd grown at least six inches taller.

Saila cried out and unleashed a beam of destructive energy. Xanos blocked it with a shield.

"Wait!" she cried out, but Saila charged her, slamming against the shield with another burst of energy.

Vitania opened her mouth inhumanly wide and began to sing.

Xanos's eyes flared. She ripped open another portal and vanished inside. It closed shut before I could see where it went.

Vitania hissed and ceased singing. "I nearly had her."

Adam sat on the ground eyes wide. "I don't understand. How did she have powers?"

"I have no idea." I shook my head. "Maybe the Sundering did something to her."

"But you were caught in it and it didn't affect you at all," Elyssa said.

"Man, oh man, this can't be happening!" Shelton slapped his forehead. "Elohim is reborn, Xanos has powers, the world is ending, and Emily is missing."

"That doesn't even sum it all up." Adam rose to his feet. "What now?"

There was only one thing to do. "Let's find Emily. The world hasn't ended yet, so we still have a chance to stop it. If all else fails, we'll portal as many people as possible to Atlantis and wait it out." As the only surviving fragment of the original Earth, Atlantis would likely be untouched by the collapsing realms.

"Wait." Adam held up a finger. "What about Alden? If Eve created a new world on a separate plane, wouldn't it be safe from the Mending, or whatever Baal calls it?"

The dim spark of hope brightened. "Yes, but we have to find it and I have no idea how we'll move billions of people and creatures there in the time we have left."

"Perhaps something like Noah's ark will suffice," Cinder said. "We cannot save everything, but we can save some of everything."

Saila wiped tears from her eyes. "I will give you my all in the time I have left before the Mending rips me from this body."

I will be the best boy ever! Cutsauce said inside my head.

Elyssa took my hand. "It's not over and we'll never stop fighting."

Shelton nodded. "We overcame Daelissa and Xanos. We can kick Baal's ass."

"Elohim thinks he's won and that'll be his downfall." Adam tapped his temple with a finger. "We've got this."

I looked into the eyes of my friends, my family, and felt a stir of hope. We were down, but not out. Elohim thought this was over, and that would be his downfall. He'd won the latest battle, but we would win the war.

ABOUT THE AUTHOR

John Corwin is the bestselling author of the Overworld Chronicles. He enjoys long walks on the beach and is a firm believer in puppies and kittens.

After years of getting into trouble thanks to his overactive imagination, John abandoned his male modeling career to write books.

He resides in Atlanta.

Connect with John Corwin online:
Facebook: http://www.facebook.com/johnhcorwinauthor
Website: http://www.johncorwin.net
Twitter: http://twitter.com/#!/John_Corwin

www.ingramcontent.com/pod-product-compliance
Lightning Source LLC
Chambersburg PA
CBHW020930260626
47169CB00006B/1651